"Tobias decided to check it out once and for all." Taft was frowning, thinking hard.

"So, where is he?" asked Mac. "I mean, is that what happened to him? He ordered the exhumation and somebody got scared? Somebody in the neighborhood or one of the Friends of Faraday? Somebody who's afraid the exhumation is going to prove Victor died of poisoning, not heart failure, and an investigation will start, so . . . they decide to stop Tobias . . . kill him . . . ?"

"Who is this somebody?" asked Taft, going with her.

"One of the neighbors? The one who killed Victor?"

"And they killed Victor because . . . he was building the three overlook houses and they couldn't stop him?"

She heard the unspoken questions in his voice. It didn't feel like enough to her either. "Okay, there's another reason, too. A different reason. I just don't know it yet. The old guard have a lot of problems with him. Maybe the answer's with them."

"So, one of them killed Tobias Laidlaw and that's why he's missing . . ."

Books by Nancy Bush

CANDY APPLE RED
ELECTRIC BLUE
ULTRAVIOLET
WICKED GAME
WICKED LIES
SOMETHING WICKED
WICKED WAYS
UNSEEN
BLIND SPOT
HUSH
NOWHERE TO RUN
NOWHERE TO HIDE
NOWHERE SAFE
SINISTER
I'LL FIND YOU
YOU CAN'T ESCAPE
YOU DON'T KNOW ME
THE KILLING GAME
DANGEROUS BEHAVIOR
OMINOUS
NO TURNING BACK
ONE LAST BREATH
JEALOUSY
BAD THINGS
LAST GIRL STANDING
THE BABYSITTER
THE GOSSIP
THE NEIGHBORS

Published by Kensington Publishing Corp.

THE
NEIGHBORS

NANCY
BUSH

ZEBRA BOOKS
KENSINGTON PUBLISHING CORP.
www.kensingtonbooks.com

Prologue

Tobias stepped out of his car into a surprisingly cold, rain-drenched night. The parking lot lights were blurred with precipitation, rain falling incessantly, dismally. His eyes searched around the darkened lot. His SUV was the only vehicle.

Throwing the hood of his parka over his head, he strode quickly across the slick black pavement. His car alarm gave a quiet *chirp-chirp* as he pointed his remote key fob at his Land Rover, locking it.

He put a palm down to his waistband, checking for his handgun, a movement he'd made twenty times since arming himself before he'd left home. The gun gave him a sense of security. Now he tracked toward the edge of the laurel hedge, his shoulder touching the wet leaves, droplets of water cascading over him as he rounded it.

Tobias was consumed with frigid fury. This ridiculous midnight meeting was imperative to set things straight if he wanted cooperation. Would he have rather met at his office? Somewhere professional? Somewhere *dry*? Of course. But he also wanted expediency and a certain amount of discretion while he decided his next move, and this was what it had come to.

His booted feet sank an inch into the muck of the soggy ground as he crossed from the pavement and over a swath of grass toward the meeting place. Ridiculous, he thought again. Melodramatic. A full moon was trying to compete with the cloud cover and mostly losing the battle.

He felt something in the air a heartbeat before he turned the corner of the hedge and—

Whack!

One moment he was standing, the next he was staggering like a drunk, unable to hold on to his footing, hands on his head. Grass, mud, booted feet spiraled in his vision; then he was on the ground, the fall's momentum rolling him over the turf onto his back, rain pelting onto his face.

I'm hit. I'm hit, he thought, disoriented. His head buzzed with pain and confusion. Something had slammed him hard.

He gazed upward into the black sky, dulled moonlight lifting some of the darkness. He squinted against the furious rain. A row of watery angels waved in and out of his vision, gazing down at him.

I can't die, he thought, frightened, struggling to rise.

"Goodbye-us, Tobias . . ." he thought he heard.

A flashlight burst on. Its beam caught on crystalline drops of rain. The blade of a shovel was raised directly above his throat, its tarnished dagger tip glimmering dully, an arrow pointing to his destruction.

No! his mind screamed. He drew a breath to shout, but it was too late. The shovel blade flashed downward, severing tissue and bone.

Angels save me . . . he silently begged as the light clicked off and darkness descended quickly.

With a gurgled sigh, Tobias said goodbye to this earth. One moment he was there, the next gone, unable to hear the whispered epitaph:

". . . and good riddance."

Chapter One

"You look fine," Mackenzie Laughlin assured her stepsister into her cell phone as she wheeled her RAV4 with its gleaming new bodywork into Taft's condominium visitor parking lot. She chose her favorite spot, which was open today, a space she'd started thinking of as her own. "You're glowing."

"Growing," Stephanie corrected sourly. "As big as an orca."

"You might be losing your sense of humor over this pregnancy," warned Mac.

"Oh, it's gone. Along with my waistline. I know it's temporary. I know I shouldn't complain. I know, I know." She exhaled on a snort of disgust. "I just didn't know it would be this hard and there are *months* left. God . . . I'll never make it."

"You will."

"I won't."

"You *will*."

"Promise?" she asked on a sigh.

"You need to do something. Have Nolan take you out for dinner."

"Oh, yeah. Just what I need. More food."

"You're eating for—"

"God, Mac, if you say I'm eating for two, I may have to kill you."

"—two."

"Argh!"

Mackenzie grinned. "Goodbye, Steph. Call me later." She clicked off, cutting short her stepsister's vague threats of ending their friendship forever.

Tucking her small notebook with the clipped-on roller ball pen into her jacket pocket, she climbed out of the RAV and headed to Jesse James Taft's front door. A one-time police officer, Taft was now a private detective, and recently he and Mac—herself a recent departee of the River Glen Police Department—had joined forces and were working together to make River Glen a better, safer place to live, one case at a time. Sort of. At least that was the way Mac wanted to see it. Taft was a little harder to read.

Truthfully, Taft was a pain in the ass. He was too good-looking, too smart, too intuitive, and too much trouble. This was the mantra Mackenzie tried to tell herself as she ignored the spark of sexual awareness between them that just wouldn't die. She knew it would be self-destructive to go that route with him, and not just because it would spoil their working relationship. Taft was the kind of guy who could break your heart without trying. Mac was constantly reinforcing the mental barrier she'd erected around her romantic notions, and so far it was still standing. Did she want more? Yes. Was she going to go there? No. Their relationship was professional and she wasn't going to jeopardize that. She knew a romance would be short-lived and she needed more than that.

She was still smiling about Stephanie, who was happy

in her pregnancy no matter what she said, as she headed to Taft's front door. Thinking of her stepsister reminded Mac of her family and her latest conversation with her mother.

"You're not going back to the department, then?" Mom had queried . . . again. She just couldn't quite hide the hope in her voice, having never really been on board with Mackenzie's choice to "protect and serve" with the River Glen PD. She'd always encouraged Mac's interest in the arts, specifically drama, which Mac had certainly enjoyed but had never believed was a solid career choice. But Mom still hoped acting would supersede her daughter's bend toward any kind of law enforcement.

"I'm not going back to the department," Mac had assured her.

"But you're with . . . Mr. Taft?"

"Well, I need a job."

"But *that* job?"

"Yes, that job."

"Pri-vate in-ves-ti-gation." Mom sounded out the syllables slowly, as if that would somehow make the idea more palatable.

"I like the work. And I'm careful."

"I just don't want to worry about you."

"I know."

Mom had gone through surgery and chemotherapy and had recently been declared cancer-free, a relief to all of them. Her remission had given her the strength to file divorce proceedings against Mac's stepfather, Dan Gerber, "Dan the Man" to Mackenzie. A great step forward in Mac's biased opinion. Even Stephanie knew how difficult her father was. But now that Mom was living alone, she was turning her attention and concern toward Mac. An unwelcome side effect. Mac, who'd helped take care of her during her recovery, had recently moved into her own apartment, and Mom was having a hard time with the change. Both of them were adjusting.

She knocked on Taft's door, grimacing at her own thoughts. She could brush Mom's concerns aside, but she understood where they came from. She and Taft had just come off two interlocking cases that had put both their lives at risk. Mac had escaped serious harm, but Taft had taken a bullet that had passed through his torso below his right shoulder, luckily missing vital organs and apparently causing no lasting harm. At least that was what Taft assured her. Mac, who had some harrowing memories of her own, wanted to argue with him about it but knew he wouldn't take her fussing over him well. She'd already tried that. And anyway, she was attempting to push it all away herself, at least for now. Postmortems were for later.

"Door's open," Taft called, and Mackenzie pushed into his condo.

She was immediately faced with a twenty- or thirty-something woman in a black jacket, a black midcalf skirt, black boots, and a mane of artfully tousled light brown hair that gave her the look of someone who'd just rolled out of bed. Her eyes were green and slanted and her lips were plump and possibly filled, but they looked a luscious, glossy pink under the lights. She was attractive and vibrant and a wholly unwelcome surprise.

Mackenzie lifted her brows. It wasn't like Taft to invite clients to his home. He met them at restaurants or parks or public buildings or their own homes. She'd never known him to bring one back to the condo. If that was what this woman even was . . . Maybe she wasn't the client Taft had called about. Maybe she wasn't the reason Mackenzie had dropped everything to come over and eagerly find out what he had in store for her work-wise.

Maybe she was . . . something else?

Mackenzie did a quick review of her own appearance, wishing she'd taken a little more care to dress up a bit, although she never did when she was expecting to be on the job, because why would she? And caring too much about her appearance was a trap in her quest to forget anything even marginally romantic as far was Taft was concerned. That was a no go and—

"Mac, this is Daley Carrera."

"Hi," Mac said, drawing a mental breath. Then, "Daley?"

The woman smiled a bit tightly. She was assessing Mac the same way Mac was assessing her. She looked vaguely familiar. "I know," she said. "Parents couldn't decide between Haley and Dana. It's been my cross to bear all my life." She looked at Taft, as if for corroboration.

"Daley's just moved into a house in Staffordshire, actually in the Villages," said Taft. "You remember."

She remembered. She and Taft had taken a look at those very homes with a real estate agent, pretending to be a married couple shopping for a house a few months earlier, reconnaissance on that job she'd shoved to the far reaches of her mind.

"She's been harassed by the neighbors and is looking for protection," said Taft. He was wearing a pair of jeans and a long-sleeved tee that fit him well and looked masculine and relaxed. He spread a hand toward Daley, silently inviting her to continue.

"I need someone to watch over me, basically. I asked Jesse, but he says he's too busy." She made a moue at him with her glossy lips. "I wasn't really expecting to have a woman be my bodyguard. I sort of wanted a man. Though my husband probably will like a woman better, I suppose."

"You're married?" said Mac with a lifting of spirits.

"For now. Whoops. I guess I've started at the end again." A shadow crossed her face. "When Leon and I moved into the Villages we immediately became personas non grata. Someone started stealing from our porch, then putting dog poop in our mailbox. I don't know what we did wrong, why they singled us out. Maybe it's just because we moved in? They're very territorial. We put in a Ring security camera, but all we've caught is someone in oversize clothes in a hoodie tied up so you can't see his face . . . or her face, hard to tell."

Mackenzie was having trouble understanding why Daley needed a bodyguard if she and her husband were still together, but okay. "You have any idea who's behind it all?"

"The whole neighborhood? They're like a nightmare. We never should have bought there. I mean, I love the house and all. It was added on to and redone last year and it's beautiful. A ranch with a hot tub and open concept. But the *people* . . ." She rolled her eyes. "They're the most unwelcoming bunch of old assholes you're ever like to meet. I'm too young for them. Too much. Oh, sure, there's one group about in their thirties or so and they're okay. But the old guard? They make all the rules and they're just awful. Leon calls them 'intractable.' They want us out." She tossed up her hands and shook her head, her brown hair shimmering in the light. "They're the only ones I can think of."

Mac lifted Daley's age range to midthirties as she told her story. "How long ago did you move in?"

"Two months. The harassment started right away."

"What about the people who lived in the house before? Maybe some resentment there?" suggested Mac.

"It was an estate sale and the heirs sold it to a flipper who sold it to us," Daley dismissed.

"Could it be anything to do with Leon?" asked Taft. "His line of work, maybe."

"There is no line of work anymore. Leon was ahead of the game on those e-cigarettes? Had a small company and sold it out to the big guys for big bucks. Before all the bad publicity. He sold before we got married and that's why he insisted on a prenup. But I'm not giving up."

"On your marriage?" Mac ventured.

"I suppose, but I was talking about the house, *my* house. I'm *not* leaving it. No way. No how."

"Where's Leon living now?" asked Mac.

"Oh, he's in the house with me. We're both there. In armed camps, so to speak. He's on one end of the wing, and I'm on the other." She nodded with her chin first one way, then the other.

Mac threw a glance at Taft. Did he really want her to take on this case? He met her gaze, but she couldn't read what he was thinking.

"Does your husband feel the same way?"

"Hard to say. We're not speaking a lot. That's why I want someone to move in with me. Before we stopped speaking, Leon joined the younger group's 'hot tub time,' not at our house, but at others'. I declined. Is it a sex swap thing?" Daley's arched brows lifted a bit higher. "Who knows? But probably. And yes, these are the *good* people. The younger group. Leon's twelve years older than I am, so it makes him feel virile, I guess."

"Just to be clear. It's only the older group you think are harassing you."

"It's those vicious ones in their fifties or sixties or whatever. I'm telling you, they're awful people."

"If you've already got a Ring, that's helpful. Have you related your harassment to the police?"

"Oh, sure, I'm reporting dog poop," she said dryly.

"Well, it sounds like there was theft involved, too."

She lifted a shoulder dismissively. "Small packages I ordered online. My makeup. Are the police going to do anything?"

Taft explained, "Daley and Leon are separating and she wants to feel safe in her own home while they work toward a divorce."

"He's trying to screw me out of everything. I signed the prenup, yes. But he owes me the house. That's what he promised when we bought it. That was our deal. Once I own it, I may have to sell it, but for now we're both camped out there. Do I want him to leave? You bet. I really wanted Jesse to move in, but he says he's too busy."

Clients and most people in Taft's circle called him by his last name. Hearing his first name on Daley's lips sent frissons along Mac's nerves.

"Move in?" Mac repeated.

"Just until Leon goes. After that I want a neighborhood watch, but not *those* neighbors. I want someone to watch *them*. I want someone to be with me and on my side twenty-four seven." Her gaze was still on Taft, as if she could will him to do her bidding. She didn't appear to want to hire Mackenzie any more than Mac wanted to be hired.

"There already is a neighborhood watch," said Taft.

"For all the good it's done me. Nobody really cares." Daley snorted.

Mac was about to suggest that she could maybe keep an eye on Daley and Leon's place from her RAV when

Daley said, "I need someone in the house with me. I need a buffer between us."

Mac could visualize herself caught in the middle of a domestic dispute between the feuding husband and wife. She pictured Daley throwing pots and pans at Leon, and she had an inner-eye view of herself ducking while kitchen cutlery flew overhead.

No. Dice.

"How's Leon going to feel about someone moving in?" she asked.

"Well, he'll hate it, of course, but like I said, I think he'd prefer a woman to a man, so there's that." She sized Mac up. "I really could use someone bigger and stronger, with more psychological heft, you know what I mean?"

"Mackenzie might surprise you," said Taft.

"I agree I might not be the right person," Mac responded at the same time.

Taft almost smiled. "Daley, how much are you willing to pay a bodyguard?"

"You're really not going to do it, are you?" She looked at him with pleading, spaniel eyes. He calmly awaited her answer, and Daley sighed and named a figure that made Mac's mercenary little heart skip a beat.

That was a lot of money.

Still . . .

Mackenzie met Taft's gaze. The bastard knew her weak spot.

You are going to regret this. . . .

"Okay," she said, inwardly cursing herself while already counting up how much she could probably make. No use standing on ceremony while there were bills to pay.

Chapter Two

Daley and Mackenzie exchanged information, but it took a while afterward for Daley to finally mosey out of Taft's condo. She was reluctant to depart, her gaze lingering on him a little too long, in Mac's biased opinion, as he held the door for her. As soon as she was gone, however, Mackenzie gave her "partner in crime" a long, hard look.

"What?" Taft asked, but that tiny smile on his lips was growing.

"Okay, who is she and what's the real story here? I understand she's married and getting a divorce, but what's the history? She definitely wanted you, not me."

"We've known each other a while," he said again.

A pause. When he didn't go on, Mac said, "Oh, thanks, Taft. That explains it all."

"There's nothing really to tell. We dated. It was short-lived. We left friends."

"Hah."

He lifted his palms and shrugged.

Mackenzie really wanted to delve deeper, but clearly Taft wasn't going to give her much more. And anyway, she needed this business relationship to work out. Nothing else would work between them. She'd been warned plenty about Taft. Unsolicited advice had poured in from everyone and anyone who knew both of them, most of it warnings to her to be extra careful. Not only was he supposedly unavailable emotionally, he had a reputation for working just inside the law . . . with maybe a step or two over the line from time to time. Mac had bought into most of the rumors at first, but she'd seen a different side of him than the gossip, an honorable side. And, well, she liked him.

"Daley wants someone to look after her for a while, and I thought you might like the work," said Taft.

"You had no intention of ever taking the job."

He slowly shook his head.

"No?"

"I'm not going to move into her house and be her bodyguard, if that's what you're asking."

"That's exactly what I'm asking. You were never going to do it, but it's okay for me to?"

"You said you wanted work. This is work."

"Yes . . ."

"But?"

But I'm not working with you.

She lifted a hand in acquiescence. "Okay, just give me some background, then, so I know what I'm walking in to."

"So, you do want the work."

"Yes, Taft. I want the work," she fairly snapped.

She could tell he was getting an inner hardy-har-har out of this, but she wanted to work with/for him, and if this was what was available, she shouldn't look a gift horse in the mouth . . . much.

He settled onto the couch, easing himself into the cushions. She fought back asking him if he was all right. It hadn't been that long since the bullet had ripped through his pectoral muscle, but she knew he wouldn't take kindly to her solicitation. She'd already been down that road.

"I met Daley about six or seven years ago. Even then, Leon was kind of around. He and Daley weren't dating, but his business was already doing well—exceptionally well—and he was getting offers to sell. Daley and I were casually seeing each other, but she . . ." Taft hesitated, clearly deciding how to proceed. After a moment he said, "She started looking at Leon differently as he succeeded, and I suppose I encouraged it."

"You wanted out of the relationship."

"'Relationship' is too strong a word."

"How about you didn't want her to get the wrong idea, so you kept her at arm's length."

"It just seemed like a natural move for her . . . and for me."

"Taft, I can relate. You didn't want to face the breakup that was coming, even though in your mind you weren't really together."

Taft seemed to want to argue but only said, "It was a long time ago."

What justified a "long time ago" in Taft's mind? Mackenzie wondered. She'd heard all about his apparently myriad ex-relationships/girlfriends from those same well-meaning friends and acquaintances who'd questioned what she was doing in his orbit. Even her old "friend" Donnie Gillis from her days of drinking/reconnaissance at the Waystation had read about her recent exploits and felt the need to address her about Taft when they happened to run into each other in downtown River Glen one afternoon.

"You and that ex-cop got something going?" Gillis had demanded. As ever, he was in cowboy hat and boots and pretending he was some kind of badass when it came to roping in women. He'd considered Mackenzie as his own even though she'd busted him for DUI twice while working for the River Glen PD. He apparently held no animus toward her and, considering their "day-drinking" afternoons, when Mackenzie was actually on the job working on surreptitiously following a couple who liked to hang out at the Waystation, as some kind of proof that he and she were together.

"You're both ex-cops, that it?" he'd asked when Mac had decided she didn't need to answer him. Gillis, however, seemed to feel he deserved answers.

"We were working on a private case."

"Oh, like PIs?" He'd squinted at her as if he was doing a serious reassessment. She could tell he thought it was a bad, bad idea.

"Well, as you said, neither of us is with the department anymore." Taft had quit two different forces, unable to fit the mold of an officer of the law. So far Mackenzie had only quit the River Glen Police Department, and even so, recently she'd been invited back. However, she had no intention of returning unless her finances became so crippled that she desperately needed a real job. She really wanted to be part of Taft's investigation business. Currently she was like a trainee of sorts, and she sensed the bigger problem was Taft really didn't want to involve her in his business, worse now since the last case. He felt responsible for her at some level, a fact he'd alluded to without outright saying so. She bristled at the idea even now; however, Taft also seemed to think she was a capable investigator, so it was difficult to work up serious indignation.

Now she looked at him and said, "I'm doing this body-guard/neighborhood harassment job because of the money, and only because of the money."

"Reason enough."

"Yeah, but you don't want to do it."

"They can't all be interesting."

Well, that was true enough.

"Want a Goldie Burger?" he asked.

Goldie Burgers were a local institution with terrible burgers and great buns, but everyone around loved them anyway. Mac and Taft defaulted to Goldie Burgers on a regular basis because neither of them leaned into cooking.

Mac picked up her phone to order.

Two hours later, after she and Taft had made short work of the burgers, she drove away from his condo and took a turn past Daley and Leon's house in the Villages neighborhood before planning to head to her apartment. The house was a U-shaped ranch, light gray with what looked like new, black fiberglass windows. The driveway was made of pavers that matched the house color, and a concrete sidewalk a few shades darker curved toward the front door from the street. The mailbox was black metal on a wooden post, not nearly as impressive as some of the others that lined the street, some full-on brick structures that sometimes incorporated their neighbors', a few painted with flowers and vines, several on carved wooden bases. None were as plain as the Carreras'. Mac made a mental note to ask about it because it appeared to recently have been put in place. Was this related to the dog poop delivery? Or had the mailbox needed to be replaced?

The sky was threatening, low and gloomy, as Mac wheeled into her designated spot at her apartment complex. She hurried toward the outdoor stairs to her second-floor unit as fat raindrops landed on her head. Another slid, icy cold, down the back of her neck, and she shivered as she made her way inside, slamming the door behind her and turning the lock. Why was it that one drop of rain could find its way under her collar every time and chill her to the bone? And when was June going to live up to its reputation as a summer month?

Shaking off the chill, she glanced down her short hallway. The doors to both bedrooms were open and boxes lined the walls. One day she would open those boxes and put their contents where they belonged, but today was not the day.

She went to the kitchen sink and washed her hands. The thought of the Carreras' mailbox infused with feces was enough to keep her at the faucet far longer than necessary.

She wandered to the second bedroom, where she'd put her laptop on a card table she'd squirreled away from her mother, seating herself on one of the three chairs she'd also managed to collect. She'd asked Mom where chair number four was, but it appeared Dan the Man had taken it with him. It was hard to become indignant about this poaching of her mother's belongings when Mac was guilty of the same thing, but she managed it, saying in a very judgy voice, "What else of yours has he liberated?" to which Mom had replied with a shrug, "Probably a lot of things."

She inputted her data on Daley Carrera into her laptop. She still used her notebook in the field, or sometimes the "Notes" app on her phone, but it was always best to write it into her computer, where she could add impressions and extra information she wouldn't take the time to jot down in the moment. As a layperson now, she was still figuring out her modus operandi, but however she gathered data, she still preferred to have it transferred to her laptop, where she basically wrote up reports for herself now instead of the department.

It didn't take long to input what little she had and when

she was finished she stared at what she'd written. It did no good to wish and hope that Taft would open up and embrace her as a worthy partner, or at least employee of sorts; that wasn't the way things were. And the hell of it was that it wasn't even a matter of him thinking she needed to be seasoned: *that* she might be able to combat. He believed in her skills. It was more that he was a solo act and wasn't good about delegating, and there was a little bit of macho bullshit mixed in where he worried about her safety as well.

Muttering to herself, Mac went into her bedroom, flopped on her bed—still just a mattress on the floor—and switched on the television. The cable guy had gotten her at least that far, so she turned to the news, found that depressing, and settled on a story about the cicadas that had made a mess out of the Northeast a few seasons back. They hatched every seventeen years. *Seventeen years*. Calculating how many times this would happen in her own lifetime, Mac was kind of disturbed it was so few.

Punching her pillow, she closed her eyes, letting the TV run, and even though it was way too early to go to sleep, she drifted off, vaguely worrying that she might not be able to sleep in this bed, such as it was, for untold days, maybe weeks . . . maybe longer, while she was playing bodyguard.

Morning came fast. Though it felt like she'd just closed her eyes, Mac jumped out of bed as if she'd been discovered in a nefarious act. She didn't even want to think of how many hours she'd been out.

Quickly, she packed up some belongings in an overnight bag for her trip to the Carreras'. She figured it was mostly reconnaissance at this point, and she planned to take short trips home during the course of the job. She wasn't going to be with Daley twenty-four seven, no matter what she thought. That would drive them both insane. Daley had been ambivalent when Mac had asked her when she should arrive, which made it seem like this bodyguard job was as flaky as it had sounded when Daley had posed it at Taft's place.

But . . . money. Rent. Gas. Food. What the hell. It was a job.

Cooper Haynes stared blankly at the computer screen on his desk, his mind busy elsewhere. He was supposed to be writing up a report on the burglary attempts by a recent graduate of River Glen High, someone his daughter, Marissa, had shared a class or two with before he graduated, but he kept thinking of other things. Several other things, as a matter of fact. On the one hand, his mind was on his fiancée, Jamie Whelan Woodward, whom he was half-living with, his belongings slowly migrating from his house to hers; on the other, he was thinking about the auditory witness to a fight between two men at a construction site that had resulted in one of them falling to his death from the second story. That witness had sworn she'd heard two voices arguing, but had later recanted that she'd heard anything at all, then had firmly placed the blame on a man who had slipped into a coma and died, so there could be no corroboration. Debra Fournier had changed course almost from the moment she'd admitted hearing the argument, certainly from the moment Cooper had shown up to take her testimony. Since then, Chief Bennihof and the department as a whole had ruled Granger Nye's death an accident, so there would be no further investigation. Case closed. Except Cooper wasn't satisfied with the decision.

"You done there, Detective?" came the female drawl.

Elena Verbena, Cooper's partner, was seated at her desk. She'd taken over his old partner's spot, and now he looked across at her. Her dark curls had been scraped back into a severe bun, her favorite work "look."

"Almost."

Actually, he'd written exactly two sentences. He'd tried to concentrate, but Jamie's face kept popping into his vision, and then Emma's, her sister's. Emma, the victim of an assault in her youth that had left her with permanent brain damage, was a unique and oddly endearing soul, a far cry from the teasing, maybe even manipulative, teenage girl Cooper had been so enamored with years earlier. After his marriage to Laura fell apart he'd thought himself incapable of falling in love, but then he'd remet Emma's younger sister, Jamie, and here he was.

"Hey, Coop, I'm heading out." Bryan "Ricky" Richards, an officer with the River Glen PD who was jonesing to be a detective bad enough to follow Cooper around like an imprinted duckling, cruised by Cooper's desk. "You need an extra hand . . ." He lifted an open palm, tacitly volunteering himself.

"I've got that covered," Verbena said coolly before Cooper could answer.

Richards left with a short chin lift of acknowledgment and Verbena slid a look Cooper's way. "*Coop?*"

Cooper shook his head. Richards's quirks for attention were somewhat annoying, but Verbena was damn near a man-hater and he didn't want to add fuel to that fire. Except that sometimes you just had to say something. . . .

"You're just a man-hater," he told her.

She said haughtily, "I hate everybody. Not just men."

"Liar."

To which she launched into a diatribe about how it

was just the men in the department she really objected to—excluding himself, of course—not the entire gender.

He didn't look up from his report. "Man hater."

"Richards has a degree in suck-up. He wants your job, or mine, probably both, but he knows better than to try his tricks on me."

"What tricks?"

She snorted, knowing he was just messing with her. "What about that teen burglary suspect? Blakely?"

"He's being processed. Since he was found with the stolen gear the family's got him a lawyer."

"Hmmm."

Cooper almost told her he planned to confront Debra Fournier again but didn't. He had to keep reminding himself it wasn't a case any longer. It was over, decided, done, and following up would do nothing but aggravate and enrage those who had closed it. Still, maybe he would just stop by and try to have a chat with Fournier, see if she would leak something that might lead him toward one of the others whom he suspected had gotten away with murder. She'd said she'd heard two men arguing just before Granger Nye took that header from the second story of a home under construction at Staffordshire Estates. Someone, or something, had spooked her into pretending later that she'd been mistaken. Nothing to hear here. Then she'd rushed to pin the blame on someone who couldn't be questioned.

Terrence Nye, Granger's brother, still called in from time to time, threatening a lawsuit if the police continued to "sweep the truth under the rug," as he put it, but Chief Bennihof told him in no uncertain terms that the case was an accidental death. The chief considered Terrence a nuisance, which he was. Definitely difficult. No, Terrence hadn't won any friends at the department, but like him, Cooper felt the true story was yet to be learned. He knew, however, that if he kept investigating he would be on his own.

Cooper briefly thought of Mackenzie Laughlin and Jesse James Taft, who'd both been as skeptical as he that Granger Nye's death was an accident. Since Mac had once been with the department, and Taft had put in a couple of stints as an officer of the law as well, once even with the River Glen PD, their opinions carried some weight. Granger Nye's death had been peripherally connected with an investigation the two of them were involved in as well. Should he count on them, maybe share information, such as it was? He knew without asking what the chief would think of that.

Maybe you should just let it go.

Cooper headed through the back door and looked around the police vehicle lot for his favorite ride. Not there. On his days on, usually everyone left that particular vehicle be. It was kind of an unspoken rule that certain officers preferred certain vehicles and, if possible, the rest moved on to some other choice. Ricky Richards might've taken Cooper's, which wasn't a crime but another sign that he was trying to be Cooper. The whole mentor/disciple song and dance Richards put on was an act that Cooper easily saw through. Richards didn't care about him one way or another. He just wanted his job, so he might've taken Cooper's ride and would claim innocence later.

It was about time to call it a day anyway, so he headed for his Trailblazer. Interviewing Debra Fournier would be on his own time, and he had reasons for heading straight home tonight, so it would have to be later. He was eager to see Jamie and move their relationship forward in a meaningful way, but he was also kind of mentally dawdling, engaging in a kind of masochistic personal torture for no good reason he could name.

Shaking his head at himself, he drove directly to the house on Clifford Street that he shared with Jamie, parking on the maple-lined street rather than the driveway. Jamie's daughter, Harley, was driving now and he'd quickly recognized it saved a lot of time moving cars if he parked on the street.

He strode up the driveway past the dogwood in the center of the yard and around the house to the back door, letting himself inside. Jamie was a teacher at River Glen High School, newly promoted from substitute to full staff. Tonight was a celebration of sorts. Harley, Marissa, and Emma were all coming to dinner and Jamie was serving up Emma's favorite dish—pasta—as they'd missed Emma's April birthday and were using it as an excuse to celebrate.

Cooper pushed through the door to hear the sound of female laughter and then Harley's voice above the rest, "Aunt Emma, you're *ancient*. Forty-two? That's like Social Security, right?"

And Emma, answering in her flat monotone, "You're teasing me."

"Of course I am. Everyone knows you have to be forty-five before you can collect."

Another peal of laughter, this time from Marissa, who Cooper suspected knew next to nothing about Social Security or anything outside their high school experience, TikTok, or Instagram. Cooper himself had just learned about "Popcat," a video of a cat photoshopped to open and close its mouth in a wide circle and make a popping noise, a TikTok sensation that made no sense but apparently had once been a viral explosion. However, just as soon as

Cooper became aware of whatever was in the zeitgeist, those viral moments became passé as the next big thing arrived, and so it went.

"I think I have to be sixty-five," said Emma. "Or maybe later."

"Let's not worry about it now," responded Jamie, who looked up as Cooper entered the kitchen from the back of the house. Her warm smile of greeting reminded him with an electric buzz of his nerves, what lay ahead.

"Hi, Cooper," greeted Emma as Harley, Marissa, and Jamie did the same.

"What are we having?" he asked.

"Nothing for a while. You're early." Jamie pointed to the oven. "Baking a chicken to go with pesto, tomatoes, and angel-hair pasta. A mash-up of Emma and Harley's choices."

Marissa piped up. "And mine."

"That's right. Marissa ordered the dessert."

"Dessert?" said Cooper with a lift of his voice.

"Don't get too excited," warned Marissa. "It's just cookies. But really big ones. With M&M's in them."

"That's worth getting excited about," Harley argued. And the two girls went off on the pluses and minuses of various cookies, with Harley turning up her nose at peanut butter, Marissa's favorite.

"When are you coming back here?" Cooper asked Emma.

Emma cocked her head. She'd moved to Ridge Pointe Independent and Assisted Living with her dog, Duchess, this last year but was thinking of moving back in with Jamie and Cooper and Harley again. As Cooper took a seat, Duchess came over and sniffed his hand. Cooper got in one pet before Duchess reseated herself by her mistress's side.

"I think we might stay," said Emma.

"At Ridge Pointe?" She'd been adamant the last time they'd spoken that she was coming back to Jamie's.

"It's almost fun," she said.

"Almost fun?" Jamie repeated. She was bending down to peer through the window of the oven, but turned and gave her sister a questioning look.

"Not a ringing endorsement," said Harley. Cooper had been thinking the same thing, one of Jamie's phrases that Harley had picked up.

"Duchess likes it better here," Emma said after a moment of thought.

"And you?" Jamie asked her.

"The cat is my friend now."

"Twinkletoes?" Marissa put in to this non sequitur.

Emma winced. Cooper expected her to remind his daughter—stepdaughter really, but he never thought of her that way—that she abhorred that name, but Emma managed to just say, "Humph" and nod.

"Something happened to it, but at least the cat came back. I was kinda worried about it," said Harley.

"Me too," said Emma.

Harley speared a couple of olives with her fork from the antipasto tray that Jamie had set out. As soon as Harley was in, Marissa did the same. Emma examined the olives critically and said, "They're not the black ones."

"No, they're not, but they're good," Jamie said equably, used to her sister's ways.

"Is the cat's welfare the reason you're hesitating about moving back?" asked Cooper. Twinkletoes seemed to be a resident, along with all the elderly and/or compromised in some way people, like Emma, who made their home at the facility. According to what he'd learned from Emma and

Harley, who worked part time at Ridge Pointe, the cat was a prognosticator of when someone was about to die. It would curl up in the resident's bed beside them a few days before that person's death. It wasn't always accurate—it liked sleeping with whoever would take it in, apparently— but it was correct enough to give the occupants the willies and the staff a hint to what may be coming.

Emma said, "If I move back, I would like the cat to move with me."

"Seriously?" Harley stared at Emma. Cooper couldn't tell whether it was a good stare or a bad one.

"It's just creepy," said Marissa, making a face.

"It's just a cat," said Emma.

"Is it, though?" asked Harley.

"Yes." Emma was firm. "It is."

Jamie gave Harley "the eye" and Harley slid out of her chair and said to Marissa, "Let's go upstairs until dinner."

The two girls disappeared and Emma gazed after them, a line of consternation etched into her forehead. "If it's not just a cat, what is it?"

"It's just a cat," Jamie agreed briskly. "And if you want the cat to come here, the cat can come here. You can even name it something else."

Cooper looked at Jamie. When her mother died she left Jamie the house and the express wish that she take care of Emma. Jamie had moved back to River Glen from Los Angeles and done just that. Her mother had managed to save enough money to provide for Emma's continuing care and though there was initial worry that that nest egg had been misappropriated by the lawyers in charge of Irene Whelan's estate, everything had eventually worked out. It had then been Emma's choice to move to Ridge Pointe, not Jamie's. In truth, they all preferred having Emma around.

"Maybe it won't like it here," Emma said, the line in her brow deepening. "And Duchess doesn't like the cat."

"You decide what you want to do," said Jamie.

"I decide what I want to do."

"Yes."

"Okay," said Emma.

Fifteen minutes later, Jamie pulled out two loaves of hot, crusty bread from the oven and served them with garlic butter, a salad of greens, pepperoncinis, thinly sliced red onions, and halved cherry tomatoes to go with the pesto chicken.

Cooper felt his nerves begin buzzing again as the girls were called back and they all sat down to dinner. Harley and Marissa began talking about school and his mind drifted briefly to the burglary suspect, Timothy Blakely, whose wealthy parents were unhappy with the police department as a whole and Cooper in particular, but then work faded into the background as he looked around the table, focusing on the people he cherished most in his life.

"You're awfully quiet," Jamie said as they were finishing up.

"Am I?"

"You know you are." She regarded him suspiciously.

Cooper smiled and lifted his water glass, looking around at the lot of them. Harley and Marissa had picked up their plates, but now they looked at him, set the plates back down, took their seats, and also lifted their glasses. Emma glanced back and forth and mimicked the girls. Jamie slowly raised her glass and looked at him quizzically.

"A toast to my family," said Cooper.

They all obediently took a sip of their water, and then Jamie said, "Why do I get the feeling something's up?"

Cooper pushed back his chair as he reached into his pocket. He bent to one knee and held out the ring box to Jamie, flipping open the lid. He tried to ask, "Will you marry me?" but was drowned out by Harley and Marissa, who gasped and shrieked while Emma declared, "A ring!"

Jamie got the message, though, because her hands flew to her mouth in shock and looked stunned. Her hazel eyes began blinking rapidly. Though they'd sort of talked about marriage, it had been for somewhere in the nebulous future.

"You have to answer him," Emma pointed out reasonably.

"Y—yes." Jamie choked out. "Yes!"

"Cookies!" cried Harley, jumping up to get them, nearly knocking over her water glass.

"Oh my God!" screamed Marissa as Cooper slid the ring onto Jamie's finger.

Everyone began talking at once and Duchess, confused by the sudden noise, added to it with loud barking that could probably be heard down the street. Then Jamie was in Cooper's arms. He buried his face in her thick, light brown hair and inhaled deeply, loving her soft, summery scent. He was happy in a giddy way he hadn't felt in a long, long time.

Chapter Three

Mackenzie headed for the Carreras' home in the Villages. In the back of her mind she figured Daley needed less of a bodyguard and more of a way to determine who was behind the thieving and harassment leveled at them and why. If she could figure that out, she might convince Daley she didn't need Mackenzie full time. Ergo the overnight bag instead of more of her belongings.

She called Taft on the way over, putting her phone in its iOttie holder and pressing the screen to engage the Speaker button so she didn't need earbuds. She listened to five rings before Taft picked up.

"Hi, Laughlin," he answered.

He sounded detached, so she said, "I'm on my way over to Daley's. Just planning to check it out. I think she needs someone to figure out what's going on, not a bodyguard."

"If you can convince her of that, good going."

"You sound like there's no chance."

"Daley's determined."

Mac read that to mean "stubborn," which didn't bode well. Stubborn people, in her experience, didn't listen much to logic or reason when it conflicted with their worldview. She'd wasted her breath enough times on lost causes to know.

"We never got a chance last night to talk about some other things. I wanted to ask you about Mangella," said Mackenzie.

"I don't know anything more than the last time you asked," he clipped out.

"You still working with him?" she pressed, moving past Daley to the subject she really wanted to discuss. He was tetchy about Mangella.

"I'm talking to him soon."

His tone warned her that she was treading into an area she was unwelcome. She knew she was. But he'd said he was cutting ties with the man and she just wanted him to get on with it. And she wanted to know about it. Taft was shutting her out where Mangella was concerned and she was tired of him picking and choosing when she could be left on the outside. If they were working together, she didn't think she should be blocked from the man who had once been Taft's biggest client. If they were working together, she wanted to be part of it.

And what if you're not?

She tried a different tact. "What about Andrew Best?" she asked now. If he wouldn't talk about Mangella, she would move on to another River Glen luminary with suspicious business ventures.

"Still looking into it," he said.

Yeah . . . well . . . maybe . . . She sensed he'd given up on investigating Andrew Best, leaving the prominent home builder to the River Glen Police. Best was the major developer of River Glen's newest housing development, the ultrahot Staffordshire Estates, where homes were being snapped up for over asking, a result of the blistering current

housing market. Both Best Homes and Laidlaw Construction, the company Mackenzie's stepsister's husband,
Nolan Redfield, worked for, seemed to be vying to be the
most popular builder. Each of them were offering deals—
if you could call them that—to cruise through their model
homes, and Best had a whole office building and staff
nearly on-site prepared to hold the client's hand through
the process. While Best was enticing would-be home buyers
to his subdivision, Laidlaw Construction was currently
focused on renovating high-rent office and apartment
buildings in downtown River Glen and erecting newer
brick ones that still kept with the Midwestern storefront
architecture of fiftysome years earlier, a retro look that
appealed to the young suburbanites who were moving
into the area and wanted something more "authentic" in
the area.

So far, the two companies seemed to be neck and neck
in popularity, but with slightly different customer bases.
They each had more work than either of them could handle.

But it was Best's foreman, Granger Nye, who'd fallen
from the second story of a house under construction and
died. Mac and Taft had both felt Best was either involved
in the accident or at the very least knew more than he was
telling. Mac had hoped Detective Cooper Haynes of the
River Glen Police Department would follow up on Best.
Maybe he was, but she'd heard the case was closed, so
maybe he wasn't. She and Taft had talked over Nye's
death, but they weren't being paid to look in to it. Still . . .
nagging, hangnail questions always bothered her.

"What about the witness who overheard the argument
between Nye and . . . whoever?" she asked.

"River Glen PD made it apparent we were to steer clear
of that investigation."

"I know what Bennihof wants. He wants to sweep the whole thing under the rug. They got the drug dealers, so the chief doesn't want to keep after his friend, Andrew Best."

"Since when are they friends?"

"You *know* they are. That isn't news."

"There's a connection there," Taft agreed. "But what that is hasn't been determined yet and the case is closed."

"Taft," she said, exasperated. "This isn't like you. What's the holdup? The chief and Best run in the same circles with all the other River Glen megamillionaires, such as they are."

"Laughlin—"

"You've put me off for over two months. Nothing's happening and now I'm playing BFF to one of your ex-girlfriends rather than going after the bad guys?"

"If you don't want the job, tell her. I've got a meeting."

"A meeting?"

"I'll fill you in later."

He said goodbye before he clicked off, but she could tell she'd irked him. Well . . . fine. She was irked as well. "I'll fill you in later" could be Taft's middle name.

Maybe you should just give up and go back to work at the department.

Mac pressed her lips into a thin line. She had her own history with Chief Bennihof and knew that would never be a consideration as long as he was in charge. She also *wanted* to work with Taft. He just made it so damned hard sometimes.

Tamping down her frustration, Mackenzie drove her RAV4 into the Villages. which were cheek by jowl with the newer, swankier homes of Staffordshire Estates on their west side, houses light-years apart in size and style, though affordability per square foot wasn't good for either.

The Villages—Victor's Villages, as they had been originally named—consisted of houses laid out in concentric circles accessed off a four-lane entry road—two lanes in, two out—on either side of a wooden sign that took pride of place in front of the park and was the size of a billboard, now just reading The Villages. Black-topped roads ran around the sign and the park both east and west, then fanned out to the rows of streets behind. Those roads were named alphabetically in sections. The first section were the A streets, the second the B, and Daley's house was on Calloway Court, one of the C streets. Mac didn't know how many lettered sections followed before the Villages ran into the East Glen River on the east and the high basalt fence that cut them off from Staffordshire Estates on the western side of the development.

She drove around the welcoming sign and the park, winding through the As and Bs until she found the Cs. She turned down Concordia Avenue and about a third of the way around the C arc was Calloway Court, a small street that ended in a cul-de-sac. Daley and Leon's house was the fifth one in. Mac had viewed it yesterday, but now there were two expensive vehicles in the driveway, an Audi and a Tesla, both black. In the front yard a magnolia tree was just losing its blooms, as were two towering rhododendrons. Blue Peters, possibly, Mac thought. Maybe Blue Ensigns, her mother's favorites, only now the top flowers were bedraggled and bruised from the rain and cold of May. But if this year turned out to be anything like the last few, the weather would turn soon and get hot in a hurry.

She parked on the street in front of the house. Unlike the

newer Staffordshire Estates, there weren't HOA rules about overnight parking, as far as she could tell. Just as well because there was no room for her RAV on the driveway.

She left her bag in the car as she headed for the front door up a gray-toned, brick-lined walk on exposed aggregate. At the front door she hesitated a moment before pressing the bell. Kind of a last moment of sanity. She felt the job was overkill against the harassment the Carreras had faced, but for the moment she was committed to it. And she hadn't met Leon Carrera yet, so he was an unknown.

She glanced back to the black mailbox. Two other mailboxes were in line with it. Had they been targeted as well? Daley hadn't said so. And why had the Carreras been picked out? What had—

The door swung inward and a man stood on the other side. A man with a shiny shaved head and a huge smile that seemed welcoming. Or maybe that smile was full of mischief, even malice . . . ? Or was that just how Daley had colored her husband for Mac?

"You must be Daley's friend," he greeted her in a purposeful drawl.

So, she'd told him about her.

"You must be Leon."

He held his hand to his chest and bent his head. "The same. Come on in."

Leon Carrera was tall and spent a lot of hours at the gym, if the circumference of his upper arms and breadth of his shoulders was any indication. His dark eyes were sharp and his mouth appeared to be curved in a perpetual smile. He wore a loose gray sweater that hugged his biceps and a pair of jeans that looked as if they'd seen better days but were more than likely made that way on purpose. His bare feet were in woven loafers. His casual but expensive look seemed almost too purposeful, but hey, a person's sartorial choices were their own. Her own style could be classified as "perpetually underdressed."

"Daley's out for a run, I think. She should be back soon," he reiterated. "Should be, but I really have no idea where she is, so maybe not. She doesn't tell me what she's doing, and I don't tell her what I'm doing. I'd ask where you two plan to go, but I have no right, so your itinerary is of no concern. Would you like something to drink?"

"No, thanks." She was glad she hadn't shown up with her bag. Clearly Daley hadn't let him know the true nature of her reason for being there. "Her car's out front."

"She's in the neighborhood, then. I'm gonna have a Bloody Mary. You sure you won't take one? There's wine, too, or something stronger."

"It's almost ten. Sure. I'll join you in a Bloody Mary," said Mac.

He grinned. All white teeth.

She followed him across a section of living room to the kitchen, an open concept with white cabinets, light-colored, manufactured quartz countertops, and square-shaped can lights that sent bright illumination along the work spaces. No wonder Daley wanted the house. The gleaming kitchen alone was enough to get potential buyers flocking.

"Daley said you're interested in helping us find who- ever left us our smelly, brown mailbox gift." He added a liberal dose of vodka to a premade pitcher of a tomato-y mix, then poured two highball glasses to the brim, topping off the concoction with a stalk of celery, a toothpick heavy with pimento-stuffed green olives, and a pickled aspara- gus spear.

"She did," Mac said, accepting her glass. "Salad for breakfast," she added.

"This is lunch for me. I was up early. She said she was going to bring someone home who would find out who the culprit is. That you?"

The amount of vodka, horseradish, and Worcestershire in the drink burned Mac's nose and brought tears to her eyes. "Phew," she said, setting down the glass.

Leon put his drink to his lips, his eyes on Mac, and chugged it all in one breath. She could see his throat swallow the big gulps, and within a few seconds he'd finished and set his glass on the quartz kitchen counter so hard Mac half expected it to shatter.

Mac pulled out her celery stalk and crunched into it, not sure if she was supposed to applaud or what.

Leon turned to pour himself a second drink. "Let me know when you're ready."

"Think I'll be fine with just one."

"The group around here knows how to have a good time, although Daley's a lightweight. I try to get her to join in, but to be honest, she's a bit of an albatross when it comes to having fun."

"The group?" Mac asked.

"The young guard." He stirred his new drink with his finger. This time it was sans the vegetables. Serious drinking . . . at ten in the morning.

"That's what Daley calls us anyway. The older generation she calls the 'old guard.' And they are a bunch of rigid, tight-ass rule makers."

"You're part of the young guard," she reiterated, just to be sure. Daley had said Leon was twelve years her senior and he looked to be in his late forties or early fifties, and she was trying to get a bead on what age constituted what.

He sucked some of the red mix from his index finger, leaving the digit in his mouth long seconds before pulling it out slowly. He then said, "If you saw the old guard, you'd know I don't belong there for any reason. They don't like us and we don't like them."

"Could that be who's harassing you? Someone in the old guard?"

"They'd be more likely to just slap down another rule on us. That Evelyn Jacoby . . . She looks out her window at our hot tub parties. I swear, she's creamin' those jeans even while she pretends to be appalled. She won't stop staring. I mooned her a few times at Jeannie's. She's a crazy bitch." He laughed. "She's not head of the neighborhood watch, but that's what we call her."

"Who's Jeannie?"

"A friend," he said cagily.

"And who are the neighborhood watch?" asked Mac. She could tell Leon wanted her to follow up on Jeannie further, but she sensed that would send the discussion off point. She could find out from Daley.

"The old guard, mostly. None of us want to do it."

"They don't know anything about who's behind your harassment?"

Leon gave her a hard look. "Did Daley hire you? Like actually pay you to find our sneaky asshole poop sniper?"

Mackenzie wondered if she should mention that Daley really wanted a bodyguard and it was partly because of him. Because he seemed to know nothing about it, she decided to keep that to herself. "Yes, she did."

"Well, isn't she free with my money."

Mac wasn't sure what their monetary situation was, but she chose to ignore the comment. "She said you've had mail stolen?"

Leon shrugged and seemed to shake off his objections or suspicions and just go with it. "Packages. Porch pirates. Nothing important, as it turns out, but I'd like to fill those bandits' backsides full of buckshot at the very least."

"You think it's more than one person?"

"Maybe. I don't know." He slugged down more of his drink. He was making short work of his second Bloody Mary while she'd barely touched her first. She took another sip, and the horseradish caught the back of her throat again, burning her eyes. She had to admire how unaffected Leon seemed to be.

"So, if not the old guard, who?" she asked once she sensed she could trust herself to talk normally again. Damn, those things were hot.

"We've got 'em on Ring. You wanna see?"

"Yes."

Leon showed her on his phone, where he clicked the Ring icon and pulled up a file of someone in a dark gray hoodie that was tightened all the way around their face except for a pair of dark sunglasses hurrying up to their porch around twilight and sweeping up two small packages. "Daley's makeup, apparently," he said, then scrolled to another picture of someone in the same clothes opening their mailbox and dumping what looked like a doggy waste bag inside. There was something about how quickly the person moved that made them seem young.

As if reading her mind, Leon burped and said, "Not the old guard."

"Maybe someone in their twenties or thirties, or a teenager?"

"You think that's a guy or a gal?" Leon asked.

The suspect wore a heavy dark gray or black jacket, dark pants, black shoes. There was really no way to tell.

"He or she runs off to the right, into the neighborhood," Mac observed.

"Yeah, well, they probably parked down the street. I asked around if anyone had a camera so we could see, but no one does. They were all fucking rude. I kinda hoped they'd all die."

Mac gave him a look, but he had that smile fixed on his lips.

"Oh, forget it. No one wanted to get involved. A bunch of timid mice, quivering, worrying that whatever's going on will happen to them if they say anything. Not that I think they know anything. They're just weak."

"Your neighbors are . . . the old guard?"

"Old guard, young guard. My Calloway Court neighbors aren't really either one, except Althea."

"Althea?"

"Althea Gresham. She's older than the old guard. Really old. In charge of the neighborhood watch, which is really a joke. They're just old people who don't have anything to do."

He finished his second drink, slammed down the glass, then went to the refrigerator. "I'm having a beer. Want one?"

"No, thanks."

"You're asking yourself if I have a drinking problem. Probably. I made a helluva lot of money and now I'm bored. That's what my shrink would say if I had one. I'm just living the dream." He took out a bottle of Dos Equis and popped the top with a bottle opener already on the counter. "Where was I?" he asked.

"Your neighbors."

He pointed the top of the bottle at her. "The regular old guard, not Althea. There's Burt Deevers. HOA president and his ex-wife . . . mmm . . . her name starts with a 'T' . . . I can never remember it. She doesn't live here anymore, but I think she owns part of the house? She shows up to some of the HOA meetings and—it's Tamara. That's her name. And then there's Cliff and Clarice. Cliff is like right-hand man to Burt, but Clarice . . ." He started trembling all over, wobbling his head. "She shakes like there's an earthquake inside her. And she's convinced we're all going to hell. Oh, and Darrell and Evelyn. Now there's a chilly pair. Make me and Daley look like lovebirds, which of course we are." More of his devilish smile.

"Clarice says you're all going to hell?" repeated Mac. Leon was making her a little uncomfortable, but he was a font of information, probably most of it unrelated to Daley and him, but she wasn't about to stop him if he felt like sharing.

"Clarice Fenwick. But it's Evelyn who looks down at us from her window. Jeannie's hot tub is right in Darrell and Evelyn's line of view. Half the joy in getting naked is to give her a show." He took a long pull on his beer.

"I take it Hot Tub Jeannie is with the young guard?"

"Hot Tub Jeannie. She'd like that." He chortled. "I'll have to tell her. She's with Chris right now, Chris Palminter. They have one of the old houses, the original Victor's Village plans. Most people have remodeled and fixed up and mostly screwed up the places. Luckily ours was renovated by someone who knew what they were doing. The Villages were built twenty-five years ago by this guy named Victor, who some of the old guard, the ones in charge of the HOA mostly, all knew."

Mackenzie was acquainted with some of the history of the development but again let Leon Carrera add his take to it.

"You're really interested in this?" he questioned.

"It's background. Who besides Althea is on the neighborhood watch?"

"I don't know all of 'em. Shaking Clarice and Staring Evelyn. Maybe Burt's ex, uhhh . . . shit . . . *Tamara*."

"Even though she doesn't live here?"

"Maybe she owns a rental property? You should ask Daley. She knows more than you'd ever want to about those old farts. There's some men on the watch, too. Where did you meet Daley?" he asked curiously.

"Through a friend."

"And you're going to *investigate* our prankster?"

He clearly didn't have all the particulars on Daley's reasons for hiring her. Mac was deciding if this was the time to tell him when he snapped his fingers. "Two-Timing Tamara. That's what I'll call her. She supposedly fuc—had sex with Victor. Burt found out and kicked her ass out. She wouldn't give up the house, though."

"Victor of 'Victor's Villages'?" she clarified.

"Yesiree. He's dead now, but I guess the scandal rocked the neighborhood back then. And she wasn't the only one. The old guard can sneer at us, but they've got skeletons in their own closets. Big skeletons. Victor cut a swath through them. He and Andre Messinger—Dr. Andre Messinger, as seen on TV?"

"The body-sculpting doc?"

He snapped his fingers and pointed at her. "That's the one. He and Victor purportedly ran through the women in the neighborhood. Abby Messinger . . ." He gave a wolf whistle. "She's still hot, man. I don't know how old she is. Somewhere in her fifties? Just one of those women who looks beautiful all the time. Daley really doesn't like her. She lives here with their son, Alfie, a teenager, but Andre moved to Portland . . . or somewhere. Not here anyway. He's remarried, but Daley says he's still in love with his wife. Maybe. I would never do seconds, though. One time at the altar is enough."

Mac thought Daley sure seemed to have a lot of information for someone who'd only lived in the area a few months.

"There's a whole history about some of the old guard and Victor," Leon went on. "He's been dead like fifteen, twenty years, but the way they talk, it's like he's still around."

"What about the young guard?" asked Mackenzie when Leon ran down.

"They're all okay. We're all getting together tonight. Maybe you'd like to join us at Jeannie and Chris's," he said suggestively, waggling his eyebrows.

Mac smiled faintly and Leon laughed, and that's when the door from the garage banged open and Daley swept in, still breathing hard from her run. She looked from Mac to Leon and back again, and Mackenzie saw her lips tighten.

"I see you two have met," she said.

Chapter Four

As soon as Taft got off the phone with Mackenzie, he drove to the home of his old "associate," Mitch Mangella. He'd purposely put Mac off about the man and was castigating himself for promising that she could help him take him down. He didn't want her anywhere near him. Mangella was dangerous and unpredictable. Taft had old scores to settle with the man, old scores that had tickled the back of his brain for a long time but had never been fully acknowledged, old scores he'd hidden from Mangella behind a good-natured bonhomie. But he knew now how much he'd been lied to. He'd known it all along at some level but had fooled himself into believing Mangella was more than the "mob boss" people believed of him. Now he realized that wasn't true. Mangella had shown his true colors.

Taft rubbed a hand over his face and grimaced. He'd thrust Mackenzie onto Daley Carrera more because he wanted her busy and away from Mangella than because he didn't want the job—which he didn't, but that was beside the point. Daley's bodyguard job was a convenient way to push her toward something else. In actual fact, it was a godsend. Something to occupy Mac's time. Of course she suspected what he was doing, but it was better than having her in Mangella's sights. The man wasn't taking kindly to Taft's decision to take a few steps back. It hadn't been proven yet, but Mangella had brushed close to an illegal drug operation, and if evidence revealed he was involved, that was the end for Taft. He'd lost a sister to drugs. He would not be a party to anything to do with them. And Mangella knew it. The last month and a half had been a dance between them, with Taft wanting to know what Mangella's involvement was and Mangella slipping like an eel away from any real admission of guilt.

He arrived at Mangella's house—a sprawling Tudor that rambled around a large corner lot flanked by maples and separated from the neighbors by lines of Douglas firs on either side of the "estate"—and strode determinedly up the steps. He was greeted by Prudence, Mangella's beautiful and treacherous wife, who opened the door before he could even knock.

"My, don't you look serious," she said with a smile, grabbing his hand and swinging it like they were going for a stroll.

Taft smiled. He wasn't known for being a hard-ass. He was known for bending . . . maybe even bending the law. But his anger was deep. A dark well that barely rippled on his outer countenance. At the shootout that had nearly killed him—an inch in a different direction and the bullet would have found its mark—that dark well had roiled. And the turbulence wasn't for himself, it was for Mackenzie. She'd been there and he'd suddenly feared for her life, a grip on his heart that hadn't let up even after he'd woken in the hospital, drugged and reliving the incident. Fear had taken over. Fear for her.

He'd been hiding that fear ever since and was determined to quash it. So far it hadn't worked. He'd kept away from Mackenzie as a result, which had pissed her off, he knew, but it had also kept her away from Mangella.

"There are those dimples," Prudence said, sliding him a sideways look.

"Is he in the den?"

"Of course," she said on a sigh.

The sliding doors were open to the bookshelf-lined room and she stepped through ahead of him. Mitch was at the bar, already pouring a drink for them both. He waved Taft nearer. "Prudence . . ." was all he said and she rolled her eyes and turned on one four-inch heel.

"Yeah, yeah, I'll leave you boys to it." She slid the doors closed behind her and her rapid, angry footsteps sounded across the tile entryway. Mostly she and her husband got along, even when they were fighting, playing elaborate head games with each other. But Mangella was strict about letting her in on his talks with his associates, which he apparently still considered Taft, even though they'd recently suffered a deep chasm of distrust when he'd decided Mackenzie meant something to Taft and he'd seen her as a way to get to him. Taft let it be known that Mackenzie Laughlin was off the table, but Mangella had just smiled and the chill had entered Taft's bloodstream. The dark well water was running ice-cold through his veins. He wasn't going to let this man, this associate . . . no longer even the whisper of a friend . . . do anything to Mackenzie.

Taft wasn't sure Mangella knew he'd crossed a line with him. There were no lines in his world. He undoubtedly wouldn't care anyway. But the line had been crossed and Taft had decided very clearly that it was time to take his old "friend" down. Completely. No slaps on the wrist. Total takedown.

"No, thanks," said Taft to the already poured Maker's Mark.

"What're you having?" Mangella asked, spreading his hands. The bar itself was old dark wood, scrolled with elaborate swirls and fleurs-de-lis. Mangella swore it was from an Italian bistro, brought over from the old country. Maybe it was. Whatever the case, he loved to hide behind it whenever there was a serious conversation afoot. Taft had seen him pull the same ploy with businessmen, auditors, and even the law.

"Think I'll just have water."

"Not one of those that has to wait for noon for a drink, are ya?" He grinned.

Mangella knew him better than that, but Taft shrugged. They both sensed the ground had shifted between them. Mangella just didn't know how much.

Mangella tossed ice into an old-fashioned glass and squirted water from a bartender's spigot into it. Then he thought about it a half moment and chose the same for himself. Handing Taft his glass, he clicked his own against it. "Bottoms up." He took a swallow, never allowing his eyes to leave Taft's. Moments spun by, then Mangella set down his glass and demanded, "Okay, what the fuck is it?"

Though Mackenzie's safety was paramount, it wasn't the only impetus for Taft to break with Mangella. Mangella had so far skirted the issue of distributing illegal drugs and the ongoing investigation still embroiling Andrew Best among other things, but all he said was, "Keith Silva."

Mangella lifted one brow. "Silva's bothering you? That

why you've been a ghost? You've got the job, man. You know that."

Amoral sack of shit Keith Silva had taken Taft's place on Mangella's team, but that wasn't why Taft had brought him up. "Silva's a bigger problem for you than for me. He was dirty when he was a cop and he's dirty now."

"And because I use him in my business, just like I use you," he reminded, "you've decided I'm dirty, too."

"I know who you are, Mitch."

"Anna is a friend of Prudence's . . ." he said.

Now, how did that fit in?

Anna DeMarcos was the widow of the officer Keith Silva shot dead when they were both cops. Officer Carlos DeMarcos had been Silva's partner and Silva had apparently accidentally shot him during the melee of a convenience store robbery gone wrong, and then swore the killing was just a tragic accident. The River Glen PD asked Silva to leave after a substantial government payout to Anna DeMarcos, the widow, and though Silva had initially resisted, he'd finally given in. Meanwhile, rumor had it that the lovely widow had actually put a hit out on her husband and used Silva as the weapon. Taft had tried to corroborate that rumor but hadn't gotten very far because the informant was the robber who'd committed the crime and not much of a reliable source. And then River Glen Police Chief Hugh Bennihof had eased Silva out and washed his hands of the whole affair, wanting no further stain on the department while he was running it.

So, though he had no proof, Taft believed Anna DeMarcos could very well be the architect of her husband's death, and now he'd learned the widow DeMarcos and Silva were involved with Mangella.

"Mitch, our working relationship is at an end," said Taft. No reason to pussyfoot around any longer.

"Just like that?"

"It's been coming a long time." They both knew it, but Mangella was clearly going to make Taft have to spell it out. "And then there's—"

"The girl," Mangella cut in. "Your girl."

Taft had been going to bring up Andrew Best's ties to the drug bust earlier in the year, but Mangella's words stopped him.

"Yes," he said simply. Mangella had obliquely threatened to use her to keep him in line.

Mackenzie assessed him in that reptilian way he sometimes adopted. Taft felt his chest tighten in response, but then Mangella waved a hand. "You read way too much into my simple interest in your life. If I'd known you were so touchy about her, I would have said something different. It's just words. Yours, mine. We were angry. If we have a problem, we work it out. You and I together. That's how I operate. It's how you operate. I look at it that we're having a family disagreement, an argument. You've taken it very personally." He lifted his hands, palms out. "Okay, she's your woman. Hands off."

Taft didn't want the war that was going to break out between them, dreaded it, but knew it was inevitable. He'd worked with scumbags before. The wealthy. The spoiled. The ruthless. Some of the cops hated him for it, especially because he'd been one of them once . . . actually twice. It had never bothered him much. He'd seen enough graft and favoritism and downright criminal activity within the ranks of the police—others similar to Silva—to have walked away with a clear conscience over his next choice of jobs.

"Can we get down to business now?" asked Mangella.

"That was the business."

He wagged a finger. "I need you to do something for me. I need you to talk to someone. A little discussion. Need to make my position clear."

Taft just waited. If this was the last dance Mangella insisted on, he would hear him out. Mangella had never asked Taft to shake someone down before. He'd never been so blatant in crossing the line into the gray legal area where Taft now knew Mangella mostly lived.

"You wanna know who?"

"Seems like you're dying to tell me."

"Bennihof."

Taft felt his pulse jump. "You want me to tell the chief of the River Glen Police that Mitchell Mangella needs to make his position clear?"

"The chief's getting pressure he needs to ignore."

Taft wasn't foolhardy enough to take on the police chief, but Mangella knew how much he disliked the man, so it was easy to continue talking as if he were really listening. "Who from? The mayor?"

"No, we're all friends," Mangella said with a dismissive shrug, as if Taft were veering off the point. "But Bennihof is getting squeezed and there's a . . . um . . . delicate matter that's getting in the way of him remembering his loyalties."

"What delicate matter?"

"Well, you know he's in trouble and has been making some bad choices about who his friends are. . . ."

Taft squinted at Mangella. Bennihof had been inappropriate and handsy with a number of female officers, Mackenzie Laughlin among them, and so far had managed to skate serious accusations and hang on to his job. Taft thought he was a scumbag and had urged Mac to go after the man, make him face his behavior, but there hadn't been a strong enough case to date. But maybe something had changed. Maybe something that was coming down from the mayor's office?

Mangella's dark eyes glittered and Taft said slowly, "You think Bennihof's going to bargain with something he knows about you in order to keep his job?"

"Well, there's nothing to tell about me, of course, but I don't want to suffer the bad publicity."

If Bennihof pointed fingers, Mangella would lose credibility in some of the circles in which he ran.

"I can't help you," said Taft.

"The chief's looking for a life raft. You could throw him one." Mangella spread his hands as if it were self-evident.

Taft just shook his head. Both Mangella and Bennihof had made their beds.

"Your . . . girlfriend . . . could put in a good word for him."

Taft almost laughed. Mackenzie? Mangella was way off.

"What?" Mangella asked, narrowing his eyes at him.

Taft was not going to even mention Mackenzie if he could help it, so he changed the subject, "What's going on with you and Andrew Best?"

Mangella didn't react, but it was from years of carefully controlling his every move, not because he didn't know what Taft was talking about. Mangella had told him that he and Best were considering some kind of partnership, but Best had been mired in drug-related, illegal activity at his business, trying to save his skin and acting like he'd had no idea what was coming down, so whatever deal he had with Mangella was something Mangella did not talk about to his old friend, Jesse Taft.

"I haven't spoken to Mr. Best in over a month."

"Still going into business with him?"

"His unfortunate troubles have delayed our deal. He's working on clearing things up and then we can move forward."

"Home building, or something else?"

Mangella smiled faintly. "I've known you're not a team player. Been warned about it, too."

"Silva." Taft was dry.

"I thought your inability to stay with the police boded well, but maybe it's just displaced loyalty. Should I stop trusting you?"

"Did you ever?"

"Of course I did."

"Trust has always been in short supply between us."

He looked disappointed. "Sounds like you're telling me something I don't want to hear. . . ."

"Our business interests parted ways awhile back."

Mangella's brows lifted. "You aren't *leaving*. . . . That . . . could be bad for both of us."

"I've given you reasons why I'm out. Add in Andrew Best's involvement with drugs. That's a deal breaker in itself."

"He never knew about what was going on in the company," Mangella insisted flatly, showing his first bit of temper. "And that's all taken care of now."

How had Andrew Best not known what was going on right under his nose? He was not a figurehead. He was aware of everything that went on inside Best Homes—his company—and though it hadn't been proven, he was likely to be as dirty as everyone else involved.

And Mangella knew that, too.

"Where are you going?" Mangella asked sharply as Taft headed for the door.

"Time for me to go."

"You're not talking to Bennihof?"

"He doesn't listen to me."

"He will," Mangella insisted. "When my name's mentioned."

"Goodbye, Mitch."

Mangella inhaled deeply through his nose and straightened. "A sad day for both of us," he said softly.

The warning made the hairs on Taft's arms stand on end as he pulled apart the den's sliding doors himself.

"Tell that pretty ex-cop I said hi . . ." Mangella added, a final coup de grâce.

His quiet threat trailed after Taft as he beelined for the front door. Threatening Mackenzie Laughlin was a sure way to make certain he would never work for the man again.

Prudence pounced on him while his fingers were clamped around the front door handle. "You'll be back," she sing-songed.

"You should stop playing games with him," Taft advised, unable to help himself even though he knew it was an exercise in futility. "One or the other of you will get hurt eventually."

"Like you care what happens to us."

"I do care what happens to you."

"You wouldn't be leaving if you did."

"What's your connection to Anna DeMarcos?"

She started at the question before she could pull on the mask again. "We're friends."

"How?" he asked. Anna was a cop's wife and Prudence was queen of the castle.

"Have you met her? She's a lovely person."

They stared at each other for a few moments. Prudence

had girlfriends who sometimes went a little too far in playing the games she and Mangella set up, games that sometimes had life-changing consequences for them.

"I'll see you around," he told her.

She didn't answer as he yanked open the door and headed outside and to his Rubicon. Pulling away from the curb, he glanced back at Prudence through his rearview. She stood in the doorway, her eyes following him until he rounded the corner.

His pulse was running fast and hard. He didn't have to search his emotions to know the veiled threats to Mackenzie Laughlin were at the heart of it. Still, he found himself looking forward to spending time with her, picking her brain, working through conflicting accounts by people they interviewed, just being with her . . . but now that Mangella had her in his sights, the danger level had risen exponentially and was unacceptable.

Just take her to bed and get on with it. You want to. Seems like she does, too.

Taft jerked his head around, hearing his sister's voice. He hadn't heard it in months. It made him smile in spite of himself. Helene was his muse, his conscience, his best friend. Ten years older than himself, she'd been gone about that same amount of time. Sometimes he saw her in a vision, other times she was just a voice. A product of his imagination, he nevertheless liked to think of her as real.

"I don't want a romantic relationship with Laughlin."

Liar . . .

"I can't have one because it would ruin things."

He waited for the answer, but there was none. He thought about Mackenzie, ensconced now at the Carrera household, and his nerves tightened. Maybe he'd been too hasty, maybe Daley Carrera did have a legitimate fear of whoever was targeting her and her husband, and what did he really know about Leon Carrera anyway?

You can't keep her in a glass box.

Helene or his own conscience, whatever . . . in that they were right. He had to stop acting like an overbearing parent. Mackenzie was her own person, capable and smart.

But when he thought about Mitch Mangella's cold-bloodedness, he knew it would be an uphill climb to stop himself from protecting her.

Chapter Five

"Well?" Daley said, eyeing Leon's beer and Mackenzie's half-drunk Bloody Mary. She'd stopped short upon seeing them at the kitchen island and now looked at both of them with suspicion. In tight-fitting joggers and matching layers of two tanks—the underneath one black like the joggers, the top one a rather virulent lilac—she looked fit and hard. If her hair, pulled into a ponytail, hadn't been sweat-soaked and sticking to her head, she could be in a Peloton ad.

"Well, it's eleven o'clock, my love. Happy hour," drawled Leon.

To Mac's surprise, and clearly Daley's, he suddenly strode over to her, gathered her into his arms and kissed her full on the lips. Daley's arms flailed and she came out sputtering at the end of the kiss.

"Stop being such an ass!" she declared.

"Your taste in friends is improving," Leon said, returning to his beer, putting the bottle to his lips and draining it. "Maybe we should take the cover off the hot tub." He inclined his head toward the back windows. Mac could see the gray tarp that covered the spa.

"I'm glad to see you've been so hospitable," she snarled.

"She's a detective, huh? Going to save us from the big bad neighbors."

Daley narrowed her eyes at him. He clearly knew just how to push her buttons.

"Yes," she said sourly.

"Well, good."

"She tell you she's moving in?" Daley bent down to untie her running shoes.

"Moving in? Uh, no, actually," he said, sliding Mackenzie an assessing look.

Mac had to once again curb the impulse to explain. "Daley asked me to move in temporarily."

"Since no one's helping us find out who's been targeting us, I took matters into my own hands," said Daley.

Mac wondered if this was when she would bring up the supposedly pending divorce. She'd made it seem like that was imminent as well and braced herself in case she felt strong enough to do it with Mac as a witness, but apparently Daley wasn't in any rush to clue Leon in.

"Well, I guess I'll assume you're taking the extra room," he said, his eyes narrowing on his wife, as if trying to figure out her game. He smiled faintly and slid a sideways glance at Mac. "Unless maybe you and Daley have a relationship I'm just learning about?"

"God, Leon." Daley snatched up her shoes and stomped back toward the garage door, letting it slam shut behind her.

"The woman has no sense of humor," he observed. "Did she tell you who she blames for the dog poop?"

"Does she have a theory?"

"She rails about all of 'em. Old guard and young guard alike. But the housing market's been fucking crazy for a long time and we outbid somebody. There was a couple who lost out to us. They've since bought in the As. The

Martins. Anthony Martin's been pretty rude to both of us ever since. I don't care, but Daley lets those things get under her skin." He shrugged. "The house they bought really needed a lot of work and I think they've run into whopping expenses. And the problem with the A streets is you're too close to the park. Little kids during the day playing on the equipment. Teenagers at night smoking dope, drinking, and having sex." He laughed. "The HOA is talking about an in-ground pool. Can you imagine? With our weather? A disaster. A small, loud faction of the young guard is fighting with the old. They want the pool."

Actually, there were a few months, starting in July, when an outdoor pool would be nice.

"Daley thinks this couple, the Martins, could be responsible?" asked Mac.

Daley opened the door again on Mac's question, sans shoes. "I do not! The Martins are nice people," she hissed furiously. "Why do you lie, Leon? You just love stirring up trouble!"

"You told me that Anthony was a prick."

"I was mad about the cost of the playground. It doesn't have anything to do with them."

"The HOA's putting in a new playground at the park," Leon explained. "A waste of money and time and energy, but then, we don't have any kids." To Daley, he reminded, "You said he was a prick."

"He's not," she snapped.

"She's changed her tune because the Martins are popular with the young guard. There's a whole social hierarchy here you've got to watch out for," Leon warned. "Y'see, Daley wants me to leave and for her to stay and work her way up the ladder. But I'm the one who's made friends. She froze 'em all out at first and now is trying to make nice." He smiled at his wife. "Well, I'm not leaving, love of my life. Nice to meet you, Mackenzie. I'm sure we'll meet in the hallway sometime. Welcome."

With that, he turned left down the passageway that led to the bedroom wing. The hall teed at the end and he turned left again. They heard the firm slam of a door.

"He's just trying to get to me." She looked around at the messy kitchen and pursed her lips. "He can clean that up himself." She shot another glance at Mac's unfinished drink. "He's hard to say no to, isn't he?"

"He was . . . giving me some background on your neighbors."

"I'll bet." She lowered her voice and motioned for Mac to follow her down the short hallway on the opposite side of the house from the one Leon had taken. It was behind the kitchen, an adjunct off the garage, and led to a spare bedroom that was clearly meant to be Mac's.

As soon as Mac was inside, Daley closed the door behind her and leaned against it. Mac looked around at the daybed with its blue plaid cover and matching ruffled pillows. A white wicker vanity with an oval mirror stood to one side with a utilitarian black desk chair.

"Don't let him fool you."

Mac thought about telling Daley that she'd met her share of personalities in the course of her career and that she was skeptical of pretty much everyone upon first meeting them, when Daley added, "He's threatened me."

That stopped her for a moment. "Physically threatened you?"

Daley pulled herself in tightly. "He hasn't hit me yet, but he shoved me up against the refrigerator once. Said it was my fault for being in the way."

Mac frowned but didn't respond. She needed the full story before she made a judgment call.

"He's dangerous. He may not seem like it, but just wait. He's like . . . an alligator waiting in the swamp. He'll come at you." She regarded Mac soberly. "Where's your bag?"

"It's in my car."

"Good. Bring it in and make yourself at home. I asked for a bodyguard because I need protection. I could be dead in a month."

"From Leon?"

"I don't know. Maybe. I just want him to leave. That's what I want. That's what I want you to do."

"Get him to leave?" Mac half laughed.

"Yes!"

"Daley, that's not what you hired me for. If you feel that threatened, maybe you should be the one to move out," she advised again.

"I told you, I'm not leaving."

"This has the potential to be a lot like *The War of the Roses.*"

"What do you mean?" she asked suspiciously.

"It's an old film with Michael Douglas and Kathleen Turner. A cautionary tale about people living under the same roof who grow to hate each other."

"I want the house. Leon owes me the house," she said stubbornly.

"And you've told him you're planning to divorce him?"

She opened her mouth and closed it. Opened it again, closed it again.

"I can't be here all the time, Daley," said Mac when Daley couldn't seem to get the words out.

"What do you think a bodyguard is?" she demanded.

"If you want someone twenty-four seven, you're going to have to hire someone besides me."

"Oh, for God's sake!" She straightened up, glared at Mac, then yanked open the door. Mac followed after her to head out and grab her overnight bag, watching as Daley stalked down the main hall and jigged right at the end of the hallway, where Leon had jigged left. Mac was glad she was at the complete other end of the house. However, if Daley was truly worried about Leon harming her, what good could she do so far away from them both?

Was Leon as bad as Daley painted him? Or was she just building a case against him in her mind to get what she wanted? At this point it was hard to tell. Either way, Daley wasn't being completely honest with either her or her husband.

Mac settled into the room, dropping her bag at the end of the daybed, then seated herself on it cross-legged and scrolled through her texts. None were urgent. She was just preparing to text Taft to let him know that she was in the Carrera household when Daley returned, sweeping into the room without knocking. Mac clicked off her phone, aware she was going to have to lay down some ground rules.

"We're going to the HOA meeting tonight," Daley announced.

"Oh, sure."

"I'm serious. Why are you laughing?"

"Well, I'm not part of the HOA."

"You're my bodyguard!"

"Is Leon going?"

"I . . . no. He hates those things."

"Then you're safe, right?"

"Are you trying to stay in the house with Leon?" she accused.

Actually, Mac had just not wanted to sit through a homeowner's association meeting. They were, as a rule, long and boring. The kind of assembly she'd suffered through in high school, with introductions and note-taking and dry subjects Mac had no interest in. She'd been antsy at meetings with the River Glen PD as well.

And she wanted to see Taft. She wanted to compare notes and get away from Daley and Leon. But now that the idea had been posed, she recognized the Village's HOA was a good place to get acquainted with some of both the old and the new guard. A lot of them would be at the meeting. Might as well meet the players in the neighborhood and see if anyone else had been victimized.

"Okay, I'll go with you," said Mac.

"Really?" Daley narrowed her eyes at her.

"Really."

"Good. The meeting starts at six thirty. We can walk over. There's a path through the streets and the meeting room is at the end of one of the Bs, Beacon Street, I think."

"Wonderful."

Daley chose not to question the sincerity of Mac's comment as she left as unannounced as she'd arrived. Probably thought it would be better not to push her luck.

Mackenzie flopped back on the bed and stared at the ceiling. She felt like a teenager hiding in her room. To that end, she wondered what Taft was doing and, somewhat annoyed with herself, put a call in to Stephanie, who was wandering around Nordstrom's baby department and not that interested in talking.

Okay, fine. Mac sat back up and wondered if she could

just leave and grab herself a bite of lunch, but sensed Daley might object.

"You're not a prisoner," she said aloud.

So why did she feel like one?

She definitely needed to get some ground rules going if she was going to bunk here for a while. Feeling hot and sticky, she wandered out to check out the hall bath shower. She had hours to go before the meeting. Well, she could use the time to transcribe some notes from her talk with Leon, who'd so far been far more informative than Daley.

Late in the afternoon, after he'd gone for a run, then returned and taken a shower, washing off the exercise sweat and the stink of Mangella's not-so-veiled warnings that if they weren't on the same side, they were enemies, Taft heard the familiar sound of his cell's default ringtone. He swept up the phone from his dresser, not recognizing the number. He thought about letting the call go to voice mail, but people wanting his particular expertise in solving problems learned of him mostly by discreet word of mouth and their numbers weren't in his contact list.

"Taft Investigations," he answered a bit briskly.

"Oh, yes. Hello. Mr. Taft? This is LeeAnn Laidlaw. I was given your name from a friend and I was wondering if I could meet with you . . . ? My husband . . . well, could we talk in person?"

LeeAnn Laidlaw. Laidlaw Construction was the fiercest competitor to Best Homes, both of which were building houses as fast as they could throughout the Greater Portland Area and River Glen, specifically Staffordshire Estates. And Andrew Best of Best Homes was one of those pieces of business Mangella didn't want to talk about.

"Laidlaw of Laidlaw Construction?" asked Taft.

"Yes, that Laidlaw," she admitted on a sigh.

It didn't sound like she relished having to confess the connection, which was interesting in itself. "When would you like to meet?"

"Soon, well . . . tonight, if possible? It's . . . well, it's urgent. Could you maybe come here, to my house, or do you have an office . . . somewhere?"

"Give me your address and I can be there by seven?"

"Eight o'clock would be better. I'm . . . well, I have dinner plans."

"All right. Okay if I bring my associate with me?"

A hesitation. "Is he trustworthy?"

"She is. Very."

"Oh. Okay."

LeeAnn gave him her address, and after they'd hung up Taft asked himself why he'd been so anxious to have Mackenzie with him. She'd texted that she was dealing with the Carreras and had made it clear, by what she didn't say, that she thought the whole bodyguard job was a ploy on his part to fob her off . . . which—well, there had been that component to it.

You want her with you.

This time he could almost sense his sister's spirit in the room with him. He said aloud, "She's a good investigator."

You need to get over your shit.

He nodded slowly. He did need to get over his shit.

He hit the Favorite button on his phone and placed a call to Mackenzie.

Seeing Taft was calling brought Mackenzie back to the present with a bang. She'd sneaked away to her place, pointing to the overnight bag and telling Daley she needed more things, which was the truth, and had stayed through a late lunch of grilled cheese sandwiches and crisp, fat pickles. Since returning with a larger suitcase in tow, she'd been lying on the daybed, lost in thought, almost half-falling asleep. "Hey," she answered.

"We might have a new client."

We? Mackenzie perked up. "Who?"

"LeeAnn Laidlaw."

"Laidlaw, like . . . that Laidlaw?" Mac's thoughts immediately flew to Stephanie's husband, Nolan, who was a foreman at Laidlaw Construction.

He laughed.

"What's so funny?"

"Yes, that Laidlaw. She wants to meet tonight at her place around eight p m. Does that work?"

Mackenzie thought hard. HOA meeting . . . hmmm. "I'll be there," she said. "I have to check with Daley and get free, but I'll meet you there. I don't want to hold you up if I get delayed." But she was bound and determined to vamoose from the meeting in plenty of time.

Taft gave her the address and Mackenzie wrote it down quickly in her notepad. She was pretty sure Daley was going to squawk, but if she went to the HOA meeting for a while, she should be able to shake free by eight.

"How's the job going?" asked Taft.

"Peachy. Love it."

"Have you met Leon?" She could hear the smile in his voice and smiled in return, even though he couldn't see her. She hadn't felt this strongly about a man since her last relationship, and that one had crashed and burned years earlier. No regrets about it ending, except possibly that she'd let it go on so long, but the memory of wanting to be close to someone lived on.

"Leon and I shared some Bloody Marys this morning," she said.

"Really. Daley with you?" he asked.

"She was taking a run, apparently. So, Leon and I got up close and personal, and he told me about people in the neighborhood. I'm going to an HOA meeting tonight before I'm due to meet you. I'll cut out early if I have to, and Daley can just deal with it."

"Good place to start."

"Yes," she agreed a bit testily. First Daley, now Taft. Everyone seemed ready to point out how important the HOA meeting was, something she already knew, even if she didn't really want to go.

"Leon say anything else?" he asked.

"I asked him about the harassment and he talked about the 'old guard' versus 'the young guard' of people in the neighborhood. Seems to be a bit of a war along age lines. Leon clearly considers himself in the young guard camp, though he's probably somewhere in between."

"You'll meet some of them tonight. Let me know if something grabs your attention. You can tell me when we get together."

"I will." Sensing she was losing his attention, she asked, "Have you contacted Mangella yet?" She held her breath, knowing she could get shot down.

"We spoke," he said.

"You'll fill me in later."

He actually chuckled, then said, "Eight o'clock at LeeAnn Laidlaw's."

"Sure. Yeah."

He broke the connection and she slowly clicked off,

lost in thought. That had sounded far more promising. But whenever she got too close to the Mangella issue, the curtain dropped, so she had to tread carefully.

There was a knock on the door and Daley sailed in before Mac could yell, "Come on in."

"You ready?" She eyed Mackenzie's jeans and the blue shirt Mac had been wearing all day.

"We've got over an hour until the HOA meeting."

"Well, we have to eat, don't we?"

"I was thinking about making a quick run to the hardware store," Mac rejoined.

"What are you talking about? No. We have just enough time to catch a quick bite before the meeting."

Daley was dressed in formfitting black pants and a gold shirt with a loose collar in folds. She'd combed her hair into a sleek ponytail and refreshed her makeup.

She looked good and it made Mac wonder who she thought she might see at the meeting.

"What do you need at a hardware store?" she asked.

"A locking doorknob for my room."

It took her half a beat to catch on. "I'm sorry, okay? I just want to get out of the house. Leon is driving me insane. He . . . scares me," she added.

Does he? Or was Daley just trying to make it seem that way? In truth, she seemed more pissed off than fearful.

"I'll knock next time. I will," she assured Mac. "Look, we need to eat something before the HOA meeting. These things can last a long time. So, I made a reservation at the River Glen Grill. It's in fifteen minutes. Get changed and let's go!"

The River Glen Grill? One of the nicest places, maybe *the* nicest place in town? For a "quick bite"? Not likely.

"Who's buying?" asked Mac.

"I am. Hurry," Daley said, and escaped out of the room before Mac could protest again, shutting the door firmly behind her.

Well, if Daley was buying and they were late to the HOA meeting because they were at the Grill, that was her problem. But it was time to get moving, so Mac went into a flurry of changing. She had one nice, clean, straight dress in dark gray and she shook it out, eyeing it for wrinkles. It looked okay, so she threw it on. The stretchy material fit over her body snugly. She combed her hair and grimaced at her reflection in the bathroom mirror. Some eye makeup and a bit of lipstick were required. When she was done she slipped into a pair of flip-flops and wished she'd painted her toenails. In the end she shrugged. Good enough.

She grabbed her jacket and met Daley, who was waiting impatiently near the garage door. Daley eyed Mackenzie up and down and seemed to approve. At least she didn't act like she disapproved as she led the way to her Audi.

They didn't talk a lot on the way to the restaurant. Mac knew the maître d' and some of the wait staff from her days with the River Glen PD. She had a friendly, symbiotic relationship with them that still lasted to this day. Mac had helped them with unruly customers and security, and a few times they had given her tips on crime suspects she'd been searching for in the area. The ivy-clad River Glen Grill was located in the center of town, a picturesque, brick-lined few blocks that unfortunately backed up to a neighborhood in decline. Maybe some enterprising developer like Laidlaw Construction would put it back together again. That was more their bent than Best Homes, which created subdivision after subdivision.

They pulled up in front of the restaurant, and Mac's thoughts turned to Dan the Man, who'd used her as his errand girl while she'd lived with him and her mother during Mom's convalescence from breast cancer. Mac had picked up takeout from the River Glen Grill for him and her mother numerous times, and more than once Dan had tried to stiff her with the bill. Now her mother and Dan were separated and he'd moved out and rented one of the full-floor apartments above the restaurant. How he afforded it was a mystery Mac was determined to uncover. Those apartments were some of the most expensive in town.

Which was also true of the River Glen Grill's prices. Not a place Mackenzie frequented often. She said as much as Daley turned over her keys to the valet, but Daley said blithely, "One of the perks of Leon's money."

"You haven't told him you want a divorce yet."

"Not in so many words."

"But that is one of the reasons I'm working for you. You're going to tell him that you've asked me to be a bodyguard?"

"Yesss . . ." She made it sound like a "maybe" as they entered the restaurant foyer, a Tudor motif with dark timbers that crowned above them in an ecru arch with a wrought-iron chandelier burgeoning with electric candles overhead, the contraption large enough to kill a small crowd should it fall on them.

They were ushered right in, more because Art, the maître d', undoubtedly knew the size of Daley's pocketbook, if his wide smile of greeting was any indication, than that he'd recognized Mac, though he did a double take on her. It was the outfit. Mac had never shown up in anything fancier than her work uniform or a pair of jeans and a shirt.

Once ensconced in the blood-red leather booth, Daley ordered a steak salad with Gorgonzola cheese and Mac did

the same. Stephanie was flirting with veganism, and though
Mac liked the idea of more vegetables in her diet, she was
lured by a good hamburger too often to really go there.
Besides, lettuce, tomato, onion, and pickles filled the bill.
But if Daley was going with a salad, so would she.

They didn't say much to each other, each wrapped in
their own thoughts, apparently, but about halfway through
the meal, Daley pointed her fork at Mackenzie and said,
"Leon told you about the old guard and the young guard.
Did he say who was in the HOA?"

"He said Burt Deevers was the HOA president and he
mentioned a couple other men and their wives as part of
the old guard."

"I'm surprised he said anything. He hardly knows who's
who. Maybe he thought he was impressing you. Don't
trust him. The HOA people? Burt Deevers for sure, and
Cliff and Darrell and probably Evelyn and Clarice, maybe
Tamara . . . I don't know. Could be more. I bet they know
who's doing this to us. They could be behind it for all I
know. They really hate the young guard, who Leon aligns
with."

"You don't think it's the Martins, then."

"Didn't I already say so? No! Leon just doesn't care
enough or pay enough attention to know *anything*! They're
too nice to harass us. Besides, they're in the middle of a
renovation and just wouldn't bother."

"In the Villages."

"They lost the house to us, but then found another one
near the park. That's all I know."

"You know a lot for only being here a few months."

"What do you mean?" she asked suspiciously.

"I mean, you know a lot for only being here a few months.
It's impressive."

"Oh. Well . . . I just pay attention," she said, mollified. "These are our neighbors, and I want to know if I can trust them."

"Makes sense." Mackenzie forced herself not to grab her phone and look at the time.

"But back to Burt. He's a prig. A know-it-all. He's been president forever. Keeps getting voted in by the old guard. He's divorced from Tamara, but she's still around. Doesn't say much, but she must have no social life because she's always there. I don't know where she lives, but not in the Villages, I don't think. Burt got the house. That won't happen to me."

"Mmm," said Mac, chewing a piece of steak. She wasn't sure who she'd put her money on, Daley or Leon. They were both formidable as far as she could see.

"Burt's right-hand guy is Cliff and his wife is Clarice, who's . . . well, there's something wrong with her." Daley seemed derailed for a moment, then she launched back in. "Darrell is the other one of Burt's good buddies and he's married to Evelyn, and Evelyn doesn't like anyone in the young guard. Every time she brings up anything at the meeting, it's about the sex parties. I get it. She lives right by them. But Leon always teases her about where are those parties and can he join?" She rolled her eyes. "See what I mean about him?"

"Will Leon be at the meeting? I thought you said—"

"No, no. He hates the HOA meetings. He's been to a few of them, and whenever he sees Evelyn he says something to her, like, 'Did you see me last night?' He's really proud of his cock. Did he show it to you today?"

"No . . ."

"Give him a chance. It's goddamn annoying. Whenever he does that Evelyn shrieks that he's a pervert and honestly, she's not that far off." She waved off her words. "But Leon avoids them, mostly."

"The old guard."

"Yes. Can I continue?"

"Go right ahead." Mac had finished her salad and was just waiting to head out. Daley, recognizing this, took another couple of bites, then pushed away the plate and stood up. "I'll catch the waiter on the way out," she said, then smiled at Art and complained about the service a teensy little bit, trying to act like she didn't really mean to get anyone in trouble. The service had been fine from Mac's perspective, but Daley somehow wheedled a twenty-five-dollar gratis gift certificate for a return trip out of notoriously stingy Art. The woman's wiles were impressive.

"So, Cliff is Burt's right-hand man," Daley went on as they waited for the valet. "They're both old and condescending and Darrell's even worse."

"How old are they?" asked Mac, surreptitiously checking her phone for the time: 6:15 pm. They would be late, but not by much.

"Sixties? Late fifties, maybe? They've been in the Villages since they were built. They still call them Victor's Villages. They really need to let go of the reins. The young guard want them out. but they can't seem to do anything about 'em. They get the votes, I guess, unless there's some hanky-panky at the ballot box. I wouldn't put it past them. When Leon's gone I might join with them. Who knows? I could be HOA president. I'd do a helluva lot better job, that's for sure."

Daley's black Audi was brought around and Mac saw she gave the man a teensy tip. She seemed to teeter between cheap and magnanimous. She drove them back to her house and parked in the driveway. "We've got to hurry," she said.

"I'm changing."

"What? You look great."

"I'll be quick." Mac went into her room, stripped off the dress, and found her jeans, a clean shirt, and sneakers. She'd started to rethink the dress, which brought more attention to her than she might want and the night was chilly. She hurried back outside and had to jog to catch up with Daley, who'd apparently decided she was taking too long.

Mac caught her at one of the asphalt bike pathways that wound through the development, this one taking them through the B streets. They passed Bristow and racewalked along Bijou. Daley had put a black sweater coat over her gold shirt, but she took it off and slung it over her arm as they hustled along. She'd changed into black flats from the heels she'd worn to the Grill.

She picked up where she'd left off. "Cliff isn't retired yet, I don't think. He works with machinery of some kind. But Clarice is superanxious all the time. She just shakes and shakes and doesn't say much. Trembles. A lot, and I mean all the time. I mentioned to Cliff once and he about took my head off. Said she's just fine, but no, she's not fine. Maybe he beats her or threatens her. I should find out."

"Maybe it's a condition," said Mac.

She waved a dismissive hand. "They're all just old and grouchy. Except for the young guard. Hard to believe some of these twenty-year-olds can buy a house here, but they do. Makes you wonder where they get their money."

They came around a corner to the recreation hall, which was done in a tropical Hawaiian style with dark timbers and tan, woven screens. It was more like a small meeting room, no "hall" about it. There were several unlit tiki torches in sconces on either side of the entry doors that looked like they hadn't been touched in years.

Several people were just entering as they arrived and Daley gave a little shiver and slipped on her black sweater coat again.

"Last time I was here they barely put the heat on. Good thing you have a jacket. I should've warned you."

Mac had already figured out that Daley didn't really have a lot of time to think about anyone other than herself. "Before we go in, I want to get some things straight," Mac said.

Daley was half a step in front of her. Mac's words stopped her and her head snapped around. "Now? About what?"

"My perceived job."

"Perceived job?" she repeated sharply.

"Daley, it seems like you want a companion more than a bodyguard, and that's fine, but like I said, I can't be with you all the time. Some of my time will be trying to figure out who's been harassing you."

"I know that."

"Okay. Just want to be clear. Like tonight, for example. I have a meeting after this meeting."

"What? What meeting?"

"Do you really think Leon would hurt you physically, because I didn't get that sense today."

"He charmed you. I knew it. That's what he does." She threw her arms around her waist and furiously shook her head. "That's why I wanted Jesse."

Mac fought back a flare of anger herself. "If you want me to leave right now, I'm ready."

"Oh, for God's sake. No." Her voice was a low hiss so others couldn't overhear. "Just don't be fooled by Leon."

"I'm not."

They stared at each other and Daley finally nodded.

"Good. Let's go in."

"Good." Mac forged ahead of Daley, aiming for the porch steps.

"What is this other meeting?" Daley asked, catching up to Mac as they reached the top of the porch.

"Business-related. Nothing to do with you."

"Are you meeting Jesse?"

"I'm meeting with a client," she answered testily. Every time Daley called Taft by his first name it was like fingernails scraping on a blackboard.

"Excuse me," a young woman said snippily, forcing Daley to move away from the entry doors so she could squeeze inside. Daley shot her a killing look and silently mouthed, *Bitch* to Mackenzie. "Oh, fine, don't tell me," she responded. "Go to your meeting, but be back later . . . please. I don't want to be alone tonight."

"I'll be there," Mac assured her, then Daley passed through the open doors to the meeting and Mackenzie followed.

Chapter Six

The Villages' hall was one room with three rows of chairs arced around a central lectern with a brick fireplace on the plastered wall behind it. Two men were standing by the lectern, one of them with his forearm laid across its top, his large, square hand reaching possessively around its edge. This must be Burt Deevers, the president, Mac decided. He had a square body and a thick neck, an impressive mane of gray hair and in his fifties was still a handsome man. But his fixed smile made Mac instantly mistrust him. His friend was thinner but not by much, his hair in a salt-and-pepper horseshoe with hangdog eyes and a hard mouth. Both men wore brown Dockers and buttoned shirts, one blue, one green. Mac glanced around and saw it was almost a uniform for the men of the old guard. The older women wore more colorful clothes, some in long skirts, some in slacks and jeans. The younger women were in lululemon-esque outfits, almost to a one: snug-fitting pants and T-shirts with matching zippered, hooded jackets, everything formfitting. Their male counterparts were in jeans and casual shirts—black mostly, sometimes blue.

Their hairstyles were short and clipped or longish and styled.

Daley fit right in. After giving Mac that last baleful look she'd headed inside and smoothly clicked into competitive mode, straightening up and running a finger around the edge of her ear, smoothing her ponytail as she assessed the younger women in the room.

She and Leon had both made comments about the old guard but had barely mentioned specific people in the younger group, though clearly these were the people Daley was surreptitiously studying and wanted to emulate. Mac wondered which of their number were members of the hot tub group. They all were fit, lean, and mean. Their smiles hid their feelings, while their eyes viewed anyone in their age group for attributes and flaws, assessing them quickly and thoroughly. Mac felt those eyes appraise her and move on. She knew she looked like she didn't care what she wore because, well, she didn't, but it still stung a bit.

One guy came up to her and practically said as much. "You got a great face and body," he told her, as if she'd asked. The unspoken rest of the comment was *but you do nothing with them*.

"Thank you?" responded Mac.

"I'm Chris. Chris Palminter."

Chris Palminter . . . boyfriend of Hot Tub Jeannie. "Mackenzie Laughlin."

"What brings you here? Did you buy the Podlich house on Cherry?"

She shook her head. "I'm here with Daley Carrera."

"Oh. Where's Leon?" He looked around.

"I don't think he attends these meetings much." She tried to sound knowledgeable rather then lost but wasn't sure she pulled it off.

He made a face. "Nah. He comes most times. Probably with Mariah or something. Whoops." He put his hand over his mouth and dramatically widened his eyes. "I wasn't supposed to say anything. Don't tell Daley."

"I'll try not to."

He narrowed his eyes, attempting to figure her out, and smiled like a devil. "Hmmm. What are you and Daley up to? Don't tell me. Let me guess. There's only one reason you'd come with her to an HOA meeting. Girl love. You two are cute together. Can I join?"

Palminter was tall and lean with sandy hair cut short. His brown eyes twinkled and she could tell he worked out. His shoulders strained at the seams of the blue shirt he wore.

"It's not like that."

His smile was knowing as he cocked his head. "So, what do you do, Mackenzie Laughlin? Have I met you before? Your name's familiar."

"I think this is a first."

"It'll come to me. You haven't been to one of our parties yet?"

"No."

"You've heard about them, though."

"Actually, this is my first night in the Villages," she sidestepped. The less anyone thought she knew about them the better.

"Call them Victor's Villages. The old guard hates it. Victor's name is that which will not be spoken aloud around here. He's dead and gone, but he was a player in his day, apparently. They get upset with our hot tub parties, but they weren't all so dried up and provincial once, or so I've heard. Come join us later."

Daley, who'd seen that Mac was talking with Chris Palminter, swanned over their way. "Hi, Chris," she said.

"Nice trade-in for Leon," observed Chris.

She flapped a hand at him. "Mackenzie's my . . . assistant."

He laughed.

"Truthfully, she's a private detective looking into whoever's been intimidating us. I don't feel safe anymore."

"Private detective," he repeated dubiously.

"Yes. And she was with the River Glen PD before that."

Hearing Daley throw out Mac's résumé was slightly unnerving, especially because Chris was assessing Mackenzie now, giving her a long, long look.

"Not a private detective." She tried to add that she wasn't accredited, but Daley jumped in, "Where's Jeannie? I don't see her."

"I know I've seen you before . . ." Palminter muttered.

"Maybe I pulled you over," Mac said lightly.

"Nah . . ." He suddenly swept in a breath and looked triumphant. Snapping his fingers, he said, "You're Pete Fetzler's ex! I knew I'd heard of you."

Daley turned to Mac in surprise. "You didn't say you were married."

"Ex-*girlfriend*," Mackenzie corrected, feeling blindsided. Of all things . . . She would have liked to lie and pretend she didn't ever know Pete's name, but it was too late for that. She and Pete had said sayonara to their dating life several years earlier, but they'd been together long enough for it to be a shared history that others remembered, apparently.

"Pete's a good friend of mine," Palminter said, making Mac groan inside. She'd never heard Palminter's name, but Pete had lots of good friends who had come out of the woodwork all the time. "I can't wait to tell him I finally met you."

There was a loud rapping, and Mackenzie saw Burt now had a gavel and was slamming it hard against the lectern. She half expected it to break, he used so much force.

Good grief. She had no interest in Pete Fetzler any longer. Not even close. They'd left on bad terms when Mackenzie ended the relationship, such as it was. Pete was the everlasting child. Everything was always all about him, and Mac had grown tired of living the exhausting supportive role. She hadn't heard from him in years and that was just fine. She hoped to God Chris Palminter wouldn't somehow open the door for Pete to contact her again. The further she'd gotten from that relationship, the more clearly she could see how one-sided it had been. Probably her fault as much as his, but she preferred blaming it all on him.

They all moved toward their seats, and after Burt cracked his gavel a few more times the last of the stragglers hurried to find a place to sit.

"Let's start or we'll be here all night," Burt snapped.

I won't be, Mac thought, slipping her phone from her pocket and throwing it a surreptitious glance. They were ten minutes late getting started. She would be leaving in less than an hour.

Daley pressed close to her and whispered, "What were you and Chris talking about?"

"You heard."

"I mean besides your ex-boyfriend. I got so many of those it's not even news."

Good. No need to have a postmortem on her love life after all. Daley didn't care.

Burt stared across the room with a glare on his face.

"I got invited to a hot tub party," Mac whispered to Daley as Burt brought the meeting to order.

"Meh," she said.

Burt said a few words and then stepped back to allow others to speak. First up was the man who'd been milling around by Burt's side as everyone got settled in the room. Was that Cliff or . . . Darrell? Whoever it was pretty much echoed Burt's words, but the members started tossing remarks and questions at him that they hadn't to Burt. There was an overall complaint about the company that kept up the grounds. Someone said they were all slackers, and Cliff or Darrell nodded in apparent agreement. And then a younger woman stood up and said, "I know you have an agenda, Burt, but I don't want the time to elapse without us talking about the ADA-compliant play structure."

Burt practically shoved Cliff or Darrell out of the way. "I'm going to get to it," he assured her in a tone that suggested she was being unreasonable.

"Last month you said the same thing."

"We're putting it in, Mariah. You can stop bellyaching."

Mariah. Mac's head swiveled to really examine the woman speaking. She was lithe and pretty without a stitch of makeup in a somewhat shapeless blue sleeveless dress over a short-sleeved white tee that nevertheless couldn't hide her ample breasts and shapely legs. She seemed oblivious to the fact that it was decidedly cool in the room. She was also the woman Daley had mouthed, "Bitch" about . . . and the one Chris Palminter had slyly linked with Leon. Wherever Leon was tonight, he wasn't with her—at least not yet.

Cliff or Darrell retook the microphone from Burt and said, "We've already started removing the old equipment."

"I know, Cliff," she said, unruffled. "But work has stalled." She remained standing.

So, this was Cliff. Mac made a mental note. He was a bit thinner than burly Burt with a ring of gray hair around a shiny pink pate that glowed under the lights. His hangdog eyes looked over the crowd.

"Just temporarily," Cliff assured her and Burt glowered behind him. His gaze landed on another older man who hitched up his chin in response. Some kind of message crossing between them. Mac suspected this might be Darrell, the last member of the older male triumvirate of the HOA both Leon and Daley had mentioned, although Darrell could be the other guy at the end of the row. . . .

An older woman's hand shot up. Her hair was blond, a product of bleach to cover the gray, Mac thought, and even though her face had crumpled a bit over the years, its heart shape was still evident, and her blue eyes were large and quite beautiful.

"Evelyn," Cliff acknowledged tiredly.

Darrell's wife, if Mac remembered correctly. This should be interesting. Mac looked down the row at the man she'd thought was Darrell. He was seated right beside Evelyn, so it was likely true. He was staring straight ahead at the back of the woman seated in front of him and his pugnacious jaw was set. Not a happy camper.

Evelyn stood up, as if yanked by a string. "Could someone make sure the construction equipment doesn't start before seven a.m.? It's in the bylaws and the city rules. It's just so loud."

"Y'know we abide by the rules, Evvie," Cliff assured her.

Burt looked as if he could barely stand having Cliff at the lectern. He had to pace a few steps behind him and as he did, Darrell and the man at the end of the row both got to their feet and went to stand by the wall, closer to the proceedings. The man at the end of the row had a gray goatee he liked to stroke. He wore thick, tortoiseshell glasses that looked slightly foggy, as if they needed a good cleaning. He left Darrell and moved toward the brick fireplace in order to confer with the HOA president, who had stopped pacing and joined him. Neither said anything to the other. They both faced forward, waiting.

Evelyn said, "Well, I've heard noise long after it should be stopped and before it should start." She darted a look at a younger woman whose riot of gold-streaked, light-brown hair swept over her shoulders. The younger woman turned and raised her eyebrows at Evelyn in a look of challenge. Her face was thin and a bit shrewish, but she wore a big smile. Evelyn swept up the bait. "And just because someone has a hot tub doesn't mean the party can go on all night! Ten o'clock on weekdays. Midnight Friday and Saturday, which is really too late, but it's in the bylaws. We should change those, and we should really all be looking out for our neighbors."

The younger woman with the hair coughed into her fist, but you could plainly hear her expel, "Bullshit." Hot Tub Jeannie, maybe.

Burt swept forward and Cliff stepped aside so Burt could lean into the mic. "Okay, listen, we need to move on. Like I said, the playground's going to get built. The old equipment's been taken down. Swings are up. We all know about the noise restrictions."

"And we need to meet ADA requirements," Mariah added, popping up from her seat again for a moment.

"Sure thing," said Burt.

Evelyn was still standing as Mariah sat back down. Mac put her in her late fifties. Though she still clung to her looks, the plaid blouse she wore over Mom jeans were an unfortunate choice. "Well, some of us aren't paying attention to the noise restrictions." She looked around the room meaningfully. Mac craned her neck, but if Evelyn was focused on anyone in particular, she couldn't tell.

There was a buzz of angry murmuring from the back, where most of the younger members were seated. Darrell seemed to realize he should've stayed by his wife, so he left the wall and retook his seat next to her. Grabbing her hand, he practically yanked her back down to her chair. The back of his neck was red with embarrassment or anger, but he leaned into her and said something that, although she lifted a dismissive shoulder to him, seemed to mollify her somewhat.

Burt nodded toward Cliff again, and he once again thrust his weathered face toward the mic. "Okay," he said in a kind of tired, gosh-shucks manner, which caused a ripple of amusement from the young guard at the back of the room. Cliff looked like he spent the bulk of his time outdoors, and as he talked about the construction company that was erecting the playground—neither Best Homes nor Laidlaw Construction, as it turned out—one of the young guard laughingly hollered out, "Cliff, no one's blaming you!" Mac twisted around to see who it was, but a number of the young guard, mostly men, were all grinning and hanging out together.

"No one thinks you'd be on a backhoe at six in the morning!" Chris Palminter added loudly, which caused another round of laughter. The young guard was clearly getting a kick out of teasing Cliff, who tried to act like it didn't bother him, but his face grew flushed. He lifted a hand to the crowd to indicate he was finished and found his way back to the empty chair the man with the goatee and glasses had vacated.

Mac leaned into Daley. "Is Cliff's wife here?"

"I don't see Clarice. She's usually at these meetings, but she's gotten worse, so maybe that's why she's not here." Daley glanced over her shoulder, her eyes doing a double check of the room.

Clarice Fenwick with the shakes. Mackenzie looked around as well, her gaze coming back to Cliff, who was staring down at his hands, which he was moving back and forth as if he were miming washing them. He still looked upset that he'd been made fun of by the young guard.

Burt asked the secretary to go over old business, and Mac settled in to wait as a woman with tightly permed blondish hair and a pair of glasses strung from a chain around her neck began sonorously reading the explanation of what projects were still upcoming, when the vote for funding would be, whether they should stick with their landscape company or find another, and what future goals the Villages had in store.

Old bones, old bones . . .

Clarice Fenwick held herself in a hug, her arms tight around her torso, and paced the length of her living room. Her body constantly quaked and buzzed these days and there appeared to be nothing she could do about it. She'd been to specialists. Cliff had taken her to specialists. At least in the beginning. But he'd lost interest when there was no explanation and no end in sight. She knew he just put up with her now. Oftentimes she caught that look on his face, that look that said she was a disappointment, a failure, an anchor. Then she would feel a spurt of anger and she'd fight with him. But it was short-lived, an old woman's feeble attempt to stand her ground when really, the ground beneath her feet had become slippery as an ice rink. Nothing solid.

You're not that old.

Wasn't she, though? Age wasn't just a number, no matter what anyone said. Age was the years you experienced, your choices from childhood to the present, everything, *everything* you'd done. And no amount of good works, of atonement, of bending before God and begging forgiveness could undo a transgression if that transgression was evil enough.

"Old bones, old bones . . ." Clarice muttered as she paced, her mind's eye caught in a loop, seeing all of them at the homeowner's meeting as if she were there with them tonight. Cliff and Darrell and Evelyn and Burt . . . and others. . . .

She stopped for a moment, seesawing between going to church and praying for all their souls or staying here and living through the nightmare of another night in her own home, plagued by the ever-present tremors. On her knees before the altar, her body would sometimes relax and release her from her agony, but only sometimes. Not often. Not lately.

When had it all started? She couldn't pinpoint the date, but it was God's will, God's punishment. God was shaking her. Trying to make her see. But she could see already. She saw everything in crystal-clear, full daylight. She'd made choices. It was her fault. All of it was her fault.

Officer, I didn't pull the trigger, but I put the bullets in the gun and gave it to the killer.

The gun and bullets were metaphorical, but the killer

was real, and in a court of law she would be found guilty. In the kingdom of God she was guilty.

She'd wanted children. Prayed for them. But she'd chosen a path that drew her away from everything she'd wanted in life. That unfulfilled promise was part of her punishment.

"Old bones, old bones . . ."

Clarice dropped her arms and walked into their bathroom. She opened the medicine cabinet with trembling fingers, staring at the bottle of pills that read "aspirin" but was so much more. Cliff wouldn't take pain relievers of any kind, unless you included alcohol, which he abused on the weekends when he wasn't driving his equipment, so he would never try her pills. Once or twice she'd wished he would, when he got that mean, set look on his face. Oh, he had his own reckoning with the Lord coming, that was for sure.

She lifted her shaking arm, which quaked wildly, the very act of reaching for the bottle increasing the intensity of her affliction. Her own fear, or God's will? She dropped her arm and stared at her reflection. Another lick of anger coursed through her. She was a good person. She'd done many good things. Hadn't she helped Althea when she'd broken her hip? Hadn't she sent money to the poor, as much as she could behind Cliff's back? Hadn't she prayed and prayed on her knees until she could hear her old bones cracking?

But . . . *but* . . .

She gazed longingly, angrily at the bottle of pills. Not today. She reached up to close the medicine cabinet door and her arm and hand reacted normally, no shaking at all. Sometimes that happened. Mostly, in those brief moments between sleep and wakefulness, those seconds before her vicious brain turned on . . . Just then she could lie quietly, peacefully, as she could when she was asleep, her body given a reprieve. But as soon as her senses awoke, as soon as her mind switched on and consciousness returned, then it began all over again.

At first it had been just an errant movement. A little finger she couldn't quite control. A twitching eyelid. She hadn't been alarmed. Dyskinesia wasn't uncommon. She'd even talked to Abby about it. Abby was a nurse and her husband was Dr. Andre, both of them employed at River Glen General Hospital, Glen Gen. *He's her ex-husband*, Clarice reminded herself. They were just together a lot. Maybe he was even at the HOA meeting.

But then the movements got bigger, until this spring they'd become whopping tremors she couldn't control. Cliff had started turning away from her. No longer just disappointed, he was now angry, embarrassed, horrified.

"It's not my fault this time," she chattered. "I didn't do it." She grabbed his arm and he yanked himself free. "It's not my fault!"

He'd slammed out of the house, as he was doing more and more lately.

But it wasn't her fault. It wasn't. Not this time. It wasn't her fault!

What about the shovel?

She pressed her quivering hand to her lips.

She needed to go to church. Right now. Could she get someone to drive her? No . . . they were all at the meeting. She would have to drive herself.

Chapter Seven

Finally the secretary was done with her report and the room started to stir again. It wasn't that she'd spoken so long, it was just that her droning voice made it feel like forever. Throughout her report, Evelyn and Darrell had sniped at each other in loud whispers, though Mac couldn't make out exactly what the issue was.

"I don't know why they're still together," Daley muttered to Mac. "Evelyn's always a problem. If Darrell can't take care of her, Cliff or Burt will. Such a bunch of assholes, but Evelyn asks for it. She just complains and complains. Entitlement. She was a local beauty queen ages ago, apparently. Although I agree with her about the hot tub parties. Having all those cavorting naked bodies outside your window? I'd spray 'em down with a hose if I lived next door."

"Shhh," the woman on the other side of Daley said.

Daley slowly turned her head and said, "Well, hi, Tamara. Here you are at another meeting."

Mac tried to get a look at Burt's ex, but the woman sat back. With Daley in the way, all she caught a glimpse of was a thick mass of bleached blondish hair and a side view of a rather frigid smile.

Burt called up the treasurer, another woman, who walked to the lectern and launched into a discussion about the budget. She was livelier than the first woman and a few years younger, somewhere between the old and young guards, Mac guessed. The HOA had apparently recently ratified an assessment to cover the cost of the new playground and a new roof and siding for the very building they were currently all seated in. More grumbling, this time throughout the room. No one wanted to pay extra for the repairs.

"Thanks, Penny," Burt said as she relinquished the mic and walked back to her seat.

A much older woman stood up, using the back of the seat in front of her as support.

"Althea," Burt acknowledged her.

"The neighborhood watch has vacancies," she announced in a gravelly voice. Her gray hair was cut short against her head and her skin had the soft, papery look of the elderly. "We have young people and some older, so don't think you're the wrong age. All volunteers are welcome."

"Thank you, Althea," Burt said as she slowly sat back down. Though he didn't do anything overtly to give himself away, Mac had the definite feeling he was just humoring her.

Another woman tentatively raised her hand. "Abby," Burt addressed her. His tone was far kinder now than it had been all night. Leon had mentioned Abby, too. Married to the body-sculpting doctor, with a teenaged son? Mac had written down the information in her notes but had left her pad back at the house. Mac tagged Abby in maybe her early fifties. She had a delicate face and wore her long, light-brown hair clipped at her nape. Her blouse was blue, simple and expensive by the look of it, and she wore a pair of white capris and sandals. She was shivering, and Burt motioned her to stand up so he could see her. She looked around carefully. Another man, one who'd been hovering around the edges of the old guard and had seated himself beside Abby, took off his lightweight jacket and stood up to put it over her shoulders. She tried to shake her head, *no*, but he put it on her anyway, lifting both palms in a hands-off gesture that said he was powerless to take it back, then reseated himself. Abby accepted the jacket with ill grace, even though she was cold. Was this the doctor husband? It didn't seem like it, for some reason.

"I was wondering about the vandalism? Has there been any more on that?" asked Abby. "We had a bike stolen."

Daley stiffened beside Mac and leaned forward to pay close attention.

Burt's gaze flicked from Abby to Daley and back again. "We didn't know about the bike, Abby. We're looking into all of it."

Daley suddenly snapped loudly from her seat. "How? What are you doing?"

"The neighborhood watch has been alerted. If anything else happens, we'll know about it." Burt nodded to Althea.

"The neighborhood watch," Daley repeated under her breath, making it clear just how effective she thought they were.

Abby had reseated herself and Burt seemed to think that issue was over, so he moved on to the three members of the architectural committee. All three were middle-aged women and as they each took their turn discussing the dos and don'ts, mostly don'ts, of the building codes of the Villages, Mac leaned into Daley once more and asked,

"Who's the guy with the goatee by the fireplace? Friend of Burt's?"

Daley craned her neck to look around Burt. "I don't know his name or where he lives. He's been at meetings before."

From Daley's other side, Tamara said icily, "Dr. Herdstrom is the River Glen medical examiner."

Mac squinted at the man. Dr. Sandy Herdstrom, the ME? She'd seen his picture before, but he looked older in person. "Does he live here?" she asked Tamara, who once again sank back in her seat and pretended she hadn't heard her.

Daley turned to Mac and rolled her eyes. She mouthed, *Another bitch.*

Mac checked her watch. Seven thirty-five. She'd spent more time than she wanted to at the meeting already. "I'd better get going," she whispered back.

Daley shot out a hand and grabbed her forearm, holding her in place. "Don't go yet."

"I don't want to be late."

"Something could happen to me on the way back to the house if you leave me. I could be attacked. Who knows who's been doing this?"

Mackenzie gave her a long look, checking for veracity. "Want me to get someone to walk you home?"

"I want you to walk me home!"

"Then get up. Because I'm leaving," Mac said as she got to her feet. Daley knew about her upcoming meeting and was purposely being a pain in the ass.

"Wait. Wait." Daley scrambled after Mac, who was already heading for the back door. There was a crowd of younger men who'd chosen to stand directly in front of the exit and Mac had to wait for them to mosey apart before she could get through.

"Leaving so soon?" asked Chris Palminter as he stepped to one side.

Mackenzie just smiled at him as she pushed outside into a rush of cold air. There was even a hovering threat of rain.

Daley clattered down the stairs behind her and followed her onto the path. "Wait up, for God's sake. I know you said you were leaving early. I just can't go home to Leon by myself. Take me with you. I'll feel safer."

"I'm not taking you with me to my meeting."

"How will you feel if something happens to me?"

"I'll walk you back, but I'm leaving you at your door."

The finality of her words seemed to finally penetrate Daley's skull. She caught up to Mackenzie and shook her head as they retraced their steps along the path. "Okay. Fine. Tonight I can go home. Leon isn't even there. He goes out every Thursday with friends. I just don't want to be alone."

This was probably the most honest thing she'd said to her to date. Mac hadn't realized she'd been holding her breath until she expelled it in a rush.

"Come back after?" Daley begged as they got to Mac's car. "I'll be up. Okay? I really do feel like something bad's coming."

"I'll be back after my meeting, but Daley, if you need a fulltime bodyguard it has to be someone other than me."

"No, no. This is fine."

So it was less about being afraid of Leon and more about feeling alone? How was that going to go after the divorce?

"We'll work something out," said Daley as she hurried

along the path beside Mac. "Before you leave, wait until I'm inside, okay?"

"Okay."

As they reached the C streets and then Calloway Court, Mac waited by her SUV and watched as Daley headed up the walkway to her house and let herself inside. Mac could track her progress as she turned on lights in a succession of rooms, heading, apparently, to her bedroom. Even though it stayed light till nearly ten this late in June, the cloud cover had added a fake twilight.

Mac drove away, her thoughts on Daley. The woman was eely. Hard to pin down on what she really wanted. Beneath her posturing, her fear and anxiety seemed real enough. She claimed it was directed at Leon, and maybe some of it was, but there was also the neighborhood harassment, and Daley hadn't been trying to make herself any friends at the HOA meeting.

Mac turned out of the Villages and as the miles slid beneath her tires, she forgot Daley, Leon, and the neighborhood and looked forward to the new case Taft had finally brought her in on.

Emma straightened the dish towels hanging from the handle of Jamie's stove. One of them was wet from Jamie wiping off the knives she cleaned by hand because she didn't put them in the dishwasher. Jamie thought the dishwasher wasn't good for the knives.

Knives. Emma felt her chest grow tight and she saw those eyes again. She didn't say it. She didn't say it. She didn't say it . . . but she wanted to scream it. *I see his eyes!*

Her chest was rising fast and falling, fast and hard.

Nooooo. She didn't want Jamie to see. She was over that. Never, almost never had those feelings anymore.

"Duchess," she whispered. Then louder, "Duchess!"

Her dog heard her from upstairs and came running down the stairs to stand beside her. Emma gripped into the fur at the back of the black and white mutt's neck.

Jamie appeared at the top of the stairway and looked down at her. "Everything all right?" Emma didn't respond and her sister came flying down the stairs. "You okay?"

"Duchess is my guard dog."

"What happened?" Jamie asked sharply. Her hair was escaping its loose bun and she looked kind of untidy.

"What happened to you?" Emma asked.

"Emma, you shouted for Duchess. Are you okay?"

Emma took in a deep breath and let it out again. That's what therapists made you do. "I'm okay."

Jamie closed her eyes and smoothed back her hair with both hands. She looked kind of unhappy.

"You're unhappy," Emma told her.

"What? No. I'm fine. It's all good. Thanks for finishing up the dishes." She looked around the kitchen, but Emma kinda thought she wasn't seeing anything. "Harley's going to take you home. Cooper's . . . um . . . he's working on a case. I think I'm going to go back upstairs."

Emma had a cold feeling. "You don't want to get married."

Jamie whipped around, staring at her. "Untrue! I do want to get married. More than about anything." She glanced at the ring on her finger and Emma looked at it, too.

"I'm sorry. I've just got stuff on my mind. Don't worry, Emma. That's not it."

"What is it?"

"I just . . ." She made a face. "I'm just tired and kind of . . . well, just tired."

"You called Ridge Pointe my home," said Emma. "You want me to stay there."

"Only if you want to. I'm having trouble reading you, Emma. You seem like you want to stay there some of the time. I just called it your home because that's where you're living right now."

Emma thought that over. Jamie was not herself. "I'm having trouble reading you," she said back to her.

The loud bang of an upstairs door sounded and Harley came down the stairs, singing to herself. She smiled at Emma. "Ready? C'mon, Duchess." She slapped her knees and called to the dog, but Duchess stayed with Emma. Realizing she was still clutching the dog's fur, Emma slowly released her fingers and watched as her sister went back up the stairs Harley had just come down.

In the car, Emma said, "What's wrong with Jamie?"

"What do you mean?"

Emma was once again clinging to Duchess, but it was because of Harley's driving. She did not make Emma feel comfortable.

"I'm having trouble reading her."

Harley shot her a look. "Who? Mom?"

"She looks kind of messy."

"Hey, none of us are a fashion plate today. I've gotta take a shower when I get back. By the way, I'm working at your place tomorrow. I don't think Twink likes me. Should I try to make friends? In case you bring her to our house?"

"She's not very friendly."

"Maybe Twink won't want to come."

"Jamie said she still wants to marry Cooper," said Emma.

"Well, of course. Why? Was there a question about it?"

"Do you think I should move back?

"Did Mom say something to you?"

"She said you were going to take me home."

Harley smiled. "And I am. Right? I'm taking you home."

"You think Ridge Pointe is my home."

"Well, yeah. Right now Ridge Pointe is your home. Is that what this is about?"

"I don't know what this is about," said Emma.

"Emma, you're not making a lot of sense. That's okay. I can roll with it, but I'm not catching on. Is there something bothering you? Something specific?"

Harley took a corner a little wide and Emma clung onto her armrest. "I don't want to talk while you're driving."

"Sorry."

They didn't say anything more until they got to Ridge Pointe Independent and Assisted Living. Duchess jumped out of the car and headed for the glass front doors. Through the panels, Emma could see the cat had approached the door, probably wanting to be let out. She placed her white paws on the door and started meowing, her little mouth pink against her black face. One look at Duchess and she was gone like a shot, tearing back inside and down one of the halls.

"Not too friendly," agreed Harley, rolling down her window so she could still talk as Emma slid outside after Duchess.

Emma looked back at Harley. "Jamie is unhappy. Maybe I should stay here."

"Don't worry about it. Whatever's going on with Mom, it's not about you. Bye, love," said Harley with a British accent as Emma pulled open one of the glass doors that led into Ridge Pointe, and Harley put the car into gear.

Jamie said Harley was trying to be British. Emma thought

that was not going to work. Harley was American like the rest of them.

Inside Ridge Pointe, Emma took Duchess to their room. The dog had already been outside and fed and she jumped onto the end of Emma's bed and watched as Emma headed back into the hallway. Duchess was a good dog who had learned that sometimes she couldn't go everywhere with Emma.

Emma looked for the cat—Twink, as Harley called her, which was way better than Twinkletoes—by the door to the kitchen, where the cat liked to hang out. No one was around, though. The kitchen was closing. She couldn't find the cat. After a time she went back to her room and settled onto her bed with Duchess and turned on one of the cooking channels. It was good to watch cooks prepare food.

Duchess whined and looked at the drawer where Emma kept the doggy treats. Emma slid off the bed and Duchess jumped after her. Duchess sat eagerly by the drawer as Emma pulled out one treat for the dog and then a Fudgsicle for herself from the freezer above her refrigerator.

Though she'd become careful about giving Duchess too many treats, it was always better to watch cooking shows while you were eating.

Chapter Eight

Mackenzie parked her RAV across the street from LeeAnn Laidlaw's house, a two-story traditional that looked as if the exterior had been upgraded recently, with stained cedar siding and espresso fiberglass windows. Taft's Rubicon was nowhere to be seen, so she surmised she'd beaten him there. Maybe he'd gotten tied up with something. Maybe traffic had stalled him. Whatever the case, she thought about waiting in her car but felt too antsy. She should have stuck around to ask Abby Messinger about her stolen bike, but it was on her list for tomorrow.

LeeAnn Laidlaw answered the bell almost as if she'd been standing behind the door. Her disappointment at seeing only Mac was readily apparent. She glanced past her, eyeing the driveway and road, and then rather reluctantly swung open the door.

"I'm Mackenzie. Laughlin. I work with Mr. Taft," she introduced herself.

"Yes, he told me his assistant would be coming. He clearly isn't here yet." LeeAnn looked her over as she waved Mac off the porch. "May I call you Mackenzie? Please come in."

"Sure."

Mac followed the shorter woman inside. LeeAnn wasn't much over five feet, a tiny brunette with an expensive haircut that tapered down the back of her neck. She looked back at Mac nervously as she led the way down an engineered, gray wood hallway. Anxiety had widened her brown eyes and she looked a little like a scared doe.

The hallway led into a great room that, in turn, looked through a wall of windows to rolling hills of bright green grass, heading down a slope. A kidney-shaped in-ground pool sat to one side, surrounded by concrete and groupings of cushioned outdoor chairs, the water riffled and gray under the cloud cover and coming night. Everything about this house and grounds had that well-tended contractor "dream home" look to it, but then, Laidlaw ran a construction business.

"Would you like an iced tea? I have decaf at this time of day," she said, already heading to the huge refrigerator that dwarfed her even more.

"That would be great. Thanks." After starting the day with a Bloody Mary, she was glad LeeAnn wasn't offering up cocktails.

She brought the drinks, handed one to Mac, then gestured to several chairs for her to sit. She curled up on the couch, tucking her bare feet beneath her legs. The house was warm, but she wore a thick, cowl-necked sweater and black workout pants, and Mac could see her shiver occasionally.

"My husband's missing. I don't know quite what to say," she started in without waiting for Taft. "Tobe's been gone for three weeks, almost four now. Though he's taken off before, so it's not that strange."

She sounded like she was trying to convince herself even though she knew better. Mac waited without comment.

"He has been gone two weeks before but not three," she clarified. "Lately, though, he's been leaving more. He just seems to work less and less at the company, which is fine. He doesn't need to be at the office. He's got good people who work for him. Very good people. But he usually calls me if he's going to be longer than a week. You'll find that out. We check in. But he hasn't called. Not a word to me in all this time. When I went to Europe with friends last year, it was kind of understood that I'd call whenever I could, which was every few days, but most of the time Tobe and I aren't abroad, so we check in." She swallowed a big gulp of her tea. She'd caught Mac's eye early in the telling, but then had let her gaze slide away, as if it were too uncomfortable to look at her.

"But we don't have to call each other *all* the time. You'll find that out, too. I've been with girlfriends who call their significant others all the time, two or three times a day. It's nauseating. We just don't do that. We give each other space. But this is too long. I've tried to call him, but he's not answering, and Tobe's always only a finger or two away from his cell. He may not always answer, but he knows who's calling and when. He wouldn't ignore me this long."

Mac had been directed to a cushy, buttery leather chair and had sunk into it, holding her iced tea out in front of her to keep from spilling. She asked LeeAnn, "Where was he going?"

LeeAnn's view was out the window toward the pool.

Mac followed her gaze, seeing the gray surface dimple now under fast-falling rain.

"A business trip," she said after a long moment. "We own Laidlaw Construction. Have you heard of it?"

"Yes." It was on the tip of her tongue to tell LeeAnn that Laidlaw's foreman was part of her own extended family but decided to keep her relationship to Nolan for another time. She fervently wished Taft had beaten her to LeeAnn's.

"He wants to grow our business, but . . ." She made a dispirited gesture with her shoulders.

Mac said politely, "There are a lot of Laidlaw projects under construction. I've seen the signs everywhere."

"And those for Best Homes as well." Her voice was dry to the point of brittle. "Tobe feels he's in some kind of race with Andrew Best, but Best is . . . well, *besting* him, and enjoying it. That's what he says, anyway. I just think it's little boys fighting."

Mac heard an engine approaching, finally, and was relieved when the bell rang. LeeAnn moved quickly to answer the door and Mac stood up from her chair. The rain was falling ever faster, making a dull background noise as Taft entered. Both LeeAnn and Taft had to speak louder to be heard as they introduced themselves.

Taft and LeeAnn came into the room together. Taft's shoulders and hair were damp with rain, the earthy scent following him in. LeeAnn couldn't seem to take her eyes off him. Her lips, set in a upside-down U till now, had begun to turn that frown upside down upon viewing Taft's good looks. She seemed dumbstruck by Taft's blue eyes, rain-darkened hair, and rakish, lightly bearded jawline.

Well, yeah. He had that effect.

Taft lifted his chin to Mac as he walked in. "I ran into a delay."

Mangella? Maybe. She would ask him later.

LeeAnn asked him if he'd like some iced tea or something stronger, which, although she wasn't interested herself, kind of pissed her off, that LeeAnn hadn't even thrown that in as a possibility. Taft declined, then said, "Tell me what I missed," and LeeAnn launched into the same tale she'd told Mac.

"Where was his destination on this trip?" he asked when she wound down.

"I don't know. I've never really paid attention. It was just another business trip. Colorado maybe? It's never been a problem before."

Taft didn't say it, but like Mac, he clearly thought that was taking the keep-out-of-each-other's-way philosophy to a new level. "When was the last time you tried him on his cell?"

"Half an hour ago. I started calling him on Monday and I've called about three times a day this week. I just get his voice mail."

"Call him again," suggested Taft, and she complied. She put the phone on Speaker, allowing them all to hear the male voice recording say, "Laidlaw Construction. Leave a message," and then the beep.

LeeAnn kept her eyes on Taft as she said into the phone, "It's me again. You've really got me worried. I think I should call the authorities. In fact, I—" Taft shook his head and she cut herself off, finishing lamely, "I'm just really worried. Call me. Just . . . call me."

"Let's wait to tell him that you've hired us until you've hired us," Taft explained as she clicked off.

"I've hired you," she replied quickly.

"Let's talk about the job first." Taft was gentle, carefully negotiating the waters. She may have decided to hire him, but he was the one who picked and chose which jobs he would take. "My associate will most likely be working on your case."

Associate, not assistant, LeeAnn.

"Not you?" LeeAnn asked plaintively.

Mackenzie tried not to let it bother her too much that both Daley and LeeAnn clearly thought she was chopped liver.

"She's very capable," Taft breezed past her worry. "Before we get started, let's talk about a contract. You may not like the terms."

Mac listened as Taft negotiated with LeeAnn. She gulped a little at the steep price, though LeeAnn barely batted an eyelash. In the end, after a couple of more tries for her to get Taft to take on her case personally, she gave up and acquiesced to having Mac, as long as Taft was involved, too.

"Okay, tell us about your husband," Taft invited when they'd hammered out the deal.

LeeAnn looked lost for a moment. "I don't really know where to begin. He was a workaholic . . . now not so much . . . but he was before, and he still takes business trips."

At her pause, Taft asked, "How long have you been married?"

"About six years. Tobe was a bachelor a long time, and he's kind of still that way, I guess, sometimes. His business is his life . . . I mean, it's all he's wanted to do. . . . We thought about having children, but . . . consciously decided not to."

"Your husband is the sole owner of Laidlaw Construction?" asked Taft.

"Yes. No partners, and I'm not involved with the business." She sounded more resigned than bitter.

Taft nodded. "He took over the company from his father, Victor Laidlaw."

"That's right."

"Victor?" Mac repeated.

"Of Victor's Villages, yes. Tobe dropped Victor's name from the Villages, but it lives on. His father's been gone for some fifteen years and still reaches from the grave. Tobe is kind of obsessed, I guess you'd say. He's never been able to let the man completely die."

"Your husband inherited when his father died?" asked Taft.

"Yes. I knew Tobe then, but we didn't become involved till later." She made a face. "Is this going to help find him now? I don't see how."

"How's the business going?"

"Fine. I mean, he hasn't complained. Construction is booming. He doesn't really talk about it all that much to me." She shrugged and spread her hands, clearly not that interested in the company that funded her lifestyle.

"What else does he do?" asked Taft.

She hesitated a moment, like the question had stopped her, like the thought had never occurred to her. "Nothing, really. He doesn't golf or go to the gym. He watches some sports, but doesn't really care that much. He doesn't do much except work."

"But there's less of that now," Mac reminded her.

"Well, it's temporary, I think. Tobe has always had big dreams, big ideas. Like Victor," she admitted. "You know he and Victor built those three houses along the river? There was a big lawsuit over them?"

Taft and Mackenzie both nodded. Recent events had put those houses in the beam of a bright spotlight for them.

"It was really Tobe who built them. He was only twenty at the time. Tobe said Victor was kind of losing it over the lawsuit. He'd done the Villages when he was young and that was about it. He thought the three overlook houses were going to bring him back to prominence, but if Tobe hadn't helped him, that lawsuit would have dragged him under. Tobe saved Victor's company. Laidlaw Construction wouldn't exist without him."

"There was a group that wanted to keep that land for a park . . ." Taft said slowly.

"Oh, God, yes. Tobe said they were insane. They claimed the three new houses broke the view to the river and they brought a lawsuit against Victor's company over their construction. But there had also been that old house on the property before Victor took it down, which kind of blew their claim about ruining the view, so then they then pivoted and said the old house was a landmark, so they sued over its removal! *Then* they sued over ownership of the property, saying it was never supposed to be developed. Any lawsuit they could come up with, they filed. And it apparently went on forever. Tobe changed the name from Victor Laidlaw Construction to just Laidlaw Construction. Even with everyone suing him, Victor had a fit that Tobe changed the name. I guess they didn't speak to each other for like six months, and then shortly afterward Victor died." She closed her eyes. "Tobe's still mad at those people. Friends of Faraday. They were against any and all land development and were always picketing someone in those days."

Mac remembered seeing signs from that group blanketing the Staffordshire Estates development as it just was breaking ground. Now the three-phase development was through phase one and deep into phase two, but she hadn't seen any of their signs lately.

"So your husband's interests have been almost solely wrapped up in the business, but lately that changed," said Taft. "Do you know what happened?"

"Maybe he's just on one of his tangents for now. He's done it before. He gets an idea and goes for it." She paused and rested her chin on her fist. "He's probably ADHD or OCD or something. I always tell him he's just too smart." She smiled. The first true sign of affection for her husband.

"What's the latest tangent?" asked Mac.

She seemed to rouse herself from some fond memory. "I guess it's the same old one. Tobe won't fully accept that his father's death was from heart failure. Mostly he blames the Friends of Faraday, who actually might have killed him from the stress alone, but then he goes off on his conspiracy theories, thinking Victor was murdered." She laughed without humor. "I call them his 'flights of fancy.' But one thing they've done, that even Tobe admits, is keep him busy so he doesn't ruin the company. Tobe's great in a crisis, but the day-to-day running . . . he gets bored pretty fast and then wants to fix things, and he really only gets in the way. That's not just me talking. That's what *he* says."

"Could this latest 'flight of fancy' be what's keeping him in Colorado?" asked Taft.

"I don't even know for sure if he's in Colorado. And if he's obsessing about his father, it would be right here in River Glen. He'd check with the same old people. I don't know who's in charge of the Friends of Faraday now, or if they even still exist. Burt might know."

"Burt . . . Deevers?" Mac asked, trying to hide her surprise.

Taft gave her a sideways look.

"He was Victor and Tobe's lawyer in the lawsuit," LeeAnn said, also looking at her. "You know him?"

"He's the head of the HOA of Victor's Villages. The Villages," she corrected herself.

"For like forever, according to Tobe." A tiny line of consternation formed in her smooth brow. "Burt's a . . . putz," she said, finally landing on an apparently acceptable word. "Tobe doesn't really like him, but I guess he helped save the company, so . . ." She lifted one shoulder in a kind of surrender.

Taft asked several more questions, trying to pinpoint where Tobias had gone on his trip, but LeeAnn was tapped out of information. He then inquired if someone at the company might know where he was, and LeeAnn, who'd seemed to sink into the doldrums, suddenly became animated again.

"Don't tell them I'm worried about Tobe, please. I don't want it to get out that I think he's missing. He could just be working. I don't really know. This is why I haven't gone to the police. Please, don't go to Laidlaw Construction."

"Isn't there someone there who could help? Someone trustworthy?" Taft asked patiently.

"No." She was firm.

"The company could have made his travel arrangements," Taft pointed out.

She clasped her hands together till the knuckles showed white. "I don't want them to know anything. Please. Don't tell them. I forbid you to."

Mac sent Taft a sideways look. She was staying quiet on purpose, not wanting to get in the way of his questioning. But . . . *I forbid you to?*

Taft took the ultimatum in stride. "We'll find another way, but it'll take time."

Mac was extremely glad she hadn't told LeeAnn that she knew Laidlaw's construction manager personally. That would have put paid to the whole thing before they'd even started. But now she wondered if she could even talk to Nolan about his boss at all.

LeeAnn wilted a bit. "There's no one there I trust. Nolan Redfield runs the company and he does a good job, I think. Tobe seems to think so. Fawn is the receptionist and Judy . . . she's his right-hand woman, but I'm just the wife, y'know? They all protect Tobe and don't want to deal with me. I'm a nuisance. So, if Tobe is just taking his time, then I'll look like an idiot and they won't trust me even more."

"Which carrier does he usually fly?" asked Taft.

"He doesn't. He drives."

Taft was giving her a long look, so Mac did the same. LeeAnn had gone from stiff and fighting to limply teetering on the edge of capitulation if her body language could be believed.

Taft said gently, "Mac is going to have to check with someone to get any kind of traction on this."

She seemed to wilt even further, her body folding into the chair. "Oh, fine. Just say I've lost his itinerary. They think I'm an idiot anyway, but don't give anything else away. Okay?" She looked up at Mac, her eyes damp with emotion.

"Okay," said Mac.

She and Taft left soon after, and he walked with her to

her vehicle. The air was thick with moisture, but the rain had tapered off and stopped.

"What do you think?" she asked him.

"He could just be overstaying somewhere."

"Think it's another woman?"

"Maybe. But only if he's blowing things up with LeeAnn. Otherwise he'd stick with his usual schedule, keep LeeAnn from bringing in the calvary."

"Then, maybe something happened to him?" Mac suggested.

He nodded slowly, clearly running possibilities over in his mind.

Mac said, "I'm not complaining at all, but why am I the face of the investigation? We're not working together?"

"We are. I'm just cleaning up some stuff."

"Mangella?"

"Among other things, yes. I am working on it."

"You'll fill me in later," she said dryly.

"I know I've been mum about Mangella."

"Mum . . ." she repeated. "But you're ready to bring me in now?" At his nod, she said, "Good. When? The twelfth of never in the ballpark?"

"Laughlin, this is me, telling you, that I'm ready to lay out everything. I haven't wanted to. Mangella's tricky and ruthless, but I've been overprotective. I'm trying not to be. Trust me on this one."

"Hell no, Taft. If I don't keep prying, you'll clam up entirely."

"You have me all wrong."

"Bullshit, Taft. Bullshit."

He was hiding a smile. "All right. Tell me about the HOA and Burt Deeters."

"Deevers. You're trying to change the subject."

"Yes, I am, before the rain returns. He's the HOA president of the Villages and Laidlaw's lawyer."

"And Laidlaw is my brother-in-law's boss," Mac said, bringing the topic back around. "I'm going to check with Nolan tomorrow, and then I'm going to call Judy, or maybe just show up at Laidlaw Construction, see if she has the travel itinerary and find out what else she can tell me. Also see if I can learn anything current about the Friends of Faraday."

"Good."

"You think the old guard at the Villages knows anything about Tobias's 'flights of fancy'? Especially his theories regarding his father's death? These people were once Victor's friends."

"LeeAnn didn't act like it was a secret," said Taft.

"I'll ask Nolan tomorrow. Then maybe I'll do some 'sleuthing' around the neighborhood, to borrow a word from Leon, see if anybody knows anything."

"What are you going to say to Judy to explain why you want the travel itinerary?"

"Besides LeeAnn's 'lost' itinerary? I'd like to tell Judy that Tobias Laidlaw is missing."

"Blame the request on me," said Taft. "Say I want to talk to Laidlaw because I'm still looking into Andrew Best and Best Homes over that narcotics ring, and I want to know how things are between Best and Laidlaw."

"That might work." She paused. "*Are* you looking into that?"

"Never stopped."

Mac felt encouraged. She'd gotten way more from him

in those few minutes than she had in months. Maybe things were turning around. "I'd better go. Daley's expecting me."

"Call me on the phone on your way back," he invited as he headed to his car. "I want to hear more about the HOA and Burt Deeters."

She almost said "Deevers" but caught herself in time. He was teasing her. She'd heard the smile lurking in his voice.

She smiled herself as she climbed into her car. Things were looking up. Glancing at the time, she saw it was close to ten p.m.

I should have taken my own car. . . .

Cooper glanced at the dashboard clock of his city ride. He'd worked late and then had chosen to make a last interview, which had given him a lot of room for thought. He'd told Verbena he was finishing up rather than heading home and so therefore had taken his favorite vehicle. But the damn thing was acting up. Hesitating. The brakes spongy. It needed a serious look.

But the interview he'd just had . . .

He felt a lightening of spirit as he pressed on the brake. Maybe they were finally getting somewhere on the—

No resistance. In shock, he slammed his foot down again, but it went right down. *Shit!* No brakes! He was barreling down Stillwell Hill, headlong into River Glen proper. He shot past the old Stillwell place, which was now owned by a couple of Jamie's friends, still trying to stop the car, practically shoving the brake through the floor.

His heart rate zoomed.

Fine. He'd ride it out. There was a long stretch at the bottom of the hill before the corner.

Damn car. Damn service needed. *Damn!*

He hit the bottom of the hill with a bang, the steering wheel jumping from his hands. He grabbed at it and yanked it to the right, trying to slow momentum. The car fishtailed and turned all the way around, losing some steam but then jumping the ditch and slamming into a large fir.

Cooper pitched forward, smacking into the rearview mirror, the car shuddering.

His senses reeled. With an effort, he pushed against the driver's door which fell to the ground as if it had been hanging by a thread. He tumbled outside, recognized one leg wasn't working. Uh oh . . .

He was in a field, looking back at the ruined car.

I've got to remember, he thought vaguely.

And then he knew nothing at all.

Chapter Nine

"There you are," Daley hissed in a whisper as Mackenzie attempted to sneak quietly back into the house. She'd been sitting in the living room, in the dark, and pounced on Mac as soon as she crossed the threshold.

"God, Daley. You scared the crap out of me," Mac snapped back, also in a whisper, as she held her hand over her heart and glared through the dimly lit room at the other woman.

"You've been gone for hours. Leon could have killed me a thousand times while you were gone."

Mac had seen both the Audi and the Tesla in the driveway, so she'd known Leon was back. "I thought we agreed that you're relatively safe from your husband."

"When I hit him with divorce papers you think that's going to be pretty?"

"But you haven't yet," Mac reminded as she made her way to her room. She had to feel the edge of the wall with her hand; the hallway was extremely dark and she didn't feel like turning on a light. Daley followed, breathing down her neck.

"What took so long?" she demanded.

"Another case. I told you."

"It's been hours."

"A couple of hours," Mac agreed.

"It felt like an eternity. You know what Leon did? He warned me to be careful. To be careful!" she repeated. I think he knows what I'm planning. That goddamn prenup. If he fights me for the house, I'm going to have to find a way to break it."

"Can we talk in the morning?" Mac asked, barring the door to the room with her body.

"He isn't home yet. I had to call him on his phone. He's probably with someone." Daley hadn't flipped on the light either, but even though Mac couldn't see her expression, she could hear the annoyance in her voice.

Mariah. Chris Palminter's snide comment came back to her.

And Daley, as if divining Mac's thoughts, said, "That Mariah Copple is a broken record. Just *loves* children. That's all she talks about. Children and that *playground.* Probably climaxes to 'It's A Small World.'"

Mac decided that wasn't an aspersion on Leon, just Daley being funnier than she knew. She waited for Daley to continue the rant, but apparently that was all she had to say about Mariah, at least for the moment.

"See you tomorrow," Mac said, stepping back from the door and closing it quietly in Daley's face.

She heard retreating footsteps that grew softer as they moved out of Mac's earshot.

Twenty minutes later Mac was in bed and staring at the ceiling. Light filtered into the room from the outside: one of the streetlamps casting dancing leaf shadows above her. She'd called Taft on her way back to Daley's, but there'd been no further discussion about how to proceed in the

Laidlaw investigation. Instead it had been a catechism by Mac of who'd been at the HOA meeting and whether any of them seemed involved with the harassment of the Carreras. She'd been hard-pressed to inject enthusiasm into the conversation. She didn't really know what she was doing for Daley. Bodyguard? Not really. Investigator? Yes, but even that felt more like an excuse rather than a real job. She'd suspected from the get-go that Taft was just humoring Daley to give Mac a job and keep her away from whatever was transpiring with Mangella, and maybe Andrew Best and others.

But she played along anyway, listing for Taft all the people she'd met at the HOA meeting: President and attorney Burt Deevers; Darrell and his wife, Evelyn—Mac couldn't remember their last name, maybe she'd never heard it; Cliff Fenwick, the heavy equipment operator, and though she hadn't met his wife, she knew the name, Clarice, who apparently shook uncontrollably. Then there was Abby Messinger, the fiftysomething woman who was divorced from Dr. Andre. And Mariah Copple, who was all about the ADA playground being constructed. Althea Gresham and Chris Palminter and Hot Tub Jeannie . . .

"Oh, and the ME was there, Sandy Herdstrom," Mac had finished as she pulled to a stop just down the street from the Carreras' drive. "He seemed to know Burt pretty well. He hung behind the lectern. Didn't seat himself with the rest of us. He must live in the Villages, too. He was pointed out by Burt's ex, Tamara. Don't know why she goes to the HOA meetings because she doesn't seem to live there."

"Did you get a chance to talk to anyone about the harassment?"

"Not yet. But I'm going to check with the Messingers.

Abby said they had a bike stolen. Leon didn't go to the HOA meeting. He apparently avoids them. Daley said he goes out with friends on Thursday nights, but one of the young guard, Chris Palminter, made a crack about him and Mariah, like they have a thing going." She also remembered his comments about Pete but didn't feel like discussing her ex-boyfriend with anyone, least of all Taft.

Taft said, "She seemed pretty certain she wanted a divorce earlier."

"No kidding. She said if she couldn't break the prenup, she was going to find a way to get the house."

"Be careful," he warned.

Taft believed some of the worst crimes were made in the name of love. He'd seen romantic debacles and small-time crime families who looked out for their own. He'd mentioned horrors committed for revenge over the loss of a loved one. Mac had seen a little of that herself, but not like Taft.

"I'll watch my back," she'd answered.

She went to sleep planning out how she was going to structure her investigations the next day.

The call came in at midnight, and Jamie sat bolt upright in bed, wide awake and her heart beginning to thump with fear. Cooper hadn't come home or called. And he always called.

"Hello?" she said, gripping the cell phone with tense fingers.

"Jamie?" The voice was calm, careful, and female. Elena Verbena, Cooper's partner.

"What's happened?"

"Cooper's in the hospital. He was in a car accident. He's at Glen Gen."

"Is he all right?" she whispered, but she was shouting in her head, already having thrown back the covers and climbed out of bed.

"Broken leg. He's in surgery. Possible concussion. Maybe some broken ribs."

Jamie realized through her fog of anxiety that Elena was struggling, too. Trying to stay professional, but fighting a sinking, bone-deep worry.

"Are you at Glen Gen now? I'm coming," she said, flipping on the light and looking around blankly for her clothes.

"I'm here," she said. "He's going to be fine."

Jamie threw on the clothes she'd just taken off and tossed over the chair in their bedroom. Their bedroom. Hers and Cooper's. She felt the ring on her finger, still unfamiliar, and fought down a wave of terror that left her shaking.

Verbena had wanted to sound sure, but the thread of worry in her voice couldn't be denied. *He's going to be fine.* Jamie's worst fear about his job was that he wouldn't come home some night. This was a car accident. Maybe had nothing to do with being a detective. *He's going to be fine . . .*

She fervently prayed it was true.

The smell filtered in first. Something antiseptic. Foreign. And then a soft beep and a feeling of brain sluggishness. Had he blacked out? It was similar to the times Cooper had drunk too much alcohol and had woken up disoriented and unable to account for time.

He heard muffled voices, distorted, like through water. He tried to open his eyes and managed one. He was in a bed and sunlight surrounded the nearly closed blinds. Daylight.

An IV ran into the back of his hand. White bedding. Hospital. Emergency Room.

He forced both eyes open. The voices were in the hallway. Verbena . . . and Jamie.

Relief flooded through him. He couldn't remember how he'd gotten here, but Jamie was here. His fiancée.

"Fiancée," he whispered. Strange word. Good word. Foreign. Jamie was his fiancée.

He drifted back to the cottony netherworld he'd woken from.

Mac opened one eye. She could smell fried bacon and heard the clink of ice dropped into a glass. Leon with more Bloody Marys? She was surprised he was up before she was.

Throwing back the covers, she headed straight for the shower. Fifteen minutes later she appeared in the kitchen with combed but wet hair in her usual getup of a shirt and blue jeans. She'd added a modicum of makeup, just enough to make herself feel presentable.

As predicted, Leon was at the blender with more Bloody Marys. What was unexpected was that Daley sat at the counter, nibbling on a piece of bacon and reading the paper as if she didn't have a care in the world. Her hair, too, was wet, and she was ensconced in a fluffy, pink bathrobe.

Leon's hair was still damp as well. Mac picked up the surprising vibe that the two of them had showered together, maybe after some early morning romantic calisthenics?

Hmmm.

"Good morning," Leon greeted her, holding up the orange-red pitcher.

"Morning. No, thanks." She turned to Daley, who slid a quick sideways look her way out of the corner of her eye but didn't make any serious move to start a conversation.

"What are you doing today?" asked Leon. He grinned at her, clearly amused by the whole situation. The cat who ate the canary.

Mac planned on meeting first with Nolan, her step-brother-in-law, but that was a subject she didn't want to get into with either of the Carreras. She chose a safer subject. "I'm going to ask your neighbors if they've seen anything or anyone loitering around your house. I'll start with Calloway Court and work my way around. Might check in with some of the HOA members," she added casually. "Burt seems to know everyone."

"Burt." Leon snorted, which earned him a look Mac couldn't read from Daley.

"Something wrong?" asked Mac.

"You're better off starting with the young guard." Leon poured more mix into his glass, throwing out an anemic-looking celery stick and plopping in a new one. "Burt's full of hot air and rules. The rest of 'em are complainers. The young guard is way more fun, and they might actually know something more than which bylaw you've trans-gressed."

"Mariah Copple's a good place to start," suggested Daley. She didn't look up from her plate even though the bacon was gone. Leon didn't jump to the bait. Instead he attempted to put some scrambled eggs on her plate, which caused her to vehemently shake her head. She was right. The eggs had been sautéed within an inch of their life into a thick, rubbery mass.

"No, thanks," Mac said again when he turned to her with the eggs still on the spatula.

"You need a little something before you head out sleuthing," he said.

"I'm good."

Daley said, "I'd like to talk to you before you race away."

Mackenzie wasn't planning on being deterred from her game plan. "It looks like you've got everything under control."

"Does it?" she asked.

"I'll be back," said Mac, easing toward the door.

"Oh, let her go, darling," Leon told his wife, who'd gotten off her stool and acted like she was going to chase Mac down. "We still have things to discuss, too."

"You're an ass, Leon," Daley snapped, to which he laughed and came around the island to gather her up and squeeze her hand. He then threw her over his shoulder, hauling her off down the hall, whistling.

Mac half expected her to pound on his back, but instead she captured Mac's gaze and looked at her angrily.

Mac paused at the door. It appeared like this was some kind of game they played, but was Daley being bullied into sex? She didn't seem like the type of personality that would stand for that. Maybe this was just role-playing for them? She'd also said she was going to find a way to break the prenup. Was sex used as a means to seal the deal?

A few moments later she heard moaning coming from

down the hall. She tiptoed back across the foyer and a
few steps into the hall. It had been a while since she'd
had sex herself, but if memory served . . . that sounded
like enjoyment.

Giving herself a hard shake, she headed outside, firmly
shutting the door behind her. If she was supposed to be a
bodyguard for Daley against Leon, she was really failing
at her job.

Taft had called the man he used as a confidential informant so many times without an answer, he'd felt certain
something had happened to him. Jimmy Riskin was listed
as RISK in his contact list, though the phone number kept
changing, so when the cell rang and his name popped up
on the screen, Taft nearly dropped the phone he'd just
picked up, juggling it and swearing, slamming his shin into
his couch as he tried to save it from falling, and swearing
some more.

"Hello?" he answered cautiously, rubbing his leg. Riskin
lived a life in the shadows, and Taft, who'd wondered if he
should report the man missing, wasn't quite sure what to
expect.

"Hey, Taft," was the soft reply.

"Riskin. What happened to you?"

"Been busy. You know who you asked me about?"

Mitch Mangella, Andrew Best, Keith Silva . . . among
others. "Yeah."

"If you find me sleeping with the fishes, you'll know
who to blame."

"Don't hang up," Taft said quickly, sensing he was about to be cut off. "I could use some information."

"I'm all out, man. After this, this phone won't be working."

Riskin ran through burner phones on a regular basis. A little desperately, Taft asked, "How will I get hold of you?"

"I'll get hold of you. Just like always."

"What happened? Something happened."

There was a slight hesitation. "I mighta seen something I shouldn't," he admitted slowly.

That was kind of the nature of his job, but his careful tone came through the line and raised the hairs on Taft's arms. "What?"

"I gotta go low, man. Gotta think. Gotta move. I'll leave you a message."

There was the faintest sound of a smile in his voice. Riskin was known for being obscure, so Taft said, "Don't make this a puzzle. If you're in real trouble, you gotta give it to me straight."

"Info on the widow. I'll find a way to get it to you."

"Anna DeMarcos . . . and Silva?" asked Taft.

"Nineteen eighty-four, man. Let the evidence speak for itself."

"What?"

But he was gone.

Taft stayed frozen for several beats, his mind racing. What had Riskin seen? Something to do with Anna De-Marcos, some kind of hard evidence? Riskin knew people who knew people, but it was a dangerous game. If there was something on the death of DeMarcos's husband . . .

Taft had asked the CI for any inside information he

could acquire on Mangella and his associates, and Anna DeMarcos was a friend of Prudence's, and Silva was now working for the man.

What had Riskin learned? Taft wanted to call him right back but kept himself from doing it. He wouldn't answer anyway, and Taft didn't know what the CI had fallen into. The man would call when he could.

If you find me sleeping with the fishes, you'll know who to blame. . . .

Taft exhaled slowly. Maybe it was time to check in on Silva, see just what he was up to with Mitch Mangella and/or anyone and anything else in his slimy world.

And what was that about nineteen eighty-four? Did he mean the year? Or the book by George Orwell? Was Big Brother watching Riskin? He wished the man wasn't so cryptic, but if Riskin really felt his life was in danger, he supposed he had his reasons.

The phone rang again and this time it said River Glen PD. Now there was something he didn't see every day, the police calling him. Since he left the department the only times he'd dealt with them was in person, and mostly those were contentious meetings. "Taft Investigations," he answered, not bothering to hide his curiosity.

"Hey, Taft."

The voice on the other end was Barbara Erdlich, a friend still within the department who liked to keep that friendship on the down low, a friend whose nickname was the "The Battle-ax," a nickname she'd embraced. Normally she and Taft communicated by cell phone, but this call had come straight from the department, from which she tersely gave him the news that Detective Cooper Haynes was in River Glen General Hospital after a suspicious car accident.

Mackenzie's phone calls hadn't netted her any results. First, Nolan had said, regretfully, that he had a hellish day ahead of him and could he talk to her this evening about whatever she had on her mind? Second, Mac had learned from Fawn, Laidlaw Construction's receptionist, that Judy Wyler, Tobias Laidlaw's right-hand woman, was out of the office today and could she leave a message for her?

Strike two for two.

She had then searched for some contact for the Friends of Faraday and had learned the group no longer existed in that form. It had morphed into the Faraday Foundation, and she'd tried to contact members of the board but had only found their email addresses: three women and one man, who seemed to be the big cheese. She emailed him asking for information on their former group.

So, with the first interviews on today's agenda postponed, and while she waited for word from Joseph Mertz of the Faraday Foundation, Mac decided to head over to the B streets, where Abby Messinger lived, and knock on her door. As she approached the sprawling ranch house, which was built similarly to the Carreras' but without the extra wing, she noticed the cracked driveway and peeling paint. Some deferred maintenance there. Mac could sympathize. It was hard to keep up with home repair and it was certainly expensive. The Carreras' house was done to a T, the previous owners having redone it before they put it on the market. She idly wondered how the Martins' renovation was going on the house they'd purchased after losing out to the Carreras on their first choice.

When no one answered, Mac knocked again, then tried the bell. Made sense that no one would be home; Abby Messinger was a nurse at Glen Gen and most likely at work, and Dr. Andre didn't live with her. If Abby's son, Alfie, was around, he wasn't making his presence known. She gave up after a third try.

Walking back from the B streets, she was passed by a group of tweenage girls on bikes. School was out for the summer and the girls were laughing and calling to one another. Overhead there were still gray clouds, but patches of blue could be seen. The air was coolish but not cold, and Mac, who'd worn a lightweight jacket, took it off and tied it around her waist. Another bike shot by, this time a teenage boy wearing a hoodie, but the hood was off his head hanging at the back of his neck. She gazed at the bike, thinking. The Carreras' thief had run away, outside of the Ring's camera, but that didn't mean a bike wasn't parked somewhere, purposely out of view.

As she drew closer to the Carreras', Mac knocked on a few doors. Maybe one of them had cameras. There was no answer at the first two doors, but at the next one a harried-looking mom with three blondish kids in the five-to-nine range just shook her head when Mac asked if she'd seen anything suspicious in the neighborhood, or if she had any equipment that could possibly have caught the eye of the miscreants who'd targeted the Carreras. Two other neighbors asked if she was on the neighborhood watch and pointed out Althea Gresham's house, about two down from the Carreras on the opposite side of Calloway Court. At the last door she knocked on, an older gent with oiled-down gray hair and a red-and-white-polka-dot bow tie said,

"Althea knows ev'rythin and ev'ryone around. Once you get her goin', you cain't stop 'er. She *is* the neighborhood watch."

Mackenzie had put off knocking on Althea's door because . . . her mind went blank.

Because you made a judgment call on her last night and think you could get stuck listening to a list of grievances.

Mac felt a twinge of guilt. Well, yes, that was why. But Althea was head of the neighborhood watch, and although it sounded like she was having trouble rounding up new volunteers, maybe it was for some other reason than what Mac's snap judgment had her believing: that Althea Gresham was a stubborn pain in the ass.

Mackenzie's phone vibrated against her thigh almost the moment after she pushed the bell of Mrs. Althea Gresham's home. She'd specifically switched to vibrate and put it in her pocket so as not to have it ring in the middle of an interview. She debated on checking it, but Althea answered the door much as LeeAnn Laidlaw had the night before, as if she'd been standing behind it. Looking into her sharp blue eyes beneath a crown of white hair, Mac let the incoming phone call go to voice mail and introduced herself to the elderly woman.

"I understand you're on the neighborhood watch," she said as Mrs. Gresham moved back from the door and motioned her inside with a stop-wasting-my-time twirl of her wrist. Mac was a little surprised because she hadn't said word one about who she was and what she wanted, but she complied. Bringing up the neighborhood watch was apparently explanation enough.

"Take that chair," the older woman ordered, pointing to an overstuffed green, high-backed seat beside a brick fireplace, similar to the one in the HOA meeting room. Mac sat down on a cushion hard as slate. "Yes, I'm part of the Villages neighborhood watch." She seated herself in a matching chair that seemed to have a little more give. "And you're a *detective* of sorts, I believe I heard. You were at the meeting last night."

"I'm Mackenzie Laughlin. I've been hired by the Carreras to see what I can learn about the harassment they've been victim to."

"The dog stool in the mailbox."

"Among other things. I was wondering—"

"You think I'm too old for the watch?" she challenged.

Her sudden accusation stopped Mac for a moment. "I, no, well, no. I haven't even met any other members," Mac stumbled around.

"You haven't met Jean yet? She thinks I'm too old. Those young people don't recognize how important the watch is. It's disgusting what happened to Mr. Carrera and his wife. The perpetrators should be thrown in jail for a good long time."

Well . . . Mackenzie wasn't certain she was feeling quite the same way. Yes, she would like to find the miscreants and have them face justice, but jail for a "good long time" might be more punishment than they'd earned. Thievery was certainly a crime, and yes, she wanted any thief to be caught and face the law, but dog shit in the mailbox was something else. A mean trick. A message. A juvenile prank. She wasn't certain the harassment had reached the level of "thrown in jail for a good long time" yet.

"Jean?" Mac questioned politely. Did she mean Hot Tub Jeannie?

Mrs. Gresham lifted her pugnacious chin. "Jean McDonald. Calls herself Jeannie. You say Mr. Carrera hired you?"

Sensing that she could be treading into dangerous waters by getting too specific with Mrs. Gresham, Mac said, "The Carreras have a Ring camera, but there is no clear image of the person, or persons, who've been harassing them. Has this happened to anyone else besides the Carreras?"

"I never heard Abby Messinger say she had a bike stolen until last night."

"But no one else?"

"No."

"No? You're certain of that?"

"The watch is always watching, my dear."

Mac smiled, but there was no hint of humor in Althea Gresham's words. She was seriousness personified.

"Who else is on the watch?" asked Mac.

She hesitated a moment and her lips pursed. A sore subject, Mac guessed. "Evelyn Jacoby. She's Jean's neighbor. And Clarice Fenwick. Abby used to be on the watch, but she's too busy with work now." Althea's look said she thought she was getting the runaround.

"Is that all?" Mackenzie asked carefully.

"Carol Martin was with us for years, then they moved. She's back now but also says she's too busy. We are looking for new members," she said. "You are just a guest at the Carreras'?"

"Yeah, I don't think I qualify."

Althea nodded grimly. "Burt's ex, Tamara, doesn't live in the Villages, so she isn't a full member of the watch anymore, but she helps out. And Abby still does what she can," she added grudgingly, as if she were thinking of some way to approve Mackenzie.

"Abby is a nurse at Glen Gen?" said Mac, hurriedly

changing the subject. She could already see being part of the neighborhood watch might make her persona non grata with Althea in charge.

"Yes, Abby is a nurse. She was married to Dr. Andre, but that didn't last. Those May–December marriages seldom do. They have a son, Alfie, who's heading down the wrong path." She made a tsking sound with her tongue. "I worry about the youth of America, don't you know. It's a parent's job to make sure they stay on track to become fruitful members of the community. I'm not sure Abby has the strength for that on her own. Dr. Andre would, but he's . . ." Here she stopped and pondered a moment, possibly searching for the right words. "He's a philanderer. No nice way to say it, so I might as well just come out with it. Philandered with some of the residents who've since moved away. Abby's a lovely woman, but she's no match for him. Once he fell in with Victor, the marriage was doomed."

"Victor . . . Laidlaw?"

"Yes, the builder of our community. I would recommend learning our history, dear, if you plan to win trust and make a difference to us," she said crisply.

"I guess it's lucky I started with you, then," said Mac, infusing her voice with extra eagerness. She didn't have to fall back on drama skills to fake attentiveness. Fortuitously, Althea had moved on to the topic Mac most wanted to discuss.

Althea narrowed her eyes at Mac, who could practically hear the sniffing as the old woman tried to smell whether Mac was putting her on or not. Though she'd dreaded coming here, annoying busybodies were some of the best sources of information. Now she wanted to just take it all in.

"What did Victor Laidlaw have to do with Dr. Andre?" asked Mac.

"What do you think? Same old story. Victor was a womanizer, don't you know. Never could settle down with just one. Married a couple of them but divorced early. Built our houses and slapped his name on the neighborhood, started in on the women around, didn't matter if they were married or not. Dr. Andre joined in. Bed-hopping, that's what it was, don't you know. Dr. Andre is one of those body doctors. Has his own clinic, I hear, which is good because it wouldn't be good for them to both work at the hospital. He and Abby wouldn't speak to each other if not for Alfie."

Though this was a lot of information that probably had nothing to do with anything, when a fire hose was blasting, you needed to just step out of the way and let it happen. Besides, it was entertaining, a complete reversal from what Mac had envisioned of her interview with Althea Gresham. She itched to take out her small notebook from her back pocket and record a few notes, but Althea was just warming up, and Mac had learned from past experience that sometimes pulling out a notebook would intimidate people, the firehose shut off. She didn't want to chance stemming the flow.

"So Dr. Andre and Victor both became involved with women from the neighborhood," prompted Mac.

"Oh, yes. Victor died about fifteen years ago, but he kept after women right till the end. Dr. Andre and Abby split up over it, even though Alfie was just a baby then. I heard the good doctor's on a shorter leash with his second wife. Lives in Portland."

Mac wondered if she should try to direct her just a tad, but Mrs. Gresham had warned her to learn the history of the community, and maybe there was something to that. Still . . . "What about the HOA president, Burt Deevers?" she asked.

Mrs. Gresham's bright blue eyes gave her a hard look. "How much do you know about him?"

"Next to nothing. I just met him last night for the first time."

Althea compressed her lips. "The homeowners go to the meetings, but nothing changes. They just run it the way they want to and never listen to us." Something about the way she said that made Mac wonder if she'd tried, and been rejected, for a position on the board at one time or another. She didn't seem like the kind of person who would take kindly to that.

"Burt and Tamara moved in a long time ago—before I was here and that was a long time ago. I sold my place after my husband died. This was our rental home, so I moved into it after Rowan died. But I knew all about Burt and Tamara and Victor. Victor nearly ruined them financially about the time the Villages were being built. Some kind of investment that went wrong. I don't know about that kind of stuff. Tamara was one of the women who got involved with Victor, too." She shook her head at the folly of it all.

"But wasn't Burt Victor's lawyer?" Mackenzie asked carefully.

"I believe so. There was a lawsuit over those three houses above the river. . . ." She half turned, as if looking toward something beyond the four walls of her house.

"The overlook houses," prodded Mac.

"Burt had a falling-out with Victor." She made a sound of derision. "Victor had a falling-out with practically everyone at one time or another. Victor practically begged Burt to represent him, but there was that bad blood between them because of Tamara. She and Burt were still married at the time of the 'overlook' houses." She gave Mac a long look. "Burt defended Victor, but Victor couldn't keep his hands off Tamara, and she had her hands on him, too. Burt kicked her out, but she still owns half the house. She doesn't live here anymore, though, so she can't be on the watch."

"I think she was at last night's meeting," said Mac. She knew full well Tamara had been there, hissing to Daley that the man silently communicating with Burt was River Glen's ME, as if Daley should immediately recognize someone of Dr. Sandy Herdstrom's eminence.

"If you know her, you know what happened next," Mrs. Gresham said tartly. She clearly didn't like her narrative interrupted.

"I don't know her. She was mentioned to me."

"She resumed her affair with Victor right when Burt was defending him in the lawsuit. Victor won the lawsuit and the hand of the fair Tamara Deevers. Tamara apparently told everyone that Victor begged her to leave Burt a second time and marry him, so she divorced Burt with hardly so much as a how-do-you-do, but then Victor never put that ring on her finger. Same old Victor."

"Victor seems to still cast a long shadow over the Villages," Mackenzie observed, borrowing the quote from LeeAnn Laidlaw.

"He was a scourge. A rapscallion. A dreadful man. But he had something, apparently." She shook her head, as if it were an unending mystery.

"You said Victor won the lawsuit? I was under the impression his business almost went under over that lawsuit and his son helped him save it."

"Well, Victor was never good with money. Any he made, he lost. That's what Evelyn said Burt says. Money went through his fingers like water. Maybe his son saved the business. I don't really know."

Or care, Mac surmised. Mrs. Gresham was interested in the Villages neighborhood, which Victor Laidlaw had been a big part of, until he wasn't. Anything or anyone outside the neighborhood couldn't hold her interest.

"I understand Victor died shortly after building the overlook houses," said Mac.

"That's right."

"A heart attack?"

"All that in flagrante delecto living caught up with him," she said with asperity.

Mackenzie reassessed the older woman. She certainly enjoyed having the floor and impressing or confounding any and all listeners. Mac had a vision of her standing in front of a blackboard with a pointer and glaring out at a classroom of students, waiting for them to catch up, if they could. No words of encouragement from this quarter.

"I'd like to talk to Evelyn and Clarice," said Mac. "Do you have contact numbers for them?"

The older woman heaved herself out of her chair and slowly toddled into the kitchen. Mac also rose from her chair, noticing her butt cheeks were slightly sore from the rock-hard cushion she'd been sitting on.

Althea dug through a drawer and finally seesawed out a small, wooden recipe card box wedged inside, very much like one Mac's grandmother had bestowed on her mother. Mrs. Gresham flipped open the lid and Mac saw the cards inside were alphabetized. Not recipes. Addresses.

Quickly pulling out her notepad, Mac scribbled the phone numbers Althea rattled off as if she were in a speed contest. *Can you memorize this?* Not a chance. Mac had to ask her to repeat the numbers and she did so through tight lips. She also asked for Mac's number in return. The old lady was very competitive.

"Are any of the young guard part of the watch?" Mackenzie asked, clicking off her pen and putting the notepad and pen away.

"Other than Jean they can't be bothered," she said, tucking Mac's number into her recipe file box.

"Who do you think's harassing the Carreras? Any ideas?"

"Someone they've maybe maligned?" she suggested, lifting her brows and staring pointedly at Mackenzie.

"Is there something I don't know?" asked Mackenzie. Clearly Althea had something on her mind she desperately wanted to pass on.

She pressed her palm to her chin, considering. Mac sensed it might be an act. The lady was dying to pass on gossip, whether she believed Mac was capable of sussing out the culprit or not.

After a few moments she dropped her hand and said briskly, "Mr. Carrera is a cheater as well. He's been seeing one of the neighbors, part of the young guard, as Burt— and apparently you—describe them."

Mariah Copple . . .

Mackenzie waited for her to speak the woman's name, but she wouldn't go that far. She said instead, "You should talk to Jean. It's her hot tub that seems to get . . . the most use. Leon Carrera spends a lot of time there, but only if a certain woman's there, too."

"You think this liaison could be the cause of the harassment?"

"You should talk to Mr. Carrera about that, I would imagine," she said, just hiding a self-satisfied sneer.

Yep. Blackboard pointer.

Mackenzie said her goodbyes a few moments later as Althea Gresham appeared to be talked out, at least for the moment. She seemed to be anxiously waiting for Mac to leave, and Mac had another vision of her hurrying as fast as she could to her landline and sending out the news about the detective of sorts who was investigating the neighborhood.

As she walked to her RAV, she checked her phone message and saw that the one she'd ignored earlier was from Taft. She instantly kicked herself for not checking it earlier.

He'd left a text: Cooper Haynes suspicious car accident recovering at Glen Gen

Oh, shit.

Chapter Ten

He awoke slowly, aware almost immediately he was on some kind of pain meds. His mouth was dry without a drop of spit and he was surrounded by a cottony feeling that dimly reminded him of how he'd felt after waking up from surgery on his shoulder. Rotator cuff, ligament damage, the product of being a basketball weekend warrior.

He could hear faint noises. Soft, rhythmic beeping. Muffled voices, somewhere distant.

Cooper groaned and opened his eyes; slowly the room gained focus. A hospital room. He could see a blanket-shrouded foot . . . and his left leg, his thigh wrapped in flesh-colored bandages. Oh, that's right. Surgery.

He had no feeling in that leg. He ordered his foot to flex and saw his ankle and toes move. Relief. It still worked.

"Cooper?"

Jamie's voice, eager, worried, shaking. He turned his head to the sound of it and saw her get up from a chair by the window. Her face was gaunt. No makeup that he could see. But the downy tenderness of her jawline and the glimmer of tears in her brown eyes brought their own beauty. He'd heard her before with Verbena.

"Jamie," he tried to say, but his throat was too dry. It came out as a croak. He attempted to clear his throat and try again, but she understood what he needed, reaching for a water glass and bringing the straw to his lips. He sipped and swallowed and said with more success, "What happened?"

"You were in a car accident on Stillwell Hill last night. You don't remember? We talked about it." She looked concerned.

He vaguely remembered, sort of.

"What time is it?" he asked. His voice was stronger.

She consulted the clock on the wall that now he could see as well. "Eleven thirty," she said at the same time he recorded the time himself.

What was I doing on Stillwell Hill?

He had no memory of it.

"How are you feeling?" Jamie asked. "I'm going to get the nurse." She straightened away from him.

"No."

"No?"

"Stay . . ."

She immediately leaned back toward him, searching his eyes. "I'm right here," she said.

He lifted his left arm and pointed to his left leg.

"Broken femur," she said. "Broken thighbone," she elucidated, though he knew the femur was the thighbone. "And a concussion. Cracked ribs."

What was I doing?

"I need to tell them you're awake," she said.

Cooper closed his eyes again. "Okay."

He heard her get up and go. He sank into himself. Everything felt incredibly hard. Thinking was hard. He dragged his brain back to his last memory before waking. He'd been at work . . . he'd been with Verbena . . . staying late? He'd been leaving . . . heading home? He remembered being at the back door of the station. Reaching for the keys from the gray metal cabinet where all the station's vehicles' keys were kept. Or was that memory from some other time? He couldn't tell.

Jamie came back and a nurse was with her. The nurse asked him questions about how he felt and then whether he knew his name and what day it was. He stumbled a bit on the day. The accident was last night? He'd been injured last night? The surgery was last night? The nurse told him he was doing fine, and she said something similar to Jamie before she left the room. He figured he was at Glen Gen, River Glen General Hospital.

"When can I get out?" he asked.

"They're going to cast your leg. I don't know about the concussion," said Jamie. "What the protocol is. But you're doing fine. You heard the nurse? It was a clean break and you're on the mend."

Her eager tone was almost too eager. He realized she'd been scared. Maybe still was. But he could hear the relief, too.

"Gotta rest," he mumbled.

"I'll be right here."

And Cooper slipped back into a dreamless netherworld, one question hanging around like an unwelcome visitor: *What was I doing?*

Taft knew Keith Silva spent most of his free hours with Anna DeMarcos, so that was where he was on Friday morning, parked across from the River Glen Grill and the brick, full-story apartments above it, where Carlos DeMarcos's widow, and Silva's lover, resided. After Riskin's call, Taft figured he'd follow Silva and see what he was up to. If there was a link to be found between Mitch Mangella and the underworld of crime, Silva was it.

Taft examined the expensive penthouse apartment with a jaundiced eye. He believed the woman had gotten away with murdering her husband, Silva being her weapon of choice. And also she'd gotten away with a fat life insurance payout.

Maybe he should take his suspicions to Detective Haynes, one of the few people Taft trusted at the River Glen PD. But Haynes was now lying in a bed at River Glen Hospital. Had he been targeted somehow? He needed more information from The Battle-ax.

Taft knew he could trust Haynes. He was a straight shooter who kept himself out of department politics. He was also someone who had Mackenzie Laughlin's back, maybe even more so since she'd left the force. He knew, as Taft did, one major reason Mac had walked away from the River Glen PD was because of Chief Hugh Bennihof's unwanted attention to her and other young, female members of the department.

And Mangella asked you to shake the man down? Rein him in? Get him to change his ways? Was that what he'd been intimating?

That was certainly how Taft had taken it. Not that he was any fan of Bennihof. He'd like to see the man brought down, but he didn't want to be the one to do it at the behest of Mitch Mangella.

And Silva had taken over Taft's job and then some. He was eager to become the "fixer," although through a different methodology. Taft had tried to keep Mangella within the law, and Mangella had initially approved his efforts. But things had changed. Silva didn't really care about pesky law and order, and it appeared at heart Mangella felt the same way. He'd at least tried to be an honest citizen while Taft worked for him, but maybe it had been an act.

He went back to thinking about Detective Haynes. He'd called Mackenzie and left her a message on a text, but she had yet to respond. He knew she was busy, but he was thinking of texting her again when Silva suddenly walked out of the apartment building's main doors, just down the block from the entrance to the Grill. Silva's dull gray hair was about the shade of the June skies. The man had grayed young and let it happen rather than do anything about it, though he was fastidious about his clothing. He favored collarless shirts and light sports coats and had worn them whenever he was out of uniform, which had prompted The Battle-ax to address him as Sonny when he was still with the department. The name referred to a character from the old television show *Miami Vice* because Silva's sartorial style mimicked TV Detective Sonny Crockett's apparent on-the-job mode of dress. When Taft had been with the force she'd called him Face, after a character from another old TV show, *The A-Team.*

Now Silva strode up the street to a parking lot run by, of course, Mitch Mangella. Taft switched on his ignition and watched from his driver's side mirror. Silva appeared a few minutes later in a brown Dodge Charger and turned on the street in the opposite direction from where Taft was. Taft eased into traffic and did a U-turn one block up, out of sight of Silva, then drove back in the direction Silva had taken.

He knew Silva's address and wondered if he was heading there now, though he spent most of his time at the widow's. He followed Silva out of River Glen and across the line into Portland. His senses went on alert as they crossed the Marquam Bridge and Silva started winding through streets on the east side of the Willamette, taking them farther east. They were growing closer to the last address Taft had for Riskin. Could that be where he was going? Maybe Riskin's paranoia was well-deserved. The CI moved around a lot, but he'd last lived in a U-shaped motor court converted to apartments, a relic from the fifties that still stood even while the area surrounding it had become more and more gentrified over the years, a source of friction in the community.

Sure enough, Silva suddenly turned into Riskin's complex, the Rosewood Court as it was spelled out in pink neon script visible through the window of the end unit, which, apparently, still was an office. Taft's pulse sped up. Was Silva here to *see* Riskin? It was a small, underground intelligence community that ran through River Glen, Portland, and the surrounding area, and as Mangella's newest fixer, Silva might know of the CI. Silva wasn't here by coincidence. Had to be something to do with the man.

Taft kept the driveway into the motor court in his sight, allowing an elderly man who looked like a candidate for an eye test work his way into his car, which was parked at the curb. The delay kept Taft from having to move forward and able to keep from passing the motor court.

An impatient driver beeped at him from behind, but Taft idled beside the elderly man's Chrysler sedan. Silva, who'd parked and was walking toward the motor court's office, which showed an Apartment Available sign in the window, glanced around at the sound of the beep. Taft, in sunglasses and a black baseball cap with the logo of a Portland motorcycle shop, hoped the man didn't make him. From the way Silva turned immediately back to the office he didn't appear to think anything of it.

By the time the elderly man had herded his vehicle back onto the road, Taft had seen enough through the office window to realize Silva was engaging a young woman behind the desk whose hair was a shockingly bright red. Taft drove past and turned at the end of the block, squeezed into a spot that clipped the end of one of the resident's driveways, then jogged back to the corner to look down the street. He checked the time on his phone, waiting impatiently for Silva to leave. Silva was clearly there looking for Riskin, and if Riskin wasn't home and Silva decided to stake out his place, Taft could be in for a long wait.

But then Silva's vehicle nosed back into traffic, turning south, reversing his route. Taft half ran back to his Rubicon just as a woman in jeans and a sweatshirt that read *I'm pretty sure I don't want you near me* was staring at his bumper crowding her drive's space and talking into a phone. When she saw Taft she thrust her hands on her hips and lowered her head, as if she were going to charge him.

He took off his sunglasses and spread his hands. "I owe you twenty bucks for taking up your driveway."

"Forty," she spat back. She said into the phone, "I got this," and clicked off, glaring at Taft. She was somewhere in her fifties, he'd guess. Thick, curly brown hair. A figure fighting an extra twenty pounds. Her best feature was her eyes. Big, brown, and what he would have liked to call soulful, except they were currently swimming with anger.

"Thirty-five," he said.

She hesitated, slowly looking him up and down. He could almost tell the moment she decided she wasn't as angry with him as she'd thought. "Okay," she said, her posture relaxing into surrender.

Taft pulled out his wallet and gave her the cash. "I couldn't find a parking spot and my errand was time sensitive."

"Huh?"

"Thank you." He climbed back in the Rubicon and gave her a high sign as he left. When he rounded the corner back toward the motor court, she was still gazing after him. He tried calling Riskin to no avail, then pulled into the apartment lot and parked in the space Silva had just vacated. Riskin's apartment had been on the second floor, near the back of the south wing. He walked toward the rear flight of stairs, the one nearest his door, and took the steps two at a time. He lightly rapped his knuckles on the panel and the door swung inward, unlocked and unlatched.

The apartment was empty, apart from minor detritus on the floor, a few papers and a full trash can. There were some playing cards scattered on a dusty shelf; rings where you could see something had once stood. Taft checked the galley kitchen of the small studio and the bathroom, his ears alert for the sound of anyone entering. Had Silva been here? Had he known Riskin was gone? Or was he the reason Riskin had said, "Gotta move" in their phone conversation. Taft had taken it as a measure of his anxiety, but it looked as if he'd meant it literally. Was Silva the reason? Riskin's info had something to do with the widow, so Silva was likely at the heart of Riskin's change of address. Taft had no idea where the CI was now; did Silva?

As Taft was heading out, a young woman stood in the doorway. "What are you doing here?" she demanded. She was tattooed and pierced, but it was her brilliant red hair that IDed her. The girl from the office

"The door was open," said Taft.

"I have someone coming to clean."

"Looks like Riskin moved out. Do you know where he went?" he asked hopefully.

She just stared at him, sizing him up. "You need to leave," she said, locking the door after him. "The cleaner's late."

She turned on her heel and headed back toward the office.

Mac's cell rang again as she entered Daley and Leon's house. She'd texted Taft, asking for more information on Cooper Haynes, but he hadn't gotten back to her yet. Now she glanced at the number, expecting it to be him, but it was Jamie Woodward, the woman Cooper Haynes lived with, returning her call. Mac didn't know Jamie well, but she had a relationship with Jamie's sister, Emma Whelan, who'd been instrumental in helping her out of a tough situation on Taft's and her last case. A more unlikely ally probably couldn't be found, but it had cemented a friendship between them.

"Hello, Jamie. Thanks for returning my call. It's Mackenzie Laughlin. Emma gave me your number. I just heard about Detective Haynes's accident and I wanted to make sure he's okay." Mac stepped across the threshold. Daley was nowhere to be seen, but through the sliding glass door she saw Leon lounging in the deck's hot tub. He was lying back, elbows on the tub's edge, his eyes closed, a faint smile on his lips.

"He's doing okay. Thank you," said Jamie.

Daley suddenly surfaced from somewhere between his legs and moved up on him for a rather aggressive kiss. Her nude back and the top of her buttocks were in Mac's line of sight, and Leon's hands were beneath the frothing water, doing something that caused Daley to squirm and wriggle.

Mac drew in a breath in surprise, then said, "Um . . ." She backed toward the front door she'd just entered, then sidled down the hallway toward her room. "I don't mean to bother you. If there's anything I can do, let me know."

"I will." She then went on to say he'd had surgery on his leg and would be in a cast but should be fine. The worry in her voice said differently.

"Is it possible to see him?" she asked, trying to get a handle on what was really going on.

"He should be home soon. He also has some cracked ribs and a concussion. . . ." Her voice broke a bit and Mac sensed this was her real worry.

She wanted to pepper Jamie with questions but understood the terrible strain she was under. Mac just needed to know he'd be all right. She'd worked with Cooper and always considered him a stand-up guy, and though her ex-partner, Ricky Richards, was now trailing Cooper like a bad smell, Cooper seemed to understand Richards's limitations.

It sometimes felt like Cooper was the only one left at River Glen PD who mattered, and now he'd been injured.

"As I said, if you need anything, let me know. I mean it," said Mac.

"I will. Thank you, Ms. Laughlin."

"It's Mackenzie. Mac."

"All right, Mac. I'll let him know you called."

Mackenzie wanted to ask why his accident was "suspicious," but maybe Jamie wasn't the right person to ask, and she could tell she wasn't ready for a full postmortem on the crash—at least not yet. They hung up and Mac slipped into her bedroom. Once again she wondered what the hell she was doing here. Daley sure didn't act like she needed a bodyguard to protect her from her husband. Maybe Leon had cavorted in Hot Tub Jeannie's spa, with Mariah Copple or someone or *someone* else, but it didn't preclude him from enjoying a frothy dip with his own wife.

Hearing footsteps down the hall, she listened hard. Neither Leon nor Daley had a real job at the moment, so maybe splashing through the morning in a hot tub together was a usual thing. If Daley was really planning to serve the man with papers, her methodology was unique. Or maybe it wasn't. If she really believed Leon would do her physical harm, maybe this was an act?

"Oscar worthy," she muttered beneath her breath. But possible.

Footsteps headed her way and then there was a knock on the door.

"Yes?"

The door cracked open and Daley stuck her wet head inside. "Where've you been?"

"At Althea Gresham's."

"Really?" Daley shrugged and shook her head. "What were you doing there?"

"I'm the newest member of the neighborhood watch."

"Good for you," she said, taking Mac at face value. "I'm

going to tell Leon this afternoon. I need you to be with me when that happens. Don't go running off somewhere, all right? Who knows what he'll do."

Mackenzie just looked at her, unable to find anything useful to say.

"Did you hear me?" she demanded.

"Yeah . . . okay . . ."

"What's wrong?"

"You tell me. What kind of a relationship do you two have?"

Daley opened the door wider and came inside. She was now wearing a robe and still nothing else as the gap flipped open, showing a smooth swath of skin from shoulder to hip before she tugged it closed. She shut the door carefully. "Keep your voice down. I can't live with Leon. He's a cheater. I'm not going to be with a cheater."

"I'm struggling to understand what 'be with' means."

"I'm not going to be able to break the prenup. All I really want is the house. I want him to give me the house. That's what he said he would give me."

"You don't have it in writing, though."

"No."

Oregon was not a community property state. If the house was in Leon's name, then it was Leon's, which it sounded like it was. A verbal promise, if there was one, wasn't likely to be enough. Add a prenup onto that and Mac wasn't sure what Daley's legal options were, but they didn't sound great.

"You need a lawyer," she said.

"You think I don't know that? I've got a lawyer. He's standing by and as soon as Leon's served, away we go. But if Leon would just follow through on his promise . . ."

"That's what the hot tub fun is all about? You're hoping he'll . . . be good to you?"

"Jesus, Mackenzie. You're spending too much time on Leon and my problems. It's not what I asked you to do."

"Uh . . . it's almost exactly what you asked me to do."

Daley looked as if she were going to fly into a full-blown rage. Mac braced herself, but in the end she just warned Mac not to leave again and then stalked back out of the room, not bothering to close the door.

Mac tried to make sense of it all but just shook her head and gave up. Whatever. She thought about texting Taft again, but instead pulled out her notebook and checked the numbers Althea Gresham had given her for other members of the watch. Only two of them, Evelyn Jacoby and Clarice Fenwick. Mac had seen Evelyn last night and considered calling her first, but her fingers punched in the number for Clarice Fenwick. Daley had told her to call Mariah Copple, but with the pending blow-up when Daley gave Leon the ultimatum, it felt safer to keep with her interviews of the old guard before she tackled the young. It was probably all an exercise in futility anyway, but there was the off chance someone would say something about Victor that would point in the direction of where Tobias was.

After several rings, the phone was answered. "Hello?" a cautious male voice answered. Ah. A landline. This was undoubtedly Cliff.

"Hello, Mr. Fenwick. This is Mackenzie Laughlin. I'm staying with the Carreras and trying to help them—"

"I know who you are. You're that detective." The faint sneer in his words couldn't be missed. "You were at the HOA meeting last night."

"I was," she agreed. "I came with Daley."

"I don't know what you think you can do."

"Well, I don't know either, actually. But I won't know till I try."

"Why are you calling me? You should be calling Abby Messinger. You heard her, didn't you? She's missing her bike."

"I was actually calling for your wife, Clarice."

"Clarice!"

He sounded so undone, she quickly told him about meeting with Althea Gresham and wanting to meet with other members of the neighborhood watch.

"Clarice isn't on that anymore. She quit a long time ago. Althea shoulda told you that."

"Is Clarice there?" asked Mac.

"Nope, she's . . . no, she's, she's not available."

"Okay . . ."

"She was in a little car accident last night and she's kinda shook up. I don't think you need to talk to her anyway. I don't know if you know this, but my wife is not well, and she doesn't like talking to strangers."

"Oh." Mac pulled the phone away from her ear and looked at it. Cliff was talking faster and faster. Nothing like his slow, aw-shucksing from the night before. She touched the Speaker button.

". . . .waste of time. Just kids prankin'. Someone like yourself probably has plenty of the other things to do."

"Okay, well, tell Clarice I called. Thanks." Mackenzie clicked off.

The old guard was sure a touchy bunch.

* * *

Clarice jumped when Cliff slammed down the landline. She hugged herself close and shut her eyes. She heard him enter the bedroom, where she sat in the rocker. He didn't say anything. She could tell he was staring at her. She had a bandage over her eye and a goose egg on her head. It wasn't a big accident. Just a fender bender. She'd left the church without feeling any better and gotten back into the car. She had trouble getting the vehicle in gear for some reason and then as she was pulling out of the parking lot, the nose of her car was clipped by a young driver whose car spun around in a circle before stopping. The driver had driven forward and come up on Clarice's side. With quivering hands, she'd rolled down her window.

"You hit me, you dumb fuck!" he'd screamed at her and Clarice had broken into tears. He'd roared away before they could exchange insurance information. She'd driven home and Cliff was there and didn't scream at her about the car, but his face was white, his mouth a line of disappointment. She told him she'd tried to exchange insurance, but the kid hadn't let her.

"Probably had a suspended license or no insurance," he told her flatly.

"I'm . . . s-s-sorry," she'd said.

"Pull yourself together, Clarice," he told her. He didn't yell at her like she'd expected. But she could tell he wanted to. He really wanted to.

"I need to atone."

"Goddammit!"

She clapped her hands over her ears, but she could still hear him yell, "What happened to you? *Stop shaking!* Get a fucking grip. It's been years, Clarice. Nothing's going to happen if you keep your mouth shut."

"It's not my fault this time, but it was. It's—"

"*Shut up!*" he roared. "It's no one's fault. Stop thinking that way and shaking yourself sick. You can stop this."

"I can't," she said meekly.

"You can. You have to." He grew more serious, less angry, but more intense. "You have to. You have to, Clarice." He took her shoulders in his callused palms. She used to love the feel of his rough hands sliding gently over her skin. Now she felt how easy it would be for him to crush the bones in her shoulders. *Old bones, old bones* . . .

He dropped his hands. "You have to or I don't know what's going to happen to you."

Chapter Eleven

Taft put on his most winning smile for the red-haired woman behind the counter. He'd debated on whether to follow after her after she caught him inside the unit, or break back into the place, see if he'd missed anything. He'd tried phoning Riskin again, but the number was out of service.

He asked a man who'd come out of a unit down the way about Riskin, but his answer was a shrug. In the end Taft had decided to check in at the office and throw himself at the woman's mercy. He wasn't sure he would succeed. Her eye makeup was somewhere between avant-garde model and Halloween demon, and she met his smile with a hard-eyed stare.

"I'm a friend of Jimmy Riskin's. I've known him for years. Jesse Taft," he said.

She considered him for a long moment. Taft waited while she made up her mind whether he was shining her on or not. He could have concocted some story, he supposed, but after catching him in Riskin's apartment she was bound to dismiss anything he said.

"You don't seem like you know him."

"I do," said Taft. But how well really? Riskin had been

difficult to reach. Long, long times of no communication, then bits of info, a couple of sentences at a time.

"The other guy said they were friends." She looked through the window and down the way toward Taft's Jeep, which was parked in Rifkin's spot, the number 209 painted in school-bus yellow on the concrete.

"The other guy who was just here? He's no friend of Riskin's," said Taft.

"I don't think you are either."

"Friends might be pushing the nature of our relationship," conceded Taft.

"Uh-huh." More silent speculation on her part.

"I'm not kidding about being worried about him." *If you find me sleeping with the fishes, you'll know who to blame.*

"I don't get involved with the tenants."

"You don't have a forwarding address for him?"

"Nope."

"I just want to know he's okay."

She took that in, and he could practically feel her rolling it around in her head, deciding whether he was speaking the truth. Maybe she started to believe in his sincerity, maybe she liked his looks, maybe she just decided she was bored and ready for any kind of activity. Hard to tell. Whatever the case, her attitude subtly changed. "Who was that first guy who was looking for him?" she asked.

It was Taft's turn to size her up and decide how much he wanted to say. "He didn't give you his name?"

"He acted like a tough guy."

"He is a tough guy. And someone without Jimmy's best interests at heart."

"He asked me the same questions you are."

"He's looking for him for different reasons than I am."

She made a sound of agreement.

Encouraged, but knowing he might be pushing the envelope, Taft pulled out a card, one that just had his name and cell number on it, and set it on the counter. "If Mr. Riskin should return, or you find out anything about him, or that first guy shows up again, would you let me know?"

She didn't take the card It sat like a small white rectangle on the faux wooden counter. But she didn't say no. He wanted to ask her if she was the manager, or if she was just working for whoever was, but he didn't. One thing he'd learned early on as an investigator was to read the person you were interviewing. This woman would not be pushed. She was quiet and careful and suspicious.

"The first guy gave me a card, too."

"Ah. He wanted you to let him know when Mr. Riskin returned."

She nodded. "I told him I wouldn't do that."

"How did he react?"

"Like I expected." There was a hardening around her eyes.

"Be careful," he warned before he could stop himself.

The faintest of smiles at the corners of her mouth, gone in an instant. "I do all right."

"Well, if you see Jimmy . . . Mr. Riskin, let him know I'm looking for him."

She didn't answer, but she picked up the card. He glanced back at her through the office windows as he left. She was turning the card over in her fingers.

Mackenzie held her cell phone tightly in both hands, willing herself not to call Nolan again. He'd said he would call her. He had no idea of the urgency she felt.

She tossed the phone on her bed and then lay back, grabbing a pillow and holding it over her face to cover the scream of frustration that boiled from within her. She managed to keep from shrieking like a banshee, but just. She'd had a late lunch with the Carreras, who'd ordered a home delivery of sandwiches from a nearby shop, which were really good, and Mac, who'd told herself she should resist and make a passive-aggressive statement about this self-imposed prison, tore into her bánh mì as if she'd been starved for a month. Daley picked at hers, opening up the bread and making a moue at the sandwich's insides, while Leon watched his wife with a small smile flickering on his lips and ate his in a couple of big, male bites that impressed Mac at both their expediency and lack of messiness. As it was, she was yanking up paper napkins from a woven box on the counter with nearly every bite.

Once lunch was over it was back to the waiting game. Mac had reluctantly agreed to stay with Daley while she hit Leon with the news that she was leaving him, but Daley couldn't seem to pull that trigger.

Maybe she could push things along . . .

A soft knock sounded at her door. Mac threw off the pillow and got to her feet. She opened her door to find Daley right behind it. Progress, she thought as Daley stepped inside. At least she'd warned her before barging in. Mac got that same sense of familiarity again as Daley paced to the center of the room. In a black shirt and jeans, her hair straighter, less artfully tossed, her hands clenched together, Daley whispered, "I can't do it. I'm too scared."

"Maybe you just don't want to end the marriage," suggested Mac.

"What's that mean? Are you trying to force me to make a decision that could affect my whole life?"

Mac held up her hands. "You're right, it's all a master plan. I was hoping you'd hire me so that I could be in the background, orchestrating your divorce. That's what this is about."

"Shhh." She looked over her shoulder even though Mac's words had been issued in a tight whisper. "I'm sorry. Okay? I'm sorry. I just can't go through with it today. I'll try again tomorrow."

"Well, I won't be here."

"Where will you be?"

"Daley." Mac was fast losing patience, had lost patience.

"Fine. Go. Leave me," said Daley.

Mac bit back a retort as she scooped up her purse, throwing the strap over her shoulder.

"Well, where are you going?"

"I'm going to check with the Martins," she said, off the cuff. They were probably employed, too, but at least it was an exit line she thought sounded pretty good.

"I told you, they're fine."

"Yeah, well, maybe I'll learn something. I'll be back later. If you're really worried about Leon," which was getting harder and harder to believe, "go somewhere." *Do something.* She didn't say it, but she thought: *Go for another round in the hot tub.*

As if she'd read her mind, Daley muttered, "If Mariah's around, Leon'll be moving from our hot tub to Jeannie's tonight."

"Maybe you should go, too," Mac said as she headed for her vehicle. She could walk to the Martins, but she wanted her RAV with her when she headed out to see Nolan, which she planned to do as soon as he was off work.

She drove out of the Bs and into the A streets. Abernethy was directly across from the park, which was an expansive half circle divided by trees and a tall, riotous hedge. At one end was an eight-sided gazebo with a white lattice skirt and on the other, quite a distance from the Martins' home, which was almost directly across from the gazebo, was the playground construction Mariah Copple had complained about. A swing set was up, but there were no seats hanging from its overhead bar. Proportion-wise, for all the crammed houses that fanned out from it in deepening semicircles, the park was exceedingly large. Though the Villages were on more expansive lots than its newer neighbors to the west, Staffordshire Estates, where the houses took up almost every square inch of ground, they still were fairly packed in. Mac was no expert, but she could see where an enterprising developer might think the park could be shaved down considerably to make room for more houses, were the HOA to decide to make some ready cash.

Mac parked across the street from the Martins', next to the hedge that muted noise and kept the houses on Abernethy from staring at the playground.

She crossed the street. The Martins' renovation was taking up half their home. One end was broken open, lonely posts reaching skyward like accusing fingers, plywood and Visqueen screening off the rest of the house from the elements. It was two story, rather than the sprawling ranch they'd lost out to the Carreras, and its renovation was extensive. Maybe they were DIYers and had no problem living through the pounding and sawing and general mess and confusion while their house was under construction, but Mac was glad it wasn't her problem. Mom had renovated and changed and redecorated all the years Mac was growing up, and it had been enough to drive them all batty.

The Martins' brick-lined walk curved around the edge of the yard to several steps and a platform cement porch. With a riot of salmon, yellow, and red roses, their heavy heads drooping a bit over the edge of the grouping of clay pots. Mac closed her eyes and inhaled deeply. She suddenly felt a pang of longing for her apartment. She would love to have roses in pots on her small deck off the back. She might even be able to keep from killing them if she was careful.

Mac knocked, and a few minutes later the door slowly swung in the length of a chain. A suspicious blue eye peered out and looked Mac up and down. A female voice asked tartly, "Yes?"

"Hi, I'm Mackenzie Laughlin. I'm looking into some neighborhood crime, and I'm checking with neighbors to see if they've seen anything."

"You live here?"

"Well, yes," she said.

"Where?"

"On one of the Cs. Callaway."

Her eyes narrowed. "Which house?"

"I'm staying with the Carreras."

Immediately the face pulled away from the door and Mac started talking fast. "I've been hired to find out who's harassing them. I'm just checking with everyone—"

The door slammed shut.

Well that hadn't worked.

"Mrs. Martin?" called Mac.

No answer. Mac sighed. It had been that kind of day.

Until something broke maybe it was time to start focusing on the young guard, though she might have more luck connecting with them over the weekend.

Emma tried to coax Twink into her room, but Duchess was behind Emma, and though the dog wasn't barking, she was whining and generally worrying the cat.

"Stop it, Duchess," Emma said, turning around in the doorway to give her dog a hard look.

The cat took that moment to trot off down the hall. Emma looked after her. "This isn't going to work." She turned back to Duchess, who'd dropped her head to her paws and gazed up at her with big, doggy eyes.

Emma barely noticed. Ever since Jamie had called and said Cooper was in the hospital she'd been feeling bad. She could feel those bad old feelings rising up, trying to take over her brain again. She knew now how to keep them behind a wall. A mental wall, the therapist had told her. Keep the bad thoughts behind a mental wall. Emma hadn't told the woman who Jamie had recommended she start seeing that she needed to think of a big metal wall with big hinges and iron rings and a *slam* sound every time she closed it. She thought the woman, Miss Kasey, might ask too many questions. She kind of did that.

You don't have to tell them your whole life story.

Those were Jamie's words and Emma was trying to live by them, even though Jamie did want her to talk to Miss Kasey.

It was very confusing.

"Twink wants to stay here," Emma said to Duchess, who

gave one short bark, as if she agreed with the cat. "But I want to be with Jamie and Harley and Cooper."

Duchess gave another sharp yip.

"Cooper's in trouble."

Emma also knew that if she went back she would be in the way. Jamie wouldn't say so, but it would be hard for her to look after Cooper and Emma, too.

The dog's eyes had moved toward the drawer with the doggy treats. Duchess always did that but Emma only allowed two treats a day along with the dog food. Now she pulled out one small dog bone, and while Duchess's tail eagerly swept the floor, she placed it in her bowl. It was all Duchess could do to wait for the signal to eat. Emma tried to be stern, but it was hard. "Go," she said, and Duchess shot forward, chomped up the treat, and ate it in one crunch of her teeth.

Emma thought about the cat . . . and her dog . . . and Jamie and Harley, but mostly she thought about Cooper. And that reminded her of Mackenzie, who was also a cop. "Ex-cop," she said aloud. She had written down Mackenzie's number. If she had a cell phone, she would use that, but she couldn't be trusted with one. She thought she maybe *could* be trusted with one, but Jamie had told her recently that "that's a conversation for another day." She wasn't sure what day that would be, but for now she had her landline.

She rummaged around in the drawer where she kept important notes. She kept the notes in small stacks with rubber bands around them. That way they wouldn't get lost. She had to search through several neat piles before she found what she was looking for Mackenzie Laughlin. "Laff-lin," she said. It was spelled like laugh, but that wasn't right. "Loff-lin. Mackenzie Loff-lin. Mac," she said, trying it out. She had been a cop like Cooper. She could help now, too, Emma was pretty sure.

Emma pressed the numbers into her phone and waited for Mac Loff-lin to pick up.

Mackenzie heard the beep of an incoming call and checked the number; not one she knew, so she kept up with what she was saying into her own cell: ". . . if I could come by tonight and talk to you, Nolan, I've got—"

"Mac, that's what you said in your message," interrupted Nolan, "but I can't. I'm still at the office. We had a gas leak at one of the houses. Just built and something went wrong with the hookup. Gas company's on-site. One employee sick from fumes. Not seriously hurt, maybe, there's . . . could be . . . maybe some acting going on there? I don't know. Still trying to figure it out. But I can't meet with you tonight. Could we talk tomorrow or Sunday? I'm sorry. There're just a lot of things that happened at the same time."

"Sure."

"I'm sorry, Mac. Just been a tough day. Raincheck, okay?"

"Really, it's no problem."

She hung up and looked at the clock on her phone. Six thirty. She'd planned her day around meeting with Nolan and she understood completely why he couldn't meet with her, but it was disappointing. She realized she had a voice mail from whoever had called her. Touching the button to access the message, she put the phone on Speaker. Into the room floated Emma Whelan's flat voice.

"Cooper was in an accident. I think you should see him. You were a cop and so is he."

And then she hung up.

One thing about Emma: She didn't waste words. Mac smiled to herself. For someone considered mentally challenged, Emma had a way of making everything seem clear.

She changed into a dark blue collared shirt, looked in the mirror, brushed her hair, and pulled it back into a messy bun, much like she'd worn when she was with the force. She didn't think she could see Cooper at this point. It was too soon. But Emma had given her carte blanche to insert herself in Cooper's affairs, and she was going to take that as an invitation. Maybe tomorrow she could check with Jamie, or maybe Cooper's partner, Detective Verbena.

For now, she was going out. She had half an idea to stop by Nolan's and Stephanie's and be there when he returned. She wanted to see her stepsister anyway. Grabbing up her purse, she headed for the door, half expecting to be waylaid by Daley or Leon. In that she was not disappointed. She'd barely stepped into the hallway when Daley appeared from the other end of the house, walking rapidly toward her.

"Mackenzie, I can't pay you if you're never going to be around."

"Okay." Mac turned toward the front door.

"Wait . . . wait . . . for God's sake, I was only kidding. Are you meeting Jesse?"

"No."

"Leon's going to that hot tub party at Jeannie's tonight. I'm going, too."

"You are?" That was a surprise.

"Mariah's going to be there. Wouldn't you go, if you were me?" she challenged.

"I don't know. Would I?"

"Yes! Yes, you would. In fact, I want you to go with me tonight."

Mac lifted her hands. "Nope."

"If we're there, they'll keep their clothes on."

Mac almost laughed, but she could tell Daley was being dead serious. "I'm not going to a hot tub party," she said. She had a strong memory of Daley and Leon in their own hot tub and it really didn't make her want to join in on the fun.

"You don't have to get in."

"I'm pretty sure I'm not even invited."

"Everyone's invited. That's just the way it is," said Daley. "No one gets an actual invitation. These parties have ramped up since summer started."

Mac glanced out the window to the grayish skies, but there were patches of blue. Maybe summer was finally getting the message.

"When will you be back?" she asked.

"I don't know."

"It's not till later. Nineish."

"Daley—"

"You don't have to get in," she repeated. "You can meet the young guard. Don't you want to keep investigating? This is your chance. A lot of them'll be there. A lot of 'em." Before Mac could pose another objection, she added, "I don't want to go alone. But I don't want Leon to go alone either. Say you'll come with me. It's a great opportunity to meet and greet."

Mackenzie mentally sighed. Daley was in a schizo-phrenic kind of struggle with herself over Leon. Mac didn't want to be a part of it, but she already was. Once again she told herself she never should have taken this assignment.

"I'm not stepping a toe in the hot tub," warned Mac.

"Sure. Great. That's what I said. Just go with me, okay?"

"Okay."

Daley was relieved. "But you might want to bring your suit just in case," she added as Mac stepped through the door and closed it behind her.

Taft sat on his couch. His mind was full of images and thoughts and some knotty problems. He wondered if he should have kept following Silva. He'd been distracted by Silva's turn into Riskin's place and then further derailed by learning Riskin still lived there. Riskin had indicated Taft would know who to blame if something happened to him. What had he uncovered? And what was that cryptic nineteen eighty-four comment?

What the hell had Silva been doing at Riskin's? If anything happened to Riskin, Keith Silva was to blame. Riskin had mentioned the widow, Anna DeMarcos, and it was her place where Taft had picked up Silva. He should go back there, to her place, maybe stake it out because Silva spent a lot of his time with her.

He realized he needed some help. Picking up his cell, he called Mackenzie. She answered on the first ring.

"Taft," Mac said as a way of greeting. She was in her car, driving toward Stephanie and Nolan's.

"Have you had dinner?"

"No."

"Are you anywhere near Pizza Joe's? If you pick up a pizza and bring it my way, I'll pay you back."

An offer she couldn't refuse. "On my way," she said, signing off. It was a little depressing how glad she was to change her plans and head to Taft's, but whatever. It was smarter to wait to meet with Nolan when he was ready than to push the issue and, well, she really wanted to talk to Taft.

She ordered a straight pepperoni pizza and then, as she was paying, asked to add mushrooms and onions to it.

She waited rather impatiently for the pizza to finish baking, then inhaled deeply as she carried the box out to the car. The spicy scent of pepperoni and the sweet pungency of the onions made her mouth water. She hadn't realized how hungry she was until now.

At Taft's she set the box on his kitchen counter and watched as he placed an empty beer bottle by the sink, then rummaged in another cupboard for a bottle of red wine. Mac thought he looked tired but knew better than to say as much. He'd spurned her solicitation these past few months. He wasn't going to take lightly to it now.

"So, how's it going?" he asked as he slid a paper plate her way, put one in front of himself, and poured them each a glass of wine. She was seated at the counter and he was standing across from her.

"How's what going?" she mumbled around a bite of pepperoni, mushroom, and stretchy mozzarella. She was momentarily distracted by the pizza. Normally she was a purist about pepperoni but the mushrooms and onions were okay.

"Life in the Villages." Taft mowed through his first piece.

"I haven't been able to talk to Judy yet, or Nolan. I've been getting some background information on Victor Laidlaw. Apparently he's infamous around the Villages according to Althea Gresham. Maybe I'll know more after tonight, but being stuck at the Carreras' . . . this thing with Daley . . . I don't even know what the hell it is. *She* doesn't know what it is."

Taft slid a second piece of pizza onto his plate.

"Something funny?" she accused, watching him, sensing he was hiding a smile.

He shook his head. "Tell me about how it's going with the Carreras so far."

She kinda wanted to argue with him, sensing he was enjoying her pique over being stuck at the Carreras' far too much. But . . . she did as he asked. Explaining about Daley and Leon's relationship, then relating her conversation with Althea Gresham and how Mrs. Martin had slammed the door in her face when she'd learned Mac was the Carreras' guest. "Daley just wants someone to hold her hand," said Mac. "You, preferably, but she's not letting go of me either. Is she scared of Leon? If she's just placating him, I give her four stars. It's a stellar performance. She says she wants to serve him with papers. She was going to tell him today, but she chickened out, or changed her mind. It's hard to tell." She stopped talking and took another bite of her pizza. Taft was almost through his second piece. "So, what's with you?" she asked, wiping her fingers and picking up her stemless wineglass.

"You know my CI I told you about? Jimmy Riskin?"

He'd said so little about his confidential informant, Mackenzie set down her glass and tried to put a merely interested look on her face when in reality she saw this as a huge step in the right direction. "You mentioned him."

"He hadn't contacted me in a while, then today he did." He picked up his wineglass, then looked at Mac again, his blue eyes narrowing slightly. "I was following Keith Silva and he went to Riskin's place—what was his place;

the apartment's been cleaned out. I talked to the girl in the office after she'd blown off Silva. She seemed to get that I didn't mean Riskin harm."

"But she didn't trust Silva." Mac wasn't surprised Taft had talked his way around whoever was in charge. She also knew what Keith Silva was like; he'd been with the department a short time while she'd been there. "I wouldn't either," she added.

"Riskin told me he was going to get some information. Something about Anna DeMarcos, probably had to do with Silva. Riskin's paranoid, but with Silva chasing him down, he probably has reason to worry.

"What was it about Anna DeMarcos?"

"I don't know. He didn't get that out." He hesitated, then asked, "What does 'nineteen eighty-four' mean to you?"

Mac searched his face. "Like the book? Big Brother?"

"Possibly." He shrugged.

"It's a year . . ." she said, lifting her palms.

"Riskin said 'nineteen eighty-four' before he hung up. He's cryptic. Too cryptic."

Mac knew that Silva had slipped into what had once been Taft's position as Mitch Mangella's right-hand man when Taft backed away from the man, but she wasn't completely sure how Taft really felt about that. A few months ago he'd been almost glad to pass the torch, but . . .

"Do you think Silva's interest in Riskin has something to do with you?" she asked.

"It has to do with the widow, but Silva does know Riskin works for me."

"That's what I mean."

"Maybe," he allowed. "I tried calling Riskin, several times. He's already gotten rid of his burner. I'll give it a day or two, see if he calls. I don't think he ever had much in that apartment, but there's nothing there now."

Mac thought he had a right to be worried.

"So, what are you going to do about Daley? Sounds like you're about ready to hang it up," he said, changing the subject. He drank from his wineglass again.

"I'm going to Hot Tub Jeannie's with Daley later tonight. Bathing suits optional, I hear."

"Planning on getting naked?"

"Yep. That's all I want to do."

"Good interviewing technique."

"Haven't talked to the young guard yet. Might as well be open with them."

He let the smile find its way to his lips, deepening his dimples beneath his close-cut beard.

They finished their meal and Mackenzie reluctantly refused a second glass of wine. Taft insisted she take the cash he pulled out of his wallet to pay for the pizza as she started to feel kind of cheap about the whole thing and tried to refuse.

"Let me know how it goes," Taft said as he walked her to the door.

"I'll give you the bare facts."

"Can't wait."

She thought she heard a guffaw after the door closed behind her. She smiled herself as she headed to her RAV.

Chapter Twelve

As Mac drove onto Calloway Court, a bicycle approached coming the other way and slowed down near the Carreras' house. As soon as the rider saw her, they abruptly turned onto a side street that led toward the D homes, the last tier of streets that ran in a semicircle from the main entry and park.

The rider wore a hoodie over their head and dark clothing and disappeared from view in a wink.

Mackenzie gazed after the rider as she headed toward the house. Before she got to the porch the front door was suddenly thrown open from the inside. Daley, brown hair pulled back into a ponytail, was dressed in a black bikini with a sheer white, long-tailed blouse thrown over as a cover-up. "He doesn't want me to go!" she cried and flung an arm back toward the house, where Leon, clad in swim trunks and zipping up a nylon jacket with one hand, a bike helmet in the other, stood in the open doorway. The look on his face was hard to interpret. Anger? Frustration? Something else?

"I don't care if you go or not," he said tautly, his normally arch manner completely missing. "I'm riding my bike."

"You just want to fuck 'em all, don't you?" she screamed.

He turned his back on her and stomped toward the door to the garage.

"You see?" she said miserably.

Mac stepped into the foyer and into the fray. "Do you not want to go now?" She tried to keep the hope out of her voice.

"No! I'm going. I'm not going down without a fight!"

"Maybe take a breath here."

"You're siding with him!" she accused, glaring at Mac. "I knew it. I knew he'd win you over, too."

"I'm not won over," Mac snapped. "But you're not doing yourself any good. Do you want him? Be honest. It doesn't seem like you want a divorce."

"I want him to want *me*, but he wants everybody else!" She stumbled into the living room and collapsed into a chair. "Don't cry. Don't cry. Don't cry," she said to herself, crying.

Mac shut the door and said, "I'll get you a glass of water."

"No." She lifted her head, sniffling, touching the tears from her face with the pads of her fingers. "Get changed and we'll go. Hurry."

"You said I wouldn't have to get in," she reminded her.

"Just get a suit on. *Please*. You don't have to get in. You just have to look like you will."

"I already feel like a party crasher."

"I told you. It's not that way. Oh, shit. I've got to put myself together." She climbed to her feet again and headed rapidly down the hall toward her own bathroom.

Mac turned the other way, toward her room. Police work had never been this trying.

Fifteen minutes later they were driving the short distance

to Jeannie's house. Daley was wearing heels and didn't want to walk. Mac worried that she wasn't emotionally fit to drive, but she returned from her makeup ministrations determinedly in control. Mac had put on a one-piece, which she'd thrown in at the last minute when she'd packed as a matter of course, only she was wearing a black sweatshirt over it and had no intention of taking it off. She also had on her jeans because it still wasn't the warmest weather out. No rain, but the air felt heavy and cool as night slowly dropped.

The party was in full swing at the back of Jeannie's house. Twinkling lights were strung overhead and the large hot tub was frothing and humming, already occupied by four or five people. Other guests were clustered in groups along the concrete patio, some by the refreshment table, where chips, salsa, and guacamole reigned alongside a clear plastic tub filled with ice, soft drinks, cans of beer, and bottles of various types of white wine. Red wine stood in neat rows of bottles, still unopened, vying for space with bottles of tequila and margarita mix. It was serve yourself, and as Mac and Daley entered, Chris Palminter was just sloshing tequila into a tumbler with a dash or two of mixer, followed by a slice of lime.

He spied Mackenzie, his face breaking into a slightly drunken smile. "It's zee cop," he declared. "Looking fine, I might add."

Mac was covered up and had done next to nothing with her looks, so she highly doubted that. Palminter was a born schmoozer.

He shrugged Daley out of the way as he corralled Mac. Daley gave him a burning look, then moved over to where Leon was holding court with several younger men and women, including Mariah Copple. He was regaling them with some story Mac couldn't hear and they were listening politely, but it did not appear anyone was paying close attention. Mac peered over Chris's shoulder to keep an eye on Mariah, who was wearing a rather demure blue one-piece with a matching blouselike cover-up. Her hair was down and white hoop earrings peeked out as she turned her head. For reasons she needed to examine more closely later, Mac couldn't picture her as this femme fatale everyone seemed to suggest she was.

"I talked to Fetzler," Chris said. "Told him I met you. He was interested. Kept bringing the subject back to you. I kept talking about anything else and then he'd sneak it back to you."

Mackenzie wasn't sure how she felt about that. It was gratifying to hear her ex-boyfriend still thought about her, but it was merely anecdotal. She had no interest in rekindling anything with Pete. Not a romance, not a friendship. "Huh," she said.

"Yeah, huh," he said, completely misinterpreting her disinterest as something else. "If I'd known you were going to be here, bet he woulda dropped everything to come."

It was really unfortunate that Palminter knew about her ex. "Pete and I are happily apart."

"Sure you are."

"Hey, Chris!" The yell came from Jeannie, who was waving him over to the hot tub. She was in a white bikini that showed off a deep tan and a nice figure as she climbed the steps on the side of the tub to dip a toe in. Spying Mac, Jeannie smiled and called, "Come on in!"

Mac held up her hand and yelled, "Thanks for inviting me!"

Jeannie flapped a hand at her. "Everyone's invited! Help yourself to food and drink!"

As Mac moved toward the table of refreshments, she smelled the distinctive skunklike scent of marijuana and saw a group of younger men standing by the corner of the patio. She caught some movement at the house next door, a curtain clutched by a hand moving across a second-story window. The hand was pulling the curtain back a bit, but the person wasn't visible. Mac saw the window was open. It was hard to see because there were no lights on in the room behind, but the person could probably hear the din of the party.

The view from the window was right above the hot tub.

"Hi," a female voice said at her elbow as she poured herself a glass of Pinot Gris into a clear plastic cup. Mac turned to find Abby Messinger standing beside her. Her light brown hair had blond streaks in it. Up close, she had wide-set, greenish eyes, and age lines were visible, but she could have passed for being in her forties, though Mac knew she was a good ten years or more older than the bulk of this crowd.

"Hi," Mac said back to her.

"I heard Chris say you're the cop who's investigating the things that happened to the Carreras. I'm Abby Messinger. I live on one of the Bs. Barranca."

"Mackenzie Laughlin. Ex-cop," she clarified. "I know. I stopped by your place today to talk to you."

She looked startled. "Why?"

"You said you had a bike stolen. I'm trying to help out Daley Carrera . . . and her husband. They've had packages stolen off their porch. Just wanted to ask you about the bike."

"Oh. Alfie left it unchained when he was playing baseball

with some friends. He knows better." She looked past her and said, "Jeannie invites us 'oldies,' but apart from Claude and me, no one shows up."

"Claude?"

"Claude Marfont." Her tone was dismissive.

An older man, gray hair combed sleekly, wearing swim trunks and a black suede zipped-up jacket, strolled over to them. He was the man who'd offered Abby his coat. He couldn't seem to take his eyes off her as he approached.

"Claude, let me introduce you to Mackenzie. She's the cop Andre told me about."

"Oh, yeah?" He barely looked at Mac. Only had eyes for Abby.

"Ex-cop," Mac corrected.

"You know, Daley and Leon are great people, but they really . . . how do I say this? They come on a little strong?" said Abby. "The Martins can't seem to get over losing the house to them. My ex, Andre, said there was an escalation clause where the Carreras outbid the Martins. Any bid the Martins made, the Carreras topped it."

Mac had gotten the impression from Althea that Abby and Andre weren't really on speaking terms, but that didn't seem to be the case. "So, the Martins gave up."

She shrugged. "Now they're in the middle of this renovation, which is probably going to cost them more, but what could they do? Leon has tons of money and he wasn't backing down on the sale. The whole thing created really bad feelings." Her smile was brittle. "But what do I know? Talk to Jeannie. She's the one who knows the ins and outs of real estate. I'm a nurse."

"You're at Glen Gen?"

"Twenty-five years. Hard to believe when I put it like that. You're friends with Daley?"

"We know each other," answered Mac, trying to read her tone.

Claude said to Abby, "Can I get you a drink?"

"Sure." Abby seemed to be looking anywhere but right at him. The vibe was clearly *Get lost, buddy*, but Claude didn't notice, or chose not to notice, because he was squarely fixated on Abby.

"You brought up the stolen bike at the HOA meeting," said Mac. "I thought it was because it was stolen from your house."

"No. Excuse me. Claude? I don't want a drink. Thanks." She moved toward the refreshment table, which was loaded with chips, dips, and fruit and vegetable trays it appeared people had brought. Mac, rightfully so, felt like a freeloader and determined she would nurse her wine as slowly as possible to make it last and not take another. She was a little annoyed with Daley for so blithely ignoring some rules of etiquette and dragging Mac with her.

Mac saw that Leon's group had broken up and he was now standing near Mariah, who was talking animatedly. Drifting closer, Mac realized Mariah was passionately describing the ADA playground equipment that was being held up, apart from the swings, which were already in, although not to her specifications.

Leon was listening politely, but he seemed to be thinking about something else. He touched her shoulder with a quick squeeze, kind of like a handshake, said something to her that Mac couldn't hear, then moved away. She gazed after him, seemingly annoyed.

"Hi, I'm Mackenzie," she introduced herself to Mariah. "You're Mariah?"

"Um, yes." She focused on Mac. She had amazing

cornflower-blue eyes and a pretty, heart-shaped face. "You're staying with Leon?"

"And Daley. Yes. I heard you talking about the playground equipment."

Immediately she zeroed in on Mac as if she'd said something incredibly important. "Yes, I was. Do you know about it? My sister has a daughter who is in a wheelchair. A condition from birth, and I want her to be able to play here. The HOA has agreed, but it's such a frustrating process . . . so slow. . . ."

Mac stood by in silence as Mariah went on and on about the benefits of the ADA compliant playground and her own love of children, that she was sending money to help them to several organizations around the world. Once Mac murmured, "You're really amazing" as a means to break the flow, but it didn't slow Mariah down in the least. After that Mac just gave up and listened, and it went on a long while. At one point she caught Leon's eye and saw him shrug and shake his head. It was becoming clearer that Leon's interest in Mariah was a figment of Daley's overactive imagination.

Daley unknowingly rescued Mac by grabbing her arm and telling Mariah, "I've got to talk to my friend," and dragging Mac away from her.

"Thanks," said Mac.

"What were you talking about for so long?" demanded Daley.

"I don't think she and Leon are having an affair," said Mac. "You were not wrong about Mariah's interest— *consuming* interest—in taking care of children."

"Leon doesn't care. She's pretty and hot in that goody-goody way."

"I'm not sure that's true."

"Oh, fuck." Daley watched Leon unzip his jacket and step into the hot tub with a group of young men and women.

After a moment she shed her white overshirt and joined them.

Abby had moved to where Jeannie, now out of the tub and wearing a long-sleeved sweatshirt that came down to her knees, her hair wet and pulled back from her face, was pouring herself another drink and laughing with Chris Palminter. Abby glanced away from Jeannie and froze. Mac followed her gaze and saw a teenage boy with long, blond hair wearing swim trunks that looked massive on his skinny frame and a dark blue sweatshirt zipped up to his neck, picking his way barefoot across the exposed aggregate patio.

Mac moved closer as Abby practically stalked forward to meet him. "This is an adult party, Alfie," she said tightly.

The kid's eyes were on the hot tub and he couldn't seem to bring them back. Mac glanced over to see that one of the young women was practically bursting out of her bikini top. Alfie wasn't the only male in the group who'd noticed. Count Leon in on that. Alfie was just the least adept at managing to make it look like his eyes weren't bugging out of his head.

Claude appeared at Abby's elbow. "You gotta toddle outta here, Son."

Alfie shot him a virulent look as Abby said tightly, "I've got this, Claude."

Once again Claude lifted his hands in that don't-mind-me-I'm-just-trying-to-help way that was fast becoming his signature move.

Alfie said to his mother. "You told Dad nobody needs an invitation here."

"Adults, Alfie. Adults!"

"Dad's on his way."

"Oh, for God's sake." Abby's head swiveled back and forth as she looked around the patio. "He's too old." Hearing herself, she snapped, "I'm too old. C'mon. We're leaving."

There was something familiar about Alfie, Mac thought, her own eyes examining him closely. A tattoo peeked out from beneath the left arm of his gray sweatshirt. There was a hood attached to the sweatshirt, but he'd tucked it down the back of his neck. She imagined what the hoodie would look like if it were on his head and the light bulb went off. "I'm pretty sure I saw you on a bike earlier."

He didn't answer her. Didn't even look at her.

Abby sucked in a breath and expelled it. "Probably. He got a new, *expensive* bike after the last one was stolen. You gotta go, Alfie. I mean it. I'll be right behind you. This isn't a kid's party."

He looked up at her resentfully through long, blond bangs and said, "I'm not a kid."

"Well, you're not an adult either," said Claude. "Your mom told you to do something."

"Claude!" Abby rounded on him. "I can handle my son."

"Why don't we all leave?" he suggested, moving a little way away from them.

The man was so clueless, Mac almost felt sorry for him. Abby looked ready to strangle him, or Alfie, maybe both.

"Could you be polite enough to say hi?" Abby asked her son, inclining her head toward Mac.

He glared at his mother and hunched his shoulders.

"This is that detective I was telling you about," she said, ignoring his ire. "The one staying at Daley's and Leon's."

Mac opened her mouth to explain she was not a detective in the way Abby meant it, but Alfie suddenly straightened, as if jolted by a cattle prod. He snapped to attention like a soldier, didn't look at Mac, mumbled something about how unfair it all was, then hightailed it back across the pebbles the way he'd come, unaware now, or uncaring, of the sharp stabs to his feet.

"You have any kids?" Abby asked her.

"No."

"You love 'em so much, sometimes you want to kill 'em."

Mac made some noncommittal sound, then asked, "Your ex-husband is on his way?"

"No. He can't be." She turned back to the table and poured herself a glass of Pinot Gris. She'd clearly changed her mind about the drink and it didn't appear she was leaving as quickly as she'd said she would. Claude had taken a few steps away, but he was still keeping tabs on her. "Andre is no kind of father. He thinks he's Alfie's age. Maybe younger. He doesn't have time for Alfie. He doesn't have time for anyone. His ego takes up all the space around him. If he shows up, it will be because he thinks he can end up in bed with one of these girls, but good luck with that."

"You're not . . . dating Claude?"

Abby gave her a look of near horror.

Mac changed the subject. "So, it appears there's no connection between Alfie's stolen bike and the Carreras' porch pirate."

"I don't see how." She pressed her lips together.

"Does your ex live around here?" Mac asked.

"Portland. West Hills. Nice house, with a view of the

city. He moved from Glen Gen to his own clinic, and good riddance. Got married to a bitch on wheels, and those wheels are a Porsche. She's determined to keep him in check. Hah."

Daley appeared at Mac's side. "I'm ready to go."

Her white overshirt was back on and sticking to her wet skin. Abby moved off and Mac reminded, "You said I could talk to the young guard."

"Yeah, well, I've seen enough."

Leon was in a serious discussion with the woman bursting out of her bra top. At least he was giving her all his attention.

Daley rolled her eyes toward the heavens and shook her head. "When are you seeing Jesse again?"

"Oh, I don't know," said Mac, surprised enough to stumble over her words a bit.

"I want to come with you next time."

"To see Taft? We just work together."

"You're not romantically involved?"

"No . . ."

"So, it's okay by you if I ask him out?"

"Can't stop you," said Mac lightly, fighting back instant feelings of ownership.

"Okay. Good. Ready?"

Hell. Dealing with Daley was *hell*.

As they were starting toward the car, out of the corner of her eye Mac saw the curtains at the house next door twitch again. "Is that . . . Evelyn? What's her last name again?" she asked, inclining her head toward the second-story window.

Daley looked in that direction. "Jacoby. Is she hiding in the dark again?" She peered closer. "What a peeping

Thomasina. You saw her last night, right? The old guard, I swear. They're all sickos."

Mac flicked a glance at the window of the Jacobys' house, but it was just a dark rectangle, the curtain still. She dropped her gaze to the hot tub, where alcohol was having its effect. Everyone was louder, drunker, less inhibited. As she watched, a woman who was being teased by one of the men sank under the bubbles to her chin. Grinning, she suddenly thrust up an arm and threw out her bikini top. It landed in a wet plop onto the patio. Everyone in the hot tub howled with laughter.

Mac glanced up. Was there another twitch to the curtains?

It looked like Evelyn Jacoby had put the "watch" in neighborhood watch to another use. Or maybe it was Evelyn's husband, Darrell, one of Burt Deever's right-hand men.

"They're at it again." Evelyn peered around the curtain, darting another look out the window, pulling back only to peek again.

Darrell restrained himself from looking. His inner eyelids were already burned with the memory of that Lauren woman's round, luscious breasts. She was always stepping in and out of Jeannie's hot tub like a fucking goddess. His cock, rather reluctant these days, stirred.

He buried his nose in the newspaper he'd already read cover to cover, the shield he sometimes held up so he didn't have to look at the old cow he'd married. "Who?" he asked. *Don't say Lauren, don't say Lauren, don't say Lauren . . .*

She didn't answer, just kept staring out the window. "They're getting naked again. There's nothing funny about it. One of these days I'm going to call the police on them for indecent exposure."

"Was I laughin'?" he asked, dropping the newspaper just a bit to glare at her. Evelyn was at her usual post, watching Jeannie McDonald's backyard, reporting to him whether he wanted to know about the shenanigans that went on or not. This was what she always, always did. Why couldn't she just stop herself? Nothing good ever came from watching the neighbors. although Lauren . . . she reminded him a bit of Evelyn, back in the day.

"I asked you who was there," he reminded her.

"Well, I don't know all their names, now do I? There are two or three men in the hot tub. Leon's just getting out. His wife left with that girl who was at the meeting, so maybe he's following them. Still a few women left in there, though. One tossed her top onto the ground. Oh, yep. There go some bathing shorts! Hot tub's heating up now that the party's breaking up. Those women, la di dah. That one . . . oh my God, she's standing up for God and everyone to see!" She turned around and caught him waiting with bated breath. "Your girlfriend," she singsonged. "Lauren."

He could feel his face heat. "Okay, *Gladys*," he muttered.

The name harkened back to that old television show, *Bewitched*, which included the nosy neighbor, Gladys Kravitz, who was always spying on her next-door neighbors.

She flicked him a smile. "Okay, *Abner*."

Abner Kravitz was Gladys's husband. To do honor to the character, Darrell felt he should be sitting in a recliner, wearing a cardigan sweater and horn-rimmed glasses, and puffing on a pipe. As it was, he was seated at the kitchen table, using the hanging overhead lamp to read, when he wasn't actually lifting the paper to keep from having to interact with her. Why had he ever gotten married? Maybe 'cause of that ole tomcat, Victor, who'd screwed 'em all in his day, had turned his eye on Evvie. . . .

She peered through the blinds again and squeaked, "There they go again! A ménage à trois, right out in front of God and everyone!"

Darrell wanted to look. He really, really wanted to look. If it was a genuine ménage à trois, he'd race over and push the hag out of the way to get a gander. But she'd lied about what she'd seen before, just to get his goat, just to get him to move, so he was torn. And he was a little uncomfortable that she might know about his interest in Lauren.

"Oh, oh, oh . . ." She took a step back, a hand to her chest.

"What?"

"My God, Darrell. That man's penis is *huge*."

He was staring at her, full-on gaping. One foot was twisted and tense, ready to propel him off the stool.

But then she couldn't hold it. She smiled. That sneaky little smile. Once upon a time he'd thought it was mischievous and cute, but those days were long gone.

He dove back behind the newspaper, angry at himself and at her. She always played these games when he showed no interest in her. She was always looking for relevance, but it just wasn't there. They'd moved into Victor's Villages when the development was first built and now their house was showing its age and so were they. Whereas most of the other homes around them had been updated and turned out like they were these little gems—lipstick on a pig, he felt—especially after they'd been surrounded by Staffordshire Estates, River Glen's newest westside development, theirs was still the three-bedroom ranch it had always been, placed on a rise above Jeannie's house with a perfect view of her backyard. It had a dank basement like some of the originals, a basement that they seldom went down to anymore, but that was its only extra amenity. Most of the homes like theirs had been scraped to the dirt and erected as new construction. All the real estate people now acted like Victor's Villages had always been a part of the overall plan that had both swallowed them up and renamed them the Villages at Staffordshire Estates, no more Victor's Villages. Victor Laidlaw was no longer even a footnote, thank God. The man had been evil. A useless piece of human garbage with a restless cock.

Darrell snapped his newspaper shut as his thoughts turned dark.

"Oh, they have no shame!" Evelyn moaned, pretending horror but actually titillated. "That man's pulling Lauren up and down on his penis, up and down, up and down, oh my *God* . . ."

That did it. Darrell clambered up from his chair and bulldozed her away. Her eyes were glued to the scene below. He gazed over her shoulders, his eyes raking the scene below. But no one was in the hot tub. The party was indeed over.

Evelyn trilled out a peal of laughter, doubled over, flapping a hand at him, almost unable to catch her breath. He backed away from her, embarrassed. She'd seen through him. He could feel the throbbing heat in his face. He wanted to throttle her, or maybe pull her up and down on *his* penis. Up and down, up and down . . . Her words had brought him back to life real quick. But he was angry, too. Women. They weren't like men. They were mean-spirited and devious. Untrustworthy. Hadn't she proved that?

All of a sudden her laughter cut off, as if she'd turned

a switch. Darrell braced himself for whatever was coming next.

"I know what happened," she whispered.

The hairs on his arms lifted. She was an uppity bitch for sure. And getting downright weird. Out of control. Like Clarice Fenwick, only more calculating. What had happened? She used to know her place. But now . . . now all of the women he and Cliff and Burt had married were loopy, unstable hags.

"What do you mean?" he asked carefully.

"I *know.*"

Her attitude scared him a little. Things were getting kind of flaky. Evvie's emotions were wingin' back and forth like a goddamn whipsaw. She was unpredictable, unsafe. Half-crazy.

He went back to the table and stared down at the open newspaper, the words bright and clear under the brilliant light, but his gaze was unseeing. Beside the newspaper was a jumble of trash mail. From beneath a hard hat, Andrew Best beamed his big smile up at Darrell from a slick cardboard flyer. Best Homes wanted to buy their house. No real estate fees. No inspection. No problem. Because their house was one of the few originals, it was "wanted." Hardly a day went by without some piece of snail mail arriving, touting all the reasons they should *sell and sell now!* If they'd had children, they could leave the place to them, but that was a subject neither of 'em talked about anymore. There was nothing and no one but the two of them and this house.

"Hey," Evvie said, sounding in control again.

"Yes, dear," he said contemptuously.

"You can't take a joke? These people are turning our

neighborhood into a sex playground and you don't care? You just wish they'd ask you to join them?"

"I don't think they'd want to see my wrinkly, white ass."

She came around the table to stare him down. Darrell's stomach tightened at her intensity. Geez, God. Sometimes he just didn't know what she was thinking and it made him uneasy. She knew better than to make waves . . . didn't she? Things didn t turn out well for those who did. She knew better. *He* knew better. But she sure seemed to be forgettin' lately, not as bad as that palsied Clarice, but bad.

"Get her in line," Burt had warned him in his rasping voice.

"You want to be in the hot tub," she accused him now. "You want to be the one inside the whore."

"Christ, Evelyn."

"I know, Darrell. *I know.*"

And then she gave him that smile again and came up behind him, placing her crone hands on his shoulders, digging in painfully. He had a sudden memory of her hands long ago, soft and warm, rubbing his cock, while her lips, those red, red lips, smiled from the back of the convertible as she waved to the crowd. Prettiest girl in the county. He'd been burstin' his buttons he was so proud she'd looked at him, though now he knew it was because she'd thought he had a little more dough in his pockets than he had, maybe 'cause he'd been braggin' a bit.

"I love you," she whispered in his ear now and took his lobe between her small, even teeth. His blood froze.

"Evvie, goddammit."

Her teeth slid away. "I know, you fucker . . ." she whispered, before sailing off toward the bedroom. Darrell remained at the table, unsettled. Who did she think she was, makin' him feel this way? So damn . . . *impotent.*

His gaze moved from the newspaper across the kitchen to the knife caddy sitting on the counter.

If she didn't pull it together, he would have to make her. She was untrustworthy. Coming apart at the seams. A liability.

Get her in line.

Chapter Thirteen

Taft's cell phone rang in the early hours of the morning. He was half-awake already after suffering through another restless night. Since he'd taken the bullet under his shoulder, coupled with his decision to turn on Mangella, he'd lost the ability to sleep, which had been his superpower before.

He reached for the phone on his night stand, squinting through the dark at the number. No one he knew. The phone rang again in his hand and he answered, "Taft."

There was a moment of silence when he heard stuttered breathing. The sound chased any cobwebs in his head away. "Who is this?" he asked.

"Mister . . . um . . . it's Deena, from the Rosewood Court."

Taft was already out of bed, sensing an urgency the female voice hadn't expressed in words. Rosewood Court. The name of Jimmy Riskin's motor court. The office girl? "Deena," he said, placing the voice. "What happened?"

"Your friend . . . is dead," she said, her voice dropping to a whisper.

"Jimmy Riskin?"

"He's hanging in the storeroom. From a pipe."

Taft was in the act of grabbing for his clothes and his wallet, but her words froze him. For a moment he didn't breathe. He visualized the odd, scruffy man who'd lived in the shadows . . . *lived* . . . past tense.

He pulled himself together. "Have you called the police?"

"No . . ."

Taft thought hard. Riskin was dead. Hanged. *Sleeping with the fishes.* "Were you the one who found him?"

"I . . . yes . . ."

"Does anyone else know?"

"No . . ." Her voice quavered. "I called you. You told me to call you."

"I'm glad you did. I'll be there. Give me . . ." Shit, it was going to take a while, but there was no traffic to speak of at this hour. "Twenty, thirty . . . um . . . twenty. I'll be there in twenty."

"He killed himself," she said in shock.

"See you soon."

Taft was in his Rubicon under five minutes, driving through the faint first streaks of daylight just at the speed limit. Couldn't afford to get pulled over. Killed himself? There was nothing in Jimmy Riskin's character that suggested that was true. The man had a strong sense of self-preservation, uniquely attuned, given his dangerous profession.

Keith Silva.

Taft's face set in hard lines. This was no suicide.

Mackenzie opened her eyes at the unmistakable sound of the blender in the kitchen. Bloody Marys again? No. They didn't require a blender.

She glanced at the clock. 5:30. Leon was up awfully
early, unless this was some Saturday morning ritual she
didn't yet know about.

She pulled herself out of bed and headed straight for
the shower.

She was under the spray and therefore missed the
screen flash of her silenced cell phone and Taft's call.

The Rosewood Court was quiet as a tomb as Taft
wheeled into the lot. No movement apart from the flickering pink neon script that spelled out the complex's name
inside the office's front windows. He parked in a visitor
spot. He would have preferred the street to make this trip
more anonymous, but he was going to have to contact the
police anyway, as soon as he had a look for himself. Riskin
was his CI. And he wanted to know what had happened
before the Portland police were called in.

The sky was a dove gray by the time Taft tested the
office door. Locked. He knocked lightly. No lights shone
from inside other than the pink neon glow.

Almost immediately Deena appeared from the shadows
inside. She opened the door for him and immediately
locked it behind him with a dead bolt, then motioned him
down a back hall. He walked behind her carefully, senses
on alert. He'd twisted the bear's tail with Mangella and the
man's reach was vast, way beyond the limits of River Glen.
Had he used Silva as his messenger?

She took him past a room with a desk and a swivel chair
and a credenza covered with scattered papers. A sleeping
bag and pillow lay on the floor, lashed together with a
bungee cord. They moved past that room farther down the
hall to a back door that was double bolted. As she undid

the locks, she said quietly, "I'm not supposed to sleep here," which explained the rolled-up bedding and possibly why she was on duty so early.

Outside, they went down three concrete steps. Directly ahead was a separate building, old enough to look as if it had been in place before the motor court built up around it. It was a garage of sorts, Taft thought, as Deena slipped a key into the lock with shaking fingers. She pushed the door inward and stood back. "He's in the back," she whispered. "Light switch on your right."

Carefully, gingerly, one hand poised to pull his Glock from where it was strapped at his hip, beneath his jacket, Taft took a step forward, his fingers reaching for the light switch. He flipped it on and the place flooded with light from overhead fluorescents hanging from chains. It was one room divided by chain-link fencing that ran floor-to-ceiling and separated out cubicles of storage. Forgotten or discarded items were stacked in each locked unit, but Taft's vision was over the top of them to the rear of the room, where he could see a bent head hanging from a rope attached to an overhead, galvanized iron pipe.

He quickly moved down the narrow walkway between the units. He lost sight of the hanging man who was apparently inside the last unit, his vision obscured by left-over or forgotten furniture that worked as a screen between the storage cubicles. As he drew closer, he felt the familiar tingling of nerves that warned him of danger. He half expected a trap. Pulling his gun, he led with it the last few steps.

But he was alone as he stood in front of the last unit. The body hung limp. The storage unit's chain-link door was unlatched. Taft didn't have to touch the body to know the CI was dead. It was Riskin. Deena had said it was, but he'd needed to see for himself. He lowered his gun and pushed aside the door with its barrel, then slipped it back in the holster, never taking his eyes off the hanging corpse.

He felt numb and detached. The sense of loss would come later. Followed by anger. This was Silva's doing at someone's behest. A paid assassination.

He'd called Mackenzie, but she hadn't answered. He'd wanted to check with her about someone she said she'd seen in the Villages, but now he wanted to wait. To think.

He stepped forward, his hands behind his back, and visually examined the body. If this was a crime scene—and he fervently believed it was—he had to steer clear of leaving any trace of himself other than what he would tell the police. He'd touched the light switch and that was all.

But . . . there were boxes behind the body in the storage unit. Hastily opened and closed again, one with a partially askew lid. Riskin's doing, or someone looking for something?

He moved gingerly around the body toward the boxes, his gaze focusing on the one whose lid looked hastily replaced.

Don't do it. Don't screw up evidence. It'll come back to bite you in the ass.

He didn't pay attention to Helene's warning, bringing his hands forward and covering his right one with the cuff of his jacket. The one lid was slightly higher than the rest. Could've been Riskin, but he was betting it wasn't. Lifting the lid, he saw the papers within had been shoved around, edges bent back or crumpled. A hurried examination? Probably in vain; Riskin wouldn't leave anything as damning as hard copies lying around.

But you're looking anyway.

He put back the lid and checked a second box, then a

third. Nothing. They were empty except for a few barbells, some books on investing, even more on physical training. Where were Riskin's belongings? Where had he moved? Taft knew of no relatives. The CI had made it clear he was living off the grid from friends and family, if there even were any.

He could feel time ticking away inside his head.

Taft took a few more precious moments to look through the boxes, but when he was sure he hadn't missed anything, he retraced his steps to find Deena shivering outside the garage door. Her eyes were huge. "I gotta leave or I'll be fired," she said. "Tony'll be here soon."

"We need to call the police. And they'll need to talk to you."

"Why? I can't talk to them," she declared, alarmed.

"Did you hear anything last night? Voices?"

"No."

But she was lying. He knew liars well enough to catch one. He was a liar himself, at times. A good one.

"You didn't hear anyone go into the shed?" He hitched a thumb to the storage unit as he led her back up the stairs into the office building. He didn't want anyone seeing them standing outside.

"Uh-uh."

"Tell me about last night."

She lifted her shoulders and splayed her palms. "I was supposed to leave at nine. Close up. But sometimes I stay . . . over."

"Did you see the man who came earlier again? The one we talked about?"

"No." She stared at him in the semidarkness of the hallway, her eyes black and liquid. "Isn't it a suicide?"

"When did you find the body?"

"This . . . morning. Just before I called you."

He waited, but finally prompted patiently, "What made you go look?"

"I heard something earlier . . . woke me up."

"What time?"

"I don't know. Two thirty maybe? I heard a clunk. So I turned on the outside light. I didn't know what it was, but I guess it was Mr. Riskin. I thought somebody might be breaking in. Look, I can't tell anybody about it 'cause they'll know I was here."

"What happened after you turned on the light?"

"Nothing. That was it. I went back to my sleeping bag."

"Did you turn off the light?"

"Not till I called you." She peered at him anxiously. "It's not suicide?"

"The medical examiner will make that determination."

"But you think it's murder."

"It's time I called it in," he said. Past time.

"I just want to leave."

"I wish I could tell you you could," he said, not unkindly. "But you found the body. They're going to ask questions. Of both of us."

"Ohhh . . . boy . . ." She walked back into the front office and sank onto a hard chair, one of two in front of the counter, for visitors, but not meant to encourage loitering.

Taft pulled out his cell and called in the death. He wished he didn't have to have his name attached to it, but there was no getting out of it. Jimmy Riskin's death would likely elicit many, many questions he didn't want to answer. He could see the future, and in that future he saw the law coming down at him hard because of his association with Mangella, and Silva, and a whole host of others

Riskin had investigated on Taft's behalf. One way or another, he was going to have to stay ahead of this investigation, whether into suicide or murder.

"Mister . . . ?"

Taft glanced at Deena. She'd been gazing at the floor, but now she looked up at him and got to her feet. The tiny stud in her nose winked pink. "I knew him."

"You knew Jimmy Riskin?"

"We were friends. I knew what he did and he knew what I did. He said your name. Taft?"

Taft nodded.

"I'm good with computers and I helped him, sometimes."

Taft took a moment, thinking, imagining Riskin with this girl, hunched over a laptop. "You're a hacker."

"Jimmy taught me some things, too," she said, somewhat modestly.

"There's no computer around here."

"I guess he took it with his stuff."

"But if it were found, you might be able to get into the files," said Taft.

"I would be able to," she answered confidently. They stared at each other for several moments, then she added, "But I'm not gonna tell the police that. I'm not gonna tell them about me."

Taft wasn't quite certain how to counsel her, if she would even take any advice he might give. "That might be wise," he admitted slowly.

She'd walked behind the counter with Taft, and now she moved forward and bent down to open a cupboard beneath the counter. She dug through an open box labeled Lost and Found and pulled out a dog-eared book.

"I think this is for you," she said, and handed him a copy of George Orwell's *1984*. "He said it wasn't important until it was and asked me to hold on to it. No one ever looks in the Lost and Found."

Taft looked down at the book. "You have any idea what he meant?"

"No. He was kinda weird that way."

Riskin and his puzzles. "Thank you, Deena."

A black Ford Explorer pulled into the lot and screeched to a halt outside. Taft recognized the men inside were cops. He stuck the novel in his coat pocket and braced himself. He had friends on the Portland PD, but he had a few enemies as well. He knew he was going to have a long day ahead of him.

As soon as she realized she'd missed Taft's call, Mackenzie phoned him back, leaving a voice mail when he didn't answer. She'd then texted him. So far he hadn't responded to either.

Around seven she walked into the kitchen expecting to see Leon, but it was Daley blending up a god-awful green-colored concoction. "Kale smoothie," Daley said, sipping from a glass. She indicated the still half-full blender. "Help yourself."

"No, thanks."

"You sure?"

"Pretty sure." Not in this lifetime. "I'm heading out this morning. I've got a meeting." She'd texted Stephanie that she would be over around eight.

"On Saturday?" Daley looked disbelieving.

"I'm not a nine-to-fiver. Leon around?"

"He never came home last night."

Maybe things had heated up after she and Daley left, but for all the talk of sexual escapades around the hot tub, the girl taking off her top and flinging it outside onto the patio, a woman named Lauren, was about as wild as the party had gotten, at least while Mac was there. There was a sense of wrap-up about the time she and Daley were preparing to leave.

"This just gives me more reason to leave him." She blinked several times, as if she might cry, but managed to hold it together.

Mac purposely changed the subject. "Could I get a look at that Ring video again?"

"Why? You know something?" She set down her drink and licked green goop off her lips.

"I just want to see the perp again. Put the image in my mind again."

"Well, Leon will have to get it for you. I don't know where it is or what he does with it. It's on his phone, I think."

"All right." She wanted time to pass so she wouldn't show up at Nolan's and Stephanie's earlier than she'd said. Thinking about how she was going to approach Nolan, she added casually, "You said Burt Deevers has been HOA president forever."

"Leon says the young guard are always trying to rout him out."

"The HOA meets once a month?"

"The general meeting's monthly. So are the board meetings. There's one scheduled for Monday, I think. They're always the Monday after the general meeting. There're also meetings for the architectural committee and other groups."

She made a face and poured herself some more of her green concoction. "I should probably get more involved. Maybe I could get them on my side and it would help convince Leon that he's the one who should leave." Her lips quivered and Mac could see her clench her teeth.

"Burt knew Victor Laidlaw, right?"

"A lot of 'em did. The old guard anyway. You'd be surprised how much his name gets mentioned for a guy who's been dead years and years." A pause. "Why?"

"Althea Gresham told me I needed to learn the history of the Villages."

"You listened to her?" Daley snorted. "You want to talk Villages history, go to the HOA board meeting. All the oldies knew Victor."

"Can people outside the board go?" Mac asked curiously.

"Althea goes. Listens to every word. But they're boring and you don't get to participate. I was kidding."

Mac had come full circle in her interest in the HOA. She didn't think it was that bad of an idea, watching the old guard interact with their friends on the board. "How long has it been since the dog poop incident?" asked Mac. "It was the last time you were targeted, right?"

"Right." Her question made Daley blink several times. "Two, three weeks . . . maybe four. . . ?"

"A while ago, though. Do you think it's stopped?"

"Probably not. It's one of the reasons I went to Jesse." She paused and gave it some serious thought. "The porch pirate was here a couple of times before the dog shit. I've stopped buying online because of it. I've told everyone that a private detective is looking into things, so maybe it's stopped." She didn't sound like she believed it.

"I'm not a licensed private detective," Mac reminded her tiredly.

She shrugged. "You're on the job."

Mac thought about Daley broadcasting to the neighborhood that she had a private detective working for her and thought it might be counterproductive to Mac learning who'd been harassing her. Forewarned, the villagers likely already had made their minds up about Mac.

"I'll see you later," said Mac. She didn't want Daley to revisit why she'd asked about Victor and wonder if Mac might have another agenda, which she did.

Fifteen minutes later she parked at Stephanie's and Nolan's ranch-style house and walked through a brisk June morning to the front door. She could smell bacon and fresh-baked bread as she rang the bell.

An aproned Stephanie threw open the door and, upon seeing Mac, dropped both hands to her protruding belly and said proudly, "We made breakfast for you."

"For me?"

"Normally I sleep in these days. Trying to bank sleep. They say a new baby is a killer. But I got up and made breakfast. Nolan's the one who slept late, but he's in the shower now."

Mac followed Stephanie into the kitchen. Her stepsister was not known for her culinary skills, but there was a plate of crispy fried bacon and the warm bread, a take-and-bake loaf that seemed to reach to Mac with an aroma finger. Stephanie started cracking eggs into a skillet. "Scrambled okay?" she asked.

There had been a time when Stephanie flirted with veganism, but the pregnancy had put that to bed, at least for now. "Anything," said Mac. She wasn't fussy as a rule anyway, but when someone cooked for her, it was dealer's choice.

Stephanie was serving up the plates when Nolan appeared, his dark hair damp.

"Look at this," he said admiringly.

"I'm only partially useless," said Stephanie.

Nolan said to Mac, "My wife is not useless."

"He's careful not to disparage me," she said with a smile, sitting down in front of her own plate. "I could cry or break something or turn into a shrieking monster."

"Untrue," Nolan said, forking fluffy eggs into his mouth. "My wife is perfect."

Stephanie snorted.

"I should come by more often," said Mac. She picked up a slice of bacon and bit into it. She couldn't remember the last time she'd eaten a full breakfast. A cup of coffee and a piece of toast were her usual morning fare.

"I can't wait for baby to get here," Stephanie said with a groan as she got up from the table. "The last trimester is coming up and I'm already over it."

"She loves being pregnant," Nolan deadpanned.

"She glows," said Mac. Stephanie was just one of those women who seemed to radiate health and beauty during pregnancy.

Stephanie coughed into her fist, "Bullshit. I puked my guts out."

"Once or twice," Nolan allowed. "That was it."

"Yeah, well, now it's food, food, and more food." To demonstrate, she plucked up the last two slices of bacon and stuck them in her mouth.

Nolan laughed and so did Mac. They both helped clear the table and then sat back down in their chairs. Nolan sighed and Mac recognized how tired he looked. Seeing she was watching him, he said, "Work."

Stephanie made a sound in her throat. "He left Best Homes because of work. It's just as bad at Laidlaw."

"Not as bad," Nolan disagreed. "Different." He turned his attention to Mac. "You wanted to talk about something?"

Mac would've loved to dive right in and ask about Tobias Laidlaw, but LeeAnn Laidlaw's warning rang in her ears. "I'm kind of partially living in the Villages right now." She explained as clearly as she could about her job with Daley. It was kind of a murky endeavor apart from looking into the harassment. "So, I've learned some of the history of the place. It used to be Victor's Villages, and because you work for Laidlaw Construction, I wanted to ask you about it."

"Well, Tobe Laidlaw is Victor's son."

Stephanie snorted. "Tobe Laidlaw . . ."

"Stephanie doesn't like Tobe much," said Nolan.

"I see that," said Mac.

"Tobe Laidlaw isn't as bad as Andrew Best. Best is . . . a slime," she said.

"Andrew Best pushes legal boundaries," Nolan explained. "He's difficult and skirts rules, if he can. When I had the chance to move, I jumped at it."

"But Nolan runs Laidlaw all by himself. He calls himself the foreman, but—"

"I *am* the foreman," he interrupted.

"—he does everything. I don't know how Tobe supposedly saved his father's business. He must've been different then because he's useless now."

"Don't hold back, Stephanie. Tell us how you really feel." Nolan regarded her with amusement.

She sat back in her chair and folded her hands on her

stomach again. "Do you know that Tobias Laidlaw hasn't made a single decision about his company for months? Maybe years?"

She looked to Nolan, who shrugged and said, "Tobe hired me to help." It sounded like a long-standing discussion between them.

"Help? You do everything! I thought it was bad with Best Homes, and it was, but this job comes with challenges, too. The man has issues."

"What kind of issues?" asked Mac.

Stephanie nodded toward Nolan. "He has wild ideas, right? He's unstable."

Nolan said, "He's not a bad guy. He does get some wild ideas that he runs with. Probably has some undiagnosed medical issue . . . ADD or bipolar or something. He's smart but unpredictable."

"What does he do that's unpredictable?"

"Like take off for weeks on end?" Stephanie looked pointedly at Nolan.

"Tobias directs the company. Makes the decisions," said Nolan firmly, seeking to quell his wife's disparagement of his boss. He might as well have tried to hold back the tide.

Stephanie said, "He's always thought his father's death was suspicious. Victor Laidlaw died of a heart attack, but Tobe keeps circling back to it. Thinks he was murdered. That's just one of his reasons to go on a wild hair. Seeking proof of Victor's murder."

"Tobe helped Victor finish a project that nearly took Victor and Laidlaw Construction under, and his father died right afterward. It was a difficult time," explained Nolan.

"The three overlook houses," said Mac.

"You know it." Nolan nodded. "Tobe brought the company back from the brink. He can really focus when it's necessary. But . . . that was fifteen years ago, and since then, off and on, he's gotten obsessed about things like his father's death. It comes and goes."

"It's been bad lately," Stephanie clarified.

Mac was itching to pull out her notepad and scratch down all she'd heard, but she didn't want to pique her stepsister's and brother-in-law's interest too much.

Nolan said, "Tobe's on a business trip now."

Stephanie put in, "Or another wild hair."

"Was this what you wanted to talk to me about?" A line formed between Nolan's brows.

Damn LeeAnn Laidlaw's restrictions. Mac quickly said, "I'm just trying to get a feel for who might be harassing the Carreras and I ran into the stories about Victor."

"He still thinks his father's a saint," muttered Stephanie.

Nolan shook his head. "Tobe knows who his father was. He might have him on a pedestal, sorta, but he knows. There were all kinds of rumors about Victor. His friends could probably tell you some stories."

"Do you know when Tobias will be back?" Mac asked casually. She was really pushing the excuse that she was just getting some history on Victor.

"Do you?" Stephanie repeated, swiveling her head to Nolan.

"He's on an extended business trip. He drives. He doesn't fly, so it takes longer."

"He's been gone quite a while," Stephanie pointed out.

"He'll probably be back in the office next week. Judy would know," said Nolan.

And hopefully Judy would be back in the office next week as well, thought Mac. She longed to just be straight with Nolan and say LeeAnn thought he was missing, but she had to keep that to herself.

The conversation stopped and Mac could see that was about all she would get out of Nolan about Tobias without raising serious red flags about her intent. The man was missing, whether by accident or design was the question. Maybe Nolan was right and Tobias Laidlaw was on an extended road trip, possibly on a quest of some sort.

Or LeeAnn could be correct and something had happened to the man.

She thanked Stephanie again for breakfast and took her leave a few moments later. Still no return message from Taft. Hmmm. She sent him another text, asking what was up, as she got in her RAV. She waited in Nolan's and Stephanie's driveway for what felt like ages but was actually only a few minutes, then tried phoning Taft again. Her call went straight to voice mail, so she waited for the beep and said, "Nolan says Judy would know where Tobias went, but Judy was out of the office yesterday. I'm guessing she'll be back Monday. I'm kind of stumbling around in the dark about Tobias. We need to talk to LeeAnn and get her to lift her ban on interviewing the employees. I could call her, but maybe you should? Where are you?" She hesitated, thinking she should say a lot more, but until she heard from him, she was on her own. "Call me," she directed, then clicked off.

While she drove back to the Villages she rolled over what Nolan and Stephanie had said. Tobias was obsessed with his father's death. Thought he'd been murdered. The old guard certainly had strong feelings about the man, so maybe they could shed some light on where Tobias had gotten that idea. Maybe the women would be more open about what they thought about Victor.

Chapter Fourteen

It was late afternoon Saturday before Jamie managed to get Cooper home, and then it was a question of whether he could make it upstairs with his cast. The accident had snapped his thighbone and the surgery had put it back in place, but now walking was awkward, damn near impossible. He slowly shook his bandaged head at the sight of the stairs and Jamie helped him back to the living room couch, where he lay down. He felt weak, exhausted, and angry. His ribs ached. He knew he was lucky to be alive and on the mend. No seriously debilitating, long-term injuries, but this "accident" wouldn't have happened at all if his favorite city ride hadn't been tampered with.

His favorite city ride. On the phone Verbena had tried to move past that piece of information, but Cooper had gotten hung up on the significance.

Someone had wanted *him* out of the way. Verbena and the chief hadn't quite gone down that road with him yet, but it made perfect sense to Cooper. Officers had their favorite cars, but no vehicle was tagged as someone's favorite as much as Cooper's was. It was a subject of ribbing around the department.

"You okay?" Jamie asked him now, eyeing his sprawled form on her couch, which was luckily long enough to accommodate his over six-foot frame. All the bedrooms were on the second floor, so the couch was the only option. Jamie had suggested bringing a bed downstairs, but Cooper didn't plan on being immobile for long.

"I'm okay," he assured her.

"Anything to eat?"

"No, thanks." He felt dull, his brain still blanketed with painkillers, and he'd suffered a concussion. He wanted time to pass so he could feel better, could *think* again. Something had happened before the accident. Something he needed to remember. It was his gut that told him that whatever that something was was critical because his head couldn't recall.

"I'm having a half-caf coffee with cream. Want one?" Jamie asked.

He smiled faintly. He'd refused all the solicitation that had hit him straight on, so now she was coming at him obliquely. He understood and loved her for it . . . even though he'd rather have full-on caffeine. "Half caf would be great."

As she went to get him his coffee, he closed his eyes and struggled to review what had taken place just before the accident. It was a black void. Impenetrable, at least at this point.

When Jamie returned carrying a heat-resistant to-go cup with its own plastic straw, he asked, "When is Verbena coming by?"

"I think she said tomorrow." She set the drink on the end table she'd moved from the side of the couch to within his reach.

Both Jamie and Elena were protecting him. He knew

that. But the urgency he felt made him impatient and cranky. It was all he could do not to bark at her; however, that feeling faded as he looked into her doubt-filled eyes.

"I have something to tell you," she said softly.

His brain did a quick wake up and he recalled how anxious she'd seemed in the days prior to his accident. *That* he could remember. Engagement regrets? His heart did a painful lurch, especially when she twisted the ring on her left hand.

"Harley's gone to pick up Emma, who's been insisting on seeing you. I tried to talk her out of it, but you know Emma. She can be . . . intractable, so I just gave in."

Cooper waited after she stopped talking, sensing there was something further to come.

"I would've rather had another day or two off work. I've got Monday, maybe Tuesday, but after that—"

"Jamie, I'm fine," he interrupted.

"If this is fine, what does 'not okay' look like?" She smiled. "I want to stay with you."

Cooper managed a smile back. "I thought you were going to say something else. You had me worried."

"Like what?" she asked, but her eyes drifted away.

There it was. Something was wrong. He closed his eyes again. He was running out of energy. He could feel his store of strength being sapped, an ebbing wave, sucking at his reserves. It pissed him off and with an effort he reopened his eyes to see her brown ones filled with tears.

"Jamie," he said, immediately alarmed.

"I'm just so glad you're all right!" She shook her head, trying to shake off her emotions.

He reached up his arms and she carefully moved into an embrace.

"Don't worry about me," he said into her hair.

"Oh, sure. Thanks for that. Now everything's fine." She pulled back and looked at him, impatiently brushing at her tears.

His galloping heartbeat began to return to normal. Maybe he was being too sensitive. "I gotta get into some real clothes," he complained. The pajamas made him feel like more of an invalid.

"I'm working on it."

"Yeah?"

A trace of amusement crossed her face. "Hold on."

She got up and headed upstairs for a few moments. He heard a car arrive and looked out the front window to see Jamie's daughter and sister arrive. Harley practically ran up the walk to the porch steps, but Emma plodded behind her. It still bothered him that Emma had become so compromised from that accident so long ago. He always felt somewhat responsible, though the blame wasn't his.

Jamie returned with a pair of khakis with one leg cut off at the upper thigh just as Harley burst in.

"Hi, mates!" Harley greeted them, then, "Ooh, fashion. Cool."

"My sewing skills start and end with scissors," said Jamie as Emma came through the door.

Emma regarded the pants in her critical way, then she looked at Cooper. "I called Mackenzie *Loff*-lin. I told her to come see you."

"Okay," said Cooper. He wasn't sure what that was all about.

"I am not moving back," she added. "I have to protect the cat."

"Are you sure?" asked Jamie.

Harley said, "Twirk is beloved and hated. She's a very scary being. Maybe extraterrestrial."

"She's a cat," Emma clarified again.

"She is more than just a cat," Harley answered in an orator's voice. "She is the grim reaper, put upon this earth to help us mere mortals bridge to another world."

"Are you going to sleep here?" Emma asked Cooper, ignoring Harley's theatrics.

Jamie answered, "For now. Why did you ask Mackenzie to see Cooper?"

Emma frowned at her sister. "She's a friend and a cop."

Was a cop, Cooper thought. He'd known Mackenzie Laughlin when she was with the department, and even though she seemed to have partnered up with Jesse Taft, who had a somewhat adversarial relationship with River Glen PD, he would say he trusted her. And he also trusted Taft's investigative skills. He wouldn't have any trouble working with either of them, especially because neither of them was a fan of Chief Bennihof.

Something twigged in his brain. A ripple. A movement. He tried to grasp it and failed.

"What's wrong?" Jamie asked him.

"Something hurts," said Emma.

"No, I'm just thinking," said Cooper.

"It hurts to think," Emma decreed.

"No shit," said Harley, then waved her hand and intoned in unison with Emma and Jamie, "No swearing," then, "I'm off to the loo."

She headed up the stairs, humming Adele's "Rolling in the Deep."

Cooper, Jamie, and Emma all looked at one another.

"She's angling for a trip to London after graduation," explained Jamie to Emma, who was clearly at sea with Harley's new behavior.

"Angling? She's an Anglophile?" asked Emma, squinting at them.

"Well . . . ye-e-s . . ." said Jamie, unable to hold back a sudden burst of laughter. "Where did you get that?"

Emma cocked her head. "Harley said she was an Anglophile, but I told her she was American."

Cooper was fighting a losing battle with laughter himself. He started to chuckle. His ribs hurt, but he couldn't stop. He couldn't meet Jamie's eyes, but he managed a glance at her. She was looking at her sister in bafflement. To which Emma said clearly, "Harley is American."

"Yes, yes. Of course she is. I'm sorry, Emma. It's just . . . do you know how much we love you?" Jamie covered her eyes with her hand and gave into the laughter.

Emma glanced from Cooper, who was grinning and chuckling and looking at Jamie sideways with love in his eyes, to her sister who was laughing her ass off, as Harley would say.

She'd missed something, which she often did, but it was okay because Jamie, who'd been sad, and Cooper, who'd been badly hurt, were having a good time. And Harley was still an American.

Leon came home at around one p.m. Daley had squirreled herself away in her room, nursing her hurt and anger, Mac assumed, when he strolled in from the garage, carrying his bike helmet and looking tousled, as if he'd just woken up. To emphasize that fact, he yawned as he reached in the cupboard for a coffee cup, nodding at Mac, who was seated at the kitchen bar with her laptop open.

"I was wondering if I could see that Ring video again," she said.

"Yeah?" He lifted his arms above his head and stretched, showing a bit of skin between his shirt and jeans. She wondered if she could ask where he'd been, whether that came under the heading of whatever the hell job she was supposed to be doing or if it would be off-limits.

"The poop deliverer and the porch pirate," she clarified.

"I only have one of the porch pirate, though he came twice. Camera wasn't working the second time."

"He?"

"Or she."

He pulled out his phone and pulled up the videos. Mac wished she could see it on a bigger screen but imagined it wouldn't help much. The perp wore a hoodie pulled tight around their face, a cloth mask over their mouth, and sunglasses. Not much to look at, but still . . . it reminded her of Alfie. Someone young and a bit hostile, maybe. Possibly a woman.

"I met Alfie Messinger last night. I haven't seen any other teenagers around."

"Yeah, I saw Alfie there," said Leon. "Not a lot of kids around here. Too many old people in the Villages, and the younger ones haven't gotten into the baby craze yet."

"Could you run both videos again?"

Leon did so, and they both watched them in silence. At the end Mac said, "Different shoes."

Leon grunted and they watched the two videos again. "I think it's Alfie," he said. "Kid's got a chip on his shoulder. Whizzes by on his bike in a hoodie sometimes. Damn near hit Althea Gresham."

Maybe Alfie's near miss was why Althea had said there was something strange about the teenager. She said, "I thought I'd talk to Alfie and see what he has to say."

"Good luck with that. Abby's a momma bear."

"No other teenagers, huh?" she asked.

"There are some. They don't hang around the C streets, though. If they're going somewhere, they're heading through the Bs and As, past the park and out of the neighborhood entirely." He cocked his head and added, "I already accused Alfie once."

"Of harassing you? You never said that."

"He pissed me off, so I told him to keep his thieving hands to himself and his dog shit out of my mailbox. He's got an alibi, so . . ."

Mac could imagine Leon's personality might not mesh well with a somewhat surly teenage boy's. "What's the alibi?"

"Something about his bike. I was just jabbing him, y'know."

"Abby said the bike was stolen," said Mac.

"Maybe. But Momma Bear came to the rescue, and Poppa Bear," he added, remembering. "You met Dr. Andre yet?"

"No."

"Hold on to your virginity. You're just his type. Young, good-looking, nice body."

"I don't really have to worry about my virginity," said Mac dryly.

"Your personality might put a check on him, though."

Mackenzie wasn't exactly sure how to take that, but Leon explained, "You're kinda prickly. Like you might strenuously object if he grabbed your breast or something."

"I would strenuously object."

He nodded, like she'd made his point. "Back in the day the good doctor was apparently in every warm bed when the husband was away. Surprised he hasn't been charged with sexual harassment yet."

"You're a good one to talk!" Daley's voice rang out.

Both Mac and Leon turned as she entered the kitchen from down the hall. Unlike Leon, she was sleek and dressed to kill. Her hair was gelled behind her ears, making her look angrier and more militant than usual, and her black slacks, shirt, and jacket only added to the effect.

"Hello, my love," said Leon with his characteristic smirk.

"Fuck you," said Daley.

"I'll see you both later." Mac closed her laptop, dropped it in her room, then headed for the door, senses on alert for Daley to waylay her and give her the third degree. In this case, however, Daley's attention was laser-focused on her husband. Mac was torn in between wanting to overhear whatever cat- and dogfight was coming and to vamoosing before it broke out.

She decided now was as good a time as any to stop by the Messingers' and find out more about Alfie's alibi. Like Leon, she was pretty sure he was the porch pirate. But the change of shoes made her wonder if the dog poop in the mailbox was someone else's doing. Teenage boys had a tendency to wear one pair of sneakers until they wore them out, and maybe it was a trick of the light, but the black shoes looked smaller.

Mackenzie parked across the street from the Messingers' house. Today there was a silver Mercedes parked on the street in front that may or may not have been Abby's. Mackenzie remote locked the RAV as she hurried across the street, up the walk to the front door, and rang the bell.

She heard footsteps and the door swung inward. "It's the detective," Abby Messinger sang over her shoulder in a way that made Mac look past her to see who else was there. She was barefoot, in jeans and an oversize sweater that hung down one shoulder. A man came around from the dividing wall that led to the kitchen. Tall, silver-haired,

with a commanding presence and dark eyes that slid up
and down her frame, he waited as she followed Abby inside.
The silver Mercedes, she'd bet. This must be Dr. Andre
Messinger, which was confirmed when he introduced himself, clasping her hand tightly, his eyes holding hers.

"Oh, Andre," Abby said on a tired sigh, her gaze on his
intimate handshake.

"You're a private detective," he said to Mac, with just a
hint of amusement and derision.

"Not licensed—"

"Why are you here?" Abby asked, and then she yelled
toward the hallway they'd just passed, "Alfie! Come on.
Let's go!"

"Well, as I said last night, I'm looking into the Carreras'
harassment and—"

"Is Leon still blaming Alfie for the dog shit?" Dr. Andre
interrupted.

"He'd better not be," warned Abby. "Alfie!"

"I'm here," the teenager muttered belligerently, schlep-
ping his way from the hallway and into the kitchen. "I'm
not deaf . . . yet." He was in jeans and the ubiquitous
hoodie. Gray, like the Ring video.

Dr. Andre said, "Leon Carrera better watch himself or
he could be in for a defamation suit."

"Both Leon *and* Daley," said Abby.

"I didn't do it," Alfie muttered, rolling his eyes Mac's
way. He held his head down and looked up at her accus-
ingly from the corners of his eyes. "I was stranded when
it happened."

"Of course you didn't do it," said Abby. "It's already
been established you were miles away."

"The dog poop incident," said Mac.

Abby nodded curtly. Momma Bear, Leon had said. Both

Alfie and Abby had jumped on the mailbox delivery pretty fast, almost as if they were prepared.

"What day was that?" asked Mac.

"Oh, who knows," said Abby.

"May 18," said Alfie.

They looked at each other. Abby in the silent, warning way a mother stares at her child who's committed a huge faux pas; Alfie in slack-jawed consternation.

Dr. Andre tried to smooth it over. "Has there been anything further? Maybe the pranks are behind us."

Alfie turned toward the door. "I'm gonna go see Burt."

"Oh, no, you're not. We have that meeting with the tutor," Abby snapped back. She glared at her ex. "He's not going with you, or to see Burt, or any of it."

Dr. Andre pointed at her. "It's my day."

"I don't like the tutor," Alfie declared.

Abby smiled brittlely and looked directly at Mackenzie. "Aren't you glad you came to our happy home? What was it you wanted again? We're kind of busy."

"Come on, Alfie," Andre said gruffly.

Alfie rolled his eyes to the back of his head and groaned.

"There was a bike in several of the Carreras' Ring videos," Mac tossed out. A lie, but they were so focused on Alfie and the bike, as if it somehow exonerated him, she thought she'd take a flyer.

All three Messingers stopped all motion, as if hit by a freeze ray. Abby recovered first. "You did listen to that asshole, Leon," she accused. "Alfie's innocent! He couldn't have put the dog shit in the mailbox. Didn't you hear me? He was miles away and dealing with a stolen bike. And as for Leon, he can't keep it in his pants, y'know. Tongue hanging out for Mariah, though she's such a dry stick, it's like she's made of wood. But Jeannie, and that *slut* Lauren . . ."

Andre said in a quiet, deadly voice, "Shut up."

"Mom . . ." whined Alfie.

"My son was miles away that day," she repeated. "We had to get him another bike. So, it couldn't be him. Alfie is not on that video. Got it?"

"You'll have to excuse my ex-wife," Andre said through a smile of gritted teeth.

Mac said, "There were several incidents of porch piracy as well."

"What are you saying?" Abby demanded. She swept a purse off the console table.

"I didn't do it!" Alfie declared again. "I was . . . my bike was stolen that day." He looked frantic.

"You tell Leon to keep his fat ass out of our affairs," Abby tossed back. Her cell phone, which was still lying on the console table, rang at that moment. Mac could clearly read Burt's name. "Jesus," Abby said. "Get in the car, Alfie. I mean it." She grabbed her phone and marched toward the door that Mac assumed led to the garage, slipping her feet into a pair of flip-flops. Alfie shuffled behind. The door slammed shut behind them, but not before Mac caught a glimpse of black sneakers on the step down into the garage.

Once they were alone, Dr. Andre swept an arm toward the front door, indicating Mac should precede him out. "So, you're staying with Leon," he said.

"I was hired by Daley," she corrected.

"I bet Leon can't keep his hands to himself with you around."

"Oh, he can."

He leered at her. That was the word that came to mind.

He clasped her elbow, as if to ostensibly move her along, but she felt the heat of his hand and his massaging grip and had to fight a shudder of revulsion. He was accusing Leon of being on the hunt, but Dr. Andre and Victor had apparently been openly carousing and poaching wives in the Villages long before Leon ever showed up.

"Abby said she didn't report the bike stolen," said Mac.

"You don't give up, do you?" He laughed with false heartiness. "You'd have to ask Abby. I don't live here anymore." They heard a car start up and the garage door hum and clatter as it rose upward. A moment later an angry-sounding chirp of tires heralded Abby's and Alfie's departure.

"She always usurps me when it comes to Alfie," he said, seeming more amused than angry. "Guess I have the rest of the day to myself now. How about yourself?"

"Things to do," she said as she headed out to the porch, ignoring the hinted invitation.

"If you want to find whoever did this, maybe you should check into Leon and Daley's backgrounds. They came into this community acting like they were too good for it. My wife, Linda, sells medical supplies and she ran into Leon a couple of times at business conferences before he sold that vaping business. He's always hustling. Probably someone is trying to get back at him."

His attempt to shift blame felt like a ploy to send her in a different direction. The minor thievery and dog poop bomb in the mailbox would seem a pretty juvenile means of revenge in the business world, although anything was possible.

She left the Messingers' with a pretty solid feeling that she'd found the Carreras' harassers. Both of them, Abby and Alfie.

What's the motive? she asked herself. Why had Alfie targeted the Carreras? Alfie and Abby were both so certain about where Alfie was on the day of the dog poop incident, it seemed like Abby might have been the perpetrator on that occasion. Maybe as a means to alibi Alfie? But that didn't explain Alfie's antipathy toward Leon and Daley, unless the porch pirating was just a crime of opportunity.

She wondered how he liked the score of women's makeup. Not exactly the loot he was probably looking for, if that was why he'd stolen packages off their porch.

She was on her way back to Leon's and Daley's when she saw Althea Gresham thumping a cane down the street, her expression grim. She turned around at the corner and started marching back and Mackenzie realized this was her form of exercise.

Older than the old guard.

Mac waved to the woman, who obviously couldn't recognize her inside her car. Either that or she just didn't feel like being neighborly, which was kind of counterintuitive, given she was head of the neighborhood watch.

Mac consulted her mental list of those who had known Victor Laidlaw. She would have liked to try to speak to Clarice again, but Cliff was clearly not interested in Mac interviewing his wife.

She hadn't spoken to Evelyn Jacoby yet, also of the neighborhood watch, so she drove to their house, glancing over at Hot Tub Jeannie's as she pulled up. Jeannie's place was shuttered, a ghost town today. Maybe the party would pick up again in the evening. She wished she'd asked Leon who he'd spent the night with. Not that he would tell her, necessarily. Maybe Daley would learn and clue her in.

Knocking on the front door, she formulated what she wanted to ask them, if either Evelyn or Darrell were home:

Darrell, one of Burt's right-hand men, and Evelyn, the party snoop. They'd both lived in the Villages a long time and had to have known Victor pretty well indeed. They also had a front-row seat to whatever the young guard was up to in Jeannie's backyard.

There was a twitch of curtains at a side window. Seeing it, Mac smiled in that direction. Curtain twitching appeared to be someone's signature move.

It took a few moments, then the door opened the length of a chain lock. "Yes?" the female voice asked.

"Evelyn Jacoby? I'm Mackenzie Laughlin. I talked with Althea Gresham and she said you were on the neighborhood watch with her."

"Yes?" she asked again, sounding even more suspicious.

Mac pulled out her cover story. "I'm looking into the malicious stuffing of dog poop in Leon and Daley Carrera's mailbox, and the theft of packages from their porch." She almost added she wanted to know more about Victor Laidlaw, thinking to appeal to the woman's gossipy side but held back. She needed a foot inside the door first.

"I can't help you with that," she stated flatly.

"I was hired to look into the matter, so I thought I could help resolve other neighborhood issues as well, other instances of . . . malfeasance." Was that too strong a word? Mac tried to put on a winning smile, although Leon's comment about her personality possibly being objectionable made her tone down the wattage some. She could almost get her feelings hurt over that one.

She half expected to have the door shut in her face. Would it do any good to put a foot in the doorway, given that the chain had not come off? Then the door did shut. Mac hoped it would open again, chain removed, but long moments went by and she was forced to face the fact that she'd failed to get past Evelyn Jacoby's defenses.

She'd turned back toward the street when she heard the door open again with a kind of whine as it was pulled open far enough to allow entry.

"Althea's the one who knows how to deal with *malfeasance*," Evelyn said, stressing the word slightly as Mac turned around again and headed back her way. She stepped aside to allow her inside her split-entry home, one of the few in the development. Mac followed her up seven steps to the main-level second floor. As she crossed the cream-colored carpet she glanced toward the window that overlooked Jeannie's patio and hot tub. Today the curtains were open.

Evelyn took a stand by the entry door to the kitchen, her arms wrapped around herself as she rubbed her elbows. She was either cold or nervous, and as June had finally thrown off its cool, overcast days, and the day was warm and getting warmer, Mac decided it was nerves.

Evelyn motioned her to take a seat at the table. Mac grabbed the back of a polished maple chair, which was crowned with a gingham cushion tied to the seat.

"Darrell's out with Burt and Cliff, but he'll be back soon. I don't really know how I can help you. Althea, well, she runs the watch. She's old, but she's spry. We don't really do much. Take phone calls, mostly. Small complaints." She was somewhere in her fifties, with brown hair in a chin-length bob, but there was something old school about her that seemed to put her at the same age and taste level as Althea.

"Have there been other incidents of harassment around the neighborhood?" Mac asked.

"There's always something. A broken window. They said it was a rock, but it was a baseball. Over by the new development. Kids playing where they shouldn't." She made a face.

"Who are 'they'?"

"Oh, they moved. Wanted to blame it on someone other than their kid. The new people don't stay long." Her gaze rolled past Mac to look toward the window facing Jeannie's property. "Some a little longer than others."

"I was at a party there last night," said Mac.

"Mmm."

"Did you see me?" she pressed, getting definite disapproval vibes radiating from Evelyn.

"Were you in the hot tub?"

Couldn't you tell? "No."

"Darrell finds those parties entertaining, but I could do without them."

Remembering the twitching curtains, Mac wasn't so sure she was telling the truth. "I suppose they could get old," Mac murmured.

"Night after night. I should say so."

"I understand Darrell's a good friend of Burt Deevers. Althea Gresham was saying how they've kept things running at the HOA."

"Althea said that?" she asked suspiciously, but Mac could tell she was thawing a little at the compliment in spite of herself. "Darrell, Burt, and Cliff have been together since the beginning, shaping the way things are done."

"The beginning of Victor's Villages."

"*The Villages*. It was never Victor's Villages; people

just called it that. And there's no Victor anymore, thank the Lord."

"Mmm. I heard he wasn't well-liked."

She gave a short bark of laughter. Mac could tell she was just dying to tell someone new all about the Villages, and she did not disappoint.

"Victor created the neighborhood and then thought it, and everyone in it, was his. He came on to me once. No, that's not true. He came on to me many, many times. And Clarice, and Tamara . . . probably Abby, too, though maybe Andre could keep her out of it because they were friends and in it together. I don't know how Abby put up with it as long as she did, but then, she can be hardheaded, too."

"Victor had a son."

Evelyn had opened her mouth to apparently rattle on, but she snapped her jaw shut. After a moment, she said curtly, "Tobias, yes."

"Tobias took over the business after his father died?" prompted Mac when Evelyn didn't appear to want to offer anything further. "That was the start of what Laidlaw Construction has become today."

"Yes."

Evelyn was clearly at war with herself. She wanted to freeze Mac out at the direction change of the conversation, but her natural desire for gossip overrode her pique. "And even before that, he helped build those three houses over by the river that his father started. Burt said Victor was in over his head and his son saved him. After Victor died, Tobias turned around and built that . . ." She waved her arm toward the west and Staffordshire Estates, the new, multistoried houses dwarfing the lower-profile homes of the Villages.

Noise floated up from Jeannie's property. Voices. Laughing. Evelyn rose, as if pulled by a puppeteer, and took a place behind the curtain, looking downward. Mac could picture her doing the same thing often, every day, a ritual.

With her gaze fixed on Jeannie's property, she said, "A lot of 'em have hot tubs. They don't have meaningful conversation. They just have sex. And they all congregate there," she said, pointing downward with her index finger and a snap of her wrist.

"It sounds like you don't approve of Tobias's Staffordshire Estate project." *Or much of anything else, for that matter.* "I thought there were a number of different builders involved, not just Laidlaw Construction."

"I don't pay much attention to those things," she said, having turned back to the window. Her back was straight and stiff.

"What do you think of Tobias?" asked Mac.

Several moments went by. If possible, her straight and stiff back grew even more rigid. "I don't know the man. If he's anything like his father, I don't care to know him."

"His wife intimated that he has some issues. Maybe ADHD or obsessive-compulsive tendencies."

"Why are you talking about the Laidlaws?" she asked suddenly. "I thought you wanted to talk about the harassment." She turned back to give Mac a look that she couldn't immediately decipher; then, at the sound of an approaching car, she swept from the window to the top of the entry stairs, declaring, "Darrell's home." She suddenly seemed hyperalert. Was there fear there? Or something else?

Mac followed after her, watching as Darrell Jacoby's

truck turned from the street to the left side of the driveway, apparently aiming for the left bay of the two-car garage.

"Althea said I should get to know the history, and I—"

"Althea's old and dotty," she cut her off swiftly. Then, "I shouldn't have let you in. The Carreras aren't well-liked. That Leon made his money on cigarettes and she's a hard-ass bitch."

"It wasn't cigarettes—"

"I don't really care. Just leave. Please." She pointed to the front door.

Mac took her time heading back down the stairs, hoping Darrell would appear and she could maybe get some kind of reading off him. The Althea Gresham excuse was wearing thin, and it had been slim to begin with. And maybe she was wasting her time. She needed LeeAnn to stop tying her hands.

Darrell was apparently just going to sit in his car. He never came up the stairs from the garage. With Evelyn waiting imperiously at the head of the steps, Mac had little choice but to go out the front door. She hoped Darrell would enter from the lower level and head up the steps to the landing where she dallied, but since he'd turned off the engine there'd been no sound and no appearance.

She was forced to leave. Looking back at the house, she saw both left and right garage doors were down. She couldn't see anything inside the garage and wondered if Darrell knew she was there and was deliberately waiting for her to leave.

"Who was that?" Darrell opened the door from the garage at the bottom level and looked up past the landing to the upper floor, where Evelyn still stood. She didn't immediately answer, just stared out toward the street. Darrell then hurried up the stairs as Evelyn drifted back to her usual place by the window, looking down at the backyard below.

"Oh, that detective girl?" she said offhandlike.

It was a lie. She was pretending. She didn't want him knowing she'd been entertaining the snoopy bitch.

"Yeah, the one bunkin' with the Carreras. What was she doin' here?" he demanded.

"She's looking for whoever put the dog poop in the Carreras' mailbox."

"What was she doin' *here*?" he repeated with more emphasis.

"I don't know. I guess she thought I might know something about it," said Evelyn, as if it were the last thing on her mind. He half expected her to yawn.

"You didn't talk to her about anythin'?"

"I don't know what you're getting at."

Oh, yes, you do, you lyin' she-skunk. "Clarice shakes like a cement mixer. Cliff's worried about her. Don't make me worry about you, too, *Gladys*."

"Or what, *Abner*? You might do something to me? Is that it? You're always threatening, but you can't scare me." She gave him the cold shoulder as she went back to her spying.

He stared at her for several moments. He thought about the nosy female "detective." He thought about Burt and Cliff and everything they'd shared together over the years.

He *could* scare her. She was dead wrong about that one.

"I know," she whispered again, giving him the willies.

Darrell looked at the back of her fake-blond head. He

had a momentary glimmer of an image. Red running down
the back of her head, matting her hair, smearing down her
neck. A baseball bat would do the trick.

Darrell retraced his steps to the garage. The day was
comin', she surely was.

Chapter Fifteen

Daley was waiting for her when Mackenzie returned to the house, seated on the daybed in Mac's room, still dressed for serious business, but her expression had changed from militant to . . . something less so. It was like she'd unwound a bit. It reminded Mac of how uptight she must've been, nearly day in and day out, at least since she'd hired Mac. Now she looked different.

"I did it," she said, not breaking into berating Mackenzie, which was what Mackenzie had expected. "I told him we're getting a divorce."

"You did?" Mac stared at her.

"I did." Her brow furrowed. "Do you think I shouldn't have?"

"You should do whatever's right for you, Daley."

"Oh, for fuck's sake, say what you think. You've been telling me I should just get on with it, and now you're backing down?"

"Honestly, Daley, I can't help you. You've gotta figure this out on your own."

"Thanks a lot."

"You're welcome," said Mac, ignoring the sarcasm.

She buried her face into her hands and screamed into them, the sound still loud enough to carry down the hall. Mac looked toward the door, half expecting Leon to burst in and do something.

After a moment Daley lifted her blotched face from her palms and gazed up at Mac, half tearful, half angry. "At least I got the house. It's in the prenup that it's mine."

Mackenzie didn't say anything. Daley had an on-again, off-again relationship with the truth. She'd said before that the house had only been a promise from Leon. That it wasn't in the prenup as a gift to her.

"He's leaving tomorrow. I'm going to be . . . alone." Her chin started to wobble.

"Leaving . . . for good?"

She nodded.

"Do you know where he was last night?" asked Mackenzie.

"No! He says I have no right to ask now."

"I was just thinking you might want all the cards on the table."

Daley shook her head. "I know you're going to leave me, too. Would you stay through tomorrow? Sunday? Maybe into next week? I'll pay you. I just need a transition period. Leon . . ." Tears welled, and she looked utterly miserable. "Leon is *generous*," she wailed as if it were an epithet.

Mackenzie couldn't have said how she felt. Daley annoyed her and occasionally infuriated her, and the woman certainly didn't care a whit about Mac in any way that mattered; Mac was simply someone to lean on and use, if possible. And yet Mac did feel kind of sorry for her.

"Okay."

"You'll stay?"

"For a short while, but not as a bodyguard, if that's what it ever was. I need to be able to come and go without having to ask permission."

Daley nodded. "I guess I was never really afraid of Leon," she said in a tear-choked voice, and Mac could see what an effort it was for her to admit. Closer to the truth was that she'd simply wanted some kind of validation, preferably with Taft in order to make Leon jealous, maybe. Prove her worth. She'd settled for Mac because she was lonely and miserable. She'd never wanted Leon to leave, but he'd always had one foot out the door and she'd been scrambling to hang on to the marriage, no matter how she went about it.

An hour later Mac headed out to her apartment with her laptop for some R and R. At the door she looked back to see Leon was out in the hot tub by himself, a glass of wine beside him. He waved for her to come out and join him. Daley was in her room and Mac, after a moment's indecision, walked across the living room and slid open the glass door, but she stayed standing in the aperture—a neutral area, she felt.

"She can have her divorce," he said.

"I'm not sure that's what she really wants."

For a moment he looked totally serious. No lifted brow. No arch comments. "It's all shit, isn't t?" he said. To her questioning expression, he added with a trace of bitterness, "Life."

Mac considered him for a moment, thought about the last few days spent in the Carrera household. Everything had felt sort of aimless since the moment she arrived. "Ever thought about getting another job?"

"I sold my company so I could retire early," he said.

"I'm not sure that's working for you."

"You could join me in the hot tub and we could talk about it."

Reverting back to form. And here she'd thought they were having an actual meaningful conversation.

"Goodbye, Leon." She slid the door closed behind her and headed out.

In his smartly kept-up ranch home on Arcadia Street, Burt Deevers listened to the voice at the other end of the phone, his expression hardening with each syllable. "I'll take care of it," he ground out. When the voice went on and on, he clicked off his cell in frustration, cutting them off in midcomplaint.

He tossed the phone on the end table, got off his black leather couch, and walked over to the bar, pouring himself two fingers of scotch, then tossed in another splash. He took his glass to the couch and sank back down, reaching for the remote and switching on the paused VCR. He was watching a much-viewed, taped game of one of his own high school football games. He'd had five, count them *five*, quarterback sacks in that game. When he had problems heavy on his mind he pulled out the game and watched it. He had several copies and he'd put it on CD, too. His ex-wife had made disparaging remarks about the tape, one of the reasons for the divorce. "One game," she would say. "One game." To this day she reminded him he could have the game on streaming of some kind. She constantly let him know he was a technological dinosaur. He didn't really give a shit. He liked watching on tape, even though he'd been through his share of VCRs as well. Tamara just liked to needle him, and he hated her, too. They had only ever agreed on one thing. They both hated Victor Laidlaw more.

"Rot in hell," Burt muttered, thinking of the man. Meanwhile his mind clicked away, planning. Life was a game of moves. He'd plotted most of his moves and mostly they'd worked out. But there was a kink now. And that goddamn kink was making it impossible today to enjoy his success on the field.

Stopping the tape again, he got up and ejected it from the machine, carefully placing it within its cardboard sleeve, putting it back on the shelf.

He sat back down and drank the rest of his scotch. Thought about pouring himself another.

He reached for the phone again. Fucking cell phones. Sure, Tamara was right. He was a dinosaur. But the goddamn things were like trackers, recording your every move, pinging off cell phone towers. He had to remind people of that. There was no privacy in this world anymore. Everyone was a voyeur, everyone was in their neighbor's business. You had to be careful or you could get swept up in the bullshit. Not that he would, but others he knew weren't nearly so careful.

He placed a call to Cliff's cell and got Clarice. "Hello?" she said in that frightened way she had.

His fingers curled around the phone. As pleasantly as he could, he said, "You answering Cliff's phone now?"

"He's in the garage. He can't hear it ringing over the noise. I'll get him."

Her voice didn't exactly shake, but he could visualize her. The woman was going to rattle herself into an early grave. Some kind of palsy, Cliff said, but Burt wasn't convinced. It had sprung up this spring and he would bet it was emotional. He'd told Cliff she needed drugs to calm her down and Cliff had reluctantly agreed, but Burt didn't know if Clarice had taken any yet.

"Hey, oh," Cliff said when he answered. It was a signal to Burt that he wasn't alone. Well, he knew that, because his rickety wife had answered the phone, but he let it go.

"We need to meet," said Burt.

"I'm gonna be workin' on the backhoe," he said. "Goddamn Mariah won't give us a break on the playground."

"I don't care if you're meeting with the Queen of Sheba, we got some problems to work out."

"Okay."

"Come over to my place."

"Darrell gonna be there?"

"Calling him next."

"Okay," he said again.

Forty minutes later Cliff and Clarice, Darrell, Sandy, Abby and Dr. Andre, and Tamara convened at Burt's. He was too thrifty to offer them much beyond a soft drink or water, though Cliff gazed hungrily at his bottle of scotch. Fuck 'em. He didn't need to do anything more for them. They needed to do things for him.

Sandy Herdstrom complained, "I've barely had time to take a shower. It's been a long day already. Do you know what I've been—"

"This has got to stop," interrupted Abby. "We need to stop her."

"Well, if your fool son hadn't stolen those packages," Burt growled.

"Keep your damn mouth shut!" she flared.

Andre said, "Shut up, Abby. You haven't helped things."

She rounded on him with her can of Coke, and Burt thought she was going to hurl it at him. "Who takes him to the tutor? I do. Who takes him shopping to try and get him in something besides that filthy hoodie? I do. Who gives a shit what happens to him? Not his father. Not *you*."

"I was supposed to have him today," Andre snapped back. "You always make it so I can't."

"Fuck you," she snarled.

"Back at 'cha, bitch."

"Children," Burt ground out, losing what little patience he had. "Abby says we have a problem with that detective."

"She's talking to everybody. She thinks Alfie stole those packages," Abby declared.

"I don't like it," said Tamara, her mouth a thin line.

Burt looked at his ex. She'd kept herself trim. She'd always had that pretty face and it still held up, but she was untrustworthy. He hadn't wanted to invite her over, but she was a part of this.

"She thinks Alfie put the dog shit in the mailbox, too," Andre ground out, glaring pointedly at his wife.

"I couldn't have him blamed," she declared. "I had to do something. They think it's all one person and it clears Alfie."

Burt looked at Abby. She was of about the same height and size as her gangly son. Yes, she'd been able to disguise herself as Alfie, who'd taken the items off the Carreras' porch because . . . well, Burt wasn't exactly sure why. Just because he was a weird kid, mostly. But Abby, after concocting the story about his bike being stolen and Alfie too far away to be in two places at the same time, had then stuck the shit in the mailbox to cover for him.

What mothers will do for their chicks, Burt marveled. But then Abby had a surprisingly dark side he found very appealing, if she wasn't such a fucking nutjob.

A registered nurse at Glen Gen? He sure as hell didn't plan on ending up in her care, or Dr. Andre's, for that matter. They might be capable as all get-out, but he would never trust his health to them for any reason. Good thing he was healthy as a horse.

"She talked to Evvie," said Darrell. "Came by the house. Left before I could talk to her."

Clarice and Cliff shared a look and then Clarice glanced away, quivering like a goddam quaking aspen.

"What?" Burt demanded.

"She called us on the phone. Althea gave her the number," said Cliff.

"Fuck!" Burt clenched his fists. It was a conspiracy. He rounded on Darrell. "What did Evelyn say to her?"

"Nothin'," said Darrell.

"Why isn't Evelyn here?" Burt demanded.

"She didn't say nothin' to her. She won't." Darrell's calm certainty did a lot to bring Burt's blood pressure down, but he was still uneasy.

"Why isn't she here?" pressed Tamara.

"Because she's at home," Darrell practically spit at her.

Sandy Herdstrom cleared his throat. "I hope you're not suggesting we do something about this amateur detective."

Burt felt a stab of anger. Herdstrom liked to pretend he was above it all, but he had no qualms about going after what he wanted.

"Alfie needs to stop fucking stealing," Burt told Abby, who threw up her hands and looked around at the group for support.

"He has!" she declared. "It was all a misunderstanding anyway."

Andre spoke up. "Alfie thought Leon was fooling around with Abby."

"Not true," said Abby.

"And he likes Carol Martin," Andre went on. "She was

always nice to him. But she blames the Carreras for losing that house, and now they're in over their head in their renovation, and she whined to Alfie about it, and—"

"Jesus Christ. Just get him to stop," snapped Burt.

"He has!" Abby glared at Andre. "Why are you here? Where's Linda, by the way? She usually has you on a short leash."

"I'm on no one's leash," said Andre, to which Abby cackled.

Clarice said in a trembling voice, "I started this."

Everyone turned to look at her. Abby stared at her as if she were from outer space, then threw a glance back at Burt.

Cliff said angrily, "Shut up, Clarice. That medicine. I'm taking you back to the doctor."

Clarice's shaking intensified and she reached a hand back to search blindly for a chair. "God sees all," she murmured.

Tamara said, "You need serious help, Clarice, and it's not from God."

Burt looked at them all. Morons. Clarice always talking about God. Evelyn intimidating Darrell with her *I-know* doomsday line. She might as well accompany it with organ music. And Tamara? And Abby and Andre and Alfie? Morons.

Abby said, "I've explained to Alfie that he was wrong about Leon Carrera." She gave a short laugh. "We all know he's been chasing Mariah. Who knows why."

"Because she's young and beautiful," said Clarice.

"Mariah Copple is a broken record," Cliff answered swiftly, frowning at his wife.

Darrell warned, "She should stop causin' us all problems."

Burt shot him a look. In truth, he and Darrell felt the same way about interfering women, but outward misogyny wasn't going to help them with Abby and Clarice and Tamara in the room.

"What's her name again? The detective?" he asked.

"Mackenzie Laughlin," Herdstrom said succinctly. "Formerly of the River Glen PD."

"She's not really a detective," Abby put in. "Just playing at it."

"Nosy kitties get hurt," said Darrell, misquoting *Chinatown*.

"Not until I say so," Burt warned quietly. He'd learned that the softest voice could be the biggest threat.

And it worked, for the moment at least. They all agreed to be on their toes where Mackenzie Laughlin was concerned. The only disquieting final moment was when Sandy Herdstrom held back after the others were gone and said, "The bigger problem is Laughlin's current connection with Jesse Taft. He's the private investigator, and he's one of the reasons my day blew up today."

Burt knew of Taft's reputation from the drug bust that had taken place recently involving Best Homes. "She the girl who was working with him?"

"Yep."

"What happened today?" Burt asked, feeling his nerves tingle with growing concern.

Herdstrom shook his head. "A different case. But Taft's involvement with us is not healthy."

"Dangerous," agreed Burt.

Herdstrom nodded once. "I'm going to try to divert him."

"Are he and Laughlin lovers?" Burt's mind was already plotting again.

"Likely." He headed toward the door. "Keep the others in line."

"I will," said Burt.

As soon as everyone was gone, he went back to his seat on the couch and sat there for several hours, thinking.

Chapter Sixteen

In the early evening Taft finally called Mac.

"There you are." she greeted him, trying not to sound too much like a worried parent. It had been hours and hours since his first call. "You called me early today and then . . . ghosted me?"

"I couldn't call till now. Riskin is dead. Found hanging from a pipe in a storage unit."

"Oh . . .Taft . . ." Mac murmured in shock.

"It's been a hell of a day with Portland PD. A lot of questions. You know how it goes."

Yes, she did. Suspicious death. Ex-cop on the scene. He was exactly right. A lot of questions.

He said, "I called this morning because I wanted to ask you about Sandy Herdstrom. He was at that HOA meeting you went to?"

"Uh-huh."

"He's working for Multnomah County as an assistant ME now. My experience with him is that he's influenced by people with money. He's going to rule this a suicide and it's a homicide."

She was still processing Taft's CI's death, whereas he'd

had hours and hours to think over the events of the day. "What are you saying? You think Herdstrom would deliberately misrepresent the cause of death?"

"That's exactly what I'm saying." He sounded grim.

"What happened? How did you find out?"

"Deena from the Rosewood Court called me. She was the one who discovered his body. . . ."

From there he went on to tell her about going to the storage shed and finding Riskin. Deena was apparently a kind of office girl and maybe friend of Riskin's who'd placed the call to 911. But Taft was involved, and so the rest of the day he had been with the Portland PD, who wanted to know exactly what his relationship with the CI had been, what had gone down between them, what they were working on together. Taft had carefully tiptoed around sensitive information, but he'd been vocal about who he thought was responsible: Keith Silva. Silva had killed Riskin. Taft told them he could only assume it was because something Riskin had learned about him. Like what? they'd pressed, but Taft had honestly been unable to tell them.

"Half of them believed me, half of them didn't," Taft wound up. He had friends on the Portland PD, but there were those who felt he'd gone to the dark side when he'd connected with Mitch Mangella . . . and they weren't entirely wrong.

"Are you maybe borrowing trouble?" Mac had to ask. "You don't know which way Herdstrom is going to rule."

"I know," he said.

"Okay."

"His history bears it out. If there's any question, he leans toward keeping things from being messy for people with influence. Riskin's death falls in that category. He told me he had information on the widow, who happens to be a friend of the Mangellas. Herdstrom will make it a suicide, but Jimmy Riskin would never kill himself. Not who he was."

Taft was clearly gearing up for a battle. Maybe it was his way of dealing with the man's death.

"Be careful around Herdstrom," warned Taft.

"I doubt I'll see him again, unless he's at the HOA board meeting on Monday. I'm going to crash that, I think. Did you . . . contact LeeAnn Laidlaw?" She hated to ask, considering everything he'd been through, but he answered in the affirmative.

"She'll see us tomorrow at two. I'll meet you there?" asked Taft.

"Sure."

There was silence on the phone after that. Mac almost asked if she could come over, but managed to keep her mouth shut. She'd spent a lot of time staying with him while he recovered from his bullet wound. But now things were different. A wall had gone up of Taft's making.

"I've got some things to go over with you," he finally said, hesitant.

"Yeah?" Mac's antennae rose.

"Riskin left me a copy of *1984*."

"The book? Oh! What does it mean?"

"Yeah, well, I haven't had time to really examine it. Jesus. Riskin and his puzzles. . . ." He made a noise of frustration. "What I really want to do is find Silva and have it out with him."

"But now Portland PD has him in their sights," she warned. Taft was a grown man who did not need Mac to tell him the obvious, but she sure as hell didn't want him to get in trouble.

"They're not taking my word for it. Silva and I have unfinished business."

"Well, I'll give you the advice you just gave me. Be careful," she warned.

"I will." Another pause, and then, as if belatedly realizing he'd been locked onto his own issues, he roused himself enough to ask, "How was last night?"

"Last night . . ." she mused. "Oh, the hot tub party. Fine. Not as exciting as you might think. There was a bikini top thrown out while I was there, and the whole event was spied on by the Jacobys. And . . . Daley told Leon she wants the divorce, so he's apparently moving out, which means I'm out of a job."

"And disappointed that it's over," Taft said with a faint return of his old humor.

"Devastated."

"Daley called me today, but I couldn't get back to her either."

"Daley called?"

"Probably because your bodyguarding stint is over. I'll check back with her now, and I'll see you tomorrow at LeeAnn's."

"Tomorrow," she agreed as he clicked off and she slowly hung up.

Daley called Taft?

Bullshit it was about Mac's job. Mac had a mental image of Daley inviting Taft over to her hot tub now that Leon had moved out.

"Ugh."

Again she had to force herself not to race over to Taft's . . . and what? Stake her claim? Ridiculous.

The night stretched ahead of her with nothing to do. She pulled up her laptop and tried to engage herself by turning

back to the Faraday Foundation. She had a call in to Joseph
Mertz, the director, who had not deigned to call her back.
She placed another call and got the same voice mail, and
left a slightly acerbic second request. She was bugged.
Bugged at Daley and bugged at herself. She needed to
go back to the Carreras'. She'd promised. But she didn't
want to spend the evening with Daley, alone or with Leon,
if he was still around at some level. She had to do something else.

She was in the process of coming up with what that
"something else" might be when Mom called, complaining
she hadn't seen her for a while and asking her to come over
for dinner. Mac instantly agreed, and though it would mean
trying to parry her mother's questions about what she was
doing with her life, it was better than sharing a meal with
Daley and wondering if she was moving on to Taft, which
seemed to be her plan from the beginning.

Taft hung up from his call with Daley and started his
engine. He'd been sitting in the Rubicon for over an hour,
parked on the side of the littered and empty lot behind the
River Glen Grill, watching the apartments above. Silva's
brown Dodge Charger was parked in the underground lot.
Taft had checked before he started his surveillance. But
nothing much had happened that he could see in Anna
DeMarcos's apartment. The blinds were down, light spilling
out around the edges.

He was coldly angry and fighting himself from confronting Silva. But a confrontation wasn't going to work.
It never worked with a guy like him. He had to remind
himself that no matter how good it might feel to pummel
the shit out of him, it wasn't going to help. Physical violence

wasn't generally Taft's way, but man, he wanted it bad now. Could taste it.

And you'd go to jail . . .

"I know," he ground out, not needing to hear Helene or his conscience or anyone telling him what he already knew perfectly well.

With an effort, he pulled his mind off Silva and back to the call he'd just finished with Daley. He still didn't know quite what she wanted; it appeared mainly to waver between tears and anger over her disintegrating relationship with Leon. Throughout the short conversation she'd dropped hints about coming over to his place, even though he told her he wasn't there. Maybe she didn't believe him. Whatever the case, he'd eased her off the phone as soon as he could.

He rolled down his window, inhaling the cooling night air as his mind tripped back to the image of Riskin's limp body hanging from the overhead pipe. He couldn't stop it. Wouldn't be able to until he could accept it. But he didn't want to anyway because he wanted to keep his anger stoked hot.

But under his fury he felt the weariness waiting for him. Riskin's death and the hours of interrogation and suspicion by hard-eyed policemen who knew his past and resented him for it had taken their toll.

The little slivers of light around the blinds flickered out. Were Silva and the widow making it an early night? He waited to see if the Charger would appear up the ramp from the parking lot, ready to switch on his ignition, but nothing happened. Looked like they were in for the night.

He unclenched his jaw. Hadn't realized how tense he'd been, ready to take on Riskin's killer. And Riskin wasn't the only one. Silva had killed his partner in plain sight, claiming it was an accident, and he'd gotten away with it. And then hooked up with that partner's widow.

I'm going to bring you down, you murdering sack of shit.

Taft clicked on his cell phone and put in a call to Mangella. His expression set as the call went straight to voice mail. Mangella didn't want to hear from him. Very likely because he knew Taft wanted to discuss his new right-hand man and it wouldn't be a pleasant conversation. At the beep, he said distinctly, "Tell Silva I want to talk to him. Sooner rather than later." And then he clicked off.

He tossed the phone onto the passenger seat, then hit the button to the glove box for the copy of *1984*. Would the book be more secure back in the safe? Yep. Sure would. But he wanted it with him.

Now he turned the dog-eared copy over in his hands. What was Riskin trying to tell him? The paperback had been printed decades earlier and showed its wear, the pages yellowed and fragile. There was a cash receipt for a sandwich and a beer tucked between the pages, used as a bookmark. Was that significant? Taft took out the receipt and looked it over, then examined the pages it had been stuck between, thirty-seven and thirty-eight. There was nothing he could see in the text that meant anything to him. He replaced the receipt and then riffled through the book. Several of its center pages were tightly stuck together. Taft had noticed that earlier and now gently pulled them apart. He'd half hoped, half expected something to fall out. Some miracle bit of information, a slim key, an explanatory note, *something*, but there was nothing there. He very slowly riffled through the yellowed pages again to no success.

The book was clearly a message; he just didn't know what it was. He'd held it back from the police, but had told them Silva had been looking for Riskin the same day as Taft was. Deena had said the same and given them the business card Silva left with her. The cops had jumped all over Taft, demanding to know what he was doing at Riskin's, even though they knew Riskin sometimes worked for him. They could sense he was keeping back something and had tried to break Deena, too, but she was made of sterner stuff than she looked and didn't give away anything she and Taft had discussed before the law arrived. When Taft was finally released he'd called her and thanked her for her discretion; she'd been let out a lot earlier than he was. She said she was going to be looking for another job; the motor court's owner had learned about her bunking in the back. Taft said if he found out anything, he'd let her know, a kind of unspoken quid pro quo in advance between them; Taft would keep her informed about Riskin and she might be able to do some extracurricular cyber work for him someday.

He waited for another half hour, then drove home. Mackenzie came to mind. He'd given up trying to protect her. That hadn't worked for either of them, but it didn't mean he wasn't worried about her. Mangella's chilling comments about her were still in his head. She was in the man's sights because of Taft. That was a fact.

It was better that she stuck with the goings-on at the Villages than get mired in his affairs with Silva. Safer. Except for the nagging worry that was Sandy Herdstrom, onetime county ME, now, in his twilight years, supposedly merely an assistant within the whole body, but still there. The guy had years of experience and clout and friends. How close was he to the members of the old guard? He'd lived there a long time, as long as they had; Taft had checked. But did it matter?

Taft pulled into his parking spot. He slipped the paperback in his jacket pocket again, headed into his condo, and sank onto the couch, his mind circling back to Riskin. There was a chance the ME would rule Riskin's death a homicide. Taft had been clear that he felt it was to the Portland PD. But if the ME said it was suicide, it was suicide, and Taft had a really strong sense that was the way this was going. He knew Herdstrom. But he also knew Riskin, and he was not suicidal. He valued his own skin. Wouldn't take his own life for any reason.

Still, the more likely scenario was that Herdstrom would rule Riskin's death a suicide. Sweep it under the rug. Forgo a homicide investigation that might look bad for people in power. The Mitch Mangellas and Keith Silvas who always had something to hide. The people Riskin was always seeking information on.

Taft took the copy of *1984* from his pocket, gazing at it hard, willing it to tell him what secrets it held. It stayed stubbornly silent. Was its age somehow important? Were the numbers what it was all about?

No *mazda* came to him just from holding it. He plucked out the receipt and turned it over again. Riskin did everything by design, so it had to have meaning of some sort. It was a receipt for a turkey sandwich, a bottle of water, and a side salad from a place called Cool Dawn. Pretty healthy for the likes of Riskin, but maybe he'd turned over a new leaf. Or maybe the receipt wasn't his.

After a few minutes he gave up and went into the kitchen for a beer. Whatever its secret was, he didn't need to be told it was what had gotten Riskin killed.

* **

Clarice feigned sleep next to her husband, who was on his back and snoring. She'd put one of her pills in his scotch, just to make sure he was dead out. By the sound of it, a locomotive could crash into their house and he wouldn't know.

Their bedroom was dark, illuminated only by a nightlight in the bathroom that filtered in a faint light green glow.

She slipped out of bed into the bathroom. Quietly, as silently as she could, just in case he was somehow faking it, she opened the medicine cabinet. He wasn't generally that crafty, but he'd surprised her once or twice, so she wasn't taking any chances. She pulled out her bottle of pills. Cliff had been the one to get her the prescriptions. He was the one who'd taken her to doctor after doctor, none of whom could diagnose what was wrong with her, but they could certainly prescribe sleeping aids, muscle relaxants, mood enhancers. For Cliff's benefit, she pretended to take them, but in actuality, she'd hidden them in plain sight.

Now she carefully carried the bottle with her into the hall, closing the bedroom door behind her. Cliff's snoring stuttered a little and Clarice froze, clutching the pill bottle to her chest. Had she been wrong? Had he somehow known what she was doing?

But then the snoring resumed, a loud sawing.

She went into the kitchen. She had a cell phone she never used tucked in a drawer. She'd never seen a reason for it. The landline was good enough, but she kept the cell charged and available for when "that day" came. Cliff only remembered it when he saw the monthly bill come in, but

Clarice had been hiding that evidence as well for a long time. He thought because of her illness that she couldn't do even the most basic things. It was difficult, for sure. Maddening and exasperating, but it was God's will, God's punishment, and she was more than willing to accept whatever He offered.

And she could do a lot more than Cliff knew.

Clutching the phone and the pills, she opened the back door and walked outside. It was a dark, still faintly warm evening. Best day of the year so far, but the sun had set hours earlier. It was after midnight.

She started walking. It wasn't that far to her destination. The trembling and quaking made it a battle to keep her limbs moving, but Clarice's determination was one of her greatest assets. It was, however, that very determination that had gotten her into this mess.

But it was what was going to get her out of it, too.

She took the pills dry. Choking a little as she did. Looking up at the stars. When she was certain she'd taken enough, she pulled out her phone.

And called the number Althea had given her for Mackenzie Laughlin.

Bzzzzz. Bzzzzz. Bzzzzz.

Mac threw an arm toward the nightstand and the phone she'd set on Vibrate. The damn thing was rattling around, about to throw itself off the edge like a cliff diver. What the hell time was it?

She got the phone in hand and squinted at it: 12:45? She didn't recognize the number, though it seemed slightly familiar. Who . . . ?

"Hello," she answered carefully.

"Hi, Mackenzie Laughlin. It's Clarice Fenwick."

The voice was low and careful. Mackenzie blinked in the darkness. "Hello, Clarice."

"I killed Victor Laidlaw. It's my fault he's dead. It's not my fault now, but I still have to make a full confession to God. I'm going to the park."

Mackenzie was scrambling out of bed, heart pounding, grabbing for her clothes in the dark. "The park?"

"I don't need a church. God is in nature, too."

She found the bedside lamp switch and threw the room into light. "How . . . how did you kill Victor?"

"I'll tell you at the park. I would like a witness." She clicked off.

"Shit," Mackenzie muttered. She dressed as fast as she possibly could, grabbing up her phone and sneakers and tiptoeing out the front door.

They will see you on Ring.

Too damn bad. She seesawed back and forth about calling Taft. It had been a harrowing day for him. He'd been distracted and it was no wonder why. But . . . Clarice had just confessed to killing Victor, so maybe Tobias was *right*?

She punched in his number.

"Mackenzie," he answered, sounding wide awake.

"Clarice Fenwick says she killed Victor Laidlaw. I'm meeting her at the Villages park right now. She says she needs a witness to her confession."

He took a moment, then said, "I'll be right there."

Mac hung up and realized Clarice Fenwick's voice had been clear and calm. No shaking at all. She had never met the woman, but from all accounts, that was not the way she presented.

* * *

Taft drove rapidly through the dark night. He'd been awake when Mackenzie called, still reviewing the day. He'd had an unexpected visit from Daley, who'd come knocking on his door at around seven as he was just finishing up a DoorDash plate of spaghetti, and he'd had a heck of a time getting her to leave. Apparently he hadn't been as successful as he'd thought at getting her off the phone and onto something else. She went right back to railing about Leon, with some complaints about Mackenzie sprinkled in as well. She abruptly admitted she liked Mackenzie, then broke down in tears about Leon, then asked if she could spend the night with Taft. He'd ended up putting his arm over her shoulder and guiding her out the door and back to her Audi. At her car she'd suddenly thrown herself into his arms, her whole body shaking with emotion.

"We never took things far enough," she whispered in his ear.

His first thought was, *Oh, Lord,* and as kindly as he could, he said, "It's better we didn't."

"I don't know if I feel that way."

She then placed both hands on his face and pulled him in to a long kiss, pressing her lips to his, the faint taste of her tears on his tongue. Taft felt exposed and his mind was darting around, wondering who was watching, but he didn't fight the kiss. He just let it play out rather than pull away and hurt her feelings. Daley finally recognized that he wasn't really participating and pushed herself away from him.

He'd been afraid she would lambast him, based on how volatile her feelings were these days, but she'd just smiled crookedly and said, "So, we're friends?"

He'd nodded, relieved, at the same time feeling a strange

sense of déjà vu. Daley looked different to him yet felt more familiar, and he was trying to figure out why when she said sadly, "Goodbye, Jesse," climbed in her Audi, and left.

He'd been alone and up watching mindless TV in an effort to slow down his mind when Mac's call came in, a welcome distraction. He'd headed straight for the Villages and was now driving past the welcoming sign. He drove to the east side of the park, by the gazebo, then remote locked the Jeep, the small beep sounding inordinately loud in the quiet night as he strode rapidly past the hedge and toward the playground.

A soft breeze was blowing and he could just make out the skeletal swing set, black lines against a dark background.

There was no one there.

He stopped and listened, senses on alert. Was this some kind of trap?

Then he heard voices down one of the A streets and he hurried toward them, glad for the illumination of a streetlamp ahead. The park, under construction, was a black hole.

"Clarice! Clarice!" Mackenzie's voice. Urgent.

Taft broke into a run and came into the middle of a street where Mac appeared to be fighting with another woman, except the other woman was flailing and falling. Taft lunged forward and grabbed Clarice, keeping her from throwing herself from Mac's arms.

"Thank God," said Mac.

"God knows what I did," Clarice cried, collapsing into Taft's arms as Mac staggered backward. She didn't seem to care that he was a complete stranger.

Taft expected lights to burst on inside one or more of the houses.

"She ran from me," explained Mac. "She was at the swing set and then she ran."

Clarice was leaning into Taft, crying. "I killed him," she said, her voice a mumble against his shirt.

"Think you could walk back to the park if I help you?" he asked her quietly.

She hung her head, then nodded, and the three of them slowly made their way to the swing set. Clarice stiffened as they drew nearer. "The devil's here in the dark," she whispered.

"God is in the park," Mackenzie argued sternly, making Taft's head snap around. But then Clarice seemed to listen to her, and after a moment she heaved a long sigh.

"What happened?" Taft asked Clarice. She was still leaning into him with half her weight. It was the second time in hours that he'd been a woman's emotional support.

"He took da land from us. And they let him. He slept with Tamara and Evelyn and . . . *me*. But they let him have da land, even though id was s'posed to be fur ever-one. I wanned him to die. . . ."

Taft felt her body start to melt against him. "Clarice?" he said sharply.

"Clarice?" asked Mac. "You okay?"

"Mr. Faraday gave da land to us and Vic-der took it!"

"The Faraday Foundation?" Taft questioned, even as he had to tighten his grip on her boneless body.

"I wuz a friend."

"A Friend of Faraday?" It was Mac's turn to query her.

"I wanned him to die," she repeated.

"You're overdosing," said Taft. "What did you take?"

She choked out a laugh.

"We need to call 9-1-1," said Mac urgently, pulling out her phone.

"Might be faster to drive her. My Jeep's there." He jerked his head in the direction of the gazebo.

Mac grabbed her other side without being told and slung Clarice's arm over her shoulder. The two of them racewalked her to the Rubicon with Clarice vainly trying to help by putting one foot out before it was dragged back by their speed, then another. They got her buckled into the passenger side of the Jeep before she started thrashing about. "Da park. Confess! *Confess!*"

"We're taking you to Glen Gen," said Taft as he jumped behind the wheel and Mac threw open the door to the back seat.

"Stop it, Clarice!" Mac declared.

Taft reversed, with Clarice scrabbling for the seat belt buckle. "Noooo," she cried as a bottle, rattling from something inside, tried to escape her half-zipped pants pocket.

"What did you take?" Taft demanded again, speeding out of the development and down the road to River Glen General.

"No hospidddle. No hospiddle. I wan to see God . . ."

"Jesus," expelled Mac.

Taft drove with concentration. He sped through River Glen toward the hospital and whipped into the Emergency Room lane. Mac leaped out of the Jeep as he was still coming to a stop. She was yanking open Clarice's door as Taft came around to help her. "I'll get help," he said, not waiting for the hospital staff to recognize there was an emergency.

"She's too quiet now," said Mac.

He met two orderlies with a gurney just inside the door and led them back out. Mac got hold of the bottle of pills and handed it over, saying she had no idea how many she'd taken. Clarice was a limp rag, her eyes open and staring. Whatever she was seeing, it wasn't pleasant.

She was loaded onto the gurney before she suddenly woke, as if from a coma. "I tole them. I tole them! I starded it!" Then she collapsed back, murmuring, "Ol bones, ol bones . . ."

They rushed her into the ER and Taft and Mac followed. They stood together as Clarice was wheeled through the hydraulic doors that opened into the ER examining cubicles.

"She wanted him to die, but she really believes she killed Victor Laidlaw?" questioned Mac.

"She seems to think she caused his heart attack," said Taft.

Mac, whose gaze had been focused reflectively on the doors that had closed behind Clarice, now looked at him. "She thinks because she was a Friend of Faraday and they pressured him, sued him, put strain on his heart, that she killed him."

"That seems to be what she's saying."

"And she wants to meet God because of it?" Mac's expression was disbelieving.

He nodded.

"And it took her fifteen years to need to confess? That's bullshit."

"Perception is everything," said Taft. "Do you know why she called you?"

"That's the question I've been asking myself. Why me? She said she wanted a witness, but I've never met her before. I called her, but Cliff wouldn't let me talk to her."

"Maybe she feels she can only trust a stranger," said Taft.

A doctor came back through the slowly opening doors

and walked up to them, carrying a cell phone. "Are you related to Mrs. Fenwick?"

"No. Is that her phone?" asked Mac. She'd thought she didn't own one. At the doctor's nod, she said, "I know her husband, Cliff Fenwick, lives in the Villages. I'll call him," she said, checking through her own phone's Contact List, pressing the numbers and then placing the phone to her ear.

"You have Cliff's number?" asked Taft as Mac waited for him to answer.

"Their landline. Courtesy of Althea Gresham."

The phone rang on and on. Mac was about to hang up when a groggy male voice finally said, "Hello?"

"Cliff, this is Mackenzie Laughlin. Your wife is at River Glen General, being treated for an overdose of . . . pills."

"What?" he asked.

She flicked a look at the doctor and added, "Check in with Emergency, Dr. . . . ?"

"McClain," the young doctor said.

"McClain. He has her phone."

"*What?* What did you do to her?" Cliff practically shrieked.

"Got her to the hospital," Mac snapped back at him and hung up.

She and Taft left the hospital, heading to his Jeep, and he asked, "Where's the RAV?"

"At the Carreras'. I walked to the park."

"What happened when you got there?" Taft asked, now that they had a moment to talk.

"Clarice was waiting for me near the swings, and she just freaked out. I guess it was too dark. I think I scared her when I came toward her because she jumped up and started kind of running away as best she could. She has trouble. Maybe to do with her shaking. I don't know. I caught her on the street and she was saying over and over again that she needed to confess. I tried to get her to move so we didn't wake anyone, and she started fighting me, and that's when you came." Mac got in the passenger seat and Taft started the engine. "She kept saying it was her fault. That she killed him."

Taft pulled away from the lot, heading back toward the Carreras'.

"'I tole them,'" she quoted, looking out the window reflectively. Then, "I wonder who she told, what she thinks she started."

Taft pulled to a stop behind Mac's SUV. "Somehow she had your name," he said soberly. He had that same bad feeling that had plagued him since Mangella had subtly threatened her.

"What time is it?" Mac looked at her phone and groaned. "Glad we're not seeing LeeAnn until two."

"Get some sleep," he advised.

"Back at 'cha. It's been a long day." She threw him a smile and then climbed out of the Jeep and headed up the walk to the Carreras' front door. He waited until he saw a faint light from the southern wing of the house before he drove back to his place.

When he placed the key in the lock, his front door opened of its own accord.

Heart pounding, he pushed it open hard. Flicked on the light. He'd taken his gun with him, but it was still locked in the glove box. Now he wished he had it.

He listened, but there was no sound. He slipped into the kitchen and grabbed a bottle of wine by the neck. Adrenaline was pumping through his veins. He almost hoped for the confrontation. *Come on, you asshole. . . .*

From the kitchen he moved toward the bedrooms and bath, the bottle lofted like a club.

But there was no need to use it. The place was empty, though the top drawer to his desk was fully closed, something he never did because it sometimes stuck. Someone had opened and closed it.

He glanced at his wall safe. Unbreached. Just to convince himself, he pressed the numbers and opened it. Nothing was disturbed.

He placed the book inside and pressed the numbers to lock it.

It was a four-digit safe. He looked at the numbers from zero to nine and thought about the ones he'd just entered. A random four he used occasionally. Like one, nine, eight, four. . .

The code for a wall safe? The code for access to . . . a combination lock? Nineteen, eight, four? Something . . . but where?

He pressed the digits for the safe once more and pulled out the book, flipping to the receipt. Where was this Cool Dawn sandwich shop? If there'd been an address, it was ripped off. The printed writing was faded.

"Oh, shit," he muttered, mad at himself for taking so long to see the answer.

Cool *Down*.

Wasn't that the name of the juice bar at some Good Livin' health clubs? He should know. He'd signed up for a trial membership on his last case, though he'd only used it to get inside the facility. Riskin had left other clues as well. The exercise equipment scattered among the remnants of his belongings. He just didn't seem like the kind of guy who would get into working out. Cool Down *was* the name of the juice bar/café. They were only in the largest of the Good Livin facilities, but he'd seen the name on flyers for the clubs

Looked like it was time to renew his membership.

Burt's cell phone rang and he rolled over and snatched it up in annoyance. Fucking Cliff. Fucking three a.m.

"What?" he demanded.

"Clarice is in the hospital. She overdosed. She was with Mackenzie Laughlin! And she has a *secret* cell phone!"

Burt's eyes popped open. "You'd better be kidding."

Cliff went into a burbling monologue of fear about all the pills Clarice had taken and how Laughlin had called him and told him she'd been the one to get Clarice to Glen Gen, and how they'd pumped her stomach, but it was touch and go because Clarice was unconscious and they didn't know if she'd make it or not.

Burt listened in cold fury. He told Cliff to calm down and call him if there was any change. Otherwise they would talk in the morning.

He clicked off. Just kept himself from throwing the phone across the room.

He prayed to God the bitch died.

And what *the fuck* was he going to do about Mackenzie Laughlin?

Chapter Seventeen

Sunday dawned without a cloud in the sky. Summer was officially here, Cooper thought, looking through the curtained front window. He was supremely uncomfortable after a night on the couch, though he'd insisted on staying downstairs. He had a dull headache and his casted leg, though anesthetized with painkillers, was a nuisance. The couch was well-loved and sagged a bit in the middle, but he hadn't wanted to find a way to wrangle himself upstairs and, also, he hadn't wanted to bother Jamie.

Worst of all, however, was his dulled mind. Throughout the night his brain had circled and circled and short-circuited when it came to the accident. He could almost remember the crash . . . almost. Or maybe that was a phantom thought because he'd been told what had happened.

He could recall being at the station, sitting at his desk, but for the life of him, he couldn't remember what he'd been working on.

Verbena was coming over today and some of that would be clarified, thank God.

His partner was fully aware of his cases and was

working on them as well, so everything was going to be fine.

So why did he feel so anxious and uncertain?

"Drugs," he said aloud. They messed with your mind. He could hardly wait to be free of them and this damn infirmity. Maybe then he could get his brain to recall the events right before the crash.

He'd managed a trip to the bathroom and had just returned to the couch when Jamie came downstairs, dressed and ready for the day. "You're up early," he observed. Normally his fiancée liked to relax on the weekends, and sure, this one was different, but he didn't want her changing her routine just to take care of him.

"Couldn't sleep," she said. "How're you doing?"

He shrugged. "More pissed off than anything today. What time is Verbena getting here?"

"Afternoon. She said she was going to Mass."

Cooper grunted. Elena Verbena was a practicing Catholic and he sometimes forgot that she was religious about going to church, so to speak. She was such a hard-ass that whenever he stumbled upon this aspect of her character he was mildly surprised.

"I'm making breakfast," Jamie said, her voice floating from the kitchen. "What do you want? Eggs or eggs?"

"How about eggs?" he called back.

"Good choice."

He lay back down and closed his eyes for a moment. But then his head was filled with frustrating fragments of memory that had nothing to do with the accident. He believed his car had been sabotaged. He believed it was because someone knew it was his favorite city ride. Someone had wanted him injured or possibly dead. He had no proof of any of it, but he was convinced that was the truth of it.

He was just finishing up the meal—which had turned out to be eggs, bacon, waffles, maple syrup, and coffee, more than he could currently do justice to—when Harley came into the kitchen and snatched a piece of toast, then one of bacon. "Ta!" she'd said to Jamie, then, "I'm on at Ridge Pointe today."

"On Sunday?" Jamie asked in surprise.

"Yeah, I added on a day or two. Bolstering the old college fund."

Cooper's stepdaughter had taken a summer job at a coffee shop, but Harley liked working in food service at Emma's independent and assisted living complex. She got a kick out of the mostly elderly people who lived there.

"Emma told me the cat went into a room two days ago and slept on another woman's bed with her. Wonder if she's dead now," said Harley.

"Ghoulish," said Jamie, making a face.

"Nah, it's just the flip side of life. You see it a little closer at Ridge Pointe, that's all. Later, loves!"

Jamie watched her head toward the back door and then turned to Cooper. "Have I failed her somewhere?"

"Probably."

She slid him a look. "You're getting better."

"Not fast enough. I have something I want to say. Much as I appreciate the pants, I think maybe some sweatpants. I could wear shorts, but I don't want the catcalls at the station."

Her brows lifted. "You think you're going back to the station?"

"Well, maybe not today or tomorrow. But later this week. Yes."

She regarded him seriously, some of the lightness of her expression seeping away. "I don't want you going back until they know what happened to that car."

"That's why Verbena's coming over."

"Nobody has any answers yet."

He reached for her hand and she slipped her fingers into the warmth of his. "We're going to figure out what happened."

"It makes me crazy to think this was done to you on purpose." He heard the catch in her voice.

"Ah, stop," he whispered as she came over and laid her cheek on top of his crown. He could feel her body shuddering. Was this about the engagement? "What's wrong?" he asked, though it took a lot to ask it aloud.

"I love you," she said.

"I love you, too." He pulled her back around so he could look at her directly. She looked anxious and miserable. "Do you . . . not want to get married?"

"No, I want to get married," she answered swiftly. "Definitely."

"But . . . ?"

She took a breath, held it, then released it on a long sigh, turning her gaze away from him, out through the front window. "I went to the doctor. I sort of knew you were going to pop the question, that we were heading that way, and I made an appointment to see if I could get pregnant. We talked about that," she reminded him.

"I know." He felt a buzz of fear go through him. "You all right?"

"Yes, yes. Oh, yes. Fine . . . for someone who's going to lose their uterus. It's been on the way out for years," she said with a crooked smile. "I know you wanted children. I want another with you too. I want it really, really badly.

It was so easy with Harley, but she's seventeen, and now, even if it could happen, I would be labeled a geriatric pregnancy, which would be fine, but it's not going to happen." Tears reached her eyes and she tried to blink them away.

"I don't care," he said.

"Don't be noble. You care. I know you do."

"I don't. I'm just so relieved you're okay. That's all that matters."

She dropped his hand to swipe angrily at the tears.

"All I want is you, Jamie."

"I've been so scared to tell you. I kept hoping it wasn't true. Getting other opinions. I just so wanted to have a baby with you."

"We've got Harley and Marissa," he reminded her.

"They're practically adults."

"So, we just have to learn to stand just being with each other."

She gave him a sideways look. "You seriously are okay with this?"

"Yes."

"I know you love your stepdaughter, but if you want your own, if that's important, then—"

"Jamie, I just want you."

"Oh, cripes. You're really going to make me cry." She shook her head and half laughed.

"C'mere." He pulled her carefully toward him.

"I'll try to stand you, if you can stand me," she said, her voice muffled against his chest.

"We're going to do fine," he told her.

She didn't answer, but he could feel the rapid beating of her heart, the trembling of her body. It killed him that she'd taken this so to heart. Did he want a child? Yes. Would it matter if they couldn't have one together? No.

She lifted her head and drew a breath. "Okay, I gotta get myself together. I'm not going to be crying in front of your partner. She almost scares me."

"She scares me a lot. She's a misogynist."

"Don't think you're really using that term correctly," said Jamie as she headed toward the stairs and her upstairs bathroom to scrub away the traces of her tears.

"She's a man-hater."

"Don't think that's right either. But she is scary."

"I love you," he yelled after her.

"I love you, too. Cooper Haynes And I'm very, very glad you're alive."

Mac arrived at the Laidlaw house just as Taft's black Rubicon rounded the corner. She'd been lucky not to wake Daley both before and after her late, late night with Taft, but Daley had seen fit to come visit her early this morning. Mac moaned, "Go away!" and jammed a pillow over her head.

Daley demanded, "Were you with Jesse last night?"

When Mac didn't answer, Daley declared, "You were!"

Mac pulled the pillow away long enough to say, "We took Clarice Fenwick to Glen Gen. She was overdosing."

"Clarice?"

"Yes."

"You and Jesse? How does he know Clarice?"

Mac was forced to give her a quick rundown of her midnight adventures, to which Daley said, "You called him to help you," as if that was the most remarkable part of the evening. She didn't ask anything about Clarice, anything about how she was doing, which told Mackenzie everything she needed to know about where Daley's interest lay concerning Taft.

"Yes, I called him. And I haven't gotten much sleep, so if you could give me a few more hours?" Mac replaced the pillow and even so could hear Daley stomp out of the room.

Mac tried to fall back to sleep, but she mostly dozed for an hour or two more before hauling herself out of bed and calling the hospital to find out about Clarice, where she was told the family—meaning Cliff—had requested no information be given out. Mac took that to mean Clarice was still alive.

Now, though, as she climbed out of the RAV, she could feel the effects of a short night in her decreased energy and an ache at the back of her skull. She wanted to slap herself awake but just inhaled a gulp of warm air as Taft pulled up behind her and parked. She joined him at the walkway to LeeAnn's front door and they headed in together, with Taft looking back several times, examining the road.

"Something wrong?" she asked.

"No."

"You think you're being followed?"

He hesitated before admitting, "Possibly."

His words made her glance down the street as well, an automatic reaction, but the whole neighborhood was quiet apart from the rustling of the line of maples from a soft breeze.

"Did something happen?" she asked.

Taft rang the bell, and before LeeAnn Laidlaw could reach her front door, he told her his condo had been broken into while he and Mac had been helping Clarice, and that he believed it was Keith Silva. "There's also something else, but I'll fill you in later," he added.

Mac was still processing that when LeeAnn opened her door, standing back to allow them into the entry. With the events of last night fresh in her mind, and now Taft's break-in, she was afraid she would have a hard time keeping her mind on the meeting. She did her best to clear her mind as LeeAnn again led them back to the great room off the kitchen, and they chose the same chairs they'd had before, as if choreographed.

LeeAnn was dressed in tight jeans and an oversize pink sweater that made her look petite and feminine. Mackenzie had taken her bag from the Carreras' and intended on going to her apartment directly afterward and doing her laundry and generally having some time to herself to gather her thoughts before returning. Leon was supposedly leaving, but if that was today, or tomorrow, or sometime in the near future, Mac had no idea. He wasn't around when she finally got dressed and ready to go.

LeeAnn said, "I know what you want, but I don't want Judy and the rest of them knowing he hasn't contacted me," she said, clasping her hands together. She looked more stubborn than distraught.

"We'd like to interview Judy directly," said Taft.

"That's just what I don't want," she declared.

Mac shook off the cobwebs with an effort. She said, "Nolan Redfield seems to think Tobias is still on a business trip and that he is in contact with Judy."

"Is he? It would be just like him to forget about me," she responded, her mouth an unhappy, upside-down smile. "Especially now."

"Why 'especially now'?" asked Taft. He was watching

her closely and Mac did the same. LeeAnn's attitude had changed from worry to sulking acceptance.

She gave them a dismissive wave. She'd been perched on the edge of her chair, but now she sat back into the cushions. "Okay, fine. Let them know. They've got a pretty good idea about us anyway. Tobe and I were fighting. He was getting worse and I told him he should see a doctor. It's not the first time I've said that, but he acted like I'd betrayed him, which he always does whenever I point out that he's being irrational. Then he just walked out. He's done that before, but this time is different. He's been gone too long. But I should've known he'd contact Judy. She's the one he trusts."

Her snide tone prompted Mac to ask, "Was there something more between them?"

"Judy's fifteen years older than Tobe. She's in good shape, but she's . . . well, I don't mean to be rude, but she's not that attractive. She and Tobe are a team, though. She would do anything for him." She shook her head. "Oh, do what you have to do. He's still missing. I don't know if he's ever coming home."

"You said he was getting worse?" asked Mac.

"He's never accepted Victor's death, but lately he's talked about exhuming his body. Everyone knows Victor died of a heart attack. He'd had a bad heart for years and his lifestyle didn't help, but Tobe wouldn't listen. I've tried to reason with him about it. I can't tell you how many times. He'd made up his mind that his father's death was murder and nothing was going to change it."

With Clarice's statements fresh in mind, Mac looked at Taft.

He asked, "Did he blame anything on the Friends of Faraday?"

"If he did, there would be some truth to it. Those people picketed and screamed at him all through the construction of those three houses. Victor's heart just gave out. No, Tobe blamed Victor's death on poison."

"Poison? Specifically poison?" asked Mac. This was new.

"Yes," she answered.

"That's why he wanted the exhumation of the body?" asked Taft.

"That's what he said. I didn't listen to him. You have to understand, Tobe says these things. He knows Victor died of a heart attack, but his obsessions come and go, and this one keeps circling around. I think he understands the truth, but then it comes back like a boomerang."

"You said Tobias got worse the last few months?" reminded Taft.

She nodded.

"Any reason? Something set it off?"

She lifted a hand, only to let it drop again. "Like I said before, Tobe's been going down this road awhile. He's never been diagnosed, but he's probably got one of those mental issues. Bipolar? OCD? All I know is that he can't let this one go. It came roaring back after Dolores died. His great-aunt," she explained before either of them could pose the next query. "She left him some money. Not much. There wasn't much left after all those years in assisted living, and whatever there was went to her grandson. But Tobe found a note in Dolores's room, written to her from Victor, asking her for money just before his death. Victor was going broke at the time and he wanted Dolores to save him. He also said he was being poisoned, so there it was in black and white. Again, this isn't late-breaking news, but seeing it written down, maybe that was proof for Tobe? He was so looking for it to be. I got mad and said some things I shouldn't have. But I also reminded him that Victor *always* thought someone was after him. He had a persecution complex. Tobe was the one who told me that! Back in the day, when he was younger . . . better . . . He's gotten worse with age."

"Who did Victor think was after him?" asked Taft.

"Everyone. Anyone he believed had slighted him in some way. Tobe knew that once, but it got away from him." Her shoulders sagged. "I hope it hasn't taken him over."

She looked like she was going to break down completely, but then she pulled herself back from the brink.

"So, you think Tobe's disappearance now is because he's on a quest to prove his father was murdered," said Mac.

"It could be. I don't know why he hasn't come home yet. It's just not like him."

"Did his aunt give Victor money to shore up his company?" asked Taft.

"No. She should've. She had a lot of money back then. Well, maybe she did give him some, but it was really Tobe's intervention and the bank easing off that borrowed enough time to complete the project. The Friends of Faraday lost their court case and the houses were sold, but there wasn't much left after the debts were paid, and Victor only lasted a few months afterward. Tobe built the company into what it is today from practically nothing." There was a hint of pride mixed with sadness in her words.

"Do you know how far he took the exhumation?"

She shook her head.

"Does your husband have a copy of Victor's death certificate?" asked Taft.

"Why?"

"I was going to check the name of the doctor who signed it."

"Oh, I can tell you that. Dr. Ernest Franklin. He died about a year after Victor. You think he made a mistake about the heart attack?" She snorted. "That's what Tobe decided."

They left a few minutes later; LeeAnn didn't seem to have anything further to add. At the door Taft said, "We'll see what we can find out," and she sent him a watery smile.

Outside, Mackenzie asked Taft, "You think whether Dolores gave Victor money is relevant?"

"I don't know," he admitted. "Laidlaw was focusing on his father's death again, right before his disappearance. I'd like to know more about it, too."

"He thinks his father was poisoned, meanwhile Clarice thinks she killed Victor because of the pressure the Friends of Faraday put on him."

"If Victor was poisoned, it could possibly still be traced," said Taft.

"The exhumation," said Mac.

"Did he order it? Takes a while to get approved. You've got to have a valid reason. Apply through the courts." His eyes narrowed. "But if the exhumation was granted on suspected criminal grounds, the autopsy would be performed by a medical examiner."

Mac felt a tiny jolt. "Sandy Herdstrom?"

"Could be." Taft drew a breath. "I'll try to track down

Herdstrom. See what he says about Victor Laidlaw's heart attack. See if he talked to Tobias about it."

"So, now we're thinking poison, or some other means of homicide, could be more than Tobias Laidlaw's overactive imagination?"

"We're following Tobias's footsteps to see where it leads us."

"So, who would want Victor dead enough to poison him?" posed Mac as he started toward his Rubicon.

"Didn't you hear? Everyone." He threw her a smile.

"I'll check with Nolan. He may have Judy's personal cell number. I wasn't going to push it with LeeAnn and ask if she had it, but I don't want to wait for tomorrow. I want to call her today. You said you had something to tell me?" she called after him.

"I'll fill you in later."

"Think you could do it now?"

He gave her a look, then relented, retracing his steps. "I think 1984 might be a four-digit code for a locker in Good Livin'."

"What? Really? How do you know that?"

"Superior intellect."

"Ah, yes, I forgot. Must've slipped my less intellectual mind."

"Must've."

"Good Livin'," she said, ignoring his smile. Taft enjoying himself was a powerful elixir to her feminine receptors. "I remember you signing up for a week trial membership there not so long ago."

"Which I let lapse. Didn't know I'd need it again so soon."

"So, you're going to check the lockers? How?"

"I already tried to use my old membership to just walk

into the locker rooms, but no dice. I'm going to have to re-up, and they insisted I meet with the membership team again."

"I mean, how will you know which locker it is?"

"I have some thoughts on that."

She waited.

"The pages the bookmark was in between. Either thirty-seven or thirty-eight."

She nodded. It wasn't a bad thought. "And if that doesn't work?"

"Let's keep it positive," he said with a quick smile. "I thought we could meet with someone around nine tomorrow? Start at the Good Livin' by Glen Gen, where I had my membership. It's the only one in River Glen with a Cool Down Café. I checked."

"We?"

"You want to go, right?" He looked at her. They both knew he hadn't allowed Mackenzie in on the case until now.

"Yes. Of course."

"I'll see you tomorrow," he said, and then his eyes searched the area again, causing a frisson of awareness to slide down her back. He did think someone was following him.

All the way back to her apartment Mackenzie was infected by the sense of being hunted.

Chapter Eighteen

Elena Verbena was a study in monochromatics as she knocked on Jamie Woodward's front door. Black pants, black ribbed V-necked sweater, the strap of a black purse slung over her shoulder, a black leather notebook in her hand, her hair pulled back from her face and clipped at the back of her crown while the rest of her straightened black hair hung down to the top of her shoulders.

She'd had a bad couple of nights after learning of Cooper Haynes's accident, especially upon hearing that it may have been a premeditated attack. His favorite vehicle had been tampered with, the electrical system compromised, the brakes failing. There was no question it could have resulted in death, and the thought of losing her partner had left her sick and breathless. She'd never truly thought about losing Haynes. She'd sort of drifted into the position as his second and accepted it and him. Not that they really held first and second positions at River Glen PD; it was just an understood, loose hierarchy.

And she was really angry at the unknown perpetrator or perpetrators. She'd been doing her homework since the accident, following up as best she could on what he'd been investigating. He hadn't told her where he'd been headed Friday night, but she knew he'd been following up on his own on Granger Nye's fatal fall from one of the Best Homes houses under construction. The case had been ruled an accident and there was nothing left to do, but Haynes hadn't been satisfied. He'd likely been going to interview Debra Fournier again—the woman who'd overheard the argument that took place just before Nye's fall—but Stillwell Hill, where Haynes's accident took place, was nowhere near the construction site where Nye met his death.

Haynes hadn't confided his plans to her. She might have objected to his course of action . . . she *would have* objected to his course of action—one of her own failings, she could admit that—so she knew he would sometimes just omit what he was doing rather than fight with her. And yes, nine times out of ten he turned out to be in the right. Eight times out of ten . . . maybe seven . . . but the point was, he very easily could have hidden the truth from her, and now he couldn't remember what that was.

Jamie answered the door, appearing weary. She was one of those women with that girl next door look that always seemed fresh and bright, although not so much today. Elena could never be described that way herself. "Exotic" was the consistent observation, but generally from men who were more interested in seeing her naked than getting to know *her*. That was her beef with men. That was why even Haynes accused her of being a man-hater, though she knew he was just ribbing her. But it was a fair description of her character whenever a member of the opposite sex dismissed her, or ignored her, or simply looked past her for someone else, some *man*. Yes, then she was a man-hater.

"Hi, Elena," Jamie said, stepping back to invite her in. "He's in his office."

His office proved to be the living room couch. The white cast sticking out in front of him, which covered his right leg, was a beacon that drew the eye. Beyond that, he, too, looking exceedingly tired.

"I won't stay long," she told him.

"Stay as long as you want. What have you got?"

Haynes didn't waste time when a situation was important. She liked that, too. She told him about the car, most of which they'd already gone over on the phone, and then segued into what she felt was the truth. "You were going to see Mrs. Fournier to ask her again about what she overheard in that argument between Granger Nye and our mystery man or woman just before Nye fell."

He nodded faintly. He used the economy of movement she recognized in a person who was carefully keeping his body from aching. "That sounds right. The auditory witness."

"But you weren't anywhere near her house."

Jamie had been standing in the background, but now she murmured something about leaving them alone, possibly feeling like an eavesdropper. Verbena had seated herself in a swivel chair that she could turn to look at Haynes.

"Stillwell Hill. What was I doing there?"

"Maybe coming home the long way?" she suggested. "Maybe purposely taking some time to go over things in your mind?"

"Maybe," he allowed. "But if there was something to think over, it feels like I should be able to retrieve it."

"Give it time." They both knew how injurious and devastating events could be erased from the memory, the body and the brain's natural means of deleting the horror as a means of healing. "But I thought I'd see Mrs. Fournier today. Check if you were there."

"Good." He brightened a bit.

"If you were, she should remember and hopefully tell me whatever she told you."

"Does the chief know your plan?"

Elena took her time composing an answer. Neither she nor Haynes truly trusted their boss, Chief Hugh Bennihof. There were sexual harassment rumors against the man that Elena had not personally experienced, but then, she was neither the girl next door nor particularly approachable. She believed the rumors, however. She'd seen his eyes linger a little too long on the derriere of one particular woman who was no longer with the department.

And along with those rumors were the ones that linked the chief to Mitch Mangella, River Glen's most prosperous and notorious citizen, a man who not only skirted the law but drove right through it sometimes. Unproven, of course. Bennihof and Mangella were friendly acquaintances if not exactly friends.

"I've taken over your cases and Bennihof has asked Richards to help me."

"Mmm." It wasn't a happy sound. "Does the chief know I'm still working the Nye case?"

Elena slowly shook her head. Granger Nye's fall from the second story of a half-finished Best Home in Staffordshire Estates wasn't to be reopened because Andrew Best, like Mitch Mangella, was another friendly acquaintance of Chief Hugh Bennihof.

"Good," said Haynes.

She then discussed several points on other cases they were working. Haynes was clear and aware on all of them, which confirmed to her that he was going to be just fine.

She almost exhaled in relief, but managed to keep her feelings to herself until she was outside the house. What they hadn't discussed in depth, though, what she'd purposely held back from him, was that they had narrowed down who had taken the car and that the suspect appeared to be an officer who'd kept his face averted from the cameras in a way that was no accident as he'd plucked the keys from the locked cupboard that was invariably left unlocked. The suspect knew just how to keep his face turned away to keep his identity secret. He came in the back door in a uniform, looking down, a nonregulation cap on his head, went straight to the cupboard and, after the briefest of hesitations, grabbed the keys. Of course new regulations were already in place for taking a vehicle. A stricter checkout process that required a signature, something that had been in place but had eroded over the years. It was embarrassing, and Bennihof had sworn that heads would roll . . . from his cell phone at an undisclosed weekend function. He was a great one for closing the barn door after the horse was out.

She left a few moments later and headed to Debra Fournier's.

". . . Mackenzie Laughlin at this number? Thank you."

She clicked off after leaving a message for Judy. On the voice mail she'd introduced herself and explained that she was working for Mrs. Laidlaw, who was concerned because she hadn't heard from her husband, Tobias, and wondered if Judy had been in contact with him. Then she asked her to call and repeated her name.

She was at her apartment, getting ready to head back to Daley and Leon's, but she was dallying. She'd promised she would stay on for a few days, but she couldn't quite make herself go over there. Leon was supposedly leaving today, maybe was gone already, and she knew Daley needed someone to lean on. It just was . . . tiring.

She wished Judy had answered her phone. Nolan had given her Tobias's assistant's cell number, somewhat reluctantly; he'd felt a bit like Mackenzie hadn't been straight with him in the beginning, which she hadn't, but no amount of explaining that LeeAnn's rule was she couldn't reveal the truth had convinced him otherwise. It made her feel bad. She hated being on the wrong side with the people she loved.

She made herself some peanut butter toast for dinner, part of her dallying. It wasn't the most gourmet meal for certain, but then, everything she needed, bread and peanut butter, was in her cupboard and voilà! Pop it in the toaster and dinner is served.

She hadn't heard from Daley since she left, which was a bit concerning. She'd expected her to call and demand to know when she was returning. Maybe things hadn't gone so well with Leon?

"You're really being a chicken," she said aloud.

Holding her piece of toast, she glanced down at the notes she'd written for herself, ready to transfer them to her laptop. She wished she'd known before today about Tobias's decision to exhume Victor's body; she would have asked more in-depth questions of everyone about Victor's death instead of taking in general information about the man. Not that it hurt to get other opinions, but she could have saved herself some time. Tobias believed his father had been poisoned and Aunt Dolores's note had solidified that belief. Victor had believed it, and Tobias did now, too.

Unless . . . She stopped in the process of bringing the piece of toast to her mouth.

Unless Victor's claim of being poisoned was an attempt to get his Aunt Dolores—Tobias's *great*-aunt Dolores—to loosen the purse strings?

Taking a bite, she turned that over in her mind. A form of extortion? To help pay for the mounting bills over the debacle the overlook houses had become?

Or was the fear he was being poisoned Victor's bedrock belief?

She wondered what kind of information Tobias had been gathering, if any, on his current quest to find his father's "killer." Had he talked to Dr. Herdstrom? Who else was around when Victor was building the overlook houses?

She made a note to herself to look into the events around the time of Victor's death.

She picked up her phone. She wished to high heaven Judy would call. She was tired of people not getting back to her.

She'd tried another call to Glen Gen to find out about Clarice's condition, hoping to reach someone different, but it didn't matter; she'd gotten the same cool response that the family had requested no information be given out. Again, though, it at least appeared that Clarice was still alive.

Why had Clarice called *her*? A witness to her confession, she'd said, but why not one of the old guard, her friends? Maybe Taft was right—she could only trust a stranger. Maybe those old friends of hers had something to hide and wouldn't appreciate Clarice confessing to anything.

And whoever the Friends of Faraday were, they couldn't be held liable for Victor's heart attack.

Unless they'd truly poisoned him, she supposed. But that wasn't what Clarice had said.

Of course she'd never gotten to make her full confession.

Finishing her toast, Mackenzie washed her hands, wiped them dry, then sat down with her laptop, transcribing notes into a word processing program. She then scrolled through what she'd written to date.

She was fairly certain Alfie was the Carreras' porch pirate and that Abby had been the one to leave the dog shit in their mailbox. Alfie's reasons were . . . what? Just because he could? Because he had something against the Carreras?

Abby's reasons were easier to understand. She'd donned a similar outfit to her son's and left the poop in the mailbox to protect him; then she'd relayed that whole convoluted story about the stolen bike in order to put Alfie well out of the area during the time the latest harassment occurred.

Mac needed to get Alfie alone and press him.

And Andre . . . who, like Victor, had supposedly run though the Villages wives as if they were part of his personal harem. Was he as universally disliked as Victor, even in death, seemed to be? And who were those wives? Had they moved away or were they still there? Maybe Tamara, Evelyn, and Clarice were notches on Victor's belt, but she couldn't picture Andre with any of them . . . maybe Tamara, possibly . . . he was just too slick. A social climber. Whereas the old guard of the Villages seemed homier. No, that wasn't quite the right word. Old-school, maybe? *Trustworthy?* That, at least, was the image they sought to present. Maybe Andre's attentions had been mostly on the young guard.

Whatever the case, did any of it have to do with Tobias

Laidlaw's disappearance? It didn't appear to. It seemed
more like Tobias was on one of his "wild hairs," chasing
down what he believed to be the truth about Victor's possible
poisoning, a plan of action resulting from the note he'd
found from Victor to his aunt.

Her cell phone rang and she recognized the number
she'd put in to the Faraday Foundation. Finally, someone
was calling her back.

"Hello," she answered.

"Hello, this is Joseph Mertz from the Faraday Foundation. Is this Ms. Laughlin?"

"Yes, it is. Thank you for returning my call."

"You had a question?"

"I've been . . . helping Clarice Fenwick, and she's
mentioned the Friends of Faraday a lot. She was a member
during the lawsuit fifteen years ago? She's been ill and
I'm following up on some unfinished business for her."
Mac mentally crossed her fingers. She was winging it.

"I don't know Ms. Fenwick personally. When the foundation was formed the original Friends of Faraday was,
well, practically insolvent. They'd been donated a lot of
land by Frank Faraday, but they were on the brink of
having to sell some of it to pay the legal expenses. Through
negotiations, the Faraday Foundation was formed and the
Friends of Faraday was dissolved."

"Is there a way I can reach some of those original members? Clarice would like to contact them."

"The lawsuit's public record."

"Clarice is more interested in friends she's lost touch
with. If you had a list of the members . . . ?"

"I'm sure there's one I could find," he said grudgingly.

"Any chance you could email it?" Mac pressed, and

Joseph agreed to look into it the next day, so Mac gave him her address.

She didn't quite know what she was looking for, but since Clarice's guilt was tied up with the group, it was worth examining who'd been in it with her.

Verbena knocked on Debra Fournier's front door, bracing herself for what she expected to be a hostile interview. Fournier had said she'd heard two men arguing just before Granger Nye fell—or was pushed—to his death from the second floor of the house under construction next to hers. Then, when she'd realized there was going to be an investigation and news coverage and a whole damn media circus, she'd suddenly recanted. Swore she couldn't remember anything. Later, she'd tried to say she'd recognized one of the voices of a person in the news who'd run afoul of the police, but neither Verbena nor Haynes believed that to be true. Too easy to reach for. All Debra Fournier wanted was to pull her head back into her shell and wait for the danger to pass.

Then the case was closed. Accidental death.

But it was not the end of the story as far as Haynes was concerned, and Verbena agreed with him.

When her knock wasn't immediately answered she rang the bell, hearing the tones peal *ding-dong*.

Verbena glanced around as she waited. From the Fournier front porch she could see the house where the accident had taken place, just a few over. Construction was nearly finished now, at least on the outside, the dark fiberglass windows in place, the horizontal brown siding up, a kind of chunky, gray manufactured stone surrounding the two-story entryway. Modern Prairie, the design was called, and it was hot, hot, hot in the building market right now. And the prices for new construction were staggering.

Idly, she wondered if the fact that someone had died during its construction would affect this particular home's price.

The Fournier house itself was Craftsman style, with natural shingled siding, white pillars holding up the porch, and white pane windows. A silver Mercedes SUV sat in the driveway, so it appeared someone was home.

Verbena was beginning to wonder if Debra would deign to open the door, but then she heard light, running footsteps approaching and the dead bolt unlatched. The door was suddenly flung open and a young girl of about eight, wearing bright yellow stretch pants and a T-shirt with an ice cream cone in various shades of pink and yellow as its central design, stood in the aperture. Her big blue eyes gazed at Verbena in a kind of awe.

"Hi," she said.

"Hi," said Verbena.

"Ashley! Ashley!" A harried, older female voice on the verge of anger rang out, and then Debra Fournier came into view, her brown hair trying to escape from a messy bun, one strand across the woman's left eye. "Don't open the door!" she declared even as she could see that Ashley had already blown that demand.

"Mrs. Fournier?" Verbena asked politely.

The look on the woman's face was anxiety mixed with a kind of awe. Verbena had seen it before. Her own black hair was scraped back into a tight bun at her nape. She knew she looked formidable. She prided herself on it.

"Ashley, go back inside." She grabbed the girl by her shoulders and walked her backward, twisting her around and shooing her down the hallway. Ashley resisted by taking steps forward at a snail's pace, while her head was turned around damn near 180 degrees, like an owl or a demon.

"I'm Detective Verbena with the River Glen Police Department," Verbena said, pulling out her badge. "Could I come in and talk to you for a moment?"

"What's this about?" she demanded, straightening.

"There was an accident a few nights ago. My partner was scheduled to come and speak with you . . ." A tiny white lie. No one knew if he'd actually made it to Fournier's doorstep. ". . . about the accident during the construction of the house next door."

"I've said enough about that."

"Did Detective Haynes come to see you on Friday night?" She shook her head. "No."

"Were you home?"

"Yes, I was. He didn't come here." She was positive. "I don't know what you people are doing." She glanced back at Ashley, who'd made it to the end of the entry hall and stopped. "Go on," Debra snapped, and Ashley gave a loud snort and stomped around the corner, clomping one step down on the hardwood with her sneakers, waiting another half second before clomping another, then finally disappearing around a corner.

Debra turned back to Verbena. "You need to leave me alone."

"We're trying to close the case once and for all," Verbena explained.

"I've told you everything I know! Multiple times. I don't want to be a part of this. You act like you don't believe me."

"You heard the argument that night."

"Yes! I've said so. I wish I hadn't!"

"Could you make out any of the words?"

"*No*. They were all shouting, but it was just loud, and then it was quiet."

Verbena looked at her. "All? I thought there were only two voices."

She was immediately flustered, and Verbena watched as color crept up her neck and face. "I don't know. It was an argument. They were yelling at each other. I didn't see them, I just heard them. It was . . . two voices," she said, then, with more conviction, "two voices. I already told you!"

"Could it have been three? Please, Mrs. Fournier. If we get to the bottom of this, we won't have to bother you any further."

Debra Fournier regarded Verbena with near loathing. Elena looked back at her and held her tongue. It was difficult when you wanted to reach down someone's throat for the words hidden inside, but she was learning forbearance from Haynes, who had a real knack for listening to people even when they were obviously lying.

"I'm not sure," she said quickly, as if the faster she admitted she could have been wrong would help in some way. "I was pretty sure it was two men fighting, but . . . I sort of have it in my head like it was three."

"Three men," said Verbena.

She gave one abrupt nod and looked Verbena right in the eye. "You promise this is the end of it?"

No, she couldn't promise that. "You never saw Detective Haynes last Friday?"

She shook her head. "I never answer the door anyway. I live alone. I'm just babysitting my granddaughter today. I'd remember if someone came by."

There was a crash from somewhere in the back of the house, probably the kitchen because it sounded like some kind of pottery had broken. Debra gasped and whipped around.

"I'm sorry!" Ashley cried frantically.

"Are you okay?"

"The grapes are all over the floor . . ." she wailed.

Verbena stepped outside and closed the door behind her, hearing the dead bolt snap into place.

She immediately called Haynes's cell as she headed for her car. When he answered, she said tautly, "Just talked to Debra Fournier. You never showed here Friday. You went somewhere else. But Debra's now admitting there were probably three people in that argument, not two. Granger Nye and two others. We've been lied to and it's time we got to the bottom of it."

Chapter Nineteen

Taft drove past his condo complex and around the neighborhood, checking the vehicles. He thought Silva was in for the night, but just in case, he wanted to see if the man's car was anywhere near his apartment. When there was no sign of the Charger he pulled into his lot and his designated parking spot.

At his front door he tested the handle before inserting his key. Everything appeared locked up tight.

He was barely inside when he heard the excited barking and the unmistakable creak of his neighbor, Tommy Carnahan's, front door. He'd left his front door ajar as he checked his apartment and through the open aperture raced two pugs, one black, one fawn. Tommy Carnahan, in his late seventies, dressed as ever in slacks, a nice blue shirt, and his driver's cap, stepped in behind them as Taft was swarmed by the pugs.

"Sorry, my man," Tommy said. "I was getting ready to clip on their leashes and they heard you."

"No problem." He bent down to the dogs. Blackie, the black pug, growled in his almost amusing pug way, while Plaid, the fawn pug, snuffled Taft's hands and rolled her brown eyes at him in a worried way, likely picking up Taft's tension because he was tense and alert every time he opened his door now.

"Do you have a dead bolt?" Taft asked him.

"Why, yes."

"Someone broke into my place. Picked the lock."

Tommy looked out the door. "My door's open. I was just chasing the dogs."

"Better close it."

The dogs tried to escape as they sensed their master leaving, but Taft grabbed Plaid while Blackie charged after Tommy.

Plaid whined and tugged at her collar, then plopped down and tried to look backward and up into Taft's face. "Sorry," Taft told the dog. He was their sometime dog sitter, and they knew him well, but his tension was making them nervous.

Taft heard Tommy close his door, lock it, and test it. He returned a moment later with Blackie, who raced over to Plaid, then gave Taft a suspicious look.

"Who was it?" Tommy asked again. "No, don't lie. I'm old, but I can tell when I'm about to be shined on. You know who it was?"

"Yeah." Taft had been about to lie, but he told the simple truth. "Pretty sure."

His shaggy gray-and-white eyebrows lifted. "You know why?"

"I have something they want."

"You gonna tell me what that is?"

Taft shook his head.

He nodded his understanding, then said, "We need to get some security cameras around here," as he rounded up the dogs and clipped on their leashes.

"Be a good idea."

"You calling the police?" Tommy stepped outside and looked back at Taft.

"I don't think so."

"Okay. You usually know what you're doing." Despite his words, Taft could tell the older man wondered if he was making the right choice. But Taft had no interest in getting the authorities further involved. They had Silva's name. They knew Taft felt he was responsible for Riskin's death.

"Saw Mackenzie walking from your place earlier. Sure she didn't leave the door open?"

"The break-in was yesterday. Mackenzie hasn't been here today."

Tommy pursed his lips. "Maybe it wasn't her. Looked a lot like her, but she was a ways away. Huh."

"You sure she was at my door?"

"Well, now, I just glanced. Thought it was strange she didn't say hello, but then, maybe she didn't see me. I think I need to talk to Rebecca about those security lights. Hate those HOA meetings, but she is the president."

"Yeah."

Taft watched Tommy head toward his convertible with the pugs. The top was still up and would remain that way with the dogs in the car.

He closed the door to his condo and locked it. He rarely threw the dead bolt. He felt safe enough without it. And he counted on the wall safe to keep his documents secure.

He tossed his cell phone onto the kitchen counter, placing his Glock beside it.

He'd barely taken a step toward the refrigerator and a cold beer when the cell rang.

Picking it up, he glanced at the number. Not one he knew. "Taft," he answered.

"You wanted to talk to me." came the cold voice.

He felt the hairs on his arms rise as he recognized Keith Silva's voice. "You broke into my place," Taft said, his own voice as frigid as Silva's.

"Well, now, that's a lie. You keep lying about me, it's not good for either of us."

"I know what you're looking for. I have it in a safe place."

"I don't know what you're talking about. I don't want anything from you. You stay away from me."

"Riskin gave it to me. It's not good for you . . . or the widow DeMarcos . . ."

He was prodding, hoping to scare him with what little information he had.

One thing about Silva: He couldn't keep up the oily villain persona for long. His brutish nature rose to the fore. "You stay away from Anna," he snarled.

"I don't know. She's pretty attractive. Maybe I should introduce myself."

"Just try it," he warned.

"I've got the goods on you, Silva. If you break into my place again, I'm turning it all over to Portland PD."

"If you had it, you'd turn it over now," he said.

That was probably true, but Silva didn't have to know it. "I'm keeping it as insurance."

"You're not good at bluffing," he snarled, but there was uncertainty in his tone.

"You killed Riskin, you asshole. And I've got the information he was holding to prove it Stop tailing me."

"You're a fucking liar. And fucking liars get themselves killed!"

"Like Riskin? He was telling the truth."

"Mangella still likes you. I've told him what a rat you are, though, and he's starting to believe. And I wouldn't want to be you now."

Taft felt his blood turn to ice. He knew Silva was just trying to get to him, like he was trying to get to Silva. But Mangella wasn't the same kind of thug as Silva. Mangella couldn't be pushed to make a mistake like Silva might.

"If you had anything, you'd go to the police," he said again, with a little more confidence. "No matter how tough you act, you're a choirboy, Taft. If you really thought you could pin Riskin's death on me, you would."

"The police talk to you already? Tell you what I said about you? I told them you did it. I'm holding back the information that'll nail you for now. I've got my reasons."

"You just keep on lying."

"We both know what it's like to be a cop. If they ever have enough evidence to prove criminal activity on us, it's over. Jail's a lot worse for ex-cops. You'd better hope I'm lying."

"I know you, Taft. So does Mangella." He added craftily, "And what about that girl who works for you? Sweet on her, are you? I saw you with her. Mangella says it's hands-off, but I'm not Mangella."

The ice in Taft's veins grew colder. So cold it burned. "Now, that sounds like a threat," he answered in a calm and deadly voice. "Guess we're back to the widow DeMarcos. I think I might go see her tomorrow."

Silva didn't answer, but Taft could hear his hard and

angry breathing. Jealousy was an emotion the man did not do well. Taft waited, his pulse thumping.

Silva clicked off.

Slowly, Taft set down his own phone on the counter and exhaled his breath

Fucker, said Helene.

"You got that right," said Taft.

And he picked up the phone to warn Mackenzie

The phone rang as Mac was driving toward the Villages by way of the East Glen River, telling herself she was enjoying the view when in actuality she'd taken the scenic route because she just wasn't ready to go back to the Carreras'. She was already sorry she'd signed up for a few more days of being Daley's companion.

Realizing she was close to Ridge Pointe Independent and Assisted Living, she turned the wheel into the parking lot to take the call, seeking out one of the visitors' spots, many available now as it was getting past the dinner hour. Picking up her cell, she answered, "Hey, there." She hadn't expected Taft to connect because they'd left off with a plan for the next day.

"I just got a call from Silva. We traded insults and he alluded to you. I'm sorry."

Her nerves buzzed at the news she was on Silva's radar, but it wasn't a surprise. Association with Taft had its dangers, but it was what she wanted. "So, no more cutting me out of your case?"

"Take this seriously," he said.

"Oh, I am."

There was a pause, and then he said, "Meet me for a drink in an hour or so?"

"Sure."

"High class or slumming?"

Even with the heightened danger, she felt a lightening of spirit. "The Waystation?"

"Okay, slumming," he said. "See you there."

Daley called just as Mac was about to walk into the Waystation. She thought about ignoring it and just going inside, but she owed Daley an explanation of where she was. "Hi, there," she answered.

"Do you know where Leon was last night? Who he was with? Jeannie. He was with *Jeannie*. And he lied about giving me the house. It's not in the prenup. It's up to him and, well, I guess he doesn't feel like giving it to me anymore."

"Is your name on the deed?"

"Both of our names are on the deed. If he decides to sell, I have to sell. I can buy him out, but I don't have the money. Leon is a shit. He's a liar and *a shit*. And Jeannie . . ." She made a choking sound. "I liked her! But she's . . . a conniving bitch!"

"Leon told you this?"

"Oh, yes. Before he left. I finally couldn't stand it, so I asked him. He said he was at Jeannie's. He *told* me."

"What about Chris Palminter?"

"*I don't know!* But they're not married. I'm married! Does Chris even know his girlfriend is a cheating, fucking, conniving . . ."

"Daley!" She sounded like she was going to blow and spew like a volcano.

"I know you think Leon is cute and all, and he's got money for sure, but he's not what you think. He's—"

"I didn't say I thought he was cute"

"—an asshole. A lying piece of *shit*! I want to kill him. I really do. He said he was at Jeannie's and he just smirked at me. You know what I mean. You've seen it. I know you'll probably be mad at me, but I went to see Jesse. I needed someone to hold me and I just broke down with him. I couldn't help it. I wanted to stay with him. Just stay in his arms forever. I asked to stay the night. I really wanted to." She started crying in earnest. "God *damn it*!" she declared through her tears.

Mac attempted to think of something to say. She tried not to have her mind zig away from Daley's issues with Leon to land on an image of Daley wrapped in Jesse's arms. Jesse? Oh, God. She almost moaned aloud. Now she was doing it, too.

His name is Taft. He's not Jesse. He's Taft. And he's free to do whatever he wants with whomever he wants.

Not. The. Issue.

"I'll be at the house later. I'm . . ." *Going to be with Jesse. Ugh.* It was like a sickness. All of a sudden she couldn't say his name without thinking "Jesse." And yes, it was his name, but not really, not *really.* . . .

"Well, I might not be there." It sounded like a challenge. Did Daley think she was going to be with Jesse . . . Taft? *Tell her. Tell her you're meeting him.*

But her lips stayed mum.

"Where are you going?" asked Mac as the moment spun out. It seemed like Daley was just waiting for her to ask.

"I'm not sure. There's someone I'm thinking of seeing," she said coyly.

Tell her!

"Okay, then," Mac heard herself saying. "I'll see you later tonight . . . or tomorrow."

"At least that asshole's gone for now," she said in a voice threaded with unshed tears. "I ripped out the ring. He's got it on his phone and he wants out, so he doesn't get to see what I'm doing!"

The ring? Oh, the Ring. For a moment she'd thought Daley had taken off her wedding ring, but what she'd done was disable the video equipment.

"I knew he'd screw me in the end," she said bitterly. "That's what love does for you. Don't ever love someone, Mackenzie. They'll hurt you."

Thanks for the advice, she thought as Daley hung up. She sure as hell made it hard to feel anything for her but annoyance. And okay, a bit of jealousy.

She parked at the Waystation right next to his Rubicon.

She realized she'd thought of it as *Jesse's* Rubicon. She closed her eyes and counted to ten. Daley was making her crazy.

She stepped into the Waystation, whose bar was a long slab of oak with embedded condensation rings beneath its varathaned surface. Behind was a mirror that spanned the length of the bar studded with sparkling rows of liquor bottles on narrow glass shelves. Well, sparkling might not be the adjective; the Waystation wasn't all that scrupulous about dusting.

The din of conversation was a low rumble, but she heard the soft click of billiard balls from the pool game nearest to her. Both tables were in use by men wearing backward baseball hats. She smelled french fries and onions and grilled burgers, the length and breadth of the dive bar's fare. Not as good as a Goldie, but good enough.

She looked around for Taft and saw he was seated on a

stool, talking to the bartender. She could see his three days' growth of beard, imagined the dimples that hid there, couldn't see the blue of his eyes from where she stood, but her memory was crystal clear.

She wanted to replace that image of Daley with Taft with one of her own. She wanted to kiss him deeply, the kind of kiss that went right down to the soles of your feet. She wanted to be in bed with him, bodies in rhythm, head thrown back, reaching and reaching, stretching . . .

He glanced her way. Gave her a nod that he'd seen her and pointed to a small booth for two near him that had a modicum of privacy. Mac exhaled as she stepped forward. Taft slid off his stool and waited till she got there before sliding in opposite her. He moved the jacket and the keys he'd used as a place keeper from the tabletop, replacing them with a half-drunk glass of beer.

"You clean up nice," he said.

She hadn't cleaned up at all, was still in her jeans and sneakers, so she said, "Well, I was coming to the Way-station."

He chuckled, and she realized she hadn't really seen his sense of humor for a while. They'd both been more reserved, more melancholy, since they'd each taken a turn at the hospital after their last case, and then, of course, Riskin's death . . .

Taft's natural insouciance had taken a beating, but here it was again.

He picked up the beer. "One of these? Wine? Cocktail?"

"One of those . . . and some fries."

"Way ahead of you."

He went back to the bar and placed the order as a waiter carrying a basket of fries and two greasy burgers elbowed his way from the kitchen and plunked them down on the bar, about as much service as was available here. Taft picked up the order and brought it to the table.

Realizing she was famished, Mac appreciated the burger. Her peanut butter toast was hours earlier. She watched as Taft picked up a glass of beer the bartender had just pulled, then brought it to Mac.

The whole process gave her a few minutes to get her head back on straight where he was concerned.

He bit into his burger, chewed a moment, and said, "Bet tomorrow we learn how the ME's office ruled on Riskin. It'll be Herdstrom's call."

"Suicide."

He nodded. "I gave Portland PD Silva's name. They know him, and me. They know I'm not kidding around, but when it comes through as suicide, that'll be it. I'll be on my own getting Silva."

"Is there any chance you're wrong?" She drank down the beer fast and felt her head tingle with a slight buzz. She'd taken several bites of her burger and now dug into the shared fries.

"Sure. I could be wrong," he said affably, but he clearly didn't feel that way.

"Okay. I trust your instincts."

"Really. Since when?"

"I don't know. It seemed like something to say."

He gave her a quick smile, then went to the bar to order two more beers. Mackenzie knew she was going to have to slow down if she wanted to drive home; either that or dawdle for a few hours at the Waystation.

It turned out that was just what they did. They ate their meals and Mackenzie went over everything she was working on: interviews, impressions, disparate pieces of an investigation, information that came from half working for

Daley Carrera, half gathering background on the Villages and Victor Laidlaw as a means to try to find Tobias Laidlaw. She felt her phone buzz in her pocket but didn't interrupt her own narrative to answer it.

She finished up with, "Maybe Tobias will just show up at work tomorrow. His weeks' long trips seem to be pretty ordinary. Maybe not as long as this one, but it's what he does. Maybe . . ." She had a feeling that was a long shot. "But meanwhile I've stirred up something in the Villages. Clarice Fenwick did attempt suicide. That was no accidental overdose."

"And this guy from the Faraday Foundation is sending you a list of members for when Clarice was there?"

"Joseph Mertz. Hopefully tomorrow. Maybe one or two of the members feel some responsibility for Victor's death, too?"

Mac hadn't mentioned Daley's comments about him. But it was smack-dab in the center of her forehead, and somewhere during her second beer she did bring up some of what Daley had said.

"You were right about her," said Taft. "She's all over the place."

"She said she wanted to stay with you." Mac was trying to proceed cautiously. Taft's response was almost clinical, which was heartening, but she didn't want to get ahead of herself. He and Daley had had some kind of relationship in the past. That was a fact.

"She's lonely and untethered," he added.

Okay, she would have liked a flat-out rejection better, but she'd take it. "She's not at the house. She's out somewhere, wouldn't say where."

"Well, it's not my place, if that's what you're asking."

"Of course not," she denied, though it was exactly what

she was asking. She added quickly, "She doesn't want this divorce even though she's pushing for it."

"She wants Leon to react."

"Or someone to," she murmured into her glass. The burgers were gone, their plates pushed to the side for now. There were a few cold fries left, and Mackenzie picked one up. She almost bussed the booth herself. Such was the service at the Waystation.

It was late and they were about talked out. Mac didn't want the evening to end, but it was time to go. The cool air felt welcome after the closeness of the bar and she inhaled deeply. Taft looked around at the other vehicles and the overall lot.

"Still looking for Silva?" she asked.

"Our pissing contest is escalating. Good to be careful."

She nodded and did her own quick reconnaissance. Taft had told her the man drove a brown Charger, but most of the vehicles in the lot were trucks, though there were a smattering of SUVs.

His gaze had returned to her. "You good to drive?"

She'd done her own mental check and her head was clear. "Yep."

"You sure?"

"Yeah. Why?"

"You generally don't call me Jesse."

Chapter Twenty

Had she done that? Had she really done that?

Inside her RAV, Mac wanted to bang her head on the steering wheel. Damn. Damn. Damn. Daley was killing her. She put the phone on Speaker and listened to the voice mail of the call she hadn't taken inside the bar.

"Hi, it's me," said Daley's voice. "I'm tired and just plan to go to bed. I went to . . . I did some . . . thing . . . I was just so mad at Leon. It was stupid. I don't know." Her tone was nasal and she was sniffing a little. "Where are you? With Jesse, I bet. I wanna talk, but you're not there, so I'll see you tomorrow, whenever I get up. . . ." It sounded like she just clicked off because she didn't want to talk anymore.

Mac was still berating herself about calling Taft *Jesse* when she turned onto Callaway Court and her headlights caught on a dark, hooded figure darting along the hedge that separated Daley's and Leon's house from the one next door. Was he or she on the pathway that led to the Carrera's backyard?

Mac drove by the Carreras' rather than parking. Daley's Audi was in the driveway, the only car.

She turned at the first street that led to the Ds and parked by an arched hole cut through a hedge to a neighbor's yard . . . and in that arch was a bike. A new bike. An expensive-looking bike. Dropped on its side. A replacement bike?

Alfie, you little shit.

She grabbed her keys and phone, stuck the phone in her back pocket, and hightailed it back toward the Carreras'.

As she neared, she heard the rattle of a spray can and the *pffft* of the paint's aerosol release. He was on the Carreras' porch. Hearing her, he froze for a second, then jumped down the steps and tried to tear away, but he stumbled a bit, allowing her to almost catch him.

"Stop, Alfie!" Mac used her sternest voice, though she was a little breathless. She started to slow. "You make me chase you and I'm calling the police!"

He kept right on going.

Goddammit. Mac was forced to pick up the pace. Even so, the kid was pulling away from her.

"I'm calling!" she snapped, coming to a full stop and yanking her cell phone from her back pocket. "*Your mom can't help you this time!*"

She placed the call . . . to no one. Put the phone to her ear and said crisply, "I need the police. I'm chasing vandals."

Was he slowing down?

"I'm in the River Glen Villages, Calloway Court. The address is—"

"*Okay!*" Alfie yelled. He staggered to a halt and sank to the ground, holding his ankle. Ah. Pain had stopped him, not his conscience.

Mac shut off the phone, slid it back into her pocket,

and walked purposefully toward him. "What the hell, Alfie?" she said.

"Don't tell my dad. Did you call the police? Can you call them back?" His voice was muffled. He hadn't taken down the hoodie, which was still tied up over his nose.

She gazed down at his bent head. "Why are you doing this?"

"I don't know."

"You do know. There's a reason."

"He had sex with my mom! He had sex with everyone!"

"I assume you mean Leon." She waited a moment or two, realizing Alfie was trying not to cry. "I'm not sure that's true."

"They stole their house. It was illegal, and they did it anyway! I want them to leave!"

Mac wasn't following. "Who? What's illegal?"

"They took the Martins' house illegally!"

Mac thought a minute. That sounded suspiciously like an adult voice talking through Alfie. "You're talking about the Carreras outbidding the Martins?"

"There was an escalation . . . an escalator!"

"Who told you this?" asked Mac.

No response.

"Whatever the case, you can't vandalize the Carreras' property. You can't steal—"

"It's *not their property*!"

"Alfie, it is their property. And it's not your fight. And you're in a whole lot of trouble now. How'd you get the spray paint?"

"Our garage I didn't put the dog shit in their mailbox," he mumbled. He'd now covered what little of his face that had been visible with his hands, trying to disappear.

"Your mom put it in the mailbox."

"She did not." But the words were without conviction.

"She did. You and I both know it, and I think your dad knows, too. None of this is a secret anymore."

There was a long pause. "What're you gonna do?" he finally asked, sounding pathetic.

"I haven't decided. I'm thinking it over. Whatever happens, you're going to have to make amends with the Carreras."

He slowly dropped his hands and lifted his head. She could see his eyes, black in the pale light from a streetlamp down the block. "You didn't call the police?"

"No."

He exhaled in relief, then with more bite, "You made me think you did."

"You don't get to be outraged, Alfie."

"What do you want me to do?" he asked reluctantly.

"Go home. Get your *bike* and go home. Stop sneaking out of the house. Tell your mom you were caught, and that both of you need to come clean with the Carreras. And pay for the damage. How much spray paint did you get on there?"

"Just a little."

"And how much of Daley's eye shadow did you use?"

He blinked. "It was face cream," he said after a moment, as if the answer mattered.

Mac smiled faintly. She'd just thrown it out there to see what happened. He'd decided to answer honestly and thereby admitted he'd opened the stolen packages and, ergo, was the thief. "Okay, well, just give it all back to Daley."

"I buried it in the backyard," he said, finally undoing the string that kept his hoodie tight on his face. "I was scared you'd find it and you'd know. You've scared my mom, too. Everybody."

"Everybody?"

He got to his feet, still holding the spray can. "Burt, too. He's a good friend of mine. He was a star football player in high school. I couldn't even make the team, but we watch football together sometimes." He hesitated, then handed Mac the spray paint can.

Mac walked him back to his bike and her SUV. Neither of them said anything more. When they were at the arch, she said, "I'm going to check in with you tomorrow. This isn't just going away."

"I know." He sounded defeated.

She watched him peddle off and thought, *Everybody?*

Burt sat on his couch, flipping through TV channels with the remote, unable to settle on anything. The impromptu meeting had broken up long before. They were of one mind now. They'd better be. The fabric of their cabal had fraying ends, but he'd cauterized them. He was pretty sure . . . but not completely sure.

He swore softly and got out a copy of his football tape, rewinding to start it over. He watched for a few minutes, then fast-forwarded to the best parts, beginning with that amazing sack just before the half. It was—

With a screech of stretching plastic, the tape broke.

Fuck.

Still, the truth was, Burt's mind wasn't really on it. He was still reviewing the evening he'd had. He'd probably be really mad later, but right now his mind was traveling down pleasurable pathways, remembering surprising events he could never have predicted.

Now he lay his head back and closed his eyes, pushing yesterday's meeting and then Cliff's goddamn morning phone call out of his thoughts. His mind ran back to the women's bodies he'd recently run his hands over. Two. Two! He'd never won the ladies over like Andre . . . like Victor. . . .

The thought of Victor Laidlaw brought him unpleasantly back to the present. Fifteen years gone and still laughing in Burt's face. It didn't matter that Burt had done the legal work for him, filed all the papers to get those three lots, planned the initial countersuit against the Friends of Faraday. And what had he gotten for his effort? Jackshit. And the man had taken Tamara from him, twice. She'd come running back, all apologetic; then, when Victor crooked his finger, she'd raced back to him.

Burt's good mood started to vanish. If ever a man deserved to die, it was Victor Laidlaw. If he wasn't dead already, Burt would kill him again.

He looked again at the ruined tape. *Fuck*, he thought woefully.

Chapter Twenty-One

Monday morning Mackenzie took a shower to wake herself up and then headed out. She hesitated with her hand on the front door, then tiptoed down the hallway to check on Daley's bedroom door, which was still shut. Good. She could leave without suffering through Daley's usual third degree, and then relate what had happened with Alfie later. And she didn't have to tell her she was meeting Taft today.

Stepping outside, she examined the front of the Carreras' house. Alfie had gotten up a silver "F" and "U" before Mac had scared him enough to run. It still got the message across, but at least it wasn't in black. The silver didn't show up as much against the white porch.

Mac wasn't looking forward to another skirmish with Alfie's mother, but she wanted to put the investigation of the Carreras' harassment to bed and, well, Alfie, and Abby, needed to fess up to their misdeeds.

She drove away from the Villages, planning to meet Jesse . . . Jesus . . . *Taft* . . . at the Good Livin' health club next to Glen Gen at nine. From there they would go to another one in Portland that had a Cool Down Café inside.

If that failed, there were a number of other smaller Good Livin's scattered around River Glen and Greater Portland.

She arrived at Good Livin' way too early. A product of wanting to get out of the house. She looked over at the hospital and thought about Clarice. What the hell. She had time.

Locking the RAV, she walked across the parking lot to Glen Gen, thinking it might be harder for the hospital gatekeepers to fob her off if she was there in person. Putting a smile on her face, she said earnestly to the woman at the reception desk, "Gosh, is it too early to see my aunt? Aunt Clarice Fenwick?"

The woman smiled in return. "Not necessarily. Do you know her room number?"

"I don't," said Mac regretfully, glancing around. "Oh, is your gift shop not open yet? I'd love to get her flowers. Yellow roses are her favorite, but any color really."

"They open at nine. You could maybe come back down and get some."

"Great idea!"

"I don't see your aunt's name. I'm sorry. Could she have been released?"

"Oh, yes! Maybe. Probably. That would be good. I'll check with her."

The woman smiled again and Mac thanked her and left. So Clarice had survived her suicide attempt, at least for now, and had probably been taken home. Good. She would try to see if she could get past Cliff and see her later, both because she wanted to be assured she was okay and because Clarice had things to say that may be important.

Mac went back to her RAV and climbed inside, looking at the clock on her dash. Eight thirty. Judy had not called her back and she was likely at work by now. Construction companies got going early. Time to call. She decided to forego Judy's cell phone in favor of the company phone number, and she didn't have to wait long before her call was answered by a bright, female voice. Fawn. The receptionist.

"Is Judy in?" Mac asked.

"Yes. Who may I say is calling?"

"This is her Aunt Dolores. She'll want to talk to me." The aunt excuse was a good one. A close relative, but just far enough away that most people wouldn't know if it was true or not.

"Oh. Okay." Fawn clicked off and was gone for a minute, but then came back on the line and said, "I'll transfer you now."

"Thank you." So, Judy wasn't returning Mackenzie Laughlin's call, but good old fake Aunt Dolores did the trick. Maybe Judy actually knew deceased Aunt Dolores's name.

"Hello. Who is this?" answered Judy, her voice impatient and prim.

"Mackenzie Laughlin. I left a message on your cell. Did you get it? I wanted to ask you if you've heard from Tobias Laidlaw since he left. LeeAnn hasn't." Mac threw everything out there as fast as possible in an effort to keep Judy from hanging up on her.

"I did get your message," said Judy, speaking slowly now, as if her mind was working out just how much to tell.

"Have you heard from him?"

"Not recently."

"Meaning . . . not since he's been on this latest trip? Is that it?"

"He doesn't always check in with me on a daily basis." Okay, time to push a little, otherwise they could do this dance all day. "Judy . . . is he missing or not? That's what LeeAnn wants to know."

"What are you to her? Why are you using Mr. Laidlaw's aunt's name? Is this some kind of scam?"

Mackenzie had already told her on the voice mail what her relationship was to LeeAnn, but she reiterated that she'd been hired to find her missing husband before saying, "LeeAnn's worried something happened to him. It's been a long time since she's heard from him. Longer than usual. If there's some reason he doesn't want to contact her, she doesn't know what it is, so if you've heard from him, you can put her mind at rest. That's all she needs to know."

"I have not heard from him." The words seemed to burst out of her. Like she'd been just waiting to say them.

"You've been worried," said Mac.

"I don't know if you're the person I should be talking to about this, but yes, I've been worried."

"I was with the River Glen PD. You can check on me. We're all on the same page here, is my guess."

"LeeAnn told you about Aunt Dolores?"

"A bit."

"Tobias—Mr. Laidlaw—was very upset at her death. He, well, he was close to his father, Victor Laidlaw, whose own death greatly affected him. And then, when his great-aunt died, it seemed to . . . energize him . . . again . . . to . . . learn more about his father."

She was tiptoeing through words, likely torn between her fear over Tobias's disappearance and her need to protect his privacy.

But she clearly wanted to talk, so Mac said, "He found information in her effects that made him feel his father had been poisoned."

"Well, yes," she said. "But of course it's untrue. Victor died of a heart attack. But this supposed proof of foul play sent him on this mission. That's what he called it, 'his mission' to find out who . . . killed his father." She said the words as if she were embarrassed at having to utter them.

"Where was he going? Do you know what his plan was?"

"Not really. He said he was going to talk to some of his father's friends. Maybe not friends, but the people who knew him."

"People who lived in the Villages?"

"I think so, yes."

The old guard. "Do you know if he talked to anyone specifically? Or if he got that far?"

"I'm sorry. He just left."

"Did he mention he wanted Victor's body exhumed?"

"No. I don't know. He just said he was going to look in to it, and he had that determined look in his eyes that meant he wasn't going to give up. And Granger Nye's death really hurt his soul, too. That and Aunt Dolores's death about the same time. It left him in a bad way."

Granger Nye was the Laidlaw Construction foreman who'd moved to Best Homes and basically traded places with Nolan. He'd died a few months earlier from a fall from the second-story of a Best Home under construction.

Judy said, "I haven't told anyone at work, but now I think I will. I really don't want to call the police. You never know. Maybe he'll show up this week."

Though she and Taft had shared much the same conversation last night, Mackenzie kind of felt it was unlikely at this point.

Mac tried a few more questions, but Judy appeared to be tapped out. Mac thanked her and hung up, then checked her email, but so far there was no list from Joseph Mertz at the Faraday Foundation.

Taft wheeled into the lot right at nine. He got out of his SUV and so did Mac. "Let's do this," he said, turning toward the front doors of Good Livin'.

"All right. But let me tell you what went down with Alfie last night—and by the way, Clarice has been released from the hospital. . . ." She gave him a quick rundown as they walked into Good Livin' together.

Cooper was leaning on his crutches, standing in the kitchen, as Jamie fussed around, not wanting to go to the school that morning. The kids were finished with classes, but she still had some cleaning out to do in her homeroom.

"I think I went to see Andrew Best last Friday," he said.

She turned to him in surprise. "You remember?"

"No . . . just have a sense of it. I wanted to talk to Debra Fournier, but Best was pissing me off. He's eely. You can't pin him down. Verbena and I had trouble with him before. He knows something about what happened to Granger Nye. He denied being there, but now that Verbena said there were likely three voices, I think his was one of them. I'm going on that assumption. From where I came down Stillwell Hill, I could have been at Best's house."

"Okay." She glanced at his crutches. "I don't want to be a nag, but should you be standing? I'm sorry, I have to go to the school for a while."

"C'mere," he said.

"What?" She gave him the evil eye, though she dropped the towel she'd been using to wipe a dish that wasn't completely dry when it came out of the dishwasher. "Don't you dare try to hug me because if you fall over, I'm not going to be to blame."

"I'm not going to fall over." He staggered a bit as she moved closer, then started laughing at the look on her face. "Joking."

"If you weren't such an invalid, I'd push you over myself," she declared as she slipped into his arms. He leaned against the counter, pulling her with him.

"I'm not an invalid."

"Don't go in today. I know you want to. Wait another day or two. Wait till the doctor releases you."

"I'm not going in today, but I'm going to be on the phone."

Jamie nodded. That was acceptable. "I won't be gone long. Promise me you'll be good."

"I'm always good." He grinned at her. He was coming back, feeling more like himself.

"And don't tire yourself out. You need legs? Use Verbena's. Or mine, or Harley's, or something. No, don't use Harley's. She already thinks she should go into law enforcement."

"She'll change her mind after she goes to Europe," he said, inhaling her gentle floral and citrus scent.

"She'll probably become a British bobby," grumbled Jamie.

He chuckled.

"She's come a long way since we moved here. All she did was fight me then."

She sounded wistful, and he knew she was thinking about not being able to bear another child. That Harley was going to go away and that she was awfully young to be an empty nester. That she wanted a child. With him.

He cleared his throat. They hadn't explored all the

possibilities that were still left to them, hadn't really had time. Now he asked, "Have you thought about surrogacy?"

She pulled back from him. "Yes. Have you?"

"I'm just throwing it out there."

She wagged her head back and forth. "Sure, it's been on my mind, but I don't know how I feel about it. I'm thinking about it. I don't know. What about you?"

"Whatever you want."

"No, you don't get to say that. We're in this together."

"I'm up for whatever you are."

"So to speak." She smiled, and he was glad to see that mischievous spark in her eyes again. She'd been worried and distracted too long. "If I give it serious thought, you need to, too, okay?"

"Okay," he said.

After she left he put a call in to Verbena and told his partner he thought he'd been to see Andrew Best the night of the accident.

She rolled that around in her mind. "Makes sense," she said. "Any recollection of what might have been said, given that you actually interviewed him?"

"Just a feeling I was there."

"I've been wanting to get Best in for questioning for a long time, but it's been hard. You know."

Yes, he knew. She was alluding to the chief's association with Andrew Best and other River Glen notables in the business world, and how Bennihof didn't like it when their investigations got close enough to scorch the local luminaries. "We may have to go to Best on our off hours," he said.

"Yeah . . ." She sounded distracted.

"I've caught you working. I'll leave you alone."

"It's not that. Haynes, I need to talk to you about something. I'll call you later."

When I'm alone.

She didn't have to say it. He knew what the unspoken message was. "Well, I'll be right here."

"Okay."

She texted him as soon as they'd hung up. *Give me an hour.*

Something was up that she didn't want anyone else at the station to overhear.

The Good Livin' staff were new and didn't recognize Taft, so they fell all over themselves trying to sell him a membership. Mac pretended interest in their sales pitch, but her nerves were already starting to stretch at what they might find if Taft's deduction about the locker combination proved correct.

She was unable to go into the men's locker room, so she used the time to pace outside the counter while the staff looked at one another with raised brows, wondering what was up with her. She rolled her shoulders to relieve some tension, annoyed with herself that of all the situations she found herself in, this would be the one that got to her. Where was her acting background now? She just wanted Taft to be right. She wanted him to bring Silva down.

Twenty minutes later Taft came out, smiling and looking relaxed as he talked to the young man earnestly selling him on the club. "I'm in," Taft told him with a laugh, holding up a hand to stop the pitch. "Bring on the paperwork."

Mac waited while Taft offered up his credit card. The sign-up process felt excruciating, but finally he was finished. He came over to her and said, "Let's go to the Cool Down Café. You're my guest today."

As soon as they were out of earshot and heading up

the stairs to the café, Taft said, "Both thirty-eight and thirty-nine have combination locks. I thought they might be electronic, but they're old-school. I'm going back in. Here's my number."

He handed her his temporary membership card and she took a seat at the bar. "I'll just order a cranberry juice," she told him.

"Good. I shouldn't be long." He headed back downstairs to the men's locker room again. From her bird's-eye view, Mac could watch the door and see if any club member followed Taft in.

She got her cranberry juice and drank it down as if she were in a contest, never taking her eyes off the walkway to the men's locker room door. One guy stepped through the door from the weight room and turned toward the locker room.

Mac stood up. She should have been down there to distract him. What if Taft was caught attempting to open someone else's locker?

Taft came back out a few minutes later. He looked up, caught her eye, and nodded.

Hallelujah. She hurried down the steps to join him and they walked into the sunny morning together.

"Well?"

"A Jumpdrive."

"You got it? It was there?"

"Locker thirty-eight. I tried thirty-nine first and it was a no go. Just got onto thirty-eight when that guy came in."

"I was worried about him," admitted Mac.

"He hardly paid any attention to me. I was able to open it with nineteen, eight and four. Now we just gotta look at it."

"My laptop's in the car. I don't normally like leaving it in the RAV, but sometimes I don't leave it at Daley's either."

"Let's see what we got."

They climbed into her SUV and Mac pulled her laptop out of its case. She switched it on and, once through facial recognition, turned it over to Taft. He slipped the Jump-drive into the USB port and uploaded the two files that were on it.

"Hope it's not malware," he said.

Mac made a strangled sound. "Don't even say it. No. It's Riskin's files. Otherwise you wouldn't have found it."

Taft clicked on the first file. It was a note that gave an address of his belongings made out to a woman in Fairbanks, Alaska. *If you're getting this*, it said, *I'm on my way.*

"He was retiring?" said Mac.

"Could be." Taft agreed grimly.

The second file was a video. They watched it together in silence. It was shot through a window into a bedroom, a near pornographic ten-minute scene between a man and a woman making love. Riskin's camera was close enough to the window to get a detailed view and the mic picked up some of the words, although beyond some serious moaning and groaning there wasn't much said.

When it ended, Mac cleared her throat. "Well, that's not Silva," she said. "That's Andrew Best." She'd seen Best a number of times, but even if she hadn't, the billboard with his huge smiling face welcoming would-be buyers to Staffordshire Estates would have helped her ID him. This was a little more of him than she would have preferred to see, however. "Who's the woman?"

Taft's eyes had narrowed. "Anna DeMarcos."

"That's Anna DeMarcos? Carlos DeMarcos's wife . . . widow?" Mac stared at the frozen picture that would begin the file again, should they care to view it. "Boy, has she changed."

"Million-dollar makeover," said Taft.

"This isn't what you were looking for, is it?"

He slowly shook his head. "Silva thinks Riskin had something on him. Maybe he did, but it's not this. But this is dynamite in its own right. Silva thinks the widow is his. If he should see this . . ."

"Andrew Best better run for his life."

"Best is a partner of Mangella's. Silva wouldn't mess with that . . . would he?" Taft mused. Before Mac could voice an opinion, he went on. "This is a betrayal. Silva won't be able to handle that. It doesn't matter who or what. He's a bloodthirsty son of a bitch. He'll turn on anybody, anytime. I pushed him and he's after me." He flicked her a look. "And you too. But if he sees this, he'll go after Andrew Best, guns loaded."

"So, what do we do?"

Taft closed down the laptop and handed it back to Mackenzie, who stuffed it back into its case. "Let's go see Andrew Best," he said, and Mac put the RAV in gear.

Verbena's call came through almost exactly an hour later. She launched right in. "Someone's accidentally erased the tape of whoever came in and took the keys to your car Friday."

"Erased," Cooper repeated.

"It's just in our memories now. No photographic evidence of who took the car."

Cooper thought about that for a moment, then asked, "How does the chief feel about it?"

"He's making a lot of noise, but that's about it. No one's saying it, but we all think he knows something about it."

"You think the chief erased it?"

A brief hesitation, then, "More likely got someone to do it for him."

Chief Bennihof had messed around with them a lot, but he'd never done anything so blatant, so overtly criminal. "You sure?"

"No, I'm not sure," Verbena came back at him a bit testily. "But pretty convinced. Richards has been strutting around like a banty rooster, so I'm thinking he may be the tool Bennihof used. Probably thinks this'll get him the promotion. Maybe it will. I can't believe I'm saying this about the chief."

"I know."

"But it's been coming," she went on doggedly. "He's been running with Mangella and Best and others. He wants to play with the big boys." She paused, then added, "He knows you haven't given up on the Nye case."

Cooper didn't want to believe Chief Bennihof had anything to do with his accident. That was too far-fetched, wasn't it?

"How're you doing? You getting back here soon?" she asked.

If I still have a job . . . Someone had deliberately sabotaged his car. It wasn't random. So, someone wanted him out of the way. Could it be someone who had the chief in their pocket? "You think I was getting too close to Best," he said.

"That's exactly what I'm thinking. I'm going to go see him today," she stated firmly. "Anything you want me to ask him for you?'

"You could tell him we have evidence that he was one of the three people at that construction site."

"But that would be an untruth."

He heard the amusement beneath her words. "Ask him who the third person was."

"I might do that."

Cooper hung up feeling grimly satisfied that Andrew Best would be faced with Elena Verbena.

Chapter Twenty-Two

Andrew Best looked out at the view from his office: a weedy patch of dirt. Fallow land that might or might not be used for expansion of a wing of the modular building that housed his office staff. His offices weren't opulent, impressive, or first class, but then, they weren't supposed to be. They were utilitarian The opulence was reserved for the several model homes staged with outrageously expensive appointments—lighting, appliance, hardwood, kitchen and bathroom fixtures—that really weren't part of the overall Best Homes package, not to mention the furniture his wife, who considered herself an interior designer, had purchased. Pieces that cost so much he wanted to weep. In truth Mary Jo was a middle-aged woman running to fat with wispy hair and a weakness for designer handbags who'd morphed from the luscious, sloe-eyed, sexy woman with the large inheritance he'd married eighteen years earlier. That inheritance had gone into Best Homes and so her name was listed as co-owner He couldn't leave her without risking the company. Divorce was a nuclear blast that would blow his bottom line to radioactive smithereens.

And now . . . ? He was in a vise. Being squeezed for the very company he only owned half of.

If Andrew were the kind of man for self-reflection, he would recognize he was having a crisis of conscience. He'd made a business decision that could torpedo his company. Though Best Homes was having its best year ever, there'd been that dip or two a few years back that had forced him to scramble for money, and it was during one of those dips that he'd become vulnerable. Loans that had amassed huge interest. Loans he couldn't pay back. Loans Mary Jo didn't know about.

And now payment was due. He wasn't sure how he was going to pay it. He was in active negotiations and there was a little bit of light at the end of the tunnel. He would have to get Mary Jo to go with him on this, though. Would have to come clean about the loans . . .

He thought about his stolen moments with Anna, and it was a relief and a pleasure to lose himself in the memories of their lovemaking. The last year had been a shit show. All the bad things going on beneath the surface of the business bubbling up.

A knock sounded on his office door. "Come in," he stated flatly, knowing he was inviting in trouble. He had no desire to allow the River Glen Police into his business; they'd nagged him for months. But he also liked to keep up the disguise of friendly relations. There was a longer game being played by the people who mattered in this town, and if that meant entertaining one of River Glen's finest for a few minutes, fine.

He had to be on his best behavior right now or the financial hammer would come down.

He was sweating lightly as his secretary opened the door and a female detective, all dressed in black, stepped inside, her expression forbidding.

So much for friendly relations.

If Nye were still alive, this wouldn't be happening, although Andrew wasn't sorry he was dead.

"Hello, Mr. Best. I'm Detective Verbena," she introduced herself.

He didn't offer his hand. She didn't expect it, which was good. "What can I do for you?"

"Detective Haynes met with you at your house last Friday."

So she knew. He hadn't heard anything since the car accident and had thought this obsession with him finally might be over. But then he looked at her dark eyes and set mouth, the dark hair scraped back into a bun, the black jacket and shirt, the bit of holster peeking from beneath the jacket that hid her gun. He'd been tired of Detective Cooper Haynes, who just wouldn't give up even when Nye's death was ruled an accident, even when the case was closed. He'd complained about Haynes and, well, Haynes was off the case. But now . . . ?

Better the devil you know.

He didn't like this woman on sight.

Time to get rid of her. "The foreman of my company is dead, Detective," he said brusquely. "I'm running a company without a foreman and have been for months. I don't have time for this continued harassment. Yes, Detective Haynes stopped by my house, and I'll tell you what I told him: I don't know what happened when Granger Nye fell. I wasn't there."

"But you *were* there."

His heart stuttered. Did she know? How could she? He shook his head at her, not trusting his voice.

"There were three people in the argument at the construction site. Granger Nye, you, and someone else."

"I don't know where you get your wild ideas, but that's not what I've heard. . . ." But he heard his voice start to rise, could feel his face turning red.

"We have evidence, Mr. Best."

How? What? No one knew.

"Did you kill Granger Nye?" she asked.

"No!"

"Who was the third man?"

"Detective . . . ?"

"Verbena," she filled in for him.

He could feel himself start to hyperventilate. He needed this to stop. He needed to talk to Mangella right away. *This wasn't his fault!*

"You can talk to my lawyer." He practically lunged for the office intercom and said to his secretary, "Please show Detective Verbingla out of my office."

"Mr. Best, this isn't going away," she warned. "And it's Verbena."

The Best Homes office was a modular building with a set of wide concrete steps that apparently was supposed to make it look grander than it was. Mac and Taft had been there before, masquerading as would-be buyers for one of the Best Homes being built in Staffordshire Estates.

That ruse hadn't been that long ago, so Mac asked Taft, "How do you want to do this?"

"Not going to work as 'John' and 'Brooke' this time."

"Don't think so." Their alter egos were a liability.

"We'll go as ourselves. We'll probably get thrown out, but before that happens, I want Best to know we're dogging him."

"Not going to show him the video?"

"Not until I know more. But Best is in a deal with Mangella, and Keith Silva is Mangella's fixer now. I don't know how that plays out with Best and Anna DeMarcos hooking up."

"Complicated."

"Foolhardy. There's no chance it ends well. We'll go in together and play it a little by ear, in case we get stymied at the front desk." Taft's phone rang and he hesitated before answering it; he was anxious to confront Best. But then Mac saw on the screen that the call was from the River Glen PD. They looked at each other and then he placed the phone to his ear and answered, "Taft."

"Hey, Face," a female voice said, loud enough for Mac to hear. "Just heard from county. Riskin's death is a suicide."

Mac recognized The Battle-ax's voice.

"Not a surprise," said Taft grimly.

"Not a surprise at all," she answered.

"Thanks."

"De nada."

He clicked off. "You heard?" he asked Mac.

"Yep. You knew it."

"Herdstrom is remarkably predictable."

"What are you going to do?" she asked.

"I'll think about it." She could almost see him calculating his next move. "Silva will be feeling safe. I might call him and tell him I have proof that he was at the Rosewood Court, maybe a video just came to light that caught him coming and going from the storeroom. I'll talk to Herdstrom and tell him the same. They'll worry it's true."

"They'll want proof."

"Herdstrom might not believe it. It would've come to light by now, and he can always fall back on 'I made a mistake' if he's questioned about the cause of death. But Silva will bite. That's who he is. He might not believe there's a video, but he won't be certain. He won't be able to help himself. He'll have to find out. He'll do something."

"Why did Riskin take the video of Best and DeMarcos?" They'd downloaded both files to her computer and Taft had put the Jumpdrive in his pocket. Taft. Not Jesse. She was relieved to realize she seemed to be over using his first name like Daley did.

"Riskin was looking for something on Silva and probably stumbled on Best with the widow. This is recent. Silva got with her before her husband's body was even cold, but Riskin's video is of the River Glen Grill building, and Anna's only lived in those apartments since she got the life insurance money."

"So, she's cheating on Silva."

"That's how he'll take it, no matter what the situation," said Taft.

"You don't think there's any chance Riskin showed it to him?"

He shook his head. "There'd be more fireworks between Silva and Anna. He may have hinted at it, though. Riskin was in the information-trading business. He wasn't necessarily into blackmail or extortion, but he didn't like Silva. Having something on him would give him power." He thought about it for a moment. "But somehow Silva got Riskin to meet him at the storeroom in the middle of the night. Things went bad and Riskin died. Silva didn't get whatever he was looking for."

"And you more or less told him you had that information, whatever it is."

"Yep. I'm pushing on both Silva and Herdstrom."

"The Villages HOA board meeting is tonight," she reminded him. "Herdstrom might be there," she added as both of them started getting out of her SUV.

"I might tag along with you if I don't reach him."

They started for the steps. Mac mentally prepared herself for the meeting with Best. She already didn't much care for the man. Maybe it was because Nolan had worked for him and she'd been told how difficult he was, or maybe it was just that frozen, smiling face on his billboard that got to her, or maybe it was the sex video where he was groaning and pumping away that she kinda wished she could unsee. In any case, he might be one of River Glen's wealthiest and most influential citizens these days, but Mac thought he was overhyped and likely consumed with ego.

And then Detective Elena Verbena walked out the doors and down the wide, concrete steps of Best Homes. Mac and Taft stopped short halfway across the lot.

"Shit," said Mac.

Verbena, in turn, slowed her steps. "Laughlin . . . Taft . . ." she said, looking from one to the other. "What's going on?"

Mac glanced at Taft, who said, "Hi, Elena. You here on the Nye business?"

"That case is closed," she answered carefully.

"Is it closed?" he answered back.

Her eyes narrowed. Her black hair was scraped back into a bun and she had a stern, unforgiving look on her face that made her seem as approachable as an ice-crusted planet.

Mackenzie kept quiet. She still had a good relationship with Cooper Haynes that she wanted to maintain. Though she'd never had any trouble with Elena Verbena, she sensed that could change with a wrong word now.

Taft, however, apparently had no such qualms. "Let's trade information," he suggested, smiling, his dimples engaging.

She didn't thaw. "Taft, you know that's not how it works."

"If you've talked to Portland PD, you already know I think Keith Silva killed Jimmy Riskin. And I just learned the ME's office ruled it a suicide. Dr. Sandy Herdstrom doesn't always make rulings based on fact. Sometimes he's told what to put on a death certificate."

She sidestepped the issue of Herdstrom and asked, "Why are you here?"

"Somewhere in all this is the nexus between Keith Silva, Andrew Best, and Mitch Mangella."

"Mitch Mangella? Your . . . client?" she questioned.

"I did some work for him."

His tone said that was over, and Mackenzie suspected Verbena may have already known that anyway.

"What do you want with Best?" she asked.

Mac wondered how much Taft was planning on revealing to her and was a little surprised when he laid it all out.

"Jimmy Riskin left me a video of Anna DeMarcos in bed with Andrew Best. I'm guessing she's been seeing Best behind Silva's back. Meanwhile, Silva wants the information Riskin gave to me. Thinks it incriminates him. He broke into my apartment looking for it."

"When was this?"

"A few nights ago," said Taft.

"You report it?"

"No."

She shook her head at him. "Where's this information?"

"The only information I have is the sex video, but I've led Silva to think there's something more."

She absorbed that and gave Taft a long look. "Good luck with that."

"Why were you here?" Taft asked her.

Verbena didn't want to answer him. Opened her mouth to say just that. Mac could read her. But then she seemed to think it over. "What do you think talking to Best is going to get you?"

"Maybe nothing. I was just going to chat with him."

"I suggest you stay away from him. Let us do our job."

"If we learn anything," Taft said, including Mackenzie, "we'll let you know."

"Best is only talking through his lawyer, so my advice to you is stay away. But . . ." She had started to turn away, but now she stopped and said, "I'm seeing Haynes this afternoon. I'll tell him I ran into you."

Mac watched Verbena walk to her personal car, a sleek, black Audi similar to Daley's silver one. No city ride for the detective, although after what had happened with Cooper Haynes, it was probably a smart idea.

"What do you think that means?" asked Mac.

"They're hoping we learn something. Best has blocked them with his lawyer. Let's try something. Instead of going in, I want you to call Best and ask for him. When you get him, I'll take the phone."

"You want me to call," she repeated.

"Tell whoever's at the front desk that you're Anna DeMarcos and you need to talk to him."

"Ahh . . . then you'll talk to him about the video. . . ."
He smiled.

She made the call on Taft's phone and got the runaround for a bit, but once the woman at the front desk checked with Best and gave the Anna DeMarcos name, she was put through.

"Anna?" Best came on the line, sounding slightly alarmed.

Mac handed the phone back to Taft, who answered, "This is Jesse Taft. I have a sex video of you with Anna DeMarcos that Keith Silva wants. Silva broke into my home to get it, but it's safe with me for now."

"*What?*"

"Silva may not know about the video yet. He may not know you're on it. But he knows Riskin had sensitive information and he thinks I've got it now."

"Are you trying to blackmail me?" Best's voice rose with outrage and fear.

"I'm just letting you know where things stand." And he hung up.

"Now what?" asked Mac.

"Let's wait and see if anything happens."

As it turned out, they didn't have to wait long. A black Tahoe suddenly careened out of a parking spot at the end of the parking lot and ripped toward the main road, Andrew Best behind the wheel, no evidence of his big smile anywhere to be seen.

"He's scared," said Mac, switching on the engine and carefully following him onto the road. She didn't want to be seen by him, but that wasn't a problem. She had to step on the accelerator to keep him in sight.

"He knows Silva will come after him."

"Where do you think he's going?"

"Mangella."

Sure enough, he was proved right when the Tahoe turned onto the street where Mitch and Prudence Mangella lived. "The big boss."

"Best wants Silva off his ass. Drive on past," he told her. "Turn at the next block and let's get out of here."

"You don't want to get any closer?"

"Don't need to. Best got spooked and is looking for help. Now we'll see if Mangella tries to rein Silva in, if he even can."

As Mac turned around, she asked, "You think Mangella knows about Best and Anna DeMarcos?"

"Depends on whether it's supposed to be a secret. If Best's telling Mitch about my call, which I'd bet he is, he knows now."

"What about Verbena? She was probably at Best's because of Nye's death. Like you said, they haven't let it go. What about Haynes's accident? Have you heard any more about why it's suspicious?"

"Not yet."

Mac realized The Battle-ax would probably come through for him on that. "You think Haynes'll contact you . . . us?"

"Verbena said that for a reason."

They passed Glen Gen on their way to the Good Livin' parking lot. As Mac pulled in, her cell phone buzzed. "Mackenzie Laughlin," she answered, coming to a stop next to Taft's Jeep.

"Abby Messinger," a woman's voice snapped back, matching her tone. "I went to your house, but no one's answering. I had to get your number from Althea."

Althea was pretty quick to hand out her phone number.

Mac wondered if it was just to members of the neighbor-hood watch or it was an all-out broadcast.

Before Mac could respond, in a voice throbbing with emotion, Abby said, "You accosted my son last night and he told me you were going to talk to me today! I don't know who you think you are, but you should mind your own business!"

Taft had opened the door and stepped out, but now he leaned back in the still-open door and raised his brows, able to hear Abby's voice as Mac put the phone on Speaker.

"Your son was spray-painting the front of the Carreras' porch," said Mac. "He admitted to stealing the packages off their porch."

"I don't see that it's your affair!"

"It's the Carreras'. And I'm working for them."

She was breathing heavily. "I would like to see you in person," she said tautly. Then, "I'll be here all day."

"I can be there in half an hour," said Mac.

"Good." Abby hung up abruptly.

Taft said, "Mother bear."

"Leon described her the same way. So, I know where I'm going next."

"As Verbena said, 'Good luck with that.'"

"Thanks. Keep in contact," she said.

He gave her a high sign as he shut the passenger door and then looked around the lot before heading to his vehicle.

She eased the RAV out of the parking lot and aimed for the Villages and the Messinger house once more.

"Clarice . . ."

Cliff stood in front of her chair, holding her cell phone. He seemed to think it was a big deal. Yes, she'd hidden it from him, but with everything else wrong in their lives she was finding it hard to understand why this was the hill he chose to die on.

Die on . . .

She hadn't succeeded in meeting the Lord. They'd pumped her stomach and saved her. Not enough of the drugs had penetrated her blood and tissues.

"Burt and Darrell and Evelyn and Tamara and the rest of 'em are gonna stop by," said Cliff. "They want to make sure you're all right." He was sliding his fingers over the phone. He didn't know the pass code. He'd asked her for it, but she'd pretended to be in a catatonic state. She'd been pretending since Cliff took her out of the hospital. She'd seen Abby Messinger there. She'd come in early this morning even though it was, apparently, one of her days off. She'd stared at Clarice, who'd closed her eyes and wished herself to disappear. It had helped enough that it gave her the idea for the catatonic state by the time Cliff arrived.

But Abby hadn't let Clarice's closed eyes stop her. She'd leaned into her and said in a hushed voice, "Remember, we didn't do anything, Clarice. They did it all. We didn't know anything until it was too late."

That was when the trembling started again. The pills had kept her from shaking and it had been marvelous, but Abby's pleading voice had made Clarice's heart start beating a little too fast, her head fill with terrible images . . . a wet night, a bright moon, the dull silver glint on the shovel.

We did something, Abby. We all did.

"I need that Mackenzie person's phone number. Cliff said you have it."

So, Cliff had already let the others know about her attempt to leave this terrible world. Her failed attempt. That Mackenzie person and her boyfriend had saved her. She remembered feeling the comfort of his strong arms and tears formed behind her lids. She didn't want to stay, but it had been nice to feel safe.

"You can't say anything or we'll all be in trouble," Abby rushed on. "Clarice, I know you don't want to hurt Cliff or any of us. Just don't say anything . . . and try to get better."

She'd had to add on that last part. Abby might pretend to be nice, but she was as bad as Clarice was herself. They were all bad. They used to think they were good, that they were making the right choices, but they were wrong. Clarice hadn't hated Victor as much then. She hadn't recognized his evil heart. He was a flirt. Like Dr. Andre, maybe even worse, but yes, she'd flirted with him, even gone to bed with him. "Knocking boots," Cliff called it whenever he was talking about someone else. He'd never been sure about Victor and her, but he'd suspected, and he'd hated Victor for it, almost as much as she'd learned to hate him herself.

Her hatred had started when Victor wangled land from the Friends of Faraday. To this day she didn't know how he'd done it. She'd been horrified. Cliff hadn't cared, but he'd been glad to see how infuriated she was with Victor. But then Cliff turned around and *invested* with Victor in those three lots! He'd climbed onto his bulldozer and cleared them, made way for those monster houses.

And . . . and God help her, she'd gone along with it. She'd set aside her convictions and been seduced by dollar signs. Cliff had told her they were going to make a fortune on those houses, and she'd turned away from the Friends of Faraday and joined Victor's team. A bargain with the devil.

You got screwed once again, she'd told herself over the years. Ha, ha. A real joke. And then, guess what? There

was no more money left. Victor used the funds she and
Cliff and others invested with him to pay off old debts,
and there wasn't enough for the construction of the new
homes. *And the Friends of Faraday sued him!* Her friends.
Her compatriots. She couldn't tell them she was on the
other side. None of them knew that most of Cliff and
Clarice's savings were with Victor. She'd hidden that. She
was ashamed, but she'd done it . . . she'd done it. . . .

And God knew. He saw all. He knew what a fraud she'd
been.

But it didn't end there, did it, Clarice?

No, it didn't. Victor's son, Tobias Laidlaw, with the help
of Victor's foreman, saved the project through some kind
of financial restructuring she didn't understand. What she
did understand was that their investment money, all their
savings, everything they'd worked for, was gone . . . and
yet Victor still built the houses. He won, while she and
Cliff lost everything.

Clarice still hated Victor Laidlaw. Hated him for turning
her evil. For taking all her money and causing them to
scrimp and save, scrimp and save, barely make ends meet.
She hated him for using her and tossing her aside like
garbage. She hated him for turning from her to Evelyn, who
in those days was quite the looker. She had those breasts,
whereas Clarice was straight as a stick. She never really
knew whether Evelyn had succumbed to Victor's charms,
although she had that stillborn child and the rumors had
swirled that it was Victor's, not Darrell's. But rumors
were just rumors. They flourished in *Victor's* Villages in
those days, and a lot of them weren't true. But some of
them were. Like Tamara leaving Burt for Victor. *Twice.*
Clarice had almost enjoyed seeing how crushed Tamara
was. Yes, she hated Victor, but she couldn't bear being his

only casualty. Tamara had lost Burt over Victor, who'd promised her marriage and a life together, but Victor was a liar. "A lying sack of shit," Burt had called him, and Cliff and Darrell, all of them, had echoed that phrase over the years. Tamara had tried to get back with Burt after the second time she'd run to Victor, but it hadn't happened. And Abby and Andre . . . they'd lost money, too, Cliff had said. Again, it had made Clarice feel better. Collective hate. That's what they all felt for Victor Laidlaw.

"Clarice," Cliff said again now, his tone begging.

She continued to stare ahead. Poor Cliff. He'd had to work so hard all these years. Scrimping and saving, scrimping and saving for their old bones.

And it could have almost been okay. Their future wasn't bright, but their house was almost paid off. They could've maybe afforded for Cliff to retire someday. Not today, but sometime, maybe . . .

Fifteen years since Victor was put in the ground. Fifteen years to put that chapter behind them. And it almost happened!

Until Tobias Laidlaw got all worked up again about Victor being murdered. Burt said there'd been some note in Victor's aunt's will where Victor begged her for money and swore he was being poisoned. The same old rumor, only written down this time for Tobias to read over and over again, and Tobias—well, Burt said he was one of those people who made up their own truth and then looked for ways to prove it. Clarice could have told him there was only one truth, God's truth, but she didn't really know Tobias Laidlaw.

She shivered violently.

"Clarice?" asked Cliff, swimming into her vision, which

was strangely veiled and liquid now. Something wrong. Her pretend catatonia was turning into something else.

"Goddamn it, Clarice. What are you doing? We're almost there! Don't blow this for us. What's wrong with you? We've got some money saved. We've managed. We could go somewhere. Somewhere sunny Hawaii, maybe, or Mexico. Acapulco? You love the beach. We can afford a trip."

Once upon a time she had loved the beach. She'd thought he'd forgotten. He'd stopped looking at her so long ago in that loving way a husband should care for his wife that she was surprised and touched.

But he was wrong about trying to entice her with a vacation.

The only place she wanted to go now was heaven, and it was going to be a hard, long road to those pearly gates. Was it too late for her? She prayed to God every minute of every day that it wasn't. If only she'd been able to make her confession in the park. She could maybe be there by now, pleading her case. What could she do to rectify all she'd done? To break this bargain with the devil?

Confession *Confession*.

Cliff's hands were on her shoulders and he was shaking her. "Clarice! Clarice!" he was yelling.

"It was my idea to poison him," she said. "You all know it."

And then her heart slowed and slowed and she prayed for it to stop.

Chapter Twenty-Three

"Oh my God, if Claude comes over here now, I'm going to lose my shit," said Abby, stepping away from the living room window. "Goddamn it. There he is."

"You shouldn't be so nice to him," said Andre.

"Nice to him? I'm downright rude. He just won't take the message."

She could still see outside and there he was, walking up her steps, carrying a bag of something. Please, God, no more bakery goods. Claude's old-fashioned way of wooing her was to fatten her up, apparently.

"Well, get rid of him," ordered Andre.

She gave him a cool look. She hadn't asked him to be here. She didn't want him to be here. But like Claude, he kept hanging around her like a bad smell. She and Andre were locked together because of past choices, but today she didn't have time for either him or Claude. She was about to face Mackenzie Laughlin and she was on pins and needles, almost sick with fear. That damn detective, or whatever she was, was like one of those terriers who bit onto your leg and wouldn't let go no matter what you did.

Andre wandered down the hall as the doorbell rang.

Abby stalked to the door, threw it open and there was pathetic Claude, smiling like a dope, handing her the bag. "Croissants," he said.

She'd made the mistake once of mentioning she liked croissants in his range of hearing. Liked, not loved, but he was burying her in them. Luckily Alfie scarfed them down and didn't gain an ounce with his teenage metabolism.

"Thank you," she said. Tersely. Rudely.

But he didn't take the message. He just loitered on the porch, still wearing the stupid smile, hoping to be asked in. He was, unfortunately, her next-door neighbor. He'd owned a different house in the Villages, but when the one next door came on the market he'd snapped it up, paying over-listing price by over ten thousand, she knew. She'd checked on Redfin. She was pretty sure it had eaten into his meager savings, and all because he wanted to live next door to her.

When it became clear Abby wasn't going to proffer the invite, Claude cleared his throat and said, "I know you're not going in to work till later; would you like to go to lunch?"

"I can't, Claude. I'm really busy." So now he knew her work schedule? It was stalking. It really was. Claude Marfont was a stalker.

"Okay, then." He lifted a hand like he understood, a signature move.

She slammed the door after him and watched him saunter back to his house, his shoulders down in dejection.

"Get a fucking life," she muttered. Did he really think she was in his age bracket? Sure, she was older than a lot of the younger neighbors, but she wasn't *that* old. She didn't look *that* old.

He was barely out of sight when Abby saw the dark blue SUV approach and park across the street.

"There she is," said Andre from somewhere behind her. Then, "What are you going to do?"

"Nothing!" she flashed. How many times did she have to say it? "Talk to her. Get her to lay off Alfie. That's all."

"We have to do something about her. You know how Burt feels."

"All I'm going to do is get her to leave." She glared at him. How had she ever thought she was in love with him? He had one move—*one move*—a slithery, catlike approach and a purr that had, yes, made for some wild sex once upon a time, and he'd seemed like such a catch. A doctor! She'd felt so lucky! So what that he'd been banging the other nurses, as many as were willing—and there were a lot who were willing. So what? Because in the end she'd won the prize. He'd chosen *her* for his wife. Woo-hoo! Break out the champagne. Let's have a dance party!

Except he hadn't stopped cheating at all. Hadn't even slowed down. Andre had used his one move on every woman who crossed his path.

Now, she set her jaw, getting ready to do battle with the detective. But she could hear Andre *breathing* behind her. She wanted to slap him. She really did. She'd just learned that Linda had finally kicked him out, which had brought her some momentary joy. If she didn't have all these goddamn problems, she could revel in it!

Good old Andre. The body sculpting doctor. Well, he'd gotten a little too close to a number of those bodies that he went on local TV and crowed about sculpting . . . for a reasonable price. *Just look at how you'll look,* TV Andre said with that smile, touting his success stories. *Look at these bodies!* But come on, Andre, aren't all those bodies really under forty? When Linda had cut him loose she'd actually called Abby and told her that yes, she was right. Andre was a rutting piece of shit. Quite a comedown for the bitch, though Abby did appreciate the honesty.

But now Andre was camped on her doorstep again. A bigger problem than Claude the stalker. She wished he wasn't here for this upcoming interview. Thank God Alfie was at a friend's house. Her mind tripped to her son. God, how was she going to get through the summer with him around all the time? With *both of them* around?

"Don't get in my way," she warned Andre as the doorbell rang.

"Maybe I should do the talking. You're too emotional."

"Oh, fuck you. Get out of my sight."

"Like I said . . ." But he backed farther down the hall, holding up his hands. "You might need some help with her if things go sideways, Ab. That's all I'm saying."

She shook her head as he disappeared into Alfie's room. She heard the bedroom door close at the same time the doorbell rang again. She stepped forward again, stopping for a moment to smooth down her blouse. Then she lifted her chin and let the little, self-important, not-a-real detective in.

When the door opened Mac was faced with Abby Messinger's rictus smile. She was clearly not a happy camper. Alfie had put her in a tough position.

"Come in," said Abby, stepping back and extending her arm.

Regardless of the grand gestures, Abby's body language told the true story of how she felt about having Mac on her doorstep. Angry, aggressive, and hostile. Okay, well, she hadn't expected anything different.

"Could I get you something? Coffee . . . tea, maybe with some . . . ?"

"Arsenic?" asked Mac with a smile. Something about the look on Abby Messinger's face had made her pop out with it.

"Cream . . . ?" Abby blinked twice and added, "Umm . . . wine? Is it too early?"

"No, I'm fine. Thank you."

She took Mac into the kitchen and hooked a thumb toward the chairs around a square table clearly used for informal meals. Mac seated herself as Abby went to the cupboard and pulled out a stemmed glass. She then turned to the refrigerator and yanked out a half-full bottle of white wine. "Excuse me, but I need something to calm me down a bit," she said. "You accused my son of stealing and defacing property."

"I caught him in the act and he admitted it," corrected Mac. Abby seemed bent on changing the narrative.

"What do you plan to do?" She yanked out the cork with surprising strength and splashed wine into her glass.

"I haven't had a chance to talk to Daley and Leon. That is really their call."

"Is it?" She stared at Mac as she kept filling the glass. Mac almost reached forward to stop her from spilling, but Abby managed to keep from overpouring by some sixth sense apparently.

"I told Alfie to talk to you about it. Abby, I know you put the dog poop in the mailbox."

"Okay, I did it. There. I did it. You got me. I didn't want Alfie to get in trouble for his pranks. Go ahead and sue me."

She drank her wine the same way she poured it, with her eyes on Mac.

"Okay, then," said Mac, recognizing Abby's intention was to punish her. This meeting wasn't exactly going to be conducive to putting things right between the Messingers and the Carreras. "I think my part in this is concluded. Thank you?"

"Alfie was misinformed about my relationship with Leon. There is no relationship. You don't know me, but I'm not interested in cheating." She raised her voice a bit, as if playing to a larger audience.

Okay, this was at least a start. "Alfie seems to think the Martins were swindled out of the Carreras' house."

Abby made a strangled sound. "Carol Martin is over-the-top. She can't let it go! Alfie likes Carol. She used to bake monster cookies at Halloween and give them to her favorite kids, Alfie being at the top of the list. He adored her as a kid, and now he's apparently listening to her bull-shit and acting to avenge her. I've called her and told her to leave my son alone, but she doesn't listen."

"Maybe you should talk to Alfie," suggested Mac. Alfie's crimes had been fairly minor and apparently done in the name of chivalry. A little direction was all he probably needed.

"You don't need to tell me how to raise my kid."

"Okay." Mac stood up.

"Are you going to the police?" Abby suddenly demanded.

"I'm going to talk to the Carreras. As I said, it's their call."

"But they hired you. You have sway with them, I'm sure. Is there something . . . anything . . . I could help you with . . . ?"

To make this go away.

Mac looked at Abby. Momma Bear and then some. She thought about her reaction when Mac had joked about the arsenic. Tobias had been planning on meeting with the old guard about his father's supposed poisoning. Why was Mac tiptoeing around it? Abby was already in a mood to fight, so . . . "Well, I'm working on another case now that maybe you've heard something about. The disappearance of Tobias Laidlaw, Victor Laidlaw's son? Tobias believes his father was murdered—poisoned, actually—and it looks like he's on some kind of quest to prove that's true. He's been missing awhile."

Abby looked down at her glass. Then she tipped it up and swallowed the rest in a huge gulp. Wiping the back of her hand across her mouth, she said carefully, "I don't know Tobias well, but I've heard about his wild theories. No one takes them seriously."

"He takes them seriously. He apparently is looking in to exhuming Victor's body."

Her skin had turned a deep shade of pink. "I'm afraid I can't help you with that. Is there anything else?"

"I guess not. I'll talk to Daley and Leon and maybe you can work things out between your two families."

"Are you still staying at the Carreras'? While you . . . look for Tobias?" The question seemed wrung from her, like she had to ask it even though she didn't really want to.

"So far. Maybe not for long."

"It sounds like you're wasting your time."

"Well, you never know." Mac heard a thud from a room down the hall. Alfie? Or Dr. Andre? She was pretty sure it was his car that was parked on the street. "Is there anyone else who might know about Tobias? Burt Deevers maybe? He was Victor's lawyer during the lawsuit with the Friends of Faraday."

"Tobias just takes off for weeks on end. He gets an idea and runs with it and turns everybody's lives upside down. He's . . . unstable. Really. Always has been."

"I thought you didn't know him."

"I know of him," she said tautly. "We all do. He was Victor's son."

"I understand he was stable enough fifteen years ago to pull his father's business from bankruptcy and finish the three overlook houses."

"You think that was Tobias?" Another sound thudded from the other room. Mac turned toward it, but Abby ignored it and ran right on. "People worked for Tobias. They were his employees and they did the work. It was Victor's foreman who finished those houses, not Tobias. He helped Tobias secure the loan to complete the project. People lost a lot of money because of Victor, a *lot* of money . . . but what did Tobias do? Just picked up the pieces that were already there and make a fortune. If Victor had lived, he would have come out smelling like a rose, too. That company? Laidlaw Construction? Tobias lucked into it. He's never known what to do with it. It just fell into his lap."

There was silence after that.

Abby's chest was rising and falling. Mac waited a moment to see if she would keep going, but instead she seemed to come back to herself. "I'm sorry," she said. "Andre and I lost some money with Victor. I don't really know Tobias, but I know that he got something he didn't deserve." She drew a breath. "Please tell Daley and Leon that we will reimburse them for any costs they've incurred because of Alfie's pranks."

And yours. "I will."

Mac got back in her RAV and gave a last look at the

house as she drove off, noting Dr. Andre's car at the end
of the block.

When she was parked in front of the Carreras' again,
she picked up her cell and texted Taft. Just finished with
Abby Messinger. Smiling faintly, she added, I'll fill you in
later.

As she stepped out of her car, she saw two women just
coming down the steps of Althea Gresham's house, catty-
corner across the street. They saw her at the same time and
waved and turned toward her.

Jeannie McDonald and Mariah Copple. Mac shut her
car door as the two of them hurried to meet up with her.
What now?

Taft was seated in his Jeep behind the River Glen Grill
again. His calls into the ME's office and Sandy Herdstrom
had gone unanswered. He'd debated on whether to leave
the man a message and finally had, dropping his own
name along with Tobias and LeeAnn Laidlaw's on Herdstrom's voice mail. If Herdstrom had his ear to the ground,
he'd know that Taft was calling because he didn't agree
with the doctor's suicide decision on Riskin. And if Tobias
Laidlaw had actually ordered the exhumation of his father's
remains, Herdstrom, who still lived in the Villages, would
likely know why Taft and the Laidlaws might want to talk
to him about that as well.

Taft then thought about calling Silva but figured the
conversation would just devolve into insults again and
decided to hold on that.

He kept coming back to Herdstrom and realized he was
missing some information. He put in another call to LeeAnn
Laidlaw, asking for the name of Tobias's lawyer. They had

been talking all around this supposed exhumation and it was time to find out if Tobias had gone through with it. LeeAnn gave him the number, and when he reached the offices of Burns and Ledbetter LLC, he asked for Neil Ledbetter but was shunted to Neil's secretary. The secretary hedged when Taft asked to speak to Ledbetter, which made Taft figure he was in his office while she screened his calls. Taft told her that he was working for Tobias Laidlaw, which finally got him to the man.

"What can I do for you, Mr. Taft?" Ledbetter answered brusquely.

"Did you file the request for the exhumation of Victor Laidlaw's body, Tobias's Laidlaw's father?"

"Why are you asking?" he asked suspiciously.

Taft explained he was really working for LeeAnn Laidlaw, that Tobias Laidlaw was incommunicado, and that everyone wanted to make sure the exhumation request had gotten to the courts.

"You know it takes a long time to get an exhumation. There are protocols. I told Tobias this."

"Mr. and Mrs. Laidlaw understand. They just want a time estimate. Weeks? Months?"

"It's still in progress. That's all I can say."

"All right. Thank you. I'll pass it along."

So, the exhumation request had been filed. Did Herdstrom know that? Taft guessed he did. And what had he done when he'd learned Tobias was really going through with the exhumation? That he'd moved from just thinking his father had been murdered—poisoned, perhaps—and actually petitioned the courts to prove it? Had it alarmed the good doctor? Made him worry that the house of cards he'd built by providing falsified causes of death was about to come crashing down? Even if Victor had not died by poisoning, could the exhumation show proof of some kind of foul play? Enough to cause Herdstrom to take action to stop it? And what about the old guard? Clarice Fenwick blamed herself for Victor's death. What was the truth in that?

Was the exhumation the reason Tobias was now missing?

Taft rubbed his forehead. He was getting ahead of himself. For all he knew Tobias would just show up for work today or tomorrow or whenever, act like nothing had happened, and be angry at his wife for stirring up a fuss.

He checked the time. Twelve thirty. He was still working out his best approach on Anna DeMarcos. He suspected she was the lynchpin to Silva's actions. The reason to kill her husband. Maybe the reason to kill Riskin.

Info on the widow . . . Let the evidence speak for itself.

Those were Riskin's last words to him.

He started the engine and drove out of the back lot toward the front of the building, planning to get himself something to eat while he decided, maybe another Goldie burger

But lo and behold, as he drove by the River Glen Grill he saw the widow herself push out of the door that led to her apartment and into the one for the River Glen Grill.

Well. Might as well have lunch right here, Taft concluded, turning around once more and reparking in the back lot.

"She didn't answer her door, but in truth, we wanted to talk to you," said Jeannie, pointing from the direction in which they'd come, Althea Gresham's house.

Mac looked from Jeannie to Mariah, who was in another smock dress over a white T-shirt. There was something fresh-faced, farmer's daughter about her, while Jeannie wore black, skintight lululemon capris and an equally form-fitting black tank. "What about?" she asked.

"Well, we want to talk to you. and Daley, too, but . . ." said Jeannie. "Let's be honest. Daley can be a little much." She and Mariah rolled their eyes knowingly toward each other. "Leon was over the other night and all we did was talk. Daley should probably know that. She may not believe it, but that's what happened."

"That's why we wanted to talk to you first," chimed in Mariah, who put out her hand, and Jeannie clasped it. They both looked expectantly at Mac.

"Oh. Are you . . . together?" asked Mac.

"Yes," said Mariah, almost bursting with the news.

Mac looked at Jeannie, wondering about her relationship with Chris Palminter.

Jeannie must've read something on her face because she admitted, "Well, I've tried it both ways. But Mariah and I have been together awhile now. There's no involvement with either of us and Leon."

"He didn't understand at first." said Mariah.

Jeannie lowered her voice and shot a look toward the Carrera house. "Daley came flying over last night, accusing me and Mariah of all kinds of things."

"She was kind of drunk," said Mariah.

Mac said, "Well, with your hot tub parties, don't you think she may have gotten the wrong impression?"

Jeannie said, "They're not as wild as you might think. Sometimes there's some nudity, yes. Maybe some things went on that might give Evelyn Jacoby the vapors."

Mariah snorted out a laugh.

"Lauren is one sexy animal," Jeannie admitted.

"Amen," said Mariah.

"She's got a body and she knows how to use it. But Daley, the other night . . . Luckily Chris was there to keep her from throwing anything at me. My God, she had the neck of that silver vase in her hand!"

"And that thing's heavy," said Mariah.

"And expensive!"

"I hate to see someone so out of control," Mariah said with a doleful shake of her head.

"But Chris sent her on her way," said Jeannie. "Did she say anything to you?" she asked Mac.

"Um, no. I haven't talked to her today." Mac realized how many things she needed to discuss with Daley. She still didn't know about Alfie and the spray paint—well, unless she'd seen it on the porch when she went for her run.

"I'd like to be really mad at her. She was just insane." Jeannie blew out her breath. "But she needs to know that Leon is in love with her. Not anyone else, just her. Maybe that'll calm her down. Don't ask me why he's so in to her. If I were him, I'd be done with her."

"He said he's sometimes mean to her," reminded Mariah.

"Yeah, because she can be really shitty to him, you know?"

Mariah bobbed her head in agreement.

Mac was having a bit of trouble getting her mind wrapped around all the relationships. "So, Chris knows you and Leon were just talking Saturday night?"

"Oh, Chris isn't my boyfriend. We just got together a time or two," said Jeannie. "But that's all over now. We're just friends."

Mac nodded. Whatever.

"We've been kind of careful about who knows about us," admitted Mariah. "I want the ADA playground for my sister's daughter, Grace, who's in a wheelchair, but I think she could be in the Paralympics, she's so athletic and so smart. They're both coming to live with me, but Grace's father is looking for a reason to fight for custody, and he could use my relationship with Jeannie against us."

"He *would* use it against you." Jeannie was positive.

"He doesn't really care about Grace. Jeannie's right. He would use it against me."

"You know that half the people in the Villages think Leon is interested in you," Mac pointed out to Mariah.

"We kinda fostered that," Jeannie answered for her. "The old guard think they know everything and we just went with it. I tried telling Daley the truth last Saturday, but she wasn't listening. She thinks Leon cheated on her and she wasn't going to let me change her mind."

"Well, Leon was gone the whole night," Mac informed them, in case they didn't know.

"But he slept on the couch. I think he and Chris played video games." Jeannie looked at Mariah for corroboration.

"I heard them whooping it up at about three a.m.," she agreed.

The sound of a car's engine could be heard coming closer, and Jeannie and Mariah dropped their hands.

"You never know who's watching," Jeannie muttered as she eyed the car which drove past them toward the D streets.

"The neighborhood watch," said Mariah, and they both broke out laughing.

"Could they be any more useless?" asked Jeannie.

"No!" cried Mariah, shaking her head.

Mac had to smile at that as well. "Do you want to talk to Daley now? Her car's here." She was finding Jeannie and Mariah a breath of fresh air after the angry resistance she'd felt from most of the old guard over the past few days.

"Could you talk to her for us?" Jeannie asked. "I mean, it wasn't good between us on Saturday."

"It was bad," said Mariah.

"Will it be better today? I don't think so. But if it's coming from you, maybe . . ." Jeannie looked at her hopefully.

"Okay, I'll talk to her," said Mac.

"Good! It'll be good coming from you. She'll listen to you."

"Yeah, well . . ." Mac wasn't so sure.

"And come over to the hot tub again," she invited. "We'll be more fun this time. You seem like you'd fit right in."

"Thanks, but I've been told my personality needs work," Mac declined.

"Who said that? Daley? No. Leon! He said that to Mariah, too."

"That's because all I talk about is the playground." She smiled.

She knew how she came off, Mac realized. And maybe it was a way to keep unwanted, would-be Romeos at bay.

"But I do want the playground finished," Mariah added earnestly, in case she'd given Mac the wrong impression. "I thought it would never happen. They put me off and put me off. They just control everything. But then one day, *poof.* It was a go. They took out the old equipment and got the ground ready for the new one lickety-split. They got the swings up, but that's it. Right back to a snail's pace. We were kind of hoping Althea could help. She can make herself be heard in that crowd. But she's not answering her door."

"She's a pain in the ass," Jeannie said in a lowered

voice, glancing toward Althea's house. "But she's good to have on your side."

Mariah said, "The HOA board meeting is tonight. We're not on the board but we're thinking about going and putting our names in for positions."

"Just to piss them off, if nothing else. We'll never get voted in as long as they have the lock on it."

"What street do you live on?" Mac asked Mariah when there was a momentary lull.

"Devon. The D streets. The 'D List.' The house has been renovated some. but it needs quite a bit of work. But it'll be great for my sister and Grace."

"Mariah works for the school district. I used to be a teacher, too," said Jeannie. "On our salaries, we couldn't be here except we both got family money."

"If I were straight, I'd go for Leon," said Mariah matter-of-factly. "He's got money and he's a decent guy."

"But he's still in love with Daley. I don't get it, but she's attractive enough. You could be her twin," Jeannie said to Mac. "Maybe Leon likes it that she's high maintenance. Some guys do."

"I don't look like Daley," protested Mac, startled.

"Well, sort of, you do," said Mariah. "Now that she's wearing her hair straighter like yours."

Mac wasn't having it. "She's shorter than I am. Our eyes aren't the same color. We don't look alike."

"I didn't mean to upset you," said Jeannie.

"I'm not upset," Mac clarified. "I just don't look like her."

"Well . . ." Mariah rocked her hand back and forth to say "kind of," then added, "She's toned herself down lately, more like you. But you totally dress differently, so I wouldn't worry about it."

Mac had an instant memory of Leon half-heartedly coming on to her. She'd written him off as having a roving eye and that his move was merely business as usual. She'd been the easiest target because she was living with them. His attitude toward her seemed to belie their belief that he still was in love with his wife.

Did he think she resembled Daley?

Jeannie and Mariah said they needed to get going. "Tell Daley about Leon for me, okay?" reminded Jeannie as they headed out.

Mac gave her a thumbs-up, though she didn't relish the idea of talking to Daley about Leon again, regardless of what they'd said.

The voice mail that came through on Dr. Sandy Herdstrom's phone turned his blood to ice. He listened to it twice. Fear gutted him. Froze him. It took long minutes before he could even pick up the phone to call Burt. "We got a problem," he said, hoping his voice wasn't as tight and squeaky as it sounded to him.

Burt's laugh didn't soothe his nerves. It sounded slightly deranged. "Yeah?"

"Jesse Taft's digging around into a lot of things. I told you about him."

Burt was quiet. Thinking. Herdstrom hoped he was still the strategist he'd always been. That laugh had scared him.

"We need to stop him," said Burt.

Ya think?

Normally Burt grabbed hold of the wheel a little quicker. Sandy was the one who stayed belowdeck.

"Okay," said Burt, then he clicked off.

That sounded a little better, but Sandy, the cautious one, the keeper of the secrets, was still worried. He might have to go see Burt face-to-face, make sure they were on the same page. They'd managed to take care of Tobias; now they needed to make sure other loose ends were tied up.

Chapter Twenty-Four

Taft was shown to a small table about three away from where Anna DeMarcos was seated and having a glass of wine. He pretended not to notice her as he sat down, but his thoughts were on the convenience store robbery that had stolen her husband from her. Silva had fired the fatal shot that had killed Carlos DeMarcos, claiming he'd aimed for the robber but DeMarcos had stepped in his way. However, this was not the tale the robber, who'd managed to dodge the bullet and run out of the store before being caught within the hour, had told Taft. In his version, Silva had taken deliberate aim at his partner, but it was not believed.

The prize for Silva's actions appeared to be Anna De-Marcos herself. With the large payouts from the department settlement and the personal life insurance policy she had on her husband, Anna had moved tout de suite to the penthouse apartment above the River Glen Grill. Soon after, Silva had moved in with her, sort of. He still had his own place but spent the bulk of his time at her expansive apartment.

Info on the widow . . . Let the evidence speak for itself.

Riskin's message hadn't included anything about Keith Silva directly. It was about the widow. But Silva didn't act like he knew that. He sure as hell wanted the information that Taft had told him he'd found. He clearly believed Riskin had possessed incriminating evidence on him, but the Jumpdrive hadn't contained anything except evidence of an affair. Sure, it would enrage Silva, but it wasn't an indictment of his crimes. Taft had hoped Riskin had finally found something that would prove Silva had killed Carlos DeMarcos in cold blood, but that was not the case.

He ordered a roast beef sandwich on a baguette, and it came oozing horseradish. It was three times the cost of a Goldie burger, but it was pretty damn good. He watched as the widow picked at her green salad loaded with chicken, mandarin oranges, and pecans. She was far more interested in her wine.

Silva was getting mighty bold if he was doing things like breaking into Taft's apartment. It was almost like he'd lost the ability to plot and plan. He was just bulldozing these days. No finesse. Is that what love had done to him?

Taft kept a close eye on Anna, who had ordered her second glass of wine while she still had some left in her first. She waved the waiter off when he tried to pick it up.

Riskin's death was reported as a suicide, but it appeared that it was Silva who was skating on the edge, as if he had a death wish. Maybe he felt invulnerable. Maybe that was it. He was working for Mangella and thought nothing could touch him.

Anna DeMarcos felt his eyes on her and lifted hers to meet his gaze. Taft didn't look away from her spiderweb lashes, high cheekbones, and a mouth with lips thick enough to denote fillers. A beautiful woman really, so far, as long as she didn't take the embellishments too far.

A friend of Prudence and Mitch Mangella. How was it that she'd been married to a cop and was involved with another one, yet friends with the Mangellas, which seemed more appropriate? She had that champagne-and-chocolate-truffle look about her that didn't meld easily with the likes of Keith Silva. Maybe Carlos DeMarcos had been one hell of a guy and she just fell for him? Taft had only known DeMarcos by sight, and he'd had a great smile. He supposed he could buy Anna with Carlos, but with Silva? He might dress like Sonny Crockett, but that was the only "cool" factor about him. In every other way he was a thug.

Maybe Silva was just someone she needed to keep happy and maybe her extracurricular time with Andrew Best was just for her. An escape from Silva. She and Best had certainly seemed to be enjoying themselves.

He checked his phone and saw there was a text from Mackenzie. Just finished with Abby Messinger. I'll fill you in later.

He smiled, recognizing his old, reliable line.

He'd dropped his gaze from Anna DeMarcos and was now pretending not to be interested in her beyond their first locked eyes. Didn't want to be too obvious. But he could feel her eyes on him. She was either working out where she'd seen him before, if she had, or she was boldly showing some interest. He decided it was time to meet her gaze again, see if she wanted to take things a bit further. Once he did she pulled back a bit, but she didn't break eye contact.

She was deep into her second glass of wine as Taft paid his bill and got up to leave. He smiled at her, making a point of passing by her table.

"I know you," she said, and put a hand deliberately on the seat of the chair next to her, an invitation.

"I know you too," he said, pretending to hesitate a minute before taking the appointed chair. Around them was the clink of silverware and the hushed hubbub of conversation.

"You work for Mangella," she said.

"That job's gone to someone else now."

Something flickered in her eyes. Fear, maybe? "Ah, yes . . ."

"How's that working out for Keith?" Taft asked.

"I'm not sure what you mean."

"Yes, you do."

She looked at him directly. Her eyes were very green. "Okay, maybe I do. He sure doesn't like you much."

"We have that in common."

She leaned toward him, folding her arms on the table. "Your name's Taft. It's like a curse word, the way he says it."

He smiled.

She gave a small snort, then took a sip of wine, watching him. She was going to need a third glass soon.

Taft decided to jump right in. "What are you to him? A roommate? A partner in crime?"

"We don't live together." She pulled back and looked around for a waiter who spied her instantly. He was coming their way, but she just lifted her glass and he did an about-face for the bar.

"I'm going to bring him down," said Taft conversationally. "You could get in the way."

"You're going to have a fight on your hands, Mr. Taft, and I don't think you'll succeed. But I suppose you could win . . ."

"Maybe then Andrew Best will move in."

Her eyes widened a bit, but she held it together. There was a faint flush beneath her skin. "I don't know how many condo units are for sale, but if Mr. Best is interested, that's up to him," she said, deliberately misinterpreting. "It was nice talking to you."

The dismissal was curt. He got to his feet. "Nice talking to you, too. Say hi to Prudence and Mitch for me."

"I hope things go well for you," she said, but there was a bit of sarcasm to her tone.

The widow was actually more like Mitch Mangella than Prudence, Taft decided. More of the killer instinct. He was beginning to lean toward that rumor that she'd used Silva as a weapon to take down her husband.

His cell rang as he headed to his Rubicon, his eyes still searching the area for a brown Charger. He was completely aware he was on a collision course with Keith Silva. He both dreaded it and looked forward to it at the same time.

The call was from a cell phone number he didn't recognize.

"Taft," he answered. Was that Silva's car at the far end of the street? No. If Silva were here, he'd be in the underground lot. He realized it wasn't even a Charger as he looked again, and the brown shade was off.

Don't get paranoid.

"Taft, it's Cooper Haynes. Elena Verbena told me she ran into you outside Best Homes this morning. You and Laughlin were there to talk to Best."

He gave his attention to the phone. "We didn't talk to him, though. We followed him to Mitch Mangella's."

Haynes took that in, then said, "I was in an accident last Friday, maybe you heard."

"I did."

"I'm home, not at work. But if you wanted to stop by the house to discuss Andrew Best . . . ?"

Taft made a sound of agreement, then asked, "All right if Mackenzie Laughlin tags with me?"

"Bring her," he said, then gave Taft the address.

Taft pressed the Off button, then clicked on Mac's number.

Taft.

Mackenzie read the name on her cell screen, although the phone's sound was still turned off from when she'd disabled it before entering the Messinger house. She was inside her bedroom, on her laptop, transcribing notes. She'd wanted to put her thoughts down while they were still fresh, to capture her impressions before she checked with Daley, who was either still in her bedroom or still out. The house was quiet.

"Hey," she answered.

"Cooper Haynes just called. He invited us to his house for a discussion about Best. I'm going to head over there soon. You with me?"

"Yep. I promised Emma I would stop in to see how he was doing; this kills two birds with one stone."

"Verbena's at the station, so it'll just be us and Haynes."

"Okay." That was a stroke of luck.

Mac wrapped up her laptop and put it in its case. She debated on taking it back out to her SUV but ended up shoving it under the bed. Throughout the morning's happenings it had been a worry in the back of her mind. She didn't want to lose it somehow. Especially now, with the Riskin video of Anna DeMarcos and Best on it.

She headed for the front door. It didn't feel like Daley was in the house, or that anyone was, for that matter. She hesitated, then headed down the hall to her bedroom door, rapping her knuckles lightly on the panels. When there was no response she called softly, "Daley?" then carefully opened the door, giving her a hell of a lot more warning than she ever gave Mac.

The room was neat and unoccupied, the bed made. But unlike Mac hiding her laptop, Daley had left her purse on the dresser in plain sight.

If she was on a run, it certainly was a long one. Was she at one of the neighbors' homes? Hmmm. Mac called her cell phone as she headed back toward the front door. It rang and rang, but there was no answer.

After Mac climbed into her RAV she sent Daley a text: **Be back later this afternoon.**

She thought about Daley's voice mail to her, saying she'd done something stupid. What had that been? Mac hadn't been that interested in finding out. Daley was, as everyone said, all over the place. But now she was starting to wonder what that was all about. Should she leave a voice mail on her phone, explaining what Jeannie and Mariah had said about Leon's fidelity?

Nah. That was news that required a conversation. However, she could contact someone else about it . . .

So thinking, she sent a text to Leon: **Talked to Jeannie and Mariah and they told me about your real Sat night.**

That oughtta do it. Then she turned on the ignition and headed for Jamie Whelan Woodward's house and Cooper Haynes.

Ricky Richards was looking a little pale and wasn't doing his usual strutting around the station, Verbena observed as she sat at her desk. He'd gone back and forth several times, a cat on a hot tin roof. So, what was eating at him? she wondered, watching as he crossed toward the hallway that led to the break room. All weekend, what she'd seen of him since Haynes's accident had made her conclude he thought he was moving up to detective somehow. He'd slotted himself in as soon as Cooper was on leave. But now . . . ?

She got up and followed him into the break room. He was standing by his locker, staring sightlessly ahead, as if in a fugue.

"Richards," she snapped, and he jerked as if he'd been hit with an electric jolt.

"What?" he snapped back, recovering himself.

"What happened?"

"What are you talking about?"

"Don't waste my time. What happened to you? The chief let you down?"

"Hey, I'm just working here." He brushed past her on his way to where? He stopped short and seemed to forget where he was going. Then he looked up at the camera by the back door.

Verbena wasn't one to make wild guesses. She didn't play hunches. She needed empirical evidence to base assumptions on, but she could read Bryan "Ricky" Richards right now as if there was a flashing neon arrow pointing down to his head. "You erased the video."

"I did no such thing. I did not." He shook his head, his hands up.

"Who told you to do it?" He was heading for the door, but she swiftly came up behind him. "*Bennihof?*" she whispered harshly in his ear.

Richards yanked open the back door and practically ran out of the station.

Verbena waited a moment. She almost wanted to chase

him, but there was a better way. She walked back to her desk, looked at the phone, then the clock on the wall. The squad room was nearly empty, most of the officers at lunch. Richards was supposed to be manning the place, as was she, until the others returned, but he'd clearly given up that duty.

She yanked open the desk drawer where she kept her personal cell phone while at work. She thought about texting, but didn't like the idea of a written record. She also didn't like the idea of calling while in the station. There was no way she would use the desk phone.

Oh, to hell with it. Chief Bennihof had been skirting the rules for too long in his effort to play with the big boys. It was time somebody called him out on it. If he'd actually gotten Richards to erase the video . . . evidence of the man who'd taken Haynes's ride from the lot . . . evidence that could lead to whoever had tampered with the vehicle . . . *evidence of a crime against a River Glen officer of the law that could have cost him his life* . . . Well, then, all bets were off.

She was so angry her skin was buzzing. She forced herself to calm down, be smart, remember to consider every angle . . .

But *what the fuck*!

She texted Haynes: May have a lead on the video saboteur. Will let you know.

The chief himself returned from lunch a few moments later. Was he looking at her differently? Assessing her?

She slid her cell surreptitiously back into the drawer.

Burt looked at Clarice's bent head and staring eyes. Was she dead? He hoped so. Certainly, certainly hoped so. She was seated in a chair but looked like she could fall out of it.

Cliff was dithering around like a ruffled mother hen. He was clearly upset. Burt guessed if he'd been married to someone as long as Cliff was to Clarice, then . . . nah. He wouldn't feel the same. If he and Tamara were still married, he'd be over her. Woulda been for years. She was one smart and scary bitch, though, and he could appreciate her a lot more from the other side of divorce.

"She's alive," said Cliff, his throat tight. "She's alive."

"Yep." Burt could see that all right, more's the pity. He wondered where the others were. They were all supposed to meet at Cliff's and have a powwow about Clarice. A goddamn intervention. It was all set, but then Cliff had called Burt, moaning and practically screeching that he thought Clarice had had a stroke, or an aneurism or something 'cause she wasn't herself, and could Burt come over right away, ahead of the others?

And he had. But he'd been here awhile already, so where were the rest of them? Clarice was downright scary in her current state. He didn't like looking at her.

As if in answer to his question, an engine could be heard. Burt looked through the window to see Darrell's truck rattle up. Darrell nosed the dark green F-150 up the street, then came back a few minutes later and parked on the opposite side of the road. He then stepped onto the road, hitched up his pants, and crossed the street. Where the hell was Evelyn? Burt wondered. He was getting really tired of these women, *their* women, trying to turn their heads and act like they weren't any part of it. They were all part of it, no matter what they said. Even Evelyn. She could only hide so long.

As Darrell came inside, Tamara's black Explorer showed up, idling for a bit as she, too, looked for a parking spot.

"Where's Evelyn?" demanded Burt.

"Home. Where she better goddamn well stay. *Gladys* is gettin' a little cuckoo for Cocoa Puffs, if you know what I mean. I had to pull her from the window. Spends all her time lookin' down on those bodies in the hot tub, even when there's nobody there."

Darrell liked looking down at those bodies, too. So would Burt, if it came to that, if he lived next door. But why Darrell delighted in calling Evelyn "Gladys" and Evelyn in calling Darrell "Abner" from that old TV show was something Burt found particularly distasteful. He didn't think Darrell really liked Evelyn, at least not in these later years, since she lost her looks. She'd been a conquest once, a big win for Darrell, and he'd felt really lucky. Not so much anymore.

"We need a little solidarity here," Burt reminded him. "Decisions to make. Not just about Clarice. You know."

Darrell looked at rag doll, starey Clarice, and then at Cliff, who was clearly frightened. "Cliff, my man, she ain't comin' back from that."

"It's the goddamn pills," sputtered Cliff.

"Sumpin' popped," said Darrell with a slow shake of his head.

"Clarice may need a doctor," said Burt cautiously.

It was pretty obvious she needed medical assistance. It was also obvious that the three of them were not going to call for an ambulance; if they did, Clarice would be packed up back to the hospital, and who knows what would happen if she should wake up again? What might come out of her mouth? It was bad enough as it was. She wanted to confess. And that could not happen.

"That what we're gonna do? Call an ambulance?" asked Darrell. He turned a hard eye on Burt.

Burt shook his head, easing Darrell's mind.

"I'll take care of her," Cliff half sobbed, then tried to play off his weakness as a hiccup.

Tamara didn't bother knocking, just walked in. She was looking a little wild today. Burt thought. It stirred him up, and he pulled his eyes away from her and back to Clarice. The way *she* looked would shrivel a hard-on faster than iced water.

"Where's Abby and Dr. Andre?" asked Tamara. Her jeans were hugging her pretty tightly. She'd put on some weight, which was a good thing; she'd always been a little too skinny for Burt's taste. Not the desiccated stick that was Clarice, but not as buxom and rounded as she was now.

"Abby's not gonna come," said Darrell. "Thinks she's better than us."

"Andre'll be here," said Burt, though he wasn't completely sure. Their coalition was breaking apart.

"And where's Evelyn?" Tamara demanded of Darrell. The two locked eyes. They'd never gotten along. Darrell didn't much like women who spoke their mind, and Tamara couldn't keep her opinions to herself. Still . . . she'd kept herself in good shape . . .

Darrell said to Tamara, "You just worry about you."

She glared at him, then finally dragged her eyes back to Burt. "What about Sandy?"

"I got a call from him. Another problem. One we need to talk about." Burt told them about Jesse Taft's name attached to the Laidlaw exhumation. They reacted with utter silence, only broken when Andre and Abby showed up.

"Didn't think you were coming," Burt said to them.

Abby just wrinkled her nose like something smelled

and Andre asked, "What happened now?" When Burt repeated what he'd just said, it was Abby who lost it, pointing at Burt and screaming, "You promised Tobias would be the end of it! All this would go away. And now it's worse than ever."

"Ab . . ." Andre murmured.

"I wasn't a part of it. I never was," she declared, jumping back into her mantra of denial, which, frankly, was getting really old.

"Neither was Clarice," said Cliff.

Abby turned on him. "It was her idea! Hers."

"Yeah, but all of us—" Cliff started in.

"Shut up," said Abby. "SHUT UP!"

"She didn't do anything," moaned Cliff.

"It was her idea," she repeated stubbornly.

"It was all our idea," snapped Burt. "Remember that. And I said I'd take care of things and I am." They should be getting down on their knees and thanking him, not arguing like children.

Tamara was gazing hard at Burt, and he wasn't sure what to make of the look on her face. "You always say that, but you never have a plan."

"I have a plan. It's already in effect," he ground out. "Cliff, take care of your wife. Get her into bed. See that she's comfortable. Andre, give him a hand." Andre didn't argue, just helped Cliff get Clarice to her feet. They tried to walk her toward the bedroom, but she was a limp rag, her toes dragging on the carpet as they hauled her down the hall, so they put her on their shoulders, her feet dangling. "The rest of you. Go on and lead your lives. I thought we might have to have group action about what to do about Clarice, but we're set for the moment."

Abby's head was turned, as she still watched the now

empty hallway where Clarice had been taken. "She's that far gone."

"Oh, yeah," said Darrell, rocking on his feet. "We're safe from her motormouth."

"Are we having the board meeting tonight?" Abby asked.

"Of course we are. Nothing changes. No broken routine."

"Abby's right," said Tamara. The others looked at her—Andre and Cliff, too, as they had returned to the Fenwick living room. "Clarice is the one that suggested the arsenic that was found in your basement. It was her idea." Her gaze was firing into Darrell, who turned his head away from that radioactive glare.

"But she didn't do it," said Cliff. "She didn't kill him. No matter what she says. You all know it. You know she couldn't go through with it. That's not what caused her shaking. It wasn't killing Victor. You know what it is. It's what happened this spring. Clarice is innocent. She didn't—"

Tamara stepped up and slapped him, the sound a sharp, echoing rebuke. Cliff staggered backward, stunned.

Burt felt his cock twitch at his ex's show of strength, but everyone started yelling at once. *"Shut the fuck up!"* Burt had to roar to restore order. "Okay, everyone go home. We're done here."

"What about his truck?" asked Tamara.

Burt looked at her. They weren't talking about Victor anymore. "I said I've taken care of things, didn't I?"

"Is it done? Have you done it, then?"

This was Tamara's weak spot. She didn't believe he could take care of the details. "It's in the works."

Abby snorted her derision, but she'd grown pale, a ghost of her former self.

Andre looked at her and admitted, "Abby mighta said a little more than she should've today to the Laughlin woman."

Burt's head whipped around to look at her. "What?"

"What?" Abby repeated angrily, glaring at her ex. "I just told her to leave Alfie and me alone!"

"You also told her that Tobias Laidlaw was unstable and that he really didn't do anything to save the overlook project, *after* you said you didn't know him," he pointed out.

"Way to throw me under the bus, Andre. I said I knew *of* him, but that I didn't know him well."

"You were talking a mile a minute. She had to know something was up. I tried to stop you."

"Oh? By bumping the wall with your secret knock? She heard you, asshole. She looked at the wall and wondered what the hell was going on. You make everything worse," she declared.

"I told you I would help you, but you wouldn't let me. And sure enough, you blew it." His face was dark with anger.

"Oh, and who the hell are you to talk? *I* didn't use a shovel to cut off someone's head!"

There was a collective gasp.

"Jesus, Abby," said Andre.

Burt, who'd always liked Abby and tended to treat her with more respect than the others, now saw red. "What the fuck," he snarled at her in a deadly voice.

Abby shrank a bit under his fury, but lifted her chin. "She brought it up, the girl detective. She said she was trying to find Tobias, that he was missing."

"Oh God," said Cliff.

"But she doesn't know anything," Abby assured them.

"Not yet, mebbe," said Darrell. "But we gotta stop her before she does."

Burt said through his teeth, "I have this under control!" He was sorrier and sorrier that he'd brought them together again. *Morons*. They needed to stick together, that was true, but they were a bunch of crybabies. And now that Clarice did not seem to be the serious problem it had looked like, they just needed to hang together. Keep quiet. Not panic. "People are going to be looking for Tobias Laidlaw soon anyway. Better Ms. Laughlin than someone more experienced. Just act normally."

Andre asked, "What about Jesse Taft?"

The rest of them turned to Burt for the answer. He put on his lawyer face and said calmly, "I talked to Sandy. There are other people interested in Mr. Taft who have a stake in keeping him quiet. We don't have to do anything. Now go on. Pull it together. No more . . . wild accusations." He shot Abby a cold look. "See you at the meeting tonight."

Everyone filtered out and Cliff went back to the bedroom to check on Clarice. Though no one was completely satisfied with his explanations, they all at least seemed to finally be arriving at a hive mindset again. Tamara lingered a bit after the others left, but Burt had lost interest in her again. Yes, they'd had some rollicking sex last night, the first in a long time, but as it turned out, she wasn't the only woman in his life. And he sure as hell didn't need her bitch-slapping Cliff right now. Things were teetering on a knife's edge. If Cliff should tip the wrong way, what the hell would they do?

Burt drove home and headed for his tape collection as soon as he was inside.

Knockety knock knock.

He turned back to the door, aggravated.

"What?" Burt asked, finding Darrell on his porch.

"They're amateurs. But I'm not. Whatever you need, Burt, you know I can do it."

Burt looked at Darrell, really looked at him. He was out of shape and appeared more like a grandpa than a dad. He'd dabbled in businesses of all kinds. Car sales. Something down at the Portland docks. Same with forestry. Nothing had ever stuck. He'd grown militaristic over the years, hawkish, more so after each change of half-assed job. He had guns. And, like Burt, he'd felt a deepening divide between the sheep and the wolves of this world.

"Appreciate it, Darrell, but like I said, I've got this under control."

"It wouldn't bother me a-tall takin' out that pretty detective . . . or her boss. Or anyone else you might need."

Burt sensed he might be thinking about Abby. Though he was pissed at her himself, he didn't need Darrell to go all vigilante. "Leave Abby alone. She'll be okay."

"You sure?"

Would she? he wondered. She damn well better be.

"And those private dicks?" Darrell regarded him intently.

Burt wavered. He wasn't worried so much about Taft. Good old Sandy might be quivering in his boots, but he knew who to call to take care of him. But truth to tell, Burt wasn't quite as confident as he made himself out to be about the girl detective. She'd spent the last week in everybody's business. But if she should suddenly disappear, the investigation would center on the Villages, and he couldn't have that.

"For now, just make sure Evelyn doesn't go off the reservation like Clarice."

"She won't be a problem to us. You sure about the pretty detective?"

Darrell was sensing far more than Burt wanted him to. He was weird like that sometimes. Almost an idiot savant.

He felt a whisper of premonition slide over his scalp and down his back. Someone walking on his grave. The truth was, Evelyn was always a problem. Had been the weakest link in their chain until Clarice started her crazed rattle and roll and overtook her. And now this girl detective . . .

Maybe he could use a little help.

"Let me think on it," said Burt.

Darrell smirked, nodded, and left.

Burt veered from his tape collection to his scotch. He poured himself three fingers and drank it down with his eyes closed, as if he were swallowing foul-tasting medicine. He hoped he'd made the right choice. Darrell was still a moron, and morons with missions were unsafe. But if he could take care of at least one of their problems, Burt could do the rest.

Chapter Twenty-Five

Mackenzie pulled up across the street from Jamie's house on Clifford Street, admiring the old leafy maples lining the street, the feel of being in a small Midwestern town. Totally different from the rambling California ranches of the Villages.

Taft pulled in behind her and as she got out of her SUV she had the sudden desire to say, "We've got to stop meeting like this," which would sound like, and was, the kind of uninspired, juvenile remark a besotted teenager might make. She could picture Alfie saying it to some girl he ran into at school, maybe when they were opening a door together, maybe by their lockers or when he ambled by her on his bike, taking his sweet time with the front wheel wobbling, traveling so slowly to stay in step with her.

All that flashed through her mind in the half second before she just said, "Hey," which really wasn't much better. Maybe she was regressing. Maybe it was her personality defect taking over.

"We've got a lot to go over," said Taft, all business. "Let's meet somewhere after this."

"Okay."

Haynes met them at the door, on crutches. "Jamie's

clearing up things at the school. She'll be back soon, but no one's here but us now."

"How're you doing?" asked Mac. She wanted to guide him back to a seat, which appeared to be the couch, but he made it on his own.

Taft remarked, "Recovery is a hard road."

"Yeah." Haynes grunted. He was distracted and seemed to have trouble coming back to the moment. Mac hoped he was okay, as then he waved them into chairs. Mackenzie got a swivel chair and Taft a leather recliner with a lever that he did not use because he wanted to stay upright.

"Emma told me you were in an accident and said I should come see you. Didn't think I'd have another reason so soon as well." said Mac.

"You talked to Emma?" That stirred Haynes back to the present.

"She left me a message." Had that been Saturday? A lot had happened in a few short days.

"She and Harley'll be here soon, too. . . . Let's talk before they arrive. Verbena said you had a video of Best?"

"A sex video of him with Anna DeMarcos. Riskin left it for me," said Taft.

"Riskin. The suicide victim," Haynes clarified.

"That's not how I see it."

"All right. Tell me how you see it."

Taft nodded. He and Haynes knew each other well enough to trust each other, so Taft explained that he'd thought Riskin was leaving him information that would prove Silva had killed Carlos DeMarcos, but instead it had been the video of Carlos's widow with Andrew Best. "Silva doesn't seem to know what Riskin had on him. I led him to believe I had something that ties him in more."

"What you've got is a video of Best cheating on his wife with Silva's lover."

Taft nodded. "Does that work into what you and Detective Verbena are doing on the side?"

Haynes looked from Taft to Mackenzie and back. "On the side?"

"Granger Nye's death is a closed case. Unless there's something else you're working on that involves Best, I'd say that's what it is," said Taft.

Haynes spread his hands. "All right, yes. It's off the books. Not something the department is . . . uh . . . involving itself with. 'On the side,'" he agreed.

They heard doors slamming outside. Haynes looked through the window and said, "Emma and Harley are here." He glanced back at Taft and Mac. "Some things have come up. I'm waiting for a call back from Verbena. All I can tell you about Best right now is that Verbena and I think he's lying about Nye's death. No talking to anyone about this, okay?" They both nodded. "There were likely three people at that house when Nye fell. We think one of them was Best himself."

"You think it's a homicide," said Mackenzie.

"Don't know at this point. Best has friends in high places."

One of them being Mitch Mangella . . . another being Chief Hugh Bennihof . . .

"Was your accident part of this . . . ?" asked Mac, just as they heard the back door open and a cluster of footsteps. Then a dog shot into the room. Emma's wonderful dog, Duchess, who Mac knew personally. Duchess immediately snuffled Mac's shoes and then wheeled around and did the same to Taft, tail wagging furiously.

"Coulda been," said Haynes as Harley and Emma came

into the living room and Duchess raced back to her mistress, and Emma absently rubbed the dog's head.

"Well, hi, all," said Harley. "Long time no see. Are you staying for dinner? Monday night's pasta night. But then, almost every night is, right?" She turned to Emma.

"I like pasta," said Emma.

"I'm afraid we can't stay," said Mac.

"Was this police business?" asked Harley as Mac and Taft got to their feet and Duchess circled around them again.

"Something like that," said Haynes as his cell phone rang. He immediately grabbed it up from the end table, and his face grew set as he read the number. "We can discuss things further later," he dismissed Taft and Mac, then turned to his phone.

Emma walked with them outside. Duchess tried to follow, but Harley pulled her back. "You came to see Cooper," Emma said as Taft's cell started ringing as well. He gave Emma and Mac a high sign that he would be taking the call out of earshot, then headed toward his vehicle.

"We did. He seems to be mending, doing okay. I'm glad," said Mac. Her gaze followed after Taft, wondering who he was talking to. She glanced back through the front window as well. Cooper Haynes was also in a serious conversation. She didn't know what Haynes had said to Taft about this meeting, but it seemed like it was truncated— just the facts, ma'am. Haynes was distracted, and though he'd given them some surprisingly sensitive information, he seemed to want to push them out the door.

Emma said in her flat voice, "Harley said she wants to be a cop, but Jamie doesn't want her to get hurt like Cooper."

"No, of course not."

"Cooper and Jamie want a baby, but they can't have one. Jamie told me her uterus stopped working right."

"Well . . . that's too bad. I, uh, hope things work out for them," said Mac. They were really stepping into the TMI range, but with Emma, you were hovering on the far edges of what was socially appropriate at any given moment.

"You can't have a baby without a uterus," Emma informed her.

"Well, yes, that's true . . . not in the traditional sense anyway, but there are other options. . . ."

"What?" Emma regarded her with unblinking blue eyes.

Mac felt pinned under that blatant stare. She wished she'd never started this. She wished she was listening in on Taft, or Cooper Haynes, rather than discussing the private issues of Emma's sister and her apparently failing uterus. "Oh, I don't know. Surrogacy? I really couldn't say."

Emma's eyes flickered. "I know that word. I can't remember it. What is it?"

Mac could feel herself tighten up inside. She had a mental picture of Emma relating how Mackenzie Laughlin had said that all Jamie and Cooper had to do to have a baby was get someone else to make it for them.

"Emma, this is kind of private stuff your sister might not want you talking about to me."

"Jamie likes you."

"It's not really about whether she likes me or not. It's personal. You know what that means? It's your own feelings, your own issues. Sometimes you might not want others to know what you're going through. Or you might want to tell that person yourself . . . ?"

"It's personal," said Emma.

"Yes."

Taft concluded his call and turned back toward Mac.

She lifted a hand, letting him know she'd be right there. She wanted to tiptoe out of this conversation tout de suite if she could.

"I have something personal to say," said Emma.

"All right. But maybe you should ask your sister—"

"Harley is American," she revealed soberly.

Mac looked at her. For a brief instant she thought about asking her what she meant. She quelled the urge quickly, aware she could end up in some other convoluted conversation that might be even trickier to get out of. "Well, that's good to hear. It was nice to see you, Emma."

"You can come back again."

"I will. I'd like that."

Mac waved to her and hurried to meet up with Taft, who said, "Let's go to the Waystation."

"Great. Good."

"What did Emma have to say?"

"Ummm . . . she discussed having children in America?" Taft gave her a long look. "Do I want to know more?"

She shook her head.

And he let her leave it at that.

An hour later they were seated at a table in the corner, sharing fries, and Mac had ordered some chicken strips. She'd skipped lunch and she was famished. They discussed their meeting with Cooper Haynes, both agreeing the man had seemed distracted. Something had happened between the time he and Taft spoke and they'd met him at Jamie's. Mac then told him all about her day, from her meeting with Abby Messinger to running into Jeannie and Mariah, and the fact that she still hadn't connected with Daley. "I left her a message, but she hasn't responded. I'm starting to wonder what's going on with her."

She'd gotten a text back from Leon, however, who said he was going to the house around five. He wanted to talk to Daley, too.

"You going to meet him there?" asked Taft. He in turn had explained about having lunch at the River Glen Grill and his "surprise" meeting with Anna DeMarcos, and her warning to him about Keith Silva. Mac had told Taft that Anna ought to take that advice herself because she was fooling around with Andrew Best behind Silva's back.

Now, she answered, "I think I will. I want to talk to Leon, too. Find out what's really going on with him."

"You don't believe Jeannie and Mariah?"

"I believe them to a point. I just want to hear Leon's side. If he really wants to get back with Daley, I'm sure that's what she wants, too. It's maddening that they can't seem to get it together."

Taft, who'd listened to what Mac had to say, even her ruminations over feeling like she was missing something in the Abby Messinger conversation, hadn't said anything about his last phone call, even though Mac had asked. Now, he leaned forward on the table, taking a french fry, though most of them had been eaten by Mac already.

"That last phone call was Mangella," he revealed.

"Oh, really." Mac didn't know how to feel about that. Just hearing Mangella's name seemed to make her marrow grow cold.

"He warned me about Silva, too."

"He listened to Best."

"Maybe. Depends on what Best said."

"Think he told him what you said about the video?" asked Mac.

"Could be, but he sounded worried, actually, about Silva. What he might do. That was new."

"You think he's figured out Silva's more trouble than he's worth?"

Taft moved his beer glass around on the tabletop, which, like the bar, was wood varithaned so heavily the surface was thick plastic. His attention was on the smeared condensation, but he was clearly rolling something over in his mind.

"You know, Mangella doesn't call. Never. He leaves texts. So when I saw who was calling, I picked up. Didn't let it go to voice mail. He was tense. Said something like 'I made a mistake. You were right and I was wrong.' That's also something that's never happened before, admitting culpability. He told me he was sorry he'd trusted Silva, that Silva was not a company man, and that he wanted us to work out a new agreement."

"Aha," she said.

"I told him I didn't see how that could happen."

"And how'd he take that?"

"He just said, 'My advice is for you to stay away from him,' meaning Silva, and then he hung up. I actually expected more pushback."

Taft picked up his glass and took a long swallow.

"So even Mangella's worried about Silva."

"I was going to call Silva earlier but changed my mind. I want to see him in person."

"You think that's going to help?" She really didn't like the idea of Taft facing off with the man.

"I want to keep up the pressure on him."

"Oh, great idea. He's got Mangella spooked and you want to turn up the heat."

He almost smiled. "I'll push it with Anna DeMarcos,

see if she'll meet me. She was cagey at lunch, warning me about Silva, but she might want to talk. Maybe she wants out of whatever she's got going with him. Maybe she'd like to move on to Andrew Best. He's got a family, but she doesn't strike me as the kind that would care."

"I wonder what he feels about it," Mac said.

"Scared, but he didn't go to her, he went to Mangella," Taft reminded. "He wants action against Silva. I'll get us a couple more beers."

He got up and went to the bar. She hadn't finished her first beer, but it had grown warm over the course of their conversation, so fine. She'd start anew, though she didn't plan on drinking too much. She did want to meet Leon.

Grabbing her phone, she checked her email while Taft was at the bar. Joseph Mertz had finally come through with the Friends of Faraday list, and she quickly scrolled through what he'd sent. Some of the original members were a who's who of the neighborhood watch: Althea Gresham, Evelyn Jacoby, Clarice Fenwick, and Abby Messinger. There were also some names she didn't recognize. Mertz had included a copy of the lawsuit as well and Mac glanced over it. Her mind jagged on a familiar name alongside Victor's, who was also named in the suit: Granger Nye, Victor's foreman. Well, what do you know. Nye's name kept cropping up, though it made sense. After Victor's death, the man had moved from being Victor's foreman to Tobias's up till the time Nolan had switched positions with him. Nolan was now at Laidlaw Construction and Granger Nye had been with Best Homes before his death. Abby had mentioned Victor's foreman today, claiming he was the reason Tobias had succeeded after Victor's death; that it was Nye who'd pulled the company out of bankruptcy, not Tobias.

"Look at this," Mac said when Taft returned, handing

him her phone. She repeated what Abby had said about Victor's foreman saving his company from insolvency.

"Nye," said Taft thoughtfully. He handed back her phone and looked at her.

"Nye and Tobias had a falling-out, which is why Nye went to work for Best Homes a few years ago."

He nodded. "Haynes and Verbena are courting serious trouble going behind Bennihof's back on the Nye accident."

"Bennihof wants the case to remain closed."

"But they're pushing it." He thought it over. "I want to know more about Haynes's car accident."

"So do I."

"Did your brother-in-law say what Nye and Tobias fell out over?"

"I don't think he's ever known. Maybe Nye just got tired of Tobias's quirks Both he and Best can be difficult to work with, according to Nolan. And from all accounts Victor had some major issues, too." Mac glanced back at her phone. "All those people with the Friends of Faraday. They were all working against Victor on the overlook project. He used to be a friend of theirs, part of the old guard when they were all still the young guard, but he ruined the friendships . . . and then they nearly ruined him financially."

"Nearly ruined him," repeated Taft. "But didn't."

"So, Tobias, or Nye, or both, saved the company, but now Tobias wants Victor's body exhumed because he thinks his father was poisoned." She paused, then asked, "So, where is he? I mean, is that what happened to him? He ordered the exhumation and somebody got scared? Somebody in the neighborhood or one of the Friends of Faraday? Somebody who's afraid the exhumation is going to prove Victor died of poisoning, not heart failure, and an investigation will start, so . . . they decided to stop Tobias . . . kill him . . . ?"

"Who is this somebody?" asked Taft. He wasn't playing devil's advocate; he was going with her.

"One of the neighbors? The one who killed Victor?"

"And they killed Victor because . . . he was building the three overlook houses and they couldn't stop him?"

That didn't feel like enough to her. "Okay, there has to be another reason, too. A different reason. We just don't know it yet. The old guard had a lot of problems with him. Maybe the answer's with them."

"So, one of them killed Tobias Laidlaw and that's why he's missing," said Taft

"They got scared that Tobias would find out that someone killed his father. Maybe poisoned him, maybe it was something else. Made it look like a heart attack. They were infuriated about the overlook houses and other things. Livid. Done with him, so they took him out."

Taft didn't say anything, but he was clearly listening.

"And now, Tobias takes his father's note to his great aunt as some kind of serious proof that Victor was killed . . . or . . . maybe Victor *did* die of a heart attack, but this someone made an attempt on his life fifteen years ago that could've led to it, or at least they think it did. Now this someone's vulnerable. They're petrified of the exhumation, so they kill Tobias to stop it."

"You think Tobias was murdered."

"Don't you?" she asked.

He nodded grimly. "Where'd they put the body?"

"Buried? Kept on ice? Thrown over a cliff? He's been gone over a month, longer. Maybe he's in someone's freezer.

Or in a shallow grave somewhere. Clarice got a guilty conscience. She's . . *seen* something. She said she killed Victor and it's haunting her. Oh, *shit*."

Taft met her gaze. He'd followed along, at first just idly paying attention, his own thoughts about Silva taking up all the space inside his head, clamoring, drowning out everything else. But he liked listening to Mac work through her thoughts.

Taft was right with her. "Clarice went to the playground to make her confession to you."

"My God. He's under the swings." Mac leaned across the table and whispered urgently. "Mariah said they were slow as molasses about breaking ground on the playground and then all of a sudden, *boom*, they're working all the time. Ripping out the old equipment, digging into the ground. Someone complained about Cliff running the equipment before seven a.m. at the HOA meeting. Actually, I think it was Evelyn. Anyway, then they slowed down again. Body in the ground. The rush is over."

"There's one way to find out."

Mac looked at him. "How're we going to dig into the playground on a hunch?"

"Clarice. She wants to tell you."

"Yes . . . yes, she does. Have to get past Cliff to see her." She checked the clock on her phone. Two hours till the HOA board meeting. She said, "Damn. I gotta meet Leon. Maybe I can put him off." She seesawed for a moment, thinking about it. "But I should check with Daley, too."

"We'll go see Cliff and Clarice afterward. Together."

"Okay. Good."

"Mackenzie . . ."

She leaned forward, hearing the sudden intensity of his tone.

"If you're right, or only partially right, doesn't matter. You never have to be completely right to scare someone into doing something crazy to hide their crimes. If they think you're a threat, they'll put you directly in their cross-hairs. There's real danger here."

"This from the guy who plans to tweak the tail of a man who's probably killed twice already?"

"I'm just saying be careful."

"I know, Taft."

He looked like he wasn't sure he believed that. "I'd feel better if you started carrying a weapon again."

She used to keep her gun under the front seat of her car. Back when she was with the River Glen PD. She didn't like carrying one as a citizen, but maybe he was right.

"Cliff could be going to the board meeting," she said. "Maybe it will be a chance to talk to Clarice alone."

"Let's aim for that."

"I'll call you after meeting with Leon and hopefully Daley."

He gave her a nod and left her at her RAV before heading to his Rubicon.

She headed out of the Waystation and back toward River Glen proper and the Villages, running a bit late. Well, if Leon got there before she did and made up with Daley, that would be great. She didn't know why she cared. They had one helluva mixed-up relationship. Call it her own foolish romantic side, but at least it would be out of her hands.

And it would be nice if Daley gave up on Taft, too.

Leon was actually just pulling into the driveway as

Mackenzie parked at the curb, his black Tesla gleaming beside Daley's Audi.

"I ran late," he said as he met her on the front walk. He wasn't going through the back door today. A nod to Daley's ownership of the house?

"Me too. About Jeannie and Mariah . . . they say you're a better guy than you tried to make me believe."

Leon chuckled. "I offered you Bloody Marys and a possible good time . . . I am a better guy."

"They think you want your wife back."

Leon unlocked the front door and pushed it open. "Do they? Maybe I do," he said. "Hey, Luceee, I'm home," he called in a Ricky Ricardo falsetto, grinning at Mac.

The house felt as quiet as it had earlier and Leon's smile fell away. He took a breath. "She's punishing me. I've left her three messages."

"I left her one. She never got back to me either."

Leon went down the hallway to Daley's bedroom and pushed open the door Mac had left ajar after looking through the room herself.

"Well, where the hell is she?" he asked, starting to grow impatient.

"I thought she was out on a run, but that was hours ago."

"Did something happen to her?" Now he sounded worried.

Mac examined him, wondering if she was watching a well-rehearsed play. He moved from affable to testy to concerned pretty fast. Maybe Jeannie and Mariah were wrong about him. "Could she be at one of the neighbors'?"

"She hates the neighbors. That's why it's been such bullshit that she wants the house. If I gave it to her, she'd just sell it."

"Did you give it to her?"

"No." He gave her a long, hard look. "I don't want to give it to her. I don't want her to leave me."

Was it ego talking here? "So, you've been dangling it in front of her?"

Taft's words to be careful floated across the screen of her mind.

He looked away from her, his eyes traveling around the house. They fell on the hot tub, visible through the sliding glass door. It was about six o'clock, the sun just beginning to cast shadows on the tan cover over the tub. Mackenzie had seen the whirlpool covered a time or two, but mostly it was open.

A cold shiver wiggled down her back, electrifying her senses.

Leon was staring at it, too. He suddenly ran forward, and Mac jumped after him. He threw back the slider, which was unlatched, grabbed the tub lid and flung it off.

Daley lay face down, her hair a dark brown cloud around her head. Her arms were outstretched and bouncing in the frothing water. She was fully dressed in the clothes Mac had last seen her in.

With a cry, Leon reached in and yanked her up. Her face was bloated. Eyes and mouth open. Mac had to look away, ill. Daley had been in the hot tub awhile.

"Oh, God, oh, God, oh, God . . ." Leon cried, pressing her close to his chest, burying his face in her limp neck.

Chapter Twenty-Six

All hell broke loose. At least in Mac's mind.

She stumbled away from Leon and Daley. Back through the still-open sliding glass door. Reached for her phone. Who to call? The coroner's office? Cooper Haynes? All her training left her with the image of Daley's face imprinted on her retinas. Bloated. Splotchy. Starey. In the water for a long time. All day. All night?

I did some . . . thing . . . I was just so mad at Leon. . . .
What else had she said?

Mac pressed numbers, put the phone to her ear. Leon was squatted on the decking now. Daley lay like an offering in front of him. He was rocking on his toes, holding his head.

Unrelenting grief? Masterful acting?

"9-1-1. What is the nature of your emergency?"

Within minutes the police were there. She'd given them the particulars and then waited, her eyes on Leon, who kept silently rocking until the officers showed up. In a daze she'd called Taft and left a voice mail. He'd phoned right back and the next thing she knew he was there, grabbing her arm and pulling her gently away from the officer on the scene, someone she didn't know.

"Hey," he said in her ear.

She simply turned into him, pressed her face into his shirt. He smelled good. A light, citrus scent. She'd seen death before. She'd been a cop. But this was Daley. Someone she hadn't known at all until a few days ago. Someone she'd lived with and worked with and fought with. There was noise all around. Yelling. Voices.

She felt embarrassed about the way she'd felt about her. Her jealousy over Taft.

"She was dead. I should have kept him from pulling her out," she said against the soft cotton of his shirt.

"I don't know that you could've." She felt the rumble of his voice in his chest.

She realized he was holding her but watching the scene. Reluctantly, she pulled back and did the same. Leon was resisting moving away from the body. Still by the hot tub, he was the one who was yelling.

Finally he was brought inside the house. The officer was waiting for a detective. He was looking into the hot tub. The jets were turned off.

"I'm okay." Mackenzie stepped away from Taft, also embarrassed that she'd reacted so unprofessionally. She didn't want him to know that her stomach was jumping all around and she was having a hell of a time holding down her burger and fries.

A gurney was brought in just about the time Elena Verbena showed up.

"What the hell happened?" she asked Mac and Taft, her dark gaze moving from them to Leon, who'd subsided into a chair, his arms dangling between his knees.

The officer said, "There's a cell phone in the tub." He pointed to a small net with a long handle, used for removing debris from the water.

"Fish it out. Make sure you use gloves," said Verbena. "Mr. Carrera?" she said to Leon.

"She couldn't have fallen in," he said. "Could she?"

You tell me, Mac thought. It was a stretch to believe it was an accident with the top of the tub over her. Maybe she dropped her phone in. Maybe she hit her head trying to retrieve it, lost consciousness. Except the hot tub lid had been snugly in place before Leon grabbed it and hurled it away, flipping it over with force.

. . . shoved me up against the refrigerator . . .

Verbena said, "We'll get a tech team in here soon." They all watched as Daley's body was removed. There were marks on her neck. Strangulation marks, Mac thought. Her stomach acid popped again, but she mentally clamped down on it.

The officer had retrieved the phone and set it on the ground. He was rolling out the yellow crime scene tape around the hot tub.

Mac looked at Leon. He seemed devastated. In shock. And Mariah . . . and Jeannie . . . . had said, what?

. . . he's still in love with Daley . . . but man, is she high maintenance. Maybe he likes that. Some guys do . . . You could be her twin . . .

Mac clamped down even harder. Not true. Not. True. This had nothing to do with her. But that questioning voice inside her head had to ask anyway: *Did someone mistake her for you?*

* * *

"There are police cars at the Carreras'," said Alfie, white-faced and staring at his mom. He'd just come back home and thrown his bike on the garage floor.

She was clearing out some of Andre's old shit that she'd been meaning to toss for years. She was so angry at Andre. Sick of him.

You shouldn't have said all that in front of them.

Well . . . fuck 'em. It was the truth.

But they'll come after you. Not just Andre. Burt. And Darrell . . . he's always been a little off, a little rotten inside. Maybe Cliff, too, although he's surprisingly undone about Clarice.

"What are the police doing there?" she snapped. "Were you at the Martins' again? Oh, God. Leave that woman alone. You're not sleeping with her, are you?"

"Mom!" He was shocked.

She waved him away. He wasn't his father. She knew that. But it pissed her off that he was acting like Carol Martin was his mother. It *really* pissed her off.

"Pick up your bike. Treat it better," she snapped. "Why are the police at the Carreras'?" *Because of Alfie? Had that bitch, Daley, called the police?*

"Goddammit!" she snarled. She suddenly wanted to run. Away from all of this. *Run!*

Alfie straightened his bike, looking miserable. "I'm sorry, Mom."

"Get in the car."

"What?"

"Get in the fucking car!"

"Right now?" He glanced around himself, shocked at her language.

"Do it. So help me God, just do it."

She ran inside the house and snatched up her purse. The

urgency to go was so intense she couldn't think. She ran back to the car. Alfie was slowly levering himself into the passenger seat, fumbling with his seat belt. She jumped behind the wheel. Hit the button for the garage door. It jerked and creaked upward, and Abby threw the car into gear and reversed with a chirp of tires, the BMW shooting out of the garage and down the driveway

"*Mom*!!"

She slammed on the brakes at Alfie's scream. She'd heard the thud. Felt the car bump something hard.

She looked at Alfie.

"I think you killed Claude," he whispered, saucer-eyed.

Verbena asked Leon lots of questions. She did the same with Mac and Taft. No one was declaring Daley's death a homicide. Not yet at least. But they were taking precautions. Those marks on Daley's neck told another story.

Leon was white-faced, shell-shocked. He'd stood up and walked out with the EMTs who'd put Daley's body on a gurney, protesting about them taking her away. He seemed to be having trouble believing she was gone. When the ambulance doors slammed shut he returned to the chair and collapsed, holding his bald head in his hands.

They heard another ambulance speed by, its alarm sharply cut off as it neared the Villages.

Mac was feeling much the same way Leon was. Spent. Confused. Disbelieving. She appreciated Taft being there. It had been less than an hour since she'd left him at the Waystation, but life could twist so fast.

Leon finally lifted his head and looked at Verbena. "I'm not staying here. I don't live here anymore. I'm at a hotel. If you want me to come in . . ."

"Give me the name of your hotel and we'll check in tomorrow," she said and he did.

"I would never hurt her," he added, his face crumpling. "We fought, but sometimes it was . . . sexual. . . ."

"Tomorrow morning we'll want to see all of you," Verbena said, looking at Mac and Taft as well. "Okay?"

They all nodded. Verbena seemed to want to say something else to them, but she settled on, "Tomorrow," and went to the other officer to discuss the tech team's arrival.

Taft said quietly, "Get some things and let's go."

She realized he was thinking ahead. There was no way she was staying here tonight either.

"Daley removed the Ring video doorbell," said Mac.

Leon looked at her dully. "Why?"

"It's on your phone. She didn't want you spying on her."

"She was mad at me and I let her be," he said brokenly.

Verbena came back and narrowed her eyes at Leon and Mackenzie. She didn't appreciate being left out of the conversation. Mac could have told her what they'd discussed, but there was, as the detective had said, tomorrow.

Mac went into her room and grabbed her laptop from under the bed. She then threw her belongings together as fast as she could. She was leaving the Carreras'. Her short tenure here was over.

"All right if we go now?" asked Taft.

Once again Verbena seemed to want to say something more, but she just impatiently waved her hand and said, "Yes."

Mac and Taft walked outside. She was carrying her laptop and Taft had her bag. A small crowd had gathered on the sidewalk and road, gawkers at the scene of an accident. Mac sought to duck her head and get to her car, but they crowded around her. Mostly members of the young guard.

"What happened?" Jeannie asked her. "Is Daley *dead*?" She sounded rattled to the bone.

Chris Palminter stepped forward. "We had no idea. We wouldn't have come if we'd known. We had no idea. Right?" He turned to a man standing behind him, moving out of the way so he could step forward, which he did.

"Hi, Mackenzie. Bad timing, right? Sorry about that. You okay?"

She blinked. Feeling she'd fallen right down the rabbit hole. In front of her stood her ex, Pete Fetzler, looking much the same as the last time she'd seen him; maybe his hair was a little longer. "What are you doing here?"

Chris jumped in. "Jeannie said she talked to you and explained some things about us, and Leon, and Mariah, and I'd been talking to Pete about you, and it seemed like the right time to get together, maybe . . ."

Mackenzie stole a glance at Taft, whose expression was unreadable as he put her bag in the back seat of the RAV.

Pete didn't miss her look and said, "Let me call you later, all right. As long as you're okay?"

"I'm fine," she said in a voice she didn't recognize as her own. Pete Fetzler. How many years since she'd seen him? Two? Three?

"Give me your number," he said, and she went through the rite of exchanging phone numbers, even though hers— and his, as it turned out—were still the same as they'd been.

Then she broke away to drop her laptop on the passenger seat. Taft had moved toward his SUV, but his eyes were on Leon, who was still in the doorway, as if he couldn't decide what to do next.

Mac walked over to Taft and said, "What do you think?"

He kept looking at Leon. "Anything can happen in a contentious divorce."

"It doesn't feel right."

"But it's a homicide," said Taft, and Mac nodded.

Leon went back in the house and the small crowd dispersed. She watched Jeannie, Chris, and Pete wander off in the direction of Jeannie's house and realized with some surprise that she felt nothing for Pete Fetzler. Absolutely nothing.

She turned her attention back to Taft. "And if it's not Leon, I don't know. Daley wasn't threatening. She was . . . annoying." Mac shrugged her shoulders, feeling bad for maligning her. "She did say she'd done something in her last voice mail to me."

"Let's hear it."

She brought up the voice mail and they listened to it.

"Any idea where she went? She cut herself off," asked Taft.

"No. I had this crazy thought . . . maybe . . . something Jeannie and Mariah told me . . ." She didn't finish, hearing how that sounded.

"What?"

"Oh . . ." She sighed. "This is going to sound like I'm making this about me, but they told me Daley looked like me. Now. Since her hair's different. And I just thought maybe it was mistaken identity?"

Taft went utterly still.

"I've stirred up the old guard and maybe hit on something sensitive? Or there's Silva and his threats . . . ?" She peered at his shuttered face. "You're taking this seriously."

Taft didn't answer. A series of memories, like videos, were crossing his mind. Tommy Carnahan saying Mackenzie had come to his condo when he knew she hadn't, the strange sense he'd had when Daley was kissing him in the parking lot, a familiarity of person, the slope of a cheekbone, the hair . . . yes, the hair had changed. Daley had adopted Mac's look, accidentally or intentionally. Silva's threat . . .

"Go to your apartment," he told her. "Stay there till I call. Don't let anyone in."

"Wait a minute. I don't think I need—"

"I think you might be right about being the target."

"Okay . . . But I don't need to hide out, unless there's something you're not telling me?" She'd gotten her stomach under control and didn't like hearing what he thought she should or shouldn't do.

"Just what we know about Silva. He's a killer. A loose cannon. It's time I ran him down and stopped him."

"Okay, but I still want to talk to Clarice. The board meeting's bound to be well underway now, almost over. Maybe Cliff's there, or maybe he's home."

"I'll call you later at your apartment," he said, then climbed into the Rubicon and drove away.

Not the answer she was looking for.

Burt checked the clock on the wall and then looked around at the smattering of people at the meeting. The board meetings weren't usually as long as the general ones, but sometimes people—board people especially—could get stuck on the smallest of points and everything went downhill from there. As a retired lawyer, Burt could appreciate paying attention to detail, but when it came to the HOA board women . . . he just wanted them all to shut the fuck up.

And the people who were *supposed to be* at this meeting were missing.

Well, he hadn't expected Abby or Andre to be here because Abby had run over Claude Marfont and nearly killed the fool, maybe had. He was hanging on by a thread at Glen Gen. That was Andre's last text from the hospital anyway. Though Andre wasn't on the HOA board, he did own a Villages rental house, so no one complained if he showed up at the meetings with Abby, who was on the board. And Burt liked to keep him close, too. Their band would break up if it weren't for Burt, and it was clear that if that happened, they were all screwed.

Most of the chairs used in the general meeting had been stacked along the wall and the board was seated around one of the folding tables they kept in an anteroom. Penny and the three hags from the architectural committee were here. They were deep into the weeds of the bylaws. Cliff had managed to wander in, looking rather peaked. Good. He at least had listened to Burt and showed up, keeping things normal, though he probably would've rather stayed with Clarice. Clarice ... . For all her talk of atonement and confession and God, like she was ready to ascend to the next world, Clarice sure as hell seemed to enjoy hanging back here on earth with the rest of them. He wished she would speed it up a little.

Jeannie and Mariah had popped in, both declaring they wanted to run for the board. Burt had growled at them to go on the HOA website and download the procedure for applying. Like either of them had a chance. Burt had a lock on the votes. Those two, though . . . they'd gotten awful chummy. Could be a problem in the future.

He glanced over at his ex-wife. Tamara sat still and straight, though she seemed to be looking at something beyond the room. She still owned half their house but allowed Burt to stay in it. It was the deal they'd struck when he'd slammed the door in her face the second time she'd come crawling back to him out of Victor's bed. He shouldn't have given her a second chance. Shoulda forced her out of the house that first time she'd left him, but he hadn't. And she'd earned a hell of a lot in appreciation over the years. Were they to sell the house, she'd make a killing. It was too bad. He didn't mind the occasional sex with her, but the idea of sharing that much money stuck in his craw.

Darrell was here, too, though sitting a bit apart. He couldn't stand the architectural hags. When he'd showed up he'd taken Burt aside and told him about the fuck-all going on at the Carreras'. Daley Carrera was dead, found floating in the Carreras' hot tub. Kinda surprised him. He'd almost made a joke about how that should get Evelyn going. She'd be proved right about those damn hot tubs. But Darrell was touchy about Evelyn, and he seemed a little stunned by the news himself. Or a little out of it, for some reason. Burt had snapped his fingers in front of Darrell's face to get him to return. He'd almost wondered if Darrell had anything to do with Daley's death, but maybe it was an accident.

He had asked Darrell about Evelyn again. Where the hell was she? She was a part of their group, and just being absent didn't give her a free ticket out. Darrell had finally admitted Evelyn was having serious doubts over what they'd done. "It's not been good for her," Darrell had said. "Not as bad as Clarice, but she just doesn't wanna think about it."

That could be said for all of them, in one way or another. Then Darrell, in his matter-of-fact way, had said, "I think Leon killed Daley."

That answer made Burt very, very uneasy.

Darrell didn't know it. None of them knew it, but Burt had heated up the sheets with Daley. She'd come to his place last night, all fraught over Leon. She'd wanted to join the board, wanted to cement herself into the HOA, like that would keep Leon from selling the house after he left. She was all over the place. Upset, and making no sense. Cause and effect weren't really working in her mind. She'd told Burt that the deed to the house was in Leon's name alone and therefore she had no claim to it, and she was berating herself for leaving herself open and vulnerable to whatever he chose financially. But mostly she was mad at Leon, mad and hurt. When Burt offered her a scotch, she'd taken it eagerly, and then a second, and then, sipping a third, she'd picked up his hand and dropped it on her thigh. She'd looked at him a little bleary-eyed, and when he'd taken the invitation for what it was, lightly squeezing her taut flesh, she'd dragged that hand upward to between her legs. Woo-wee. Till then Burt had never thought much about Daley Carrera one way or the other. She was just another woman, although a mighty attractive one. Younger than his crowd by a stretch. But when she was there, holding his hand in place, he'd been more than happy to oblige, even though, by coincidence, he'd already had a pretty satisfying time in the sack. He and Tamara had gone at it, barely an hour earlier. It was an understood thing between him and his ex. If they felt like it, they went for it. But Tamara and then Daley a couple of hours later? That kind of thing had only happened to him when he was younger, and not that many times. Burt prided himself on not being like Andre and Victor. They liked stacking them up, maybe even working out a group thing, but Burt was more discriminating. He'd been a good-looking man in his youth and he kept himself in shape now. Still, Daley had been a surprise.

But now she was gone. Just like that. A snap of the fingers. He was having a little trouble processing that. Had to put it aside till after the meeting . . . except thoughts kept creeping in. Should he tell someone they'd been together? Get ahead of it? But then, it might not come out at all. Though if he didn't tell, that wouldn't look good, now would it?

His mind skipped to yesterday's calisthenics. Daley'd been *hot*, wanting him to go fast, fast, fast. They'd slipped from his couch to the floor and she'd moaned and thrashed about, a little different from sex with Tamara, which was nice but maybe a little predictable, although last night his ex had raked her nails down his back, a Tamara move from long ago, one he wasn't sure he welcomed back. The welts still kind of itched. Tamara had always been almost completely silent during sex. He'd found it kind of off-putting at first, then grown to love it. He'd spent a lot of time and effort trying to get her to let go in those early years, but she rarely did. Mostly he could tell she was enjoying herself by the little catch in her breathing, and those nails down his back.

So, it had felt good with Daley screaming and thrashing. Almost joyous, like riding a bucking bronco. He'd looked forward to maybe getting something going in the future . . . until she started crying for Leon. After that, he'd hustled her out the door and was glad to see the backside of her. Still, the memory of her was indelibly etched, something to review later in detail. He glanced at his ex again. Did Tamara suspect he'd had sex with Daley just after her? He hoped not. That wouldn't go over well. And the more he thought about it, the less people he wanted knowing he might have been one of the last people to see Daley Carrera alive. Much better to keep that secret.

Penny was trying to bring the architecture lady with the earlobes weighed down by fake gold earrings back on track. He saw Sandy Herdstrom standing by the back door. He'd come in about a half hour ago. Burt really wanted to talk to him, needed to know what was going on with Jesse Taft. The overhead lights refracted off the smudgy lenses of his glasses. He looked like hell, Burt realized. Haggard. Nothing like his usual self.

Oh, fuck. What now?

One of the other architectural ladies raised her hand. Why couldn't he remember any of their names? "The Martins have overstepped their bounds," she said. "They're adding onto their driveway, widening it beyond what's allowed. The bylaws clearly state the driveway can only be as wide as the mouth of the garage opening and theirs is at least two inches wider on each side."

"Excuse me a moment." Burt got up from the table. The whole damn world was coming down and these biddies were out there with their rulers. What if he just blurted out, "Fuck the rules." How would that go over?

Tamara's bleached blond head had swiveled to look at the woman, too. She felt the same way he did, he could tell. But then her eyes followed him as he headed to meet Sandy.

He had a sudden, sharp memory of Victor Laidlaw with his thick hair that really hadn't grayed that much throughout his fifties. He'd been in good shape, worked out. He liked to take the ladies out, buy 'em dinner, show 'em a good time, take 'em back to his place, screw 'em every which way but loose. He'd had good taste in women, and he treated them right for a while. He just was sloppy about ending relationships. You couldn't throw a woman over, especially for another one, without paying a price. Burt had thought Tamara had learned that the first time, but nope, she'd gone back for seconds. Now, of course, she wanted back with him, wanted to make it legal again, but Burt was never going to let a woman have the upper hand again.

He walked by Sandy and jerked his head to indicate meeting him outside. "What's going on?" he asked as soon as they were out of earshot of Penny, the three hags from *Macbeth*, and anyone else. Cliff had looked at him askance but stayed in his seat. Good boy.

Sandy spit out, "What are the police doing at the Carreras'? We don't need this!"

"It's nothing to do with us," said Burt.

"Everything in the Villages has to do with us." He glanced back at the closed doors behind them; they could barely hear the murmur of voices inside. "Especially now."

"No one's going to find out about us. I've got it under control. How are you doing with Mr. Taft?"

"I'm not involved with any of this. That is not my problem, it's yours."

Burt felt a spurt of anger. This was always Sandy's stance. And some of the women's, too. They'd all been gung ho in the beginning, but come a little adversity and they folded like a fan.

He was really, really close to pointing out to Sandy that yes, he was involved, and yes, he'd been involved since Victor Laidlaw was put to rest, when a BMW suddenly screeched into the lot and Abby Messinger came flying out. Burt knew instantly that they were in for more trouble.

Seeing her, Sandy, true to form, slithered off to the

side of the porch and began quickly walking away from the clubhouse and back toward his house.

Burt stood his ground and braced himself.

Abby saw Burt on the porch and wanted to rush up to him and slap him silly, like Tamara had slapped Cliff. It took a lot for her to pull herself back. She couldn't say why she was so mad at him, she just was.

She'd called for the ambulance after knocking Claude to the ground, then had waited for it to come and pick him up. Alfie had run back to the house to get Andre, even though Abby just wanted her ex to disappear in a cloud of smoke, never to be seen again.

Claude's eyes had flickered open as she looked down on him. He wasn't focusing very well. She'd checked his pulse. Was worried he'd hit his head. Could be a subdural hematoma, she thought, and was actually concerned for his life until he reached a quivering hand up to brush back her hair and whispered, "I followed you that night."

"What? What night?" But her heart nearly stopped.

"I saw you with the shovel."

"You . . . you didn't see me," she chattered. "I didn't have a shovel."

"Yes, you did." And then he'd smiled, the creepiest smile she'd ever seen.

She'd understood instantly that he'd been waiting to tell her this. Waiting to let her know that he had her. That she was his. That he *owned* her.

She wished she'd crushed him against the other car.

When the ambulance arrived she'd followed it to Glen Gen, driving a bit recklessly, almost as if she were drunk. Andre had showed up to offer support, but she wished he'd stayed with Alfie. It hadn't helped when Andre said he'd dropped Alfie off at the Martins' and Carol had taken him in. That bitch.

Claude was awake and talking to the nurses. The doctors decided to keep him overnight. He assured everyone that it was just an accident, making sure Abby knew how honest and forgiving he was showing himself to be. Some of the staff knew Abby, and she was told over and over again that accidents did happen and Claude was going to be okay; she didn't have to worry or feel guilty.

Andre whispered jokingly in her ear, "The old fart deserved it," to which Abby hissed, "He *saw*."

Clarice was not their only problem.

Claude was given some pain meds and wheeled off to a room. Abby managed a few more moments alone with him, hoping to question just exactly what he had seen, but he closed his eyes and blindly groped for her hand, clasping it firmly upon finding it, and then *giggling*. Bastard. Creepy old, disgusting bastard.

She'd peeled her hand from his grip and left the room. Andre had used the time he was waiting for her to chat up one of the hospital's prettiest nurses, who just happened to have the biggest tits on the floor. Abby'd seriously thought about kicking him in the balls. One swift upward shot to the nuts as she went by. Instead she mowed past him.

He tried to catch up to her, but she hurried to her car and left him to his.

And then she'd driven straight to Burt at the HOA board meeting. He was still their leader. As mad as she was at him, and Andre, and everybody, Burt was the one who would know what to do about Claude.

Her faith in him took a hit when, after explaining what Claude saw, Burt's answer was a staccato explosion of curses—whispered, because they were on the clubhouse porch, but his whispering didn't take away the power of the swear words.

"I'm going to wrap things up here and call you," he ground out. "We need a plan. We need a fucking plan."

"You're the guy who makes the plans, Burt," she reminded him.

His answer was another round of curses, which did nothing to make her feel better.

Mac drove like an automaton back to her apartment. She gave a cursory look around the lot to see if anyone was lurking or acting suspiciously, but everything appeared safe, so she hauled her belongings inside and locked the door.

She pulled out her laptop but just set it on the kitchen counter, glancing around. She felt like a stranger in her own home, she'd spent so little time there lately.

She poured herself a glass of water and drank it down. She wasn't looking forward to tomorrow. It was going to be a stint at the station. Picking up the phone, she checked the time. The board meeting was likely wrapping up. Maybe not. Depended on how long they ran. Cliff could be there, or maybe he was with Clarice.

But there was this tiny window of time she might be able to see Clarice alone and this was it. She understood Taft's warning completely. She got it. He was right. But if she didn't take this opportunity, how would she know?

She was on her way to the Villages within minutes, fully aware, that Taft was right. It might be wise to invest in a gun of her own that she would put beneath her seat again or into the glove box.

* * *

Taft took the circuitous route back to his condo, his head filled with black thoughts about Silva. The man had threatened Mackenzie. He and Mangella had both threatened Mackenzie. Silva had killed Riskin, and it looked like he'd killed Daley by mistaking her for Mackenzie. Could he be that careless? Normally, no. He wouldn't think so. But Silva lacked finesse. He might've followed Mac to Daley's. He could've known she was staying there.

Taft clenched his teeth. Should he have gone with Mackenzie to her apartment? Would Silva be so bold as to go after her after killing Daley? It had only been about a day since Daley's death. If he made that mistake, he likely knew about it now.

Taft determined he would text Mac as soon as he was in his parking spot and—

There was the brown Charger.

Parked three blocks away from his condo on a one-way residential street.

Silva was here.

Chapter Twenty-Seven

He wants to kill you, reminded Helene.

Taft almost made the sign of the cross. He wasn't Catholic, but it was a gesture he'd made for years when he spoke to his deceased sister, less so the last few years as her memory, the vision of her, slowly faded.

He pulled the Rubicon into the lot. He didn't see any sign of the man. Was Silva inside his condo again? He'd made no effort to change the locks. He almost welcomed Silva to try it again.

He checked that his gun was in place at his hip. It was there. No safety on the Glock. It was ready.

Taft got out of the Rubicon, trying to act as if he had no idea his nemesis was nearby. There were no cameras, so he was only playing for Silva as he strode toward his front door. Tommy Carnahan was probably right in asking Rebecca if the HOA would install some.

Carefully, Taft tested the lock and found it open. Not locked. Not the way he'd left it.

Silva was inside.

With one booted foot, Taft kicked open the door. It banged against the adjoining wall of Tommy Carnahan's unit before ricocheting back and slamming into Taft's open palm.

And there was Silva, sitting in the chair Mackenzie normally took, his gun resting across his knees. He casually picked up the handgun and aimed it at Taft. Taft hadn't gone for his gun upon seeing Silva's lying across his legs because he'd calculated he'd be a deadly half second behind Silva's bullet.

Taft's heart was beating slow and hard. His face was set in a hard mask.

"You need to hand it over," said Silva. "Whatever you've got." He slowly stood up, his gun, a Glock similar to Taft's, not wavering an inch.

The Jumpdrive in his pocket was lightweight. He couldn't feel it, he just knew it was there. "I don't have it here."

"Open up the goddamned safe."

"It's not in there."

"Open. The. Safe."

Carefully, Taft moved toward the safe, Silva right behind him. He could feel the man's anger like a living thing and imagined it pulsing through his veins.

Don't be rash. Keep a cool head.

He stood in front of the safe and lifted his hand to the digital code, Silva's hot breath on his neck. With a click, the door unlatched.

"Take everything out."

Taft raised his arms to obey, his mind racing.

And Silva's cell phone began to ring.

In that split second Taft threw himself sideways, toward his desk, and rolled.

"Shit!" Silva spat. He lunged for Taft, ready to slam the Glock into the side of his head like a bludgeon, but Taft was still moving, so it was only a glancing blow. Taft elbowed him in the nose and blood spurted, but this time Silva smashed the butt of the gun against his forehead and he saw stars.

Taft kicked backward for all he was worth and caught Silva's knees. He toppled over and howled in fury. Taft leaped on him and they were on the carpet, grappling for each other's throat. Silva lost his grip on his Glock, while Taft was clawing for his own. No good. Couldn't get it. He wrapped his arm right around Silva's throat and grabbed him by his silver hair, yanking his head back, looking into his hot, dark eyes. He increased the pressure. Silva's fingers dug into Taft's arm as he sought to breathe.

His phone was still ringing.

They stared at each other, Silva fighting for breath, Taft trying to contain his fury enough to keep from killing him.

Taft said softly, "You killed Daley Carrera because you thought she was Mackenzie."

"I shoulda fucking shot you when you came in!" he sputtered, and Taft squeezed harder, which cut off his words.

The sound of muffled but excited yipping came through the walls. The pugs.

Taft's eyes broke contact with him. Both guns had skittered across the floor. Out of reach. He slowly released Silva's hair but kept his arm around his neck.

He wanted to pat the man down and search for another weapon. If he kept choking him, he could make him pass out, and he was doing just that when there was a knock on his door, accompanied by more yipping and snuffling.

Silva rasped softly, struggling for air. "Didn't kill your girlfriend's look-alike. Almost did. Realized it wasn't the same woman."

"Taft?" Tommy Carnahan's voice came through the door,

causing one of the pugs, probably Plaid, the worried fawn one, to howl.

"It's okay, Tommy," Taft called. "Take the dogs and go back home."

"Did you hear me?" Silva could barely get the words out. Taft was forced to ease up the pressure.

Taft heard Tommy's door shut and breathed easier himself. He thought about it and shoved Silva away from him. Silva grabbed his throat and staggered backward. Taft swept up both guns, aiming the barrel of his at Silva and placing Silva's carefully on the desk, now shoved up against the couch.

"You're a liar," Taft snarled. "You killed Daley and Riskin."

Silva was clearing his throat, shaking his head. "Riskin came at me. I had no choice."

"You strung him up."

"Had to make it look like suicide. But it was self-defense."

"Not true. There's a video of you and Riskin. There were cameras," Taft lied.

"The fuck you say." He was trying to clear his throat, panting. "No cameras. Like there are no cameras here."

"You killed Riskin in cold blood. Just like you did Carlos DeMarcos."

"That was a mistake. He was my partner. Everybody knows that was a mistake."

"You killed him to get the insurance money for Anna DeMarcos. That's what everybody knows."

"Give me my gun and I'll go."

Taft laughed shortly.

"I'll go, man," Silva said, eyeing the barrel pointed at him. His face was flushed, but he was starting to breathe easier. He bent over, hands on his knees, inhaled a deep breath.

That was a no go. "Stand up!" Taft ordered at the same moment Silva rushed him. Taft hesitated killing the man. He wanted to. Finger on the trigger. One quick squeeze. Instead he slammed the butt of the gun down on Silva's head, much the same way he'd done to Taft, but the man feinted at the last second..

Sizzzzzzzz!

He heard the crackle of the Taser the same instant his body jerked with pain and shock. He dropped to the ground and Silva shot him again. *Sizzzzzz!*

Fucker did have a second weapon, said Helene.

Then Silva had his own gun in hand. Smacked him with it.

Lights out.

Cooper clicked off his cell and looked at Jamie, who was waiting silently by. Harley had left with Emma and Duchess to take them back to Ridge Pointe about the time he'd gotten the call. His terse responses had lured Jamie to his side.

"Verbena?" she asked.

Verbena had called him earlier to tell him about forcing Ricky Richards to stand up about erasing the video of the man who'd taken his city ride. She'd had to wait until she was outside the station to make sure no one overheard her. No one including the chief, who she thought had directed Richards. He'd heard the deep worry in her voice, bordering on fear. It took a lot to shake Verbena. He'd felt a dart of fear himself.

But this was the second call from her. He'd braced himself for it, but it was about a different animal entirely.

"There was an accident and a woman died in a hot tub," he told Jamie.

"Verbena called you to tell you that?"

"Her name was Daley Carrera, and Mackenzie Laughlin is currently living with her."

"Oh!" Jamie's eyes widened. "What happened?"

"Apparently Laughlin and Daley's husband, Leon Carrera, walked into the house together. Neither of them had talked to Daley all day. Her car was there and they discovered her body." He hesitated, then said, "Preliminary findings suggest it's a homicide."

"Oh, no . . ."

"They're coming to the station tomorrow, along with Jesse Taft. I've got to go there, too. Jamie. I can't be here another day, all day."

She nodded slowly. She was lucky he'd stayed home as long as he had, she supposed. "Does this have anything to do with the cases you're working on?"

"That's what I want to find out."

Mac pulled up across the street from the Fenwick home. The day had gone on forever and the light was finally fading. She thought about all the ruses she might use to get past Cliff if he wasn't at the board meeting. She had this mental image of herself just pushing him aside and looking for Clarice. Let him have her arrested for trespassing.

She rang the bell and it tolled inside the house for a long time, one of those ringers that ran up a scale and back down. When nothing happened, she tried a second time, grimacing at how long it went on.

She was debating on a third time when the door slowly opened. Clarice stood there, clinging to the door handle, her head oddly tilted to one side, like she couldn't hold it up, her body bent forward.

"Clarice, are you all right?" Mac asked, stepping forward quickly, afraid she might fall over on her face. She put a hand out to her and Clarice grasped her arm hard.

"Confession," she rasped.

"Is Cliff here? Let me help you inside. Should I call someone?"

Mac whipped her head around from side to side as she helped Clarice into the living room. She managed to turn her body a bit and shuffle forward, enough for Mac to see she was aiming for a particular chair, one that seemed to almost swallow her up as soon as she sank into it.

"Where's Cliff?" Mac asked. "The board meeting? I think . . . you might want to go to the hospital."

"No . . . I will see God now. Come here. Hold my hand."

She reached out a trembling palm and Mac clasped it and took a seat next to her. Clarice's grip was weak, but she was clearly determined to hang on. She couldn't, however, seem to get started.

Mac did it for her. "Tobias is buried in the playground."

Clarice's loppy head swiveled slowly her way, in that same, unsettling way a praying mantis had once turned its head to look at Mac. Not something insects should be able to do, Mac believed. "You know?" asked Clarice.

I do now . . . Mac's ears were sharply listening for sounds of Cliff. "Tobias believed his father was murdered and he was going to exhume Victor's body."

"Mr. Faraday gave us the land to save but Victor found a way to take it . . . he took everything . . . we all wanted him dead, but it was my idea. . . ." She drew a hard-fought breath.

"You poisoned Victor."

"I didn't put it in his drink," she said weakly. "But God knows it was my idea."

"Tobias was finally convinced by the note from Victor to his aunt." Was that noise outside from a car? Turning onto Beech Street?

"It was the contractor. He knew and he finally told."

"What contractor?" *Nye?*

Clarice leaned forward, and Mackenzie had to let go of her hand to gently push her back into the chair before she fell to the floor. "Clarice, I'm calling an ambulance."

"Evelyn told us about the arsenic. A forgotten bottle deep in her garage. She said she meant it as a joke, but she hated Victor. We all did, but she really did. I don't know where Evelyn is now."

"Who killed Tobias? Burt?"

"Burt brought the shovel."

"Burt killed Tobias with a shovel?" Had the car parked? Her ears were straining so hard they were almost buzzing.

"Burt hit him with the shovel and then he . . ." Her quivering, which had been largely absent, as if whatever had happened to her—a stroke? some kind of muscle lock?— had taken it away, suddenly returned in force. "He took off his head."

Mac's stomach recoiled.

"We passed the shovel around . . . he said we all had to . . . make sure . . ." A tear escaped one of her staring eyes.

Clarice's voice was slowing down. She was starting to drool. With one hand keeping her from falling, Mac used the other to pull out her phone and place the call to 9-1-1. When the dispatcher came on, she said urgently, "Ambulance needed at 434 Beech Street. Possible stroke."

Several car doors slammed. Cliff. And someone with him?

The garage door started rumbling upward.

He took off his head.

Mac ended the call and helped Clarice lean back in the chair. Clarice lifted her eyes to her. "Goodbye," she said, and the eyes rolled up into her head.

Mac couldn't run out the front door or through the garage. Taft's warning about the danger ran through her head. Not helpful. There was a sliding glass door off the back. She got to it in three leaps and slid it open as footsteps sounded on the stairs. It barely made a whisper as she closed it behind her, almost all the way. Not fully. Didn't want the door to make a sound. Tiptoed toward the back of the patio, into the yard, into the shadows of the hedges. Dark, but not dark enough yet. Could she be seen? She didn't know.

But she could see in. Cliff was there. And Burt. Mac's blood ran cold. Cliff went straight toward the bedroom, but Burt made a sound of surprise. He was looking into the living room and saw Clarice. Cliff came running back.

They lifted Clarice's loppy head and her eyes seemed to roll back and stare straight through the sliding glass door to where Mac was frozen.

She saw Burt's head start to turn and she was already running.

Taft came to in the passenger seat of a vehicle. An SUV. His Jeep Rubicon.

His head throbbed. He'd been hit hard before and recognized the sick feeling. Concussion, likely.

Silva was driving. And on the phone.

". . . couldn't take your call. But I'll be back soon. We can watch a movie . . . shouldn't be long . . . love you, too. . . ."

He clicked off and set the phone onto the console. Without taking his eyes from the road, he picked up the gun that was lying there, aimed it at Taft. "Don't do something stupid."

Taft vaguely recalled half walking, half carried to his vehicle and stuffed into the passenger seat. His hands were tied behind his back with the cord Silva had cut off his blinds. He tested his fingers. Maybe not as tight as Silva thought. The man had worked fast. Disabling Taft, then ripping through the papers in the safe. Mostly notes on his cases. Financial data. Nothing to do with Riskin.

"Where're we goin' . . . ?" Taft asked. He sounded duller than he felt. Good.

"We're going to go look at the Jumpdrive I now have in my pocket."

"It's not whad you tink."

"I know it's not a video of Riskin. There were no cameras. You've lied and lied, Taft."

They were driving up Stillwell Hill. Taft tried to think where they were going, but before he came to any conclusion, Silva enlightened him. "Andrew Best is expecting us. We have some things to take care of for Mitch."

Us? His head had cleared from the jolt of adrenaline caused by Silva's last words. Silva was going to look at the video in front of Best?

"I know you, Taft. You keep thinking Mangella likes you. That if it comes down to you or me, he'll pick you. But you're wrong. He doesn't trust you and he doesn't trust Best either. I'm going to help him out with both of you."

He chuckled without mirth. A chilling sound. And he

made it sound like he was going rogue. Never a good idea, especially when dealing with Mangella.

"So, just sit back and watch it happen," said Silva.

The gate. The gate. One of those locks on the top of its seven-foot-high frame. Her fingers scrabbled. She was on her tiptoes. Damn. Damn. *Damn!*

Her fingers reached the cold metal. She pressed down and the lock clicked up, the gate swinging out.

She was through and running lightly around the side of the house to the street. Her RAV was there. Directly in front of the house. She was on Beech Street. She could run to the Carreras' or go the other way toward the A streets and the park. She needed to call Taft. And the police. She didn't know if the old guard had killed Daley. It was possible. She hadn't had a chance to ask Clarice, but given her condition it was doubtful she would even know. But they'd killed Tobias with a shovel. One or two or all of them. And they'd probably all killed Victor with arsenic, too.

What to do? Walk? Run?

She was in the shadows. Maybe she should go through the C streets and into the Ds? But that would be taking her farther away from the exit out of the Villages. No. She would go toward the As. She started walking rapidly, past her vehicle. She reached for her phone, out of her back pocket. Text or call? No time for a text. She pressed Call.

"Where you goin' in such a hurry, Miss Detective?"

The drawl made Mac's skin crawl. A man emerged from behind a Suburban, directly in front of her.

Darrell Jacoby. Waiting outside.

Her pulse was running fast and light. Could she bluff him? "Hi, Darrell, I was—"

He lifted a gun, a .38 special, and pointed it between her eyes.

"You was wha ? Talkin' to Clarice while Cliff was gone? Seein' if she could tell you all about us? You'd better come with me. . . ." He opened the door of the Suburban, the .38 shifting.

Mac tensed, ready to spring away, knowing it was foolhardy—yes, Taft, *dangerous*—but she wasn't passively going with him.

She jumped to the side, but he grabbed her arm. She yelped and tried to wrench free, but he twisted her arm up her back so hard she gasped in shock and pain.

"Get in or I'll rip it off," he said through his teeth. The .38 was leveled at her once more.

She got in.

Andrew Best opened the door. He was barefoot, his hair mussed, his white shirt unbuttoned at the throat and un-tucked. His face was dead white.

Taft stumbled forward, pushed by Silva. His head ached abysmally and his stomach lurched. But he could think. Plan. Figure out what was going on.

"Come in here," said Best, leading them down a short hallway to a back office. The room was all wood—cherry—with carved beams crossing the ceiling. "The wife's gone. At the beach with the kids. You shouldn't be here, Silva. I don't know what you're thinking. Mitch won't like this."

"Oh, won't he?"

Silva pulled a folded set of papers from inside his jacket with the hand that wasn't holding the gun on Taft. He moved the gun to indicate Taft should sit on a roller chair that currently was parked against the wall.

Best looked concerned. "I'll call Mitch and we'll figure out—"

"Shut the fuck up," Silva said, nodding his head to one of the occasional chairs that were cozied up to the desk for Best. Best hesitated, then slowly perched on the edge of the chair as Taft, who'd also taken his time doing as Silva commanded, was pushed into the roller chair by a heavy hand.

Silva tossed the papers on the desk. "This is what you sign," he growled.

Best stared at him, and then at the papers. "I don't know what that is."

"You don't know what that is?" Silva shouted. "You made a deal with Mangella and it's time to sign. Where's your computer?" His eyes kept pinging from Taft to Best, but he never moved the Glock from Taft.

"I don't have one here."

"Laptop?"

"At the office. My wife might have one. . . ."

Silva stepped back a few paces, making sure he had both Taft and Best in his range of vision.

Best said urgently, "Mangella and I have a deal. We understand each other."

"Sign those papers or end up dying for it, courtesy of Mr. Taft here. You see, he's going to pull this trigger and shoot you. He's gonna take it upon himself to get rid of a drug dealer."

"I never knew about the drugs. I told the police—"

"Shut up, Best. You're weak. Weak. Like Taft here. He coulda shot me, but he didn't." Silva smiled coldly at Taft, whose fingers were carefully working through the bindings behind his back.

Careful, Taft warned himself.

"Sign 'em."

"I've got a deal with Mangella! This is old information!"

"Sign 'em!"

"It'll never hold up in court."

"Oh, I think it will. Sign 'em."

"I need a pen.'

"Get one."

Andrew Best rose cautiously from his chair and walked around to the back of his desk, opening the top drawer. Silva moved right up next to Taft and placed the barrel of the gun against his temple. "Or maybe Taft shoots you in a struggle for the gun and takes a fatal shot himself."

Best pulled out a pen, slid over the papers, and signed them, his throat working.

"Okay, sit down in your chair, there." Silva nodded for Best to seat himself behind his desk in another roller chair, which he did. "Put your hands on the desk."

"This is bullshit. A waste of time. Mitch and I—"

"I'm not going to tell you again."

Move the gun. Move the gun. Move it a fraction away. Taft's hands were almost free.

"You want me to look for the laptop?" queried Best. He was sweating profusely now.

Silva smiled. "You want to get away, don't you?"

"I signed the papers."

"I don't need the laptop. I know what's on this Jump-drive," Silva revealed. "You really thought I didn't know?" he asked Taft.

Did he know? Taft felt most of the bindings slip off, but he kept hold of one end. It wouldn't do for them to drop to the floor behind the chair.

"You never had anything," said Silva. "Just a safe worth of useless paper. Coulda saved myself a lot of trouble and let Riskin live."

"Look, Silva. I don't know what's going on here, and I don't want to know, but I'm no part of it." Best held up his hands and shrugged.

"Oh, you weren't the one who complained about Detective Haynes? Begged to have him taken off your ass? I did that for you, fucker. With the chief's help. But then you went and messed things up with Mitch."

"I didn't mess things up with Mitch." Best's white face grew even paler, if that were possible.

"You tried to back out."

"No . . . no," said Best, shaking his head. "I went to see Mitch today. You can ask him. We're okay. We're good now." He waved a hand at the papers he'd just signed. "Those don't matter."

"Mitch gave me a job and I'm doing it. Not like Taft, here, who wouldn't even try to get Bennihof in line."

The barrel of the gun slid alongside Taft's temple but stayed in place.

"Let me call Mangella and get this straight." Andrew spared a glance at Taft, who removed the last bit of string from his hands as Best reached toward the desk phone.

"After what you did with my woman?" asked Silva.

Best froze. So did Taft.

"See, I thought we could all watch together, but we don't need to, do we? Told you I knew what's on the Jump-drive," said Silva.

And he pulled the Glock and aimed a shot between Andrew Best's eyes.

Chapter Twenty-Eight

Darrell ran the Suburban into his garage. He'd held the gun on Mackenzie as they drove the short distance to his house. Now he said, "You stay put and I'll come around and pull you out. You move an inch and I'll kill you."

There was a truck on the other side of the Suburban, squeezed into the two-car garage. Mac stayed put as Darrell backed his large frame out of the driver's side, leaning down to keep her in his sights.

"Darrell." The voice came from outside, but he didn't take his eyes off Mac.

It was Cliff.

"Open her door and pull her out," ordered Darrell.

Cliff did as he was told, but it was a squeeze. The door wouldn't open all the way because of the big truck on the other side.

Cliff said in a tight voice, "You said you were getting rid of his truck."

Burt's voice. "He's taking it apart little by little. But Cliff's right. You gotta speed it up."

"Been busy," said Darrell as Cliff dragged Mackenzie out of the vehicle. Her arm ached, but she clenched her teeth. She glanced over at the truck. Tobias's, by the sound of it. The interior of the cab looked as if it had been stripped down to the metal.

Mackenzie was marched inside the house and straight ahead to the large basement room beneath the living room, which looked like an extension of the garage. A workbench and all kinds of roofing, siding, and general building materials were parked around the periphery. There were several folding metal chairs erected in the middle of the room. One of them was occupied by a woman's body.

"Oh, shit," said Cliff, staring.

Evelyn was seated in the chair. Tied to it.

"Don't mind Evvie," said Darrell. "She's not gonna do anything."

For sure, thought Mac. Because she was dead.

Burt said quietly, "What happened here, Darrell?"

"Well, Gladys . . . I guess she's watched her last hot tub party." He chortled a bit.

Burt was clearly disturbed. "Darrell, you didn't have anything to do with Daley, did you?"

Darrell had grabbed Mackenzie from Cliff and pulled her roughly over to the chair beside Evelyn's. She had to fight down a moan of pain at her aching shoulder as he sat her down hard. "Well, I sure thought she was this one, for a while." He gave Mac a hard shake that made her teeth rattle.

"Jesus, Darrell," said Cliff, alarmed.

"But I didn't kill her. I figured it out."

Mackenzie decided not to look at Evelyn. There was just the beginnings of the smell of rot. Burt and Cliff exchanged a look. They clearly didn't believe Darrell about Daley.

"So, now we got 'er," said Darrell, his hands squeezing Mackenzie's shoulders. "How're we doin' this? I called the girls over. They're not gonna like seein' Evvie, but they're part of this. We're all part of this. Victor, Tobias . . . Better get Andre, too."

"I gotta get back to Clarice," muttered Cliff, sidling toward the hall to the garage.

"She's gone," snapped Burt. "Darrell's right. You're part of this. Get back in here."

Reluctantly, Cliff complied, wiping some sweat from his upper lip.

"Good thing you haven't brought in the rest of that playground equipment yet, Cliff," said Darrell. "The ground's primed and ready for another body."

A knock on the door.

"That's them," said Darrell.

"I'll get 'em," said Burt.

He went back out and up the stairs just as the front door squeaked open and Mackenzie heard Abby call, "Evelyn?"

"She's downstairs," Burt informed her.

A clatter of footsteps, and there was Abby and Tamara, with Andre bringing up the rear. Burt followed them in as their eyes ran from Mackenzie to Evelyn . . . and stayed there. Abby goggled and Tamara snapped around to glare at Darrell.

"You killed her!" Her voice shook with horror.

"She took a tumble down the stairs."

"Then you pushed her!"

"She kept sayin', 'I know. I know.' You all heard her. She couldn't shut up about it. She should've stuck Tobias with the shovel like the rest of us. Instead she kept sayin' she *knew*, like we were all goin' to hell except her. Like she was so good. All bent about Jeannie and her hot tub. Tryin' to get me to look at Lauren. Well, I didn't look at

Lauren," he added quickly. "But Evvie's no better than us. We're all the same."

Mac glanced at Abby. She was pale as death. "This is out of hand. I'm not a part of this," she said.

"Shut up," said Burt. "That argument's never worked. You are part of this and always have been."

"I didn't give Victor the poison. That was Andre! I didn't do it!" She wheeled on her ex. "You always try to blame me, but you can take the blame. It's yours anyway."

"You stabbed Tobias with the shovel, though," Tamara reminded her.

They all looked at her.

She was glaring at Abby. "Stop acting like you didn't." She moved away from Abby and closer to Burt.

"And then Evvie was goin' on about losin' the baby again," Darrell said with a snort, as if there had been no break from his narrative. "*Victor's* baby."

Tamara switched her glare back to him. "It wasn't Victor's baby. How many times do you have to hear it?"

"Evvie said it was. And that's why it died," Darrell said stubbornly.

"Well, Evelyn was wrong," said Abby.

Now everyone turned to look at Abby.

"Abby . . ." Andre warned.

Abby barreled on: "Darrell, you stupid moron. The baby was Andre's. We all know it. We've known it for years. Evelyn never slept with Victor. That was just a lie that we've all learned to believe. She told you it was Victor's to protect Andre." Abby lifted her chin and gazed at each one in turn. "Okay, I've said it. We've all lied to Darrell, all these years. Well, now you know, Darrell," she finished.

Mac felt Darrell's hands clench harder into her shoulders. She sensed all the eyes on her, all of a sudden, and shifted her gaze to Burt who was staring at her in consternation. "You shouldn't have moved to the Villages," he said.

Now, there was an understatement.

"What are we gonna do?" asked Cliff.

"Put 'em both in the ground," said Darrell rather cheerily. "Gladys and the girl detective."

The instant before Silva fired at Best, Taft shoved the chair backward into him. Best ducked and Silva's shot zinged past him. Silva stumbled to his feet as Taft leaped upward, grabbing his arm.

Bang!

Another shot reverberated, and Best yipped as he slid lower behind the desk. Silva was strong and Taft's head clanged with the loud noises. He ground his teeth together and fought for the Glock. Silva was trying to turn the barrel, using his strength, gradually, gradually, pulling around.

Taft dropped a shoulder and plowed into his chest.

Bang! Bang!

Bullets tore through the wood panel, splintering it.

Silva slipped, just a little, but Taft pushed forward, slamming Silva's gun hand into the wall. Silva jerked the gun free, put it between them.

Bang!

There was a moment of silence. Taft stared at Silva and Silva stared at Taft. They were both breathing hard. Their hands were both on the gun's handle.

Taft looked down and slowly stepped backward, holding on to the Glock. Silva's fingers slipped off the gun.

"You shot me," he said. He put a hand to his abdomen. There wasn't a lot of blood yet. He hitched a step backward to the wall, using it for support.

Taft held him at gunpoint. He wanted him to die. Wanted to rid the world of the scum he was. But he was a choirboy, according to Silva. Backing up to Best's desk, he picked up the receiver of the landline. Andrew Best was squatted on the floor, his hands over his ears, unhurt.

"9-1-1, what is the nature of your emergency?"

"We need to wait till after midnight or someone'll come along. They always do," said Burt. "C'mon. Let's go upstairs. Leave Darrell with them."

Mackenzie's pulse accelerated.

Everyone looked stunned except Darrell.

"You're not going to . . ." Andre started. He couldn't look at Mackenzie.

"We can't do this! We can't do this!" Abby screamed.

Tamara walked over and slapped her, hard. Abby stumbled backward, but then came at Tamara, nails drawn. "You fucking bitch!" she screamed.

"Stop!" Burt ordered, his voice a whip, but neither of the women listened.

Mackenzie's gaze was darting around Darrell's workshop. Had been the whole time she was there. Vise, planer, lathe. Punch board with all kinds of tools. Pieces of metal on the floor, pieces of Tobias's truck. Rebar. Pieces of wood from large to small, chunks and poles and small, cut pieces with rough edges. Sawdust.

Bang!

Mac jumped. The gunshot was loud enough to make her ears ring.

"Fuck," said Burt, looking at Darrell.

Mac could smell the cordite.

Tamara and Abby had let each other go. Each breathing

hard. Each staring at Darrell, who'd squeezed off a shot into the ceiling.

Evelyn toppled forward, out of her chair, her head cracking on the cement floor.

Darrell leaped forward as if he were going to save her as Abby screamed.

Mac threw herself toward the workbench, half expecting another shot.

"Shit! Bitch!" Burt screamed, grabbing her left arm, the sore one Darrell had wrenched up her back.

Mac's right hand scrabbled on the floor. Fingers closed on a cold, cylindrical bar. The rebar. She swung blindly backward with all her force.

Crack!

Burt shrieked and grabbed his knee. She saw Darrell leveling the gun at her. His face savage.

Cliff threw himself at Darrell. *Bang! Bang!*

Tamara's mouth was an O of surprise.

Abby bolted for the stairs as Cliff fell over. Andre ran after her.

"Goddammit!" roared Burt. "You morons. You fucking morons!"

Darrell staggered. He lifted the gun, aiming it at Mac again. She'd had time to pull back and gain power and she swung the rebar at him next. He jerked backward, but not fast enough. *Crack!* She got his arm and hand. The gun flew out of his grip, skittered across the floor to Tamara's feet.

"Don't pick it up," snarled Mac, gripping the rebar. "Don't make that mistake."

Darrell was on his knees. He started laughing. Holding his broken arm and laughing.

Burt was moaning.

Tamara bent down, grabbed the .38, aimed it at Mackenzie. "Stop laughing," she ordered Darrell.

"Gonna kill her now, too?" Darrell said gleefully.

Tamara's eyes flicked his way.

"I saw you," he said. "I wasn't gonna say anything, but I saw you. I was comin' to see Burt, right there on Alameda. Out she comes, lookin' like she'd really gotten a tumble. Sorry, boss," he said to Burt, who had collapsed in a ball, his eyes closed. Blood seeped around the pants leg. "I shoulda told ya, but I didn't figure you wanted anyone to know about Mrs. Carrera. But you . . ." He laughed again, shivering a little with pain. "You," he said to Tamara. "You followed her from Burt's. Knew what she'd done. What he'd done. Thought you were the only one in his bed all these years, didn't ya? You ran off with Victor—twice— you dumb bunny. Too dumb to learn. Burt's moved on, honey. Killin' Mrs. Carrera won't change that."

Burt groaned in pain. "I hope he's lying, Tamara."

She didn't respond. Just glared daggers at Darrell.

Burt murmured, "But it doesn't matter. It's over. All of it's over."

And that was when Mac's cell phone started ringing in Darrell's pocket. She'd turned the sound back on when she'd tried to call Taft.

"It's her fault!" Tamara suddenly screeched.

Mac leaped away as Tamara pulled the trigger. *Bang!* It caught Burt in the chest, and Darrell's laughter abruptly died. Tamara turned toward Mac again, the phone singing the default ringtone.

Darrell lunged forward before Tamara could take aim again. *Bang!* Another shot rang out as Darrell plowed her down to the ground with his weight.

Mac staggered forward, took one look at the three bodies

in various stages of pain and agony. The phone stopped ringing.

She dropped the rebar with a clang against the cement, then ran up the steps and out the front door, which was wide open.

Taft stood back while Elena Verbena took command of the situation. "Quite a night," she said, her only words to Taft. But she had a lot of words for Andrew Best. Most of them put together in terse, staccato questions.

Taft had tried to call Mac several times from Best's landline. His phone had been taken by Silva, apparently, or it was somewhere in his condo, lost during his fight with Silva.

She hadn't picked up, but he'd left her two voice mails explaining where he was and what phone he was using. He'd also called Tommy Carnahan and explained about losing his phone, asking him to check with Mac. He was concerned beyond measure when Tommy told him there had been some kind of ruckus at the Villages. Neighbors calling the police about shots fired from a house on Andromeda Avenue. Bodies found in the basement. This was mere hours after an accidental death in a hot tub on Callaway Court, which might or might not be a homicide. And another resident taken from Beech Street to the hospital after being backed over by a neighbor.

And then Tommy Carnahan had called Taft back. To his text to Mac of This is Tommy. Taft's neighbor. He wants to know if you're okay. He has no cell phone.

Came Mackenzie's answer back: I'm okay. Old guard not so much.

Epilogue

The media had barely learned of Daley's hot tub death when the deaths of Clarice Fenwick, Cliff Fenwick, Darrell Jacoby, and Evelyn Jacoby were reported, along with the varying injuries and subsequent hospitalizations of Burt Deevers and Tamara Deevers.

Keith Silva's death was missed in that first flurry of news, hidden behind what was coming out of the Villages and the discovery of one Tobias Laidlaw's body buried beneath a nearly completed swing set, the first piece in the construction of an ADA playground, said playground being spearheaded by one of the residents, Ms. Mariah Copple, who was believed to have no knowledge that Mr. Laidlaw was buried there.

But the newspapers and television news crews caught up to speed, and when Jesse Taft and Mackenzie Laughlin left the River Glen Police Department the next day, both looking a little worse for wear—especially Taft, who was taken to River Glen General first but was a terrible patient and insisted on going to the police station to meet his business partner, Ms. Laughlin—they were hounded by enterprising young journalists all the way to Mr. Taft's residence, where one of his neighbors, Mr. Thomas Carnahan, warned them to keep their distance, that he would try to keep his attack dogs on leash, but they'd been known to escape . . . and, well . . . good luck to you.

Tommy's flirting with the press was a nice way to get rid of them, hopefully, as Mac and Taft were both tired and wanted to be left alone. They stayed inside for the first few days afterward, Mac back on the couch, though Taft tried to give her the bed, just like when she'd taken care of him before. But apart from her shoulder, which was getting better daily, she hadn't been as compromised as Taft. He'd suffered a concussion and been tased and acquired cuts and bruises from the fight, and this while still mending from the bullet that had nearly taken his life three months earlier. Tommy brought them food and the pugs squirreled around them, and it was all good.

On the news they also saw that several other neighbors within the Villages community had been rounded up: Abby and Andre Messinger, whose son, Alfie, was living with a neighbor while his parents dealt with their alleged crimes.

There were varying reports on what had taken place, but about three days after it all came down, one resident of the Villages, who happened to be the head of the neighborhood watch, Althea Gresham, gave the clearest account.

"You've got to know the history," the older woman said to one of the local TV reporters, a young woman with sleek, blond hair and a penchant for bright pink clothes. "Those people have lived here a long time. Longer than I have. My late husband, Rowan, and I moved in much later, but those people bought homes when the first section of this whole west-side development began.

"Mr. Victor Laidlaw was the original developer of the Villages, once called Victor's Villages. He purported to be everyone's friend but was a sneaky philanderer who used his influence to cuckold his 'friends.' His fortunes faded over the years, along with his friendships, and he was in desperate need of a new deal. Some fifteen years ago, with the help of business acquaintances and his onetime lawyer, Burt Deevers, he was able to purchase that plot of land with those three houses near the overlook. Do you know the one I mean? The Friends of Faraday, of which I was a member, objected strenuously to that decision. That land was purportedly given to us from Frank Faraday but there was apparently a loophole in the contract which Victor Laidlaw walked through. He ended up with a portion of the land, the part where the old Willoughby house stood. We filed a lawsuit, but we lost. Several of my Faraday friends took matters into their own hands, unbeknownst to me. They are alleged to have used poison— some form of arsenic, kept in the basement of one of the first houses— to slowly kill Victor Laidlaw. They invited him for meals and served it in his food. The poison accumulated over time and Victor had a weak heart and . . . and he died. His cause of death was listed as a heart attack, although there were questions all along. Rumors that poison had brought on the attack.

"Just recently, Victor Laidlaw's son, Tobias Laidlaw, concluded those rumors were true and he requested an exhumation of his father's remains. That is still pending. But those same people, Mr. Deevers among them, couldn't afford to have Victor Laidlaw's remains checked for poison and so . . . I can only speculate here . . . but it is believed that Mr. Deevers and those same people lured Tobias Laidlaw to his death. His body was discovered beneath the playground being constructed within the Villages welcome park. Sadly ironic for a wonderful place to live. The neighborhood watch is requesting cameras at every street corner and—"

Taft clicked off his television. "She's on the local news on every channel," he said as Blackie leaned his head up and gazed at him with an adoring face. "Could go national."

He and Mackenzie were seated on his couch together. Plaid snorted from Mackenzie's lap and she petted her fawn head till the dog turned her face up to her. Mackenzie wrinkled her nose and Plaid wrinkled hers back at her. Tommy, after getting them settled, was on a weekend junket to Las Vegas with a girlfriend. Just a friend, he wanted them to know. It was important to him that they remembered his one true love remained Maura, who was living in a nursing home these days in a twilight world. He went to see her regularly but had recognized there was no coming back for her from the road she was traveling, and so he chose to enjoy his life, even if it was a little sadder without her.

Mac rolled her shoulder, testing it. A twinge, but doable. "I'd like to hear more from Haynes and Verbena." They'd met with both of them at the station on Tuesday morning regarding Daley's death, though after Mac told them what Darrell had said about Tamara, they'd followed that path and learned from Burt that he believed that Tamara had killed Daley out of jealousy. "I'm kinda surprised Burt has been so forthcoming. Tamara's still not talking, but she's not denying it."

"Burt wanted to get ahead of it," said Taft. "Tough when you're the ringleader to shout your innocence."

"I hope Tamara gets the maximum." She could still picture the end of the barrel staring her in the face. "But I hope Abby gets a light sentence, for Alfie's sake," said Mac. In the meantime he was staying with the Martins.

"Did you see on the news that Claude Marfont's attorney is representing her?"

"I did. And Claude's been talking to the press from the hospital, declaring her innocence. He seems to have taken on her case like a job."

"Unrequited love?" asked Taft.

"Maybe. At least he's recovering. What about Sandy Herdstrom?"

Herdstrom had disappeared during the arrests and seemed to have been trying to run from his involvement with the crimes. He'd been discovered pretty quickly at a house he'd purchased in Idaho but now was claiming he was a victim, not a perpetrator.

"He's in too deep to wiggle free," said Taft.

Mac heard the jingle of a new text and picked up her phone. "It's Stephanie," she said. "Looks like LeeAnn Laidlaw is taking the reins at Laidlaw Construction and she's given Nolan a new title and a raise."

"Good." Taft lifted his barely touched glass of kale smoothie, the drinks they'd shared in honor of Daley earlier. Mac's idea, the ingredients brought by Tommy. Neither of them had been able to finish it.

They'd also heard that Leon had already checked with a real estate agent to list the house.

"I want Haynes to tell us more about Andrew Best," said Mac.

Taft snorted, which made Blackie snort as well. "We'll hear eventually. But Bennihof's in trouble. Maybe Mangella, too. They've got my statement on it all."

"Glad you're all right," said Mac. She'd said it before, but she couldn't help saying it again. It was almost a mantra since she'd heard the harrowing account of his abduction by Silva and the events that led to the man's death. It still had the power to chill her blood.

"Glad you're all right," he came back at her, turning to look her right in the eye. She could read an echo of her fear in those blue depths.

"I may have to rethink carrying a gun."

"Next time there might not be rebar handy, slugger," he agreed.

They smiled at each other.

Mac felt the spark that just wouldn't die sizzle to life.

Taft's senses quickened, and Helene said, *Kiss her, dummy.*

Blackie twisted his head from side to side, looking up at them, and started howling. Plaid stood up on Mac's legs, digging her feet into the flesh of her thighs and whipping her head around, barking madly, sure something was up.

"Whoa," Mac said, getting the dog to settle onto her lap again.

Maybe next time, she thought.

She glanced back at Taft, thought she saw something in his eyes, and was pretty sure he was thinking the same thing.

Cooper slid his Trailblazer to a stop on Clifford Street across from Jamie's house. A flow of maple leaves eddied down onto the hood of his SUV while mounds of gold, brown, and orange leaves lay in damp piles on the street as September turned to October.

Clifford Street brought to mind Cliff Fenwick, now

deceased. He and Clarice had died within hours of each other—minutes really—both victims of their own misdeeds.

His mind touched on the rest of the old guard who'd been involved with Tobias Laidlaw's death—the ones who'd died and the ones who'd survived and lawyered up. Burt Deevers had initially thought of representing himself, but he'd quickly changed his mind. He hadn't been much of a lawyer when he was practicing. He was probably wise to look for outside representation. So far all of them had managed to keep themselves out on bail. There was a lot of finger-pointing going on. He was glad it was not his problem.

He stepped onto the street and inhaled. It had rained for several days and the road was still damp, but the air felt cool and dry, with just a hint of autumn muskiness, the faint scent of rotting leaves.

It was almost dark. Every day getting a few minutes shorter. His leg had healed and he was back at work full bore. There was no more Chief Bennihof. Investigations, lawsuits, and accusations abounded, and Bennihof had been replaced by an interim chief named Marcus Duncan, who was around fifty, a few inches over six feet with a tendency to hunch, and a hangdog Humphrey Bogart face. In fact he looked so much like the actor that people who knew him well called him Humph. The rank and file of River Glen PD called him Chief Duncan, Verbena and Cooper among them. The department was getting back on track.

Today had been a good day, he thought, heading down the driveway to enter through the back door. Harley's car was parked in the drive, as was his stepdaughter Marissa's. Both girls were in their last year of high school now. Seniors. Man, that went fast. They'd gotten one of their classmates back this fall: Timothy Blakely, the burglary suspect whose parents had fought tooth and nail to keep their little criminal out of jail and had apparently succeeded. Cooper and everyone in the department knew the kid had committed the crime, but it was determined to be a teenage one-off. Time would tell.

But the reason today had been good was because Andrew Best had finally come clean—with his lawyer present and monitoring every word, of course—about what had really happened the night Granger Nye fell to his death.

First off, no, no, a thousand times no, Best said. No, he hadn't asked—begged—for someone to get Detective Cooper Haynes off his ass. No matter what Jesse Taft may have thought he heard that night, that was not the case. Yes, Best had complained about what he deemed harassment by the River Glen detectives, but tampering with Cooper Haynes's city ride? That had been all Silva. The papers Silva had forced him to sign? They'd been ripped up by Mitch Mangella himself. Again, Silva had been acting alone.

Cooper had had to let that one go. He was pretty sure Best had been a little more adamant about getting rid of him, but with Silva dead, there was no chance of hearing from the other side. And anyway, they knew it was Silva who'd stolen the keys and taken the car, Silva who'd had it rigged. Bryan "Ricky" Richards had erased the video at Bennihof's sideways request . . the old chief knew how to make his wishes known without actually verbalizing them. A mob boss move. Ricky had been let go from the department, but he'd avoided jail time by confessing his involvement and giving the prosecutors Bennihof.

But after professing his innocence in that matter, Best

had finally laid out the events that had occurred the night Granger Nye died.

Nye had known about the drugs being peddled inside Best Homes and had assumed Andrew Best was not only aware of the operation but heading it up. This was patently untrue according to Best; he was still peddling that narrative, and maybe it was true. Yet to be determined. But Nye had decided to engage in a little blackmail. He wanted Best to give him the house under construction as a means to keep his mouth shut. They were at the jobsite arguing about it when Tobias Laidlaw, Nye's old boss, joined them. Tobias had been looking for Nye because he claimed to have learned proof positive that his father's death was murder. He was ranting about the poisoning that would hit the papers in June when the whole plot came to light, but that night Nye hadn't known just how much Tobias believed the rumor. Suddenly here was Tobias, confronting Nye, claiming he was part of the poisoning. Nye vehemently denied it. Told Tobias he was going off on another wild conspiracy theory, just like always. Best took a few steps away from the warring men. Finally Nye declared that, okay, yes, he'd known about the poisoning, but no, he wasn't an actual part of it. Never. He liked Victor. Always had. He could name names, though, which he did: Deevers, Jacoby, Fenwick, Messinger.

Enraged, Tobias shoved him. Nye tripped, seemed like he was going to catch himself, then took a header over the edge. Not wanting any part of it, Best lammed out immediately. He didn't care what happened to Tobias, he just ran. He didn't want to tell the truth about how Nye died because he didn't want to be involved. Best was afraid maybe Tobias would call him as some kind of witness, but he never heard another word. He'd called Laidlaw

Construction once, asking for Tobias, not giving his name, but was told Tobias was on an extended business trip.

And that was the truth of that, according to Best and his lawyer, who wanted to put the whole thing to rest. Best admitted that he should have reported the truth of the accident when it happened, but he just wanted it to go away. It didn't alter the fact that it was just an unfortunate accident. Tobias was angry at Nye but hadn't meant to kill him. And as for him naming names, it was just noise without corroboration.

So, now it was for the lawyers to figure out. Cooper was just glad for the clarification. And though Best might skate some on this, he wasn't getting away scot-free. He was currently in the midst of a very expensive divorce from a soon-to-be ex-wife who owned at least half of Best Homes. As far as he knew, Best's affair with Anna DeMarcos was ongoing, but Cooper had bets on how long that might last if, and when, Best came out on the other side a much poorer man. Karma was a bitch.

Cooper entered the back door and was greeted by the smells of tomato sauce and fresh herbs. Emma's dog, Duchess, came bounding down the stairs toward him, tail wagging, as Cooper entered the kitchen. Cooper gave the dog a big scratch on the ears. Jamie, her hair up in its usual messy bun, an apron wrapped around her, looked around from checking the oven. "Lasagna," she said, shutting the oven door. "Guess who ordered pasta?"

"Can't imagine." He left the dog and came toward her, sweeping her into a bear hug and murmuring, "Mmm," into her hair.

"Well, hello there. You know you're going to get tomato sauce on yourself."

He pushed her into the counter and began kissing her

neck madly, making smacking noises. She was laughing and half-heartedly trying to push him away when Harley, Marissa, and Emma followed the dog downstairs.

Harley said, "The parental units are getting frisky."

Marissa said, "It's kinda cute and disgusting."

Emma said, "Get a room," which broke them all up.

Thirty minutes later they were all seated around the table. Cooper, not a man normally at the mercy of emotion, suddenly felt deeply moved by being with his blended family. Silently, he reached out a hand to Marissa on his left side and one to Emma on his right. Marissa took his hand and smiled at him, then clasped Harley's hand with her other. Harley then reached for her mother's, and Jamie stretched her free hand toward Emma. Emma looked first at Cooper's hand on the one side, then at her sister's on the other.

Jamie, who knew how difficult it was for her sister to be touched, said, "It's just because we're happy."

Very carefully, Emma put her left hand in Cooper's and her right hand in Jamie's.

"We're not going to pray, are we?" asked Harley.

They all looked to Cooper.

"It was just a good day and I wanted to hold on to it."

"What happened?" asked Marissa.

He thought about it all and said, "Resolution. Completion."

"You closed a case," said Harley, interested. She still hadn't given up the idea of going into law enforcement, even though she'd cooled a bit on all things British. Not that she still didn't want to go to England; she'd just determined not to be such a nerd about it. This according to Jamie, who knew her daughter well.

They dropped hands and started to eat, but Emma sat silent for a moment.

"Something wrong?" Jamie asked after taking a bite of lasagna.

Emma announced, "I've decided to be a surrogate for you and Cooper."

Harley choked on her bite and started coughing. Marissa's mouth dropped open, her forkful of lasagna suspended in the air and beginning to drip back onto her plate.

Cooper knew better than to say *anything*.

And Jamie said, "No way in holy hell!" in a very uncharacteristic reaction to dealing with the sister she loved.

Emma said in all seriousness. "I know I was in an accident that hurt my brain, but the rest of me works fine."

"I'm not . . . I can't . . ." Jamie inhaled and counted to three. "Thank you, Emma, but we can't, um, we won't . . . it's just not going to work."

"Holy shit," said Harley. "No swearing."

"Why not?" asked Emma, looking at Jamie.

Marissa said, "That's amazing, Emma. Really amazing."

"You don't know what pregnancy is like," said Jamie, coming back to herself. "It's long and can strain your body, and you have to take care of yourself—"

"I take care of myself."

"You don't even like to hug! There's a lot of hugging involved. It's not something you can do for me," Jamie struggled to explain. "But my God, I so appreciate it."

Emma looked at Jamie. Her sister's face was very intense. Emma suspected Jamie was lying to her in some way. Jamie really wanted a baby. She'd stopped talking about having one because she needed a surrogate. She'd spent all summer talking about the wedding, which was supposed to be earlier but then Cooper's leg was hurt and it didn't happen. Now they were planning for right around Christmas. But Emma would like to give them a baby, too. Just because Jamie had stopped talking about it didn't mean she didn't still want one.

"I can hug," Emma said, and got up from her chair and put her arms around her sister.

"Oh, Emma . . ." Jamie had tears in her eyes.

She was crying because she couldn't have a baby. Emma knew she was right. She needed to go see a doctor to make this happen. Maybe Harley would take her. If not, she could take the bus.

That would be her wedding present to her sister.